Connie of
Kettle Street

By the same author

Lizzie of Langley Street

Rose of Ruby Street

Carol Rivers, whose family comes from the Isle of Dogs, East London, now lives in Dorset. *Connie of Kettle Street* is her third novel.

Visit www.carolrivers.com

Carol Rivers

Connie of Kettle Street

POCKET
BOOKS

LONDON • SYDNEY • NEW YORK • TORONTO

First published in Great Britain by Simon & Schuster, 2006
This edition first published by Pocket Books, 2007
An imprint of Simon & Schuster UK
A CBS COMPANY

3 5 7 9 10 8 6 4 2

Simon & Schuster UK Ltd
1st Floor
222 Gray's Inn Road
London WC1X 8HB

www.simonandschuster.co.uk

Simon & Schuster Australia
Sydney

A CIP catalogue record for this book is
available from the British Library

ISBN: 978-1-8473-9795-9

Typeset by M Rules
Printed and bound in Great Britain by
Cox & Wyman Ltd, Reading, Berks

I dedicate this book to all the Islanders,
both past and present, in celebration of
their courage and tenacity.

Acknowledgements

My thanks to the Island History Trust Docklands Settlement and especially the Island History News which helps to keep Islanders in touch and brings memories alive of the old days. My thanks also go to my dear buddies, Chris and Bart.

Chapter One

The London Blitz
Isle of Dogs
Saturday 7 September 1940

Connie was running. Running as fast as her legs would carry her through the unlit streets of east London. Above her, the smoke-strewn sky was filled with an eerie, crimson glow. To the south, across the river, blood red flames leaped high into the air over London's Surrey Docks.

An ear-deafening bang sent a shiver through the ground. But she ran all the faster, dodging the ambulances and the firemen dousing the fires that were already spreading from the incendiary bombs. Their shouts were lost in the deafening noise of the return fire of the British anti-aircraft guns. Even the colossal barrage balloons sailing high above the city hadn't proved an effective deterrent to the Luftwaffe.

Connie hurdled a wall; sweat was soaking her pale blond hair and dripping on the collar of her old tweed coat. At the top of Kettle Street she stopped to wipe the moisture from her eyes and blinked at the sight of a lone cyclist pedalling towards her.

'What's up, Connie?' The ARP warden jumped off his bike. 'You shouldn't be out in this lot.'

'It's Billy, Mr Jackson, he's done his disappearing act again.'

'Well, you ain't got time to find yer brother now. You'd better get down your Anderson before the sods come back again. I'll keep a lookout for him on me rounds.'

'Thanks, Mr Jackson.'

The warden hopped back on his bike. 'Take care of yourself, Connie. And keep yer head down, love.'

Connie pushed open the squeaky front gate of number thirty-three Kettle Street. The sooty but sturdy semi-detached boasted a Beefeater-red front door and all four of its neat square windows were criss-crossed by blackout tape. She pulled up the length of string behind the letter box and let herself in, stood quietly in the darkened passage and listened for movement. Hearing none, she groped her way up the stairs. After what she'd found under Billy's mattress this morning, she had no doubt as to what he'd been up to.

In the boys' bedroom, she slid her hand under her younger brother's flock mattress, searching for the pile of coupons and identity cards she had discovered this morning. But now there was nothing, nothing at all, just the hard curl of the metal springs.

'Sis?'

Startled, Connie turned round. 'Billy!'

'What are you doing? Where is everyone?'

'Dad's fire watching and Mum's gone to the public shelter. I've been looking all over the place for you. Mum is worrying herself silly. Where've you been?'

He shrugged lazily, pushing back the tumble of blond curls that fell over his face. 'I was with a pal, that's all. We was having a bit of a lark when the warning went.'

'A *lark*?' Connie rolled her eyes. 'Billy, there's a war on, a real war this time. The Luftwaffe's not playing games. I suppose you're gonna tell me those coupons and identity cards I found when I made your bed this morning are a bit of a joke, too? What if it was Mum who'd discovered them and not me?'

Connie waited for an explanation. At fourteen, four years her junior, Billy was already her height and still growing fast. Although they were identical in looks, with corn-coloured hair and soft blue eyes, Connie thanked her lucky stars that up until now she didn't appear to have any of Billy's more wayward tendencies.

'You won't tell her, will you?' he said sheepishly.

'I'd be too ashamed to and that's a fact—' Before Connie could finish, a huge rumble followed by a burst of bright light lit up the house. Billy grabbed her hand and pulled her down the stairs as more explosions followed one after another. Before they reached the back door, the front one blew off its hinges and landed behind them. Connie felt the rush of wind in her face and was blown against the wall. Billy dragged her on through the kitchen and into the yard. Dazed and terrified, she tumbled with him down the slippery steps of the Anderson and into the dark, musty smelling shelter covered in sand-bags.

Connie shivered as he secured the corrugated iron door behind them. Her teeth chattered, even her bones seemed to be shaking. She wondered if they would die immediately if one of the bombs hit them, or would it be a long and lingering death? She didn't want her life to end, not now, like this. Billy pulled her down on the wooden bench. ''Struth, that was a close one,' he sighed as they huddled together. 'Stay put. I'll light a candle.'

A gentle amber glow soon illuminated the darkness. The meagre contents of the small shelter came into focus: the wooden bench they sat on, three of Dad's army blankets folded on a stool and a row of gas masks placed on a wide wooden shelf. Squeezed beside these were four chipped enamel mugs, four plates and a brown china teapot. A bottle had fallen over beside it. Billy picked it up. 'What's this, Con?'

'Phosferine tonic wine.'

Billy rubbed his hands together. 'We're all right for a drink, then.'

'Mum said it's for medicinal purposes only.'

He laughed. 'I was only joking. Come on, give us a smile, we're all in one piece, ain't we?'

'Yes, but I thought the house was coming down on top of us.'

Billy sat beside her again as the walls of the shelter vibrated. 'Mum's gonna have a fit when she sees what's happened.' He chuckled. 'I ain't never seen our front door open so quick.'

Connie admired his spirit. He was a happy kid, a character trait that endeared him to everyone. They'd grown up in poverty, knew what hardship and going hungry was when Dad had been unemployed or he'd had a bad week on the gee-gees. But Billy was bright and always on the lookout for an opportunity to make money, his natural talent aided by the outbreak of war twelve months ago. With evacuation of children in full swing, Billy had been in his element. Left to his own devices, he had relied on Connie to bail him out of the trouble that always dogged his footsteps. Now she looked at him and sighed heavily. 'Tell me the truth, Billy. Did you steal those coupons and identity cards?'

'No, Con, course not. I was just . . . looking after them for someone.' He gave a light-hearted shrug. 'Me mate Charlie asked me to keep a few things for him.'

'Why should he do that?'

'Dunno, he just did.'

'Billy, this is your sister you're talking to. I'm not daft.'

'I never said you was.'

'Then tell me the truth.'

He smiled widely, lifting his hands in a gesture of innocence. 'Come on, Con, give us a break—'

'No, Billy,' she interrupted angrily. 'I've always taken your side when you've got in trouble because I thought it was just schoolboy pranks. But today was different. I actually saw the evidence for myself.'

Slowly his smile faded and he leaned his elbows on his knees. 'I found this handbag. It was just lying around.'

'Then why didn't you take it to the police station?'

He laughed. 'You've got to be joking. I'm not that much of a mug. They'd say I nicked it.'

'Did you?' Connie knew she was being lied to and Billy's lies weren't even very clever.

'No, Con. It was like I said. Someone must've dropped it. It was there in the road staring me in the face. If I hadn't grabbed it someone else would.'

Connie wondered if he was telling her the truth. 'It's not so much what you do, Billy,' she said more gently then. 'It's the way you come out with these stories, expect me to believe them and even stick up for you. You're me kid brother. I don't want you ending up on the wrong side of the law.'

It was the emotion in her voice that made him turn and face her. 'It's too late, Con. I'm in over my head already.'

'What do you mean?'

'The handbag was kosher. But I done a really bad thing today.' His blue eyes stared emptily into hers. 'I broke in to someone's gaff.'

'You *what*?'

'I climbed in through this fanlight in the back of a pawn shop up Stepney. I'm thin, see? The right build for a creeper. Getting into places and opening doors from the inside. I didn't steal nothin' though. These other two blokes I was with did the actual business.'

Connie gulped. 'Billy, I can't believe you would do such a thing!'

'I told you I didn't steal nothing.'

'So what did you do it for then? And don't say it was just for a lark, 'cos I won't believe you.'

Billy muttered under his breath. 'I wish I hadn't told you now.'

'Well, you have, so you'd better tell me the rest.'

He looked at her sullenly. 'I was to keep a look out, that was all. They said they'd bung me a few quid. And it would have worked out if the warning hadn't gone. I ask you, for a whole year we've been twiddling our thumbs waiting for Jerry and he has to arrive today. Anyway, the old boy's gaff was upstairs. He was deaf as a post and had to be at least ninety. If the siren hadn't gone, he wouldn't have known we was there. The old geezer saw Reg and Charlie stuffing the gear in the boot of the car. He was waving this rifle, a big museum piece it looked like. I heard the first shot and nearly shit me pants. I jumped in the car. Charlie jumped in beside me and there was another shot. I didn't see what happened to Reg 'cos Charlie drove away.'

Connie blinked as she digested the fact that they were talking about a burglary in which a gun had been used. 'Billy, do you realize you've committed a crime?' she demanded when she got her breath back.

'Charlie and Reg said they'd put the squeeze on me if I didn't.'

'How could they do that?'

'I done a few jobs for Reg, see. Nothing big. Not really. You name me anyone who isn't up for a touch in wartime, Con. There's always a bit of black market to be had and you'd be a fool not to take it. We all enjoy knocked off stuff now and then, even Mum and Dad, who turn a blind eye to a few perks, so I don't see what all the fuss is about.'

'There's a difference between perks and stealing.' She stared at him coldly. 'What happened then?'

'Me and Charlie was driving through Poplar and heading back to the island. Charlie's lost his bottle and he's heading hell for leather for the foot tunnel. He lives over Greenwich, see? Well, the next thing I know is he's had it on his toes and I'm left sitting there like a lemon with me dabs all over the car.'

'What car? Who does it belong to?' Connie asked bewilderedly.

'Dunno. Charlie nicked it for the job.'

'Billy, that's terrible.'

'I told you, I got in too deep to get out.'

They sat in silence. Connie's heart pounded as she thought of the repercussions of the mounting crimes that Billy was involved in.

'You can drive, Con,' Billy said suddenly. 'You learned last year for the war effort. It would be dead easy for you to drive the motor right up to the river, then we could just push it in.'

'You are joking, I hope?'

'I ain't got no one else to ask, Con. If the coppers find that car with me fingerprints in, I'm a dead duck. I'll get me collar tugged and what will Mum do then? She'd never live down the shame of it. I couldn't do that to her, honest I couldn't.'

'Why didn't you think of that before, Billy?'

'I know. Today has taught me the lesson of a lifetime.'

'And I'm supposed to believe you?'

He reached out to grasp her hand. 'It's the truth, Con.

I want to change me ways. I just need a chance. The car is the only thing that links me with the job. No one's gonna find it in the water, not for ages, especially with Jerry doing his business. Even the divers can't see a foot in front of them on a clear day.' He squeezed her hand tightly. 'Remember as kids we'd watch them with their big bowl helmets and long pipes? You was always telling me they kept goldfish in them, remember? Happy days, weren't they, gel?'

Connie knew she was a soft touch and Billy was taking advantage of it. If he was caught, Mum would never live down the shame. Being arrested and sent to prison was something that happened to others but not to the Marsh family. As for her own job at Dalton's Import, Storage and Transport Services – well, she'd soon be brought down to earth with all the gossip that would abound. But all these things were nothing compared to the effect that prison would have on Billy himself.

He'd been such an innocent, lovely kid once, always trailing at her heels, just wanting to be with her. She was close to Kev too, but in a different way. Kevin was practical, like Mum, and self-sufficient. Billy was a dreamer and vulnerable. She didn't want to believe those days were over, that Billy was growing away from her into someone she didn't know.

She looked into his eyes. 'I must be mad to listen to you, Billy Marsh.'

He hugged her hard. 'I knew you'd understand.'

She couldn't refuse the little boy who smelled of dirt and soap and had made her laugh with his funny antics, never taking anything seriously if he could help it. She looked into his young face, at the angelic features and soft, full lips of a child. He still had bum fluff on his chin and her heart went out to the brother she adored. 'I love you, Billy Marsh. And that's my trouble. I love you too much.'

Chapter Two

The raid, which had started about four o'clock, now seemed to be over. Connie had never known such a long two hours and even when the all clear went, she didn't want to stick even her nose outside the Anderson, much less her whole body.

'Come on, this is our chance,' Billy insisted, grabbing her arm.

'But what if the planes come back,' Connie argued, 'and we're caught in the open?'

'All the more reason to hurry,' Billy urged as he struggled to dislodge the door. 'If we're lucky, Jerry might have clobbered the motor, blasted it sky high, and that would solve all our problems, eh?'

Connie wasn't sure which she was most frightened of, a return of the enemy bombers or helping Billy to dispose of the car. She was about to voice her doubts when he managed to pull open the door. Half a dozen sandbags toppled in, followed by a cloud of dust. Billy stepped over them and looked up at the house. 'Blimey, the place is still standing! That's a miracle, that is.'

Connie peered over his shoulder. Number thirty-three

Kettle Street was a pale shadow lost in the swirling dust, but all was intact as far as she could see.

'Watch your step,' Billy warned as he led the way into the house. They stepped across the fallen door and paused in the gap at the front where it had once hung. A September breeze whistled past them, bringing with it the smell of burning oil. Shrapnel, bricks and shattered glass were strewn across the little patch of grass outside and all the way down the street.

'Oh, Billy, I don't recognize our road, do you?' They listened to the distant wails of the ambulances. 'It's so eerie. Like the end of the world.'

'Yeah, well it will be if we don't get a move on.' He grabbed her hand.

'I'm scared.' Connie looked up at the sky. She couldn't see very much, only the beams of the searchlights and the immense bottoms of the barrage balloons. 'Let's wait till tomorrow.'

Billy shook his head, pulling her with him. 'Tomorrow will be too late. Come on, stick with me, you'll be all right.'

They broke into a run. Connie found it hard to breathe in the polluted air. But every time she slowed down, Billy pulled her on. The soles of their feet crunched noisily over glass and shattered roof tiles. Buckets full of sand had been left untouched in doorways and fires burned in the rubble by craters that appeared in the roads. Somewhere close by she could hear the shouts of the rescue teams working quickly before another raid.

In Haverick Street, she saw a fireplace hanging by a

whisker to the first floor wall of a terraced house. The frame of a chair lay smouldering beneath. What had once been two or three houses filled with treasured personal possessions was now a mountain of smouldering debris.

'Billy, stop. There might be people under all that.'

'Connie, we ain't got time.'

'But someone might be trapped!'

'The ARP will be along soon. They'll dig them out.'

Connie took a step forward. 'Listen, I can hear something!'

'It's only a cat or a dog,' he yelled, trying to pull her back.

But she could clearly identify a noise now, like someone moaning. If only she knew where to start! A pall of dust surrounded her as she pulled away the bricks and broken wood. Splinters dug into her skin and some of the concrete was too heavy to move. 'Billy, help me!' she cried, but when she looked round Billy shook his head.

'I can't stop, Connie.'

'Please help me, Billy.' Her hands trembled as she dug into the rubble. The noise was still there, louder now as she clawed at the pieces of plaster. Was there a human being beneath all this rubbish? And, if so, how could they help them? What would the person look like if she did find them? Would there be blood and broken limbs to contend with?

Connie suddenly stopped. The space behind her was empty. 'Billy!' she screamed. But she knew it was no use. He'd gone.

A scratching noise made her jump. She stretched out

to lift a large slate balanced precariously on the top of the pile. Suddenly a hand appeared and the fingers moved! As she lifted off more bricks the hand grew into an arm, a shoulder, and finally a head. The young girl was trapped by a piece of timber too heavy for Connie to lift.

'My baby,' the girl whimpered. 'Please save my baby.'

'Your baby?' Connie faltered. 'Where?'

'Here . . . here . . .'

But where was here? Connie wondered as a little trail of blood trickled from the girl's mouth. She tried to remember the first aid she had learned at school. But they had only ever practised on dolls and even those were lying flat on the floor. Applying bandages had been easy in the safety of the school classroom. But this was real life, with someone who must be in terrible pain. 'I'll run for some help,' she decided then, but the girl's eyes flashed wide.

'No . . . don't leave us, don't go . . .'

'But I can't help you alone,' Connie replied gently. 'I'll find a rescue team, bring them quickly—'

'No . . . no . . . time . . . please try . . .'

Connie couldn't leave her. But the roof slates were broken and sharp, the bricks heavy. How would she ever manage to free her or find her baby with all this rubbish on top? As she lifted one brick, two more tumbled down in its place.

The girl gave a sigh. Her voice was low. 'Look after my baby . . . won't you? Please, promise me . . . ?'

Connie nodded slowly. 'Yes . . . yes, I promise.'

A little sigh rattled deep in the back of the girl's throat.

Connie stared into eyes that seemed to be looking beyond her into another world. She had never seen anyone die before.

'Miss? Are you all right?'

Connie heard the voice from very far away as though in a dream. Her head swam as she tried to focus. The next thing she knew, a young man wearing an ARP helmet was patting her back gently. 'Take a deep breath. You'll feel better in a minute.'

Connie gulped in air. 'What happened?'

His arm was around her waist. 'You were going to faint, that's all.'

'Was I?'

'I'm afraid that poor girl is beyond our help.'

Connie followed his gaze, then looked away again. 'I felt so useless,' she croaked. 'She asked me to find her baby.'

'Under there?' He shook his head doubtfully. 'We'll need manpower to shift that lot.'

'Couldn't we try,' Connie protested as she struggled out of his grasp. 'Both of us together?'

He went over to the girl and gently closed her eyes. 'All right, we'll have a quick shufti and see what we can do. If the planes come back, though, we'll have to make a run for it. Now, from the angle of her body, she's lying on something and as we can't move that beam let's take the stuff from underneath her first.'

Connie tried not to look at the sad white face as she bent to help him. As they pulled rubble out they were careful not to create an avalanche. Slowly a hole began to appear.

'Can you see anything in there?' Connie asked as he went on his knees and looked in.

'Yeah, one of those big brass coal scuttles that open at the front.' The top half of his body disappeared through the gap and Connie felt like holding on to his boots just in case he might disappear for ever. But then she heard him shout and soon he was wriggling back again. This time he held a bundle in his arms.

'A baby!' Connie gasped as he kneeled on the ground and unwrapped the filthy shawl. 'Is it alive?'

'No doubt about it, he's got his eyes wide open.'

'He?'

The young man grinned. 'Well, he looks like a he to me, but then again, he might wash up like a girl.'

Connie stared at the tiny little face covered in soot. 'What do we do now?'

'We run like bloody rabbits, that's what we do,' he told her just as the siren went off again. 'Me gran's house is round the corner in East Ferry Road.' He gripped the baby against his chest and reached for Connie. 'Come on, they'll be over in a moment.'

Connie's throat felt sore as they ran. The dust and smoke poured into her open mouth. By the time they reached East Ferry Road she was panting and coughing, trying to spit out the dirt. In the distance there was the deadly drone of the bombers and the soft crump–crump of the bombs.

He pulled her towards a line of tall terraced buildings and they leaped up the steps of one of them. 'Gran, it's me!' he yelled as they entered the passage of the dark old house.

No one answered.

They stood there, breathing noisily. 'Wouldn't she be in your Anderson?' Connie spluttered.

'No, they couldn't put one in the yard 'cos of the gas pipes so close. She'll be over at me sister's house in Manchester Road. Pat wouldn't rest if Gran was here on her own.'

'Where shall we shelter then?' Connie gulped.

'Follow me.' Once more Connie was dragged along. She couldn't see anything, it was pitch black. 'This is the understairs cupboard. I'll put me torch on when we're inside.' Connie was bundled into another dark space. It smelled very old and musty. 'Hold the baby, I'll close the door.' She heard a soft bang. 'There, how's that?' The torch light went on. All she could see was cobwebs hanging from rafters.

She nodded. 'Better, thanks.'

'Are you all right?'

'Yes, it's the baby I'm worried about.'

He shone the beam in the infant's face.

'Do you think he's hurt?' she asked worriedly.

'There's nothing wrong with his lungs,' he chuckled as an almighty yell burst from a very small mouth.

'Is that a good sign or bad?'

'If he's anything like my little niece, Doris, he'll shut up as soon as milk's poured down his gob.'

'You mean he's just hungry?'

'Gran keeps Doris's bottle in the larder as she looks after the kid while Pat's at work. While I'm gone, make yourself comfortable in the armchair.'

He held her arm and Connie sank down. 'Will you be long?' she asked anxiously. 'I don't even know where I am or who you are. Though it's funny but I seem to recognize your voice.'

'And I recognize you, Connie Marsh.' He took off his tin helmet and brushed back his thick, dark hair. 'Remember me? Vic Champion, from British Street School.' He laughed, just as a tremendous bang rattled the whole house. Connie was too terrified to move as she hugged the baby against her. As more explosions followed she felt a pair of arms go around them. She snuggled into his chest and closed her eyes, the baby squashed between them.

'Sorry if I crushed you,' he apologized when they had subsided. 'No damage done, is there?' He shone the torch on the baby again.

'No. He's not even crying now. The noise must be awful to his little ears.'

'I'll go and find the bottle now.'

'Yes, but don't be too long.'

He grinned in the torch light. 'Now that's an offer I can't refuse.'

Connie blushed in the darkness. Vic Champion – she remembered him now, a keen footballer from an early age. She'd had a crush on his friend Jimmy Longman. They were always hanging around together, though Vic never seemed interested in girls, only football.

She vaguely remembered his sister, Pat, who now, apparently, had a little girl. Vic had grown into a good-looking young man, with a rather large, straight nose and lovely big dark eyes. How strange they should meet again after all this time.

In the shadowy light of the torch she saw the cupboard was full of mops, brooms and pieces of junk. The air smelled of lavender and mothballs, a not unpleasant odour that reminded her of home. Suddenly she missed her family very much. How had she come to be here in a stranger's house? And where was Billy?

The baby moved restlessly. She undid the long white gown. Two dainty blue boots poked out. Vic had guessed right. Connie rocked him, humming softly. A very strange sensation filled her. She had never experienced anything like it before, like drinking a cup of cocoa in bed, then snuggling down under the eiderdown, all cosy. Gently she gave him the tip of her finger to suck. She could feel his little tongue and the hard pull of his mouth, making her go tingly all over.

'How's the damsel in distress?' Vic teased when he returned.

Connie giggled. 'I thought you might have gone out to save another one, seeing as you're so good at it.'

'One a night's enough.' He sat down on the arm of the chair. 'Took all my strength to tether the horse and put the armour away.'

She chuckled. 'What have you got there?'

'Our Dorrie's bottle. True the milk's stone cold, but there's nothing to heat it with.'

Connie took the banana shaped bottle and pressed it against the baby's lips. 'He doesn't seem to want it,' she wailed as he refused to drink.

'He? Did you look, then?'

'Yes, his bootees are blue.'

Vic roared with laughter. 'So that's how you tell! I always wondered.'

She blushed. 'I don't know anything about babies.'

'Just follow what your Uncle Vic tells you then. It's easy.' He placed his hand over hers and pushed. 'Drink up, chum, it's all we've got.'

Connie gasped. 'That worked. How did you do it?'

'It's my magnetic charm. Animals and kids can't resist it.'

The bottle was almost empty when another huge explosion resounded. Two more followed and a shower of dust cascaded down. The bombs fell in quick succession and Vic held her tightly again, placing his arms firmly around them.

'This isn't so bad after all,' he joked when the all clear went. He sat back on the arm of the chair. His white teeth shone under an embarrassed grin.

'How long will the raids go on?' Connie asked, hoping he couldn't see her going red either.

'Getting fed up with me already are you?'

Connie laughed. 'Haven't you got a wife or something to go home to?'

'Certainly not a something,' he told her cheekily, 'and definitely not a wife. I live here with Gran.'

'Oh.' Connie nodded. 'I see.'

'What about you?'

'No, I haven't got a wife either.'

They both laughed and the relief of tension was a wonderful feeling.

'Where do you live, then?'

'In Kettle Street with my mum and dad and two brothers.' She giggled. 'And I can tell you something else.'

'Go on, I'm all ears.'

'I used to be keen on a mate of yours, Jimmy Longman.'

'Blimey, I'd have been jealous if I'd known,' he teased her, pulling back his shoulders. 'What did he have that I didn't?'

'Well, you was always showing off with that ball of yours, bouncing it on your head or your heels and getting all cocky with it.'

He laughed softly. 'I didn't have the pluck to come up and talk to you, did I? Not whilst your mate was around anyway. The one with all that orange hair.'

'Red hair,' she corrected lightly. 'And Ada's still my mate. What about Jimmy Longman?'

'Don't break your heart over him.' Vic shrugged. 'He's a married man now, with so many kids running around him it's impossible to count the heads.'

'Oh.' Connie smiled. 'Does he live round here?'

'No, in Timbuktu.'

Connie burst into laughter again. She felt that funny feeling in her tummy as she gazed into his dark eyes.

'He's dropping off isn't he?'

Connie nodded. 'Makes me feel tired myself.'

Vic patted his thigh. 'Here, lean against me.' The last thing she remembered was his strong hands pulling her against him.

In no time at all, she was asleep.

★

'Hello love, I'm Pat, Vic's sister.'

Connie sat bolt upright. A young woman with thick, dark brown hair like Vic's was smiling down at her, the baby curled in her arms. She had Vic's big brown eyes and his friendly smile.

Connie sprang to her feet. 'What happened? Did I let him fall off me lap?'

Pat laughed pleasantly. 'No, course you didn't. But you were sleeping this morning when Vic left. He should have reported in to his post last night, but you and the baby took priority.'

'I hope he doesn't get in trouble.'

'Don't you worry about that. Our Vic is big enough to take care of himself. Besides which, he's not a real warden. He's not officially old enough. But as he's waiting for his call-up and they were short of wardens in this area, they took him on temporarily.' Pat looked down at the baby in her arms. 'I've washed and dressed him in one of Doris's old vests, a gown and matinée coat. The pink mittens and bootees are the wrong colour but they'll keep him warm. He's a lovely little boy, you know.'

Connie gazed in wonder at the spotlessly pink face. The little boy was now swathed in a clean white shawl and Connie felt the urge to grab him and cuddle him tight, only preventing herself from doing so as Pat seemed to be enjoying cuddling him too.

'How old do you think he is?' Connie asked.

'He's a good weight, well nourished and cared for – about three months I should say,' Pat decided as she stroked his cheek. 'Now, how do you fancy some breakfast?'

'I'd love some. Is the raid over?'

'Yes, thank God. Where do you live?'

'Number thirty-three Kettle Street.'

'What about your family?' Pat asked as she led the way along the passage.

Connie was wondering that herself and trying to block from her mind any negative thoughts. 'Mum went to the public shelter and Dad was firewatching. Kevin, my brother, was over his girlfriend's in Blackwall. And I dunno where me other brother Billy is,' she ended glumly.

'How old is he?'

'Fourteen.'

'You know what kids are, I'm sure he'll be safe,' Pat said confidently as she led the way to the kitchen. 'The gas and electricity's working in this road, which is amazing as most other streets are turned off.'

'Will Vic be coming back?' Connie asked hopefully.

'Don't think so. There'll be a lot to sort out after the raids, including the poor dead girl you found.'

Connie felt sad when she thought of last night. Pat must have guessed what she was thinking. 'Don't let it prey on your mind, love. You saved her baby. How grateful she would be to you for that.'

The kitchen was filled with every conceivable pot and pan either fixed to the walls or standing on shelves. A wooden rack, lowered from the ceiling, was filled with vests, underpants, knickers and petticoats from which floated a strong soapy smell.

'You must be Connie.' A wrinkled old woman with a

face like a walnut smiled as she poured tea into mugs on the big wooden table. Vic's grandmother had the piercingly dark eyes of both her grandchildren. Her long grey hair was drawn back into a bun at the nape of her neck. 'You'll be needing the lav, ducks. Go through to the yard and help yourself.'

Connie hurried out, forgetting to breathe slowly. She inhaled a big gulp of acrid air. As she used the lavatory she could hear voices in the distance, people beginning to take stock of the damage. The island was waking up to reality. She wondered what slice of reality she would have to deal with herself today.

'Sit yourself down,' Gran told her when she returned. 'I've made some egg fingers, not with real egg of course, but you wouldn't know the difference. There's a mug of tea and sugar in the pot. Owing to someone's sweet tooth that's the last of our ration. There's not much left, but you're welcome to what there is.'

Pat gestured to the pretty black-haired child sitting at the table. 'This is the culprit, Doris, my daughter.'

Connie smiled at the little girl. 'How old is she?'

'Nearly two.' Pat continued to bounce the baby on her knee as Connie ate her breakfast.

'Vic says you don't know who the dead mother was?' Gran asked when Connie had finished and Pat had returned the baby.

'Not her name. She looked very young though.'

'What were you doing out in the raid?'

'Looking for my brother,' Connie improvised. 'Mum was worried about him.'

'You know, it's almost as if that baby recognizes you,' Pat said, changing the subject.

'Is he really smiling or is it just wind?'

'That's a real smile, that is, a winner. What are you going to do with him?'

'Take him to the authorities I suppose.'

'Why not wait till Vic makes some enquiries,' Pat murmured thoughtfully. 'Seems a shame to give him to someone strange. I expect they'd put him in an orphanage.'

'Would they?'

'That's where all the waifs and strays go. Why don't you keep him for a while?'

'But I don't know anything about babies.'

'It's dead easy. They just eat and sleep.'

Connie realized her two fingers were locked in a strong little grasp. She felt that tummy-twirl again and held him closer. 'I'll have to ask Mum.'

'I'll give you some of Doris's cast-offs. A couple of gowns and vests and another matinée jacket. I'll wash out his old clothes and let you have them back when they're dry. As for nappies, I've got three or four I could lend you for the time being.'

'Are you sure you can spare them?'

'Dorrie's nearly potty trained. You can have the bottle, but look after the teat. Rubber's almost impossible to find these days. And I'm afraid I haven't got any rubber knickers at all. I'll put them all in Gran's shopping basket and you can take them with you.'

'Won't Doris want her bottle?'

Pat grinned. 'As you can see, she's eating for England now and doesn't really need a bottle. It's just a comforter, that's all.'

'I hope the baby's appetite is as good as hers.' Connie sighed as she remembered the way he wouldn't feed at first.

'Try a teaspoon of mashed up or strained food. Just a little at a time. He seems in the peak of health and whoever took care of him obviously loved him.'

For a moment the three women were silent. Then Gran spoke. 'The Salvation Army are a good bet too,' she said as she adjusted the wide straps of her crossover pinny. 'They are always ready to help anyone in distress.'

They all looked at the baby. Connie stroked his little chin with her finger. He beamed the biggest smile in her direction. She felt proud, as if he were her own baby, which was daft. But Connie knew she wasn't going to be in any hurry to hand the baby over to anyone – least of all the authorities. The relatives, of course, were a different proposition.

Connie would never forget that Sunday morning as she made her way back to Kettle Street. Instead of people walking to church in their Sunday best, the scenes of devastation were everywhere. No one had expected the intense bombing and the docks had suffered badly. Many houses like those in Haverick Street had fallen, reduced to smoking piles of rubble, whilst their next door neighbours stood intact. Women and children were queuing at standpipes for water and firemen and rescue workers were out in force.

The worst sight was those who'd lost family or friends and were staring with dazed eyes into the ruins. She saw Mr Jackson, his normal role as postman now set aside as he helped to clear the obstructing masonry. The first-aiders were gallantly struggling with the chaos and had provided shelters for the walking wounded. Ambulances negotiated the debris with care.

Connie went the long way round. She felt too upset to revisit the place where the baby's mother had died. Instead she walked along Manchester Road and up to the Mudchute. The soldiers, dressed in their greatcoats and heavy boots, were repairing the battery's wooden huts. She hoped no one had suffered there, and as one of them caught her eye and winked cheekily, she smiled back, admiring their bravery.

As she walked on, she wondered what she would find when she came to Kettle Street. Was the house still standing? Were Mum and Dad and safe? And Kev and his girlfriend, Sylvie? What had happened to Billy during the night?

'You can't go that way, love,' a man shouted. 'The whole block has gone, including the butcher's and a sweet shop.'

The gravity of his words brought back the moment last night when she had looked into the girl's eyes. She had witnessed a human life extinguishing without being able to prevent it. War was a terrible thing. Why did it have to happen to innocent people?

Then, as the baby murmured softly and she gazed into the beautiful dark eyes that she thought, in daylight, might be turning blue, her spirits lifted. A moment later, she was hurrying home. As her footsteps quickened, she vowed she would never take her family for granted. And Billy was no exception. She couldn't wait to see them all again.

Chapter Three

Nan Barnes spread out her long arms and hugged Connie tight. She only realized there was a baby between them when she heard a gurgle at her breast. A big boned woman, tall and loud, her gasp was audible. 'Blimey, look at this! Is it real?'

Connie nodded, trying to glance over her neighbour's broad shoulder down the length of the street.

'What is it, boy or girl?'

'A boy.'

'What's his name?'

Connie hesitated. She hadn't thought about his name, which posed somewhat of a problem. She couldn't just refer to him as the baby all the time. 'I don't know, Nan. His home was bombed and he survived, but he was the only one in the house that did.'

'Poor little beggar.' Nan cooed at the baby, her big lips pursed together under her paisley headscarf. 'Number fifty-six along the road copped a direct hit,' she told Connie rapidly. 'Luckily the Coles weren't there, but staying with their relatives in Wales. Now, I saw yer Dad mending your door this morning, or at least attempting to. Tell him to give Lofty a shout if he wants any help. Ebbie ain't exactly nimble with his fingers, is he?'

Connie was so relieved to hear her parents were safe that she ignored Nan's tactless comments and hurried on. The Coles' house was a terrible sight with its blackened rafters still smouldering and the debris spilling on to the pavement. But Mrs Spinks from next door waved from the upstairs window and seemed none the worse for wear.

'Connie!' yelled her dad, dropping his hammer on the floor with a clatter when he saw her. 'Thank God you're safe, love!'

She melted into his open arms. He hugged her, squashing the baby between them.

They were both tearful and Connie swallowed. 'Oh, Dad, what a night! I'm so pleased to see you.'

'Where have you been? You wasn't in the Anderson when your mother got back from the shelter this morning. She thought you and Billy would be waiting for her.'

'It's a long story, Dad.' She hoped that Billy would turn up quickly this morning and put everyone's mind at rest.

Her dad lowered his bright blue eyes to the bundle she was carrying. 'What, or rather who, is this?'

Connie placed the baby gently in her father's arms. 'I'll tell you all about it when we go inside.'

Ebbie Marsh gazed down at the child in his arms. Connie watched in silence as her father bent his head, displaying a thick cluster of straw-coloured hair identical in colouring to her own. 'My, my, there's a big smile to brighten my day.' He looked up at his daughter. 'Your mother is going to be relieved to see you walk in that door, Con.' He laughed at his own joke. 'Well, walk over it anyway.'

As Connie went in Olive Marsh raced out of the kitchen. 'Constance! Where on earth have you been? I was so worried!' As usual, her appearance was immaculate, Connie noted as she embraced her mother, hugging the slim, slightly stiff shoulders covered in a smart green blouse. Not a hair was out of place, the glossy brown pleat at the back of her head secured by an army of pins. 'I would never have asked you to look for your brother if I'd known what was ahead of us.'

'He'll be home soon,' Connie replied and, before her mother could ask more, she nodded to the bundle in her father's arms. 'Look what I found.'

'A baby? You *found* a baby?'

'Yes, a little boy.'

'When? Where?'

'Last night, as I was . . . er . . . looking for Billy,' she fibbed. 'Some houses had been hit in Haverick Street. I found this poor girl in the ruins, but she was trapped and before I could help her, she died.'

Olive gasped. Her father frowned. 'And this baby survived?'

Connie nodded. 'Goodness knows how. He was shut in a coal scuttle under a table. A warden came along and helped to dig him out. Well, he's only a temporary warden, a boy I knew at school called Vic Champion. Luckily his gran lives just round the corner and we had to run with the baby and take shelter there. This morning Vic's gran and his sister Pat gave me breakfast,' she ended breathlessly.

'Vic Champion?' her father repeated. 'I remember him! He stood out, that lad did. Smashing little footballer. Faster than all the rest of the lads put together. He could dribble a ball like no one's business.'

'Yes, yes,' nodded his wife impatiently, 'but what happened to your brother, Constance?'

'You know our Billy, Mum.' Connie shrugged lightly. 'He was off with some pal when the warning went.'

'I'll bet it was with that Joey Donelly!' her mother exclaimed. 'Messing about on the river again. One day he'll fall in, I know he will. I've forbidden him to go near those barges yet he still does exactly as he likes. Ebbie, you're going to have to put your foot down with your son, and that's a fact.'

'Calm down now, love,' her husband soothed. 'It was pandemonium yesterday. None of us knew what we was doing, especially as you insisted on going to the public shelter when I'd set up the Anderson especially.'

'That contraption is a death trap,' Olive Marsh pronounced shortly. 'How you can stand there and advise your family to use it, I really don't know.'

'Is there a cup of tea going?' Connie broke in as she took the baby from her father. He gave her a wink.

'Of course.' Her mother nodded. 'Go in the front room and sit yourself down. Dad's made a fire and lit the paraffin stove. There's a kettle on top of it, heating slowly, but it should be boiled soon. We've no gas and the water's turned off, but I remembered to fill the kettle and two saucepans before I left yesterday.' She frowned at the baby. 'Does that poor child need feeding?'

Connie nodded. 'I expect so. Vic's sister, Pat, has a little girl called Doris and Pat gave me her bottle to use and some clothes to borrow. They're all in this shopping basket.'

'In that case, we'd better get cracking,' Olive decided, taking Gran's basket and hurrying off to the kitchen.

'What are you going to do with the boy?' Ebbie asked as he accompanied his daughter into the front room.

'I don't really know, Dad.' Connie sank into the big fireside chair and was immediately enveloped by warmth. As one who was used to her full eight hours sleep, she was feeling the lack of it now. 'I'll have to ask Mum.'

'Did you see what happened to the Coles' house?' her father asked as he sat on the couch and rolled a cigarette. 'Lucky they were away.'

Connie nodded sadly. 'There was a whole street sealed off as I walked home.'

'Saint Cuthbert's took one, you know.'

'Oh dear. Whatever will the congregation do now?'

'It's anyone's guess.' He paused. 'Nan Barnes told your mother the Islanders was bombed too. I shan't be going down there for a quick one at the weekend, will I? And Surrey Docks was alight from end to end. The coast and the city took the brunt of the bombing this summer, but nothing like the inferno of the docks tonight.' He inhaled deeply, lifting his head to blow out a slow stream of smoke. 'Looks like we're in for a repeat performance tonight.'

33

'P'raps it won't be as bad,' Connie said optimistically.

Her father shook his head woefully. 'You'd have thought the devils would have caught their breath after nabbing Poland, then invading France and her neighbours. But oh no, they annihilated us at Dunkirk, then gave our RAF lads hell in the air over Britain. Now we're told to expect them on the beaches, or sailing up the river!'

'We'd never let them land, Dad!' Connie stared at her father, who looked very tired. Even his sprinkling of chocolate freckles did little to lift his fair, slightly grey skin.

'No, we'd give them a run for their money, all right.'

Connie felt a shiver of dismay. Was there really a chance that Britain would be invaded? There were always threats and rumours abounding, but so many had been circulating since the beginning of war twelve months ago that the fear of invasion had receded. Now last night's activity had changed the picture again.

'Did you have a bad night, Dad?'

He nodded. 'Couldn't keep up with the fires. Those incendiaries were everywhere. The Luftwaffe just followed their path, dropping bombs all over the place, and the balloons never seemed to make a difference.'

Olive walked in and lowered a tray on to the table. 'Drink up whilst it's hot, you two, we can't afford to waste tea, no matter how weak it is.'

Ebbie held out his arms. 'Give him to me, Connie. I'll hold whilst you pour, love.'

'Don't you go getting broody now,' his wife warned

him sternly. 'You're a pushover when it comes to kids. You'd have another one tomorrow if it was humanly possible.'

'Yeah, well thank the Lord it's not,' he muttered as the baby brought up a loud burp, his bald head wobbling on his shoulders. 'That's it, kiddo, better up than down. Wish I could do the same, but I'd get a right chewing off if I did.'

'Manners maketh man,' Olive agreed swiftly. 'Start as you mean to go on, that's what my moth—' Her mouth fell open as she stared at the door. 'Billy! Oh my God, look at the state of you!'

Connie turned to see her brother framed in the doorway. His jacket and trousers were unrecognizable under the stains of what looked like oil and grease. His boots and socks were caked in mud, but he had a smile on his face that was dazzling.

'Mrs Spinks said I could borrow this.' Billy lifted a bucket, talking as if he was carrying on a conversation from five minutes ago. 'She was up by the standpipe and said she thought I needed a wash more than she did.'

'Too right you do, son.' Ebbie nodded, wrinkling his nose at the smell drifting into the room.

'You're filthy,' Olive wailed. 'Oh, Billy, you've been on them barges, I knew it!'

Connie leaped up from her comfortable seat. 'Don't say a word,' she whispered as she grabbed the bucket from his hand. 'I'll get him scrubbed up, Mum,' she called brightly. 'Keep the tea warm for us.'

Pulling Billy with her, Connie hurried to the downstairs

bathroom. She blessed the day three years ago, when the council had seen fit to install one in the house. It was nothing fancy, but the large white bath and basin were accompanied by a real flushing system, not like the smelly old toilet they'd used for years in the backyard. The rabbit-sized rats that it attracted had overwhelmed the district and after an outbreak of several unpleasant diseases all the property maintained by the council had been converted. The bathroom was unheated, freezing in winter, and the iron window frames were already rusting. But it was the one room in the house that afforded a degree of privacy. Connie slid the bolt on the door as Billy began to peel off his clothes.

'You gonna scrub me back, then?' Billy laughed as she tipped the cold water in the basin

'I just wanted to tell you what I said to Mum about last night,' Connie replied crossly as she gathered the filthy garments.

'What was that then?' Billy sank his head into the water, splashing it noisily over himself.

'I said you went off with a mate. She thinks you've been down the river on the barges with Joey Donelly. So I should keep to that story if I were you.'

'Thanks, sis.' Billy rubbed the bar of Puritan soap vigorously over his stick-like arms and skinny chest.

'So what happened, then?' Connie demanded, annoyed at his apparent indifference.

'When?'

'When do you think? When you ran off and left me.'

'Con, I had to get rid of that motor.'

'For your information I found a girl under all that rubble.'

He stopped drying himself on the thin towel and stared at her. 'You mean there *was* someone there?'

'She was . . .' Connie felt tears rush to her eyes. 'I couldn't help her. It was too late . . .'

'Oh, Con,' Billy murmured, putting his wet arm around her. 'I'm sorry, I wouldn't have buggered off if I'd known that.'

Connie shook him off. She sniffed back the tears. 'Well, excuse me, Billy Marsh, but I find that hard to believe. Thanks to you, her baby could have been overlooked. If it hadn't been for a friend of mine helping me to search, he'd probably be dead by now too.'

'You mean little Baldy sitting on Dad's lap? I wondered where it turned up from.' Billy stood shivering in his underpants. 'So who's this friend of yours then?'

'Just a friend, that's all. Now, what happened to the car?'

'I ditched it.'

'But you can't drive.'

'That was the least of me worries. There was no one around so I let off the hand brake and pushed it to the first bit of high water I found. What happened next was the iffy part. Jerry suddenly appeared and the wharf went up like a powder keg. I was blown in the water, right on top of the car. Honest, Con, it was like a bog, all oil and burning wood, and it stank of petrol. That's what you can smell on me clothes. Somehow I got myself out.'

'Billy, you could have drowned.'

'I know. I don't mind admitting it was a close call. But I'm a lucky so and so, Con, you've said it yourself.'

She shook her head despairingly. 'You'll need all the luck going if Mum ever finds out.'

'Well, she won't, will she?'

Connie put her hands on her hips. 'That depends on whether or not you behave yourself.'

'Connie, I swear I'm not getting in no more trouble. Scout's honour an' all that.'

'You wouldn't know a scout if you saw one.'

His teeth chattered under his grin. 'I'm bloody freezing, gel. Is the lecture over?'

'Get upstairs and dress yourself. I'll sort out your dirty clothes. And remember what I told Mum and Dad. You'll have to fill in from there.'

'You're a smasher.' He kissed her cheek. 'I'll bet that friend of yours thinks so too, don't he?'

Before Connie could reply, he shot out of the door.

By the time she returned to the front room, Kevin was home. A fresh pot was brewed and thick slices of bread and dripping prepared. The family sat round the fire in the front room, with the baby, this time, on Kevin's knee.

'He's a little cracker.' Kevin's broad-featured face broke into a smile as he bounced the baby up and down. 'What's his name?'

'We don't know,' Connie said, refilling the mugs.

'What about Baldy?' Billy laughed.

'Lucky,' her dad suggested, puffing hard on his cigarette. 'After what you told us about how he was found.'

'Lucky's not a proper name,' Olive commented. 'His

relatives would have something to say about that.'

'We won't know who they are,' Connie pointed out, 'till Vic finds them.'

Kevin quirked an eyebrow. 'Vic, eh?'

Connie rolled her eyes. 'Don't you start.'

'So you was with Sylvie last night, was you, bruv?' Billy asked, and everyone stared at Kevin.

'Well yes, sort of.'

'And what's that supposed to mean? Was it just the two of you in the shelter?' Olive asked directly.

'No, Sylvie's auntie and two cousins were with us.'

'I'm relieved to hear it.' Olive folded her arms. 'Now, as we're all back together again, we had better decide what to do tonight if those planes come back.'

'Chances of another raid are strong.' Ebbie nodded.

'Then we'll all go to the public shelter together.'

'I'd rather stay here,' Billy protested gloomily.

'No you won't, young man,' his mother insisted. 'You'll come with me to Tiller Road. I like to be with other people, I feel safer.'

'Why doesn't Dad take you along, Mum? Me and the boys can stay here. After all, Dad got the Anderson all ready for us.' Connie didn't care for the small garden shelter, but it was preferable to a public one and would be bearable if her brothers were with her.

'I'm going over to Sylvie's shelter,' Kevin objected, spoiling that particular plan.

'Well, I'm sorry, but I'm not for it,' Olive decided. 'We're a family and families stick together.'

Ebbie sighed, holding up his hands. 'Tell you what,

kids. Give Tiller Road a chance, for your mother's sake. Then, if any of you have a serious objection on your stay there, we'll give it serious consideration tomorrow.'

Reluctantly Kev nodded his approval as did Billy. None of them wanted to upset their mother. Connie gazed down at the baby. She didn't like the thought of a public shelter at all. But she didn't want to be left on her own either. Not that she would be if she stayed. She would have – Lucky! She looked at the baby's smiling face. It was not just herself she had to consider now. She was in charge of another little soul, albeit temporarily.

Most of her friends from school had married, very often their first boyfriends. When invited round to their houses, she had wondered how they managed, kids and grown-ups alike all thrown together in a couple of rooms.

She would be nineteen next year and had no ring on her finger. Much to her mother's dismay, she was deter-minedly pursuing a career. Hadn't Mr Burns told her that she was indispensable? Dalton's Import, Storage and Transport Services was a well-regarded name. She wanted a future without the threat of poverty that had blighted her own parents' lives and those of nearly everyone else on the Isle of Dogs.

It might be a dream, but she would rather have a dream than a failure, where the glamour soon wore off and a girl was trapped for the rest of her life.

'Connie?' Her mother's voice made her start.

'Yes, Mum?'

'That child's going red in the face.'

'What does that mean?'

The room erupted in laughter, followed by an awful pong.

There was no let up for the East End that night. The bombers returned, wave after wave, dropping their lethal cargoes over the docks. Connie had no chance to wash the baby properly or invent a crib. As the siren sounded the warning, the drone of aircraft followed.

'Right, we make a dash for it, all together,' Ebbie shouted and everyone dropped what they were doing. 'Bring your gas masks and a blanket each, and, Connie, let me hold the baby whilst you get him ready.'

Ten minutes later, breathless and flushed, the Marshes were being herded like sheep into the public shelter in Tiller Road. Connie made up her mind as she was pushed and shoved and forced to create a shield around the baby with her arms that this would be her one and only night here. It was far worse than she had imagined. Not even the Anderson could be as bad as this. The crush of bodies, the lack of privacy and the unpleasant smells were enough to make her appreciate the shelter at home.

When the noise of the bombing became unbearable a man began to sing, or rather yell. Others chimed in. Connie knew people were terrified and were trying to cover their fear. But the nervous, false singing only made things worse. Squashed as they were on benches, chairs and mats on the ground, the shelter was starved of oxygen. She tried to feed Lucky from Doris's bottle, but her hands jumped as the explosions shook the ground underneath them. All night, she rocked him or pressed him against her, trying to comfort him. Between Jerry and the internal unrest, morning couldn't arrive too soon for Connie. When day broke, she was almost too exhausted to move.

'You've got work at half past eight,' Olive reminded her as they packed up their belongings and struggled into daylight. 'What are you going to do with the child?'

Connie had been hoping her mother would volunteer her help. 'I don't know, Mum.'

'Well, it's obvious isn't it? I'll have to look after him. But you must ask Mr Burns for time off so that you can take him to the Welfare people tomorrow. I'm sorry, he's a nice little chap, but he isn't our responsibility. And anyway, I'm sure they'll soon turn up a relative or two.'

The glimmer of hope that Connie had been cherishing now extinguished. Without her mother's help, she couldn't look after the baby. Her work came first.

The Marshes were silent as they turned the corner of Kettle Street. No one knew what they would find. But good news met them in the form of Nan, who was sweeping the glass and tiles from the pavement outside her house.

'You're back safely!' she cried excitedly. 'Well, you'll be pleased to know we're all in one piece. Our house, yours, the whole street.'

Connie saw the tears of relief glisten in her mother's eyes. Even her brothers started running towards home, punching each other playfully as they went.

Number thirty-three was a welcome sight. Connie walked towards it, wondering how she was going to get through Monday when she felt so tired. More than anything she wanted to curl up in her nice warm bed and sleep. Her body felt battered, her neck and face stiff, her arms bruised where she'd held Lucky for so long. But she was still breathing and that was what counted.

An hour later, she was hurrying down Kettle Street, dressed in her working clothes. Her naturally wavy blond hair was drawn up at the sides and pinned in a neat roll over her forehead. The white blouse and skirt beneath her coat were regulation wear for the office and her shoes sturdy heeled brogues. The stockings that she had preserved so carefully were now past their prime, but Mr Burns held high standards of dress for his staff and Connie always made certain she observed them.

As she turned into Westferry Road, a tall figure hurried towards her. Vic Champion cut a handsome figure in daylight, his dark and now dustless hair slicked back across his head. His shoulders looked even wider under the smart, single-breasted, grey and tan checked overcoat.

'Vic, what are you doing here?'

'Looking for you. I've brought these.' He handed her a brown paper parcel. 'From Pat. The baby's dry clothes.'

'Oh, thanks, but I'm on my way to work. Mum's looking after the baby today.'

He took her arm. 'Where do you work?'

'At Dalton's, the transport people.'

'My car's round the corner. I'll drive you there.'

'You have a car?'

He nodded. 'I don't know for how much longer though. What with the petrol so short.'

A few minutes later, she was being chauffeured in a comfortable green Austin to her place of work. She hadn't been in a car since her driving lessons last year. After Britain declared war on Germany, she had taken ten lessons with an elderly instructor from Poplar who offered his services free as a contribution to the war effort. Connie wanted to help her country if necessary, by enlisting, with driving as one of her skills. But Mr Burns had persuaded her out of it, remarking dryly that the work she was doing was more important, if a little less glamorous. And as there were very few cars on the roads due to the petrol rationing, it seemed to have been a pointless exercise.

Vic drove them through the cluttered streets, his big hands capably steering the vehicle. There were few other motorists about, mainly fire engines and their crews and lorries being piled high with debris. He made several detours as roads were too obstructed to pass. The East End was waking up to the next round of clearance, cleaning, and fighting innumerable fires.

'Where do you work?' she asked curiously.

'Wapping, in the PLA offices. Have done since I left school. Dead boring really, but it pays well.'

'That's important,' Connie acknowledged.

'It's a respectable job, as Gran would say. It was her who pushed me into it. She said it would be a waste to work on the merchant ships, which is what I wanted to do. Not that I hope to be there much longer. I've put in for the navy.'

'Yes, Pat said.' Connie frowned. 'Have you always lived with your Gran?'

'Since we were kids.' He nodded. 'Mum and Dad died when we were young.'

'That must have been awful.'

'It would have been without Gran. Which reminds me, I made enquiries at our post about the baby's mother. The tenant of the house was a Miss Elsie Riding, an elderly spinster, who lived alone. She also died during that raid – her body was found quite close to the girl. As for the people in the house next door, luckily they evacuated last month. There was only one woman, a few doors along, who had noticed a young girl going in and out of Elsie's. She didn't know who she was. Apparently Elsie kept herself to herself.'

'There must have been some identification. Everyone carries a bag, or papers of some kind.'

'Nothing that our blokes have found yet.'

'But who could she be, then?'

'I'll check the list each day. It's updated after each raid, so someone of her description and the baby's might turn up. How's Laughing Boy, by the way?'

'Dad suggested we call him Lucky and it's sort of caught on.' Connie smiled as Vic stopped the car outside Dalton's. 'Thanks for the lift.'

'My pleasure.' He grabbed her wrist as she went to get out. 'Connie, are you free on Saturday?'

'Why?' she asked stupidly.

'We could go for a drive.' He laughed shyly. 'Though with the raids as they are, I appear to be asking you out at the worst possible time in history.'

'I've got to work in the morning,' she said quietly.

'The afternoon then. About two?'

She nodded. 'I'll wait on the corner.'

He was still smiling as he drove off, leaving Connie to wonder if he really had just asked her out on an official date.

The tall wooden gates of Dalton's Import, Storage and Transport Services were still intact, as was the huge wharf-side warehouse behind them. The transport department where Connie worked was located to the rear and she hurried there eagerly amidst the early morning rush.

The faces that looked at one another held expressions of surprise and joy, as colleagues hugged, patted backs and even shook hands at the fact they were still alive. Amongst them was Connie's best friend, Ada Freeman, a slim young woman with long auburn hair who pushed her way through the throng to grab Connie in a warm embrace.

They hugged and linked arms as they made their way to the shipping office. They had so much to tell one another that they didn't at first see their boss, Alfred Burns, inspecting his watch.

'Good morning, Connie . . . Ada.' He nodded as they filed by, giving them a businesslike smile, as usual.

'Good morning, Mr Burns,' they chorused, also as usual.

'A nice morning, isn't it?'

'Yes, Mr Burns.'

'Glad to see you in.'

It was not surprising to Connie that her manager's last remark was his only concession to the previous thirty-six hours of high drama. Even the bombing had not altered his routine or the expression on his deadpan face. Short and dapper in his pinstriped suit and waistcoat, he kept his finger firmly on the pulse of the shipping office. Connie was thankful that her little world at work had not been disrupted, even by the Luftwaffe.

She wanted to tell Ada all about Vic and Lucky, but by the time they were sitting on their tall stools and facing their ledgers and typewriters on the narrow shelf they both worked on, Leonard English, the head clerk, was doing the rounds. After loudly allotting them their instructions for the day, he lowered his voice to a whisper.

'Are you both all right?'

'Yes, thanks, Len.' Connie smiled as she opened her ledger, blowing away the dust that seemed to have covered the entire planet since the bombing began. 'What about you and your mum?'

He gave a little shrug, his thin face and pale blue eyes wearing a perpetually hungry expression. Connie always felt he deserved a good meal. Len lived with his eccentric mother, who was now the topic of his conversation. 'Mother didn't approve of last night at all,' he said soberly, as the girls tried not to laugh. 'She's thinking of complaining.' He gave them a droll smile. 'I told her to go ahead, I'd pay her ticket to Berlin. And you know what?'

'What?' both girls whispered.

'She accepted.'

The giggles were rife as Mr Burns glanced up from his

desk. 'Everything all right over there, Mr English?'

'Yes, thank you, Mr Burns.' Len gave them a wink and said in an exaggerated voice, 'We'll get on with the processing of goods, Miss Freeman, Miss Marsh. The bargees will be assessing their loads before the weigh-in. We'll carry on as normal and if there are any, er . . . disturbances, the cellars below are open to staff. Now, who is going down to meet the deliveries?'

'It's me this week, Mr English,' Ada said in a high-pitched, squeaky voice that almost had Connie hooting again.

'Very good.' Len leaned over their ledgers in pretence of scrutiny. 'See you girls in the canteen.'

When he had gone, Connie glanced at her friend sitting a few feet away. Ada was still trying not to laugh, her green eyes sparkling as she kept her hand over her mouth. Connie did the same and looked away. Exhaustion, relief, disorientation and fear were to blame for their heightened states, and in Connie's case a tingling anticipation of Saturday.

At one o'clock, she and Ada made their way to the canteen. Len was waiting for them. Over hot mugs of tea and slightly stale spam sandwiches, they swapped tales of the last two unbelievable days. Connie's discovery of Lucky and the night spent under the stairs in Gran's cupboard was enough to make Ada's eyes pop out from their sockets. Len said the drama quite eclipsed his own. The one story Connie didn't relate, though, was of Billy and the burglary. Even to Connie, the incident was beginning to fade into realms of fantasy.

*

Just after lunch, Mr Burns instructed them to pack away their books. 'Due to unforeseen circumstances,' he explained briefly, 'we are closing early. The time lost will be made up by arrival at work in the morning and every day thereafter for two weeks, at eight o'clock prompt.'

'I saw some official-looking bods arriving in a big black jam jar,' Len whispered as Connie and Ada completed their work and closed their ledgers. 'I'll bet it's to do with them.'

'What could they want?' Connie wondered aloud.

'I've a feeling we'll all find out soon enough,' Len said nervously.

'And why should we have to come in early for two weeks?' Ada demanded as they went to put on their coats.

'I've never known Mr Burns to let us off early before, not even in the summer when the city was bombed,' Connie agreed as they hurried to the gates.

'Yeah, but our planes were giving Jerry a run for their money then. Last night it was all one way, and sadly not ours.'

'Look after yourself,' Connie said as the two girls stood together in the mild September afternoon. 'Will you be seeing Wally?'

'We only met for half an hour yesterday because I had to help Mum with me three younger sisters. I gotta see him tonight or I'll bust,' Ada sighed bleakly. 'We can't even kiss without Dad breathing down our necks lately, let alone have a bit of how's your father. What about your new bloke?'

'He's not my bloke, Ada. I told you, he was at British Street School with us.'

'Well, I don't remember him.'

'You wouldn't. He wasn't your type.'

'What do you mean by that?'

'Only that he was in the football team and older than us. You never watched any of the matches. You was always hanging round the bike sheds having a fag when they were on.'

'S'pose I was. But you're seeing him on Saturday, aren't you? What's that if it not going out with someone?'

Connie smiled. 'It's certainly not a bit of how's your father.'

'You'll never know till you try it,' Ada responded with a wink. 'And in my opinion it's the best thing since fried bread. And I'd eat it every day if I could. Fried bread, I mean.'

Connie gasped. 'Ada Freeman, you be careful!'

Ada grinned, tossing back her red hair. 'I want a bit of fun whilst I'm young enough to enjoy it.'

'Just as long as it's fun you want and not babies,' Connie warned.

'Hark at you,' her friend cried as she took her leave, 'you're looking after a kid and you haven't had any fun getting it. T'ra now. See you at eight o' clock tomorrow morning!'

Connie watched Ada's little bottom under her raincoat wiggle off into the distance. Trust Ada to put the situation into perspective. But she was wrong on one count. She hadn't had fun in finding Lucky, it had been a traumatic experience all round. But from the moment the baby smiled at her, something inside her had changed. Added to this was the appearance of Vic, who today she had spent a good deal of time thinking about.

If only she could keep Lucky a little longer! Then Connie had an idea. Perhaps he had won over her mother's heart, just as he had hers. Perhaps her mum would be holding him tenderly in her arms, an entranced smile on her face.

'Constance, we'll manage him somehow,' she would say.

Almost breaking into a run, Connie set off for home. Her heart was much lighter than it had been at the beginning of the day.

Chapter Four

'He's had wind all morning,' Olive complained as she stood in the kitchen, holding the baby over her shoulder. 'I haven't been able to get on with a thing. Crying continually he was.'

Connie, breathless from hurrying home, took the baby in her arms. She rocked him gently, gazing into his little red face. If she had entertained any hope of the infant charming her mother, it had now disappeared.

'Did he drink his milk?'

'Yes, but I don't think it agrees with him. He was probably breast-fed.'

'Oh dear. Does it make much difference?'

'Not in wartime,' her mother said briskly.

'Pat suggested he might eat mashed or strained food,' Connie offered unwisely, regretting the remark as soon as she'd made it.

Her mother's eyebrows jumped to her hairline. 'And where would I find the time to mash and strain food,' she demanded shakily, 'when I haven't even had a spare moment to prepare your father's dinner?'

'Is the gas on?'

'Yes, but I don't even know if we'll have time to eat. Not if we want to get down to Tiller Road before that dratted siren goes off.'

The subject of the public shelter was weighing heavily on Connie's mind too. And now it was broached, she braced herself for the opposition to follow. 'I'd prefer to stay in the Anderson, Mum, with the baby of course.'

Olive gasped. 'Rubbish, Constance. You're coming with us.'

'I'm sorry, but Dad said if we had any objections to voice them. Public shelters aren't for me, Mum. I know you feel safer there, but I don't. It was like being trapped in a sardine can, with all the fish still wriggling. I didn't get a wink of sleep all night.'

'And you think you'll fare any better in that rabbit hutch outside?' Olive said scornfully.

'I don't know. But I'm willing to try.'

Her mother opened her mouth to speak, but then her face crumpled. 'Oh, this dreadful war! Look what it's doing to us. Driving families apart who should be standing shoulder to shoulder.'

Despite the sorrow in her mother's voice, Connie saw the funny side. 'It was more like bum to bum in Tiller Road. The farts were bouncing off the walls like tennis balls.'

'Oh, this is not a joke!' Olive dabbed her eyes with the hem of her pinny. 'I don't know what's to become of us, I'm sure.'

Connie put her free arm round her mother's shoulders.

'As soon as Dad and the boys come home, you'll feel better.'

'Much hope of that!' Olive wailed. 'Billy's probably down the river again, the little devil, despite your father giving him a right ticking off after Saturday. And Kevin – well, words fail me! He's going straight from the factory to the Nobbs's house. I ask you! Preferring someone else's home to his own.' She looked indignantly at Connie. 'It's not right you know, he's only fifteen. That girl will latch on to him if he's not careful.'

'Our Kevin knows what he's doing,' Connie answered quietly. 'He's sensible – like you. He knows what he wants out of life.'

Olive looked askance. 'And what choice does a woman have in this world? If she's a wife and mother she is everyone's property but her own. You put yourself last and your family first. Is it so wrong to expect a little loyalty now and then? You never ask for anything in return. Just a little peace occasionally. A moment or two to get your thoughts together. And then what happens? The war, that's what.' Red in the face, she heaved in a quick breath. 'Now, I know this poor child couldn't help crying, but I'd forgotten how much attention babies need. Feeding, changing, washing out the nappies and drying them – the work is endless.'

Connie was aware that any moment now one of her mother's 'turns' was on the cards, curable only by an early night and the household treading on eggshells, a remedy that in wartime was highly unlikely to be available.

'Anyone at home?' Nan and Lofty Barnes ambled into the kitchen, filling the small space with their large bodies.

'What's up, me old china?' Taking one glance at Olive's flushed face, Lofty dropped his tool bag and pulled her into his arms.

'Don't suffocate the poor bitch,' Nan rebuked her husband. 'What is it, Ollie? Tell us what's wrong.'

'Nothing, nothing!' Olive pushed herself from her neighbour's clumsy embrace, hurriedly repairing the damage to her hair. 'Things got on top of me for a bit, that's all. But I'm fine now,' she ended through gritted teeth.

Nan raised an eyebrow at Connie.

'The baby had wind,' Connie offered, doing her best to sound calm and unperturbed.

Nan held out her arms. 'Give him to me, love. Olive, why don't you go upstairs for forty winks? Connie, make yer mum a nice cup of rosie and take it up to her. Lofty, off you trot and get that door back on its hinges. Now, me and the kiddy will be in the front room out of everyone's way.'

'I don't want any tea, thank you, Constance,' Olive said indignantly.

'Please yourself, ducks.' Nan winked at Connie and disappeared into the hall.

Alone with her daughter, Olive whispered, 'Nan means well, but she hasn't had a day's illness in her life and doesn't know what it's like to feel out of sorts.'

'Why don't you go to the shops, then?' Connie suggested. 'A breath of fresh air always cheers you up. I'll peel the veg and there's a tin of spam on the top shelf. By the time you get back, dinner will be ready.'

Olive, looking brighter, grasped her handbag. 'Well, I have been saving up me coupons. Enough for . . . let me see, four ounces of tea, that'll make a nice change, having a strong cup instead of dishwater. And four ounces of jam would make us a good breakfast through the week instead of dripping . . . just lucky that I saved last week's meat rations too, due to Kevin being over at *that* girl's house for his meals.'

Connie took the grey coat from the peg on the kitchen door. 'It's not cold, but you'd better put this on.'

'Quite right, dear, I don't want a chill.' Olive slid in her arms and turned down the collar. 'You always seem to get these complaints when the weather turns.'

Connie gently ushered her from the kitchen. Once on her own, she felt like a hearty sigh herself. She heated the milk for Lucky and took the bottle to Nan. Five minutes later he was feeding nicely and the front door was a screw away from total repair.

Other than Lofty's whistling, the silence was golden. Connie absorbed it as she stood at the sink peeling vegetables. She couldn't wait to give Lucky a cuddle and knew that later, in the Anderson, she would be holding him close. By which time her mother would be installed in a public shelter, the most torturous form of existence Connie could imagine!

Had she made the right decision after all? Connie wondered that night. She was sitting, petrified, next to Billy in the Anderson. The bombs that had been dropping incessantly since dusk were pounding the earth like giant footsteps across the land. Every impact sent a vibration through the ground, but at least Billy was beside her and the baby was asleep after screaming his lungs out for the past two hours.

Thanks to the Valor paraffin stove that her father had transferred from the front room, she was able to heat the milk. In addition to the candles, a Tilley lamp and Dad's old army hammock had been resurrected from the attic. Billy had also produced a contraption for the baby to sleep in. A crude wooden crate balanced on four small, rusty wheels attached to an iron frame.

When a sudden lull in the bombing came, Billy gave a hefty sigh. 'He's gone off, at last.' He nodded at the slumbering child swathed in a blanket, his pink face illuminated by the glow of the candle. 'The cart's done the trick, eh?'

Connie nodded, her ears still ringing. 'Where did you find it?'

'The rag and bone yard. Well, the wheels anyway. I stuck the bit of wood across the metal and tied on the rope so's you can pull it along.'

'You can be useful when you try.'

'I thought I better get back in your good books.'

'Oh, so that's your game.' Connie relented a little. 'Well, you've made a start, so don't go blotting your copybook.'

'I don't intend to.' He gestured to the hammock strung from one end of the shelter to the other. 'Get your head down and I'll take first watch.'

Connie felt a little shudder of delight at the mention of sleep. She had been treading air all day and was ready to fall asleep sitting up. But Billy's sudden concern worried her. 'You're not thinking of doing another bunk, are you?'

'Not likely. I'm a changed man, now.'

'A man, eh? You was just a fourteen-year-old kid yesterday.'

Billy grinned. 'Seen your bloke then?' he asked mischievously.

'If you mean Vic Champion,' she huffed, 'he's not my bloke. I told you, we went to school together.'

After a small silence, Billy nudged her arm. 'Connie?'

'What?'

'Lend us three bob, will you?'

Connie's jaw dropped. 'I thought you was after something!'

'Only till next week. I owe the bloke for them wheels.' He nodded down at the baby's cart.

'Those rusty old things cost three shillings!'

Billy looked insulted. 'Every bit of metal's going on the war effort. I was lucky to get them.'

Connie picked up her bag and opened her purse. 'I suppose, as it's for the baby . . .'

'Thanks, Con. You're a sweetheart.'

'So you keep telling me.'

Billy stuffed the money in his pocket. 'Come on, I'll show you how to get in the hammock. Me and Kev used to muck about with it in the yard. It's a right laugh, I can tell you.'

Connie placed her foot in Billy's cupped hand. He heaved her into the hammock. They were both laughing as she swung precariously to and fro. 'Hold on, I'll push your bum in!'

'You leave my bum alone, Billy Marsh,' Connie giggled, wriggling herself into place and snuggling down. If only Billy was always like this, the brother who made her laugh and was kind and considerate. She could hardly believe this was the same boy who had abandoned her in Haverick Street.

As she looked up into his laughing face, she wondered again if she was being naïve. Was he really going to change his ways? A concern that soon disappeared as she fell fast asleep.

Early next morning there was a bang on the door. It took her a few minutes to roll out of the hammock and stand upright.

The door came open with a creak, letting in the smoke and fumes, but Nan's smile was as cheerful as ever. 'Tea up, ducks,' she cried, pushing a tin mug into Connie's hands. 'I'd make one for your brother too, but just look at those two. Fast asleep by the looks of it.' Billy was curled on the bench, snoring loudly. Lucky lay snoozing in the cart beside him.

Connie stepped outside. 'Nan, you're a lifesaver.'

'Thought I'd drop by before yer mum and dad arrive home.'

Connie sat down on the sandbags and Nan perched beside her. 'Well, as you can see, we survived another night,' Nan said as they gazed up at the house. 'Did you manage any kip?'

Connie stretched her stiff body. 'More than the night before. I tried to take Lucky in the hammock with me when it was really noisy but I had to wake Billy and ask him to hold the hammock. It swings everywhere. And the milk took ages to warm, by which time Lucky was screaming his head off. When I changed his nappy he did a pee all over the place.'

Nan roared with laughter. 'That's men for you. Untidy buggers.'

Connie sipped her tea. 'I wonder if Mum and Dad and Kev are all right.'

'Course they are. Now, I'm here to ask you a specific question. What are you going to do with the baby today?'

All night Connie had been wrestling with the problem, which was the true reason for her sleeplessness. But in spite of all her thinking she had come up with only one solution. 'I'm not going into work,' she confided miserably. 'Mr Burns would have a fit if I asked for time off. I'll say I was sick. As I can't expect Mum to look after Lucky in her state of health, I'll have to do as everyone says. Take him to the Welfare people.'

Nan made a little snort. 'Poor little sausage.'

'I know. But what else can I do?'

'I could look after him for you.'

Connie looked up in surprise. 'Would you, Nan?'

'We got on like a house on fire yesterday, 'scuse the pun. He finished his bottle, didn't he, and survived?' She patted Connie's arm. 'I won't see sixty again, love, but

I'm not geriatric. Me and Lofty never had any kids but I'd like to do me bit for the war effort in whatever way I can.'

'Oh, Nan, what a relief!'

'You're partial to this little lad, ain't you?'

Connie looked at Lucky in his cart and her heart melted. 'He's such a good baby.'

'Yeah, well, life is full of surprises, girl. Now, do you want me to take him on?'

'Tell you what, I'll feed and change him, then we'll stop at your house on the way to work, if that's all right? About half past seven as I have to be at Dalton's for eight.'

Nan stood up. 'Just walk right in, the door's open.'

'Shall I bring the cart?'

'No, don't bother, Lofty'll rig something up.' She took the mug from Connie and disappeared into the mist.

Connie wanted to jump for joy. She could keep her promise to Lucky's mother, at least for the time being. Of course, she couldn't expect this to be a permanent arrangement – her excitement faded a little at the thought – perhaps the same thing would happen with Nan as had happened with her mother. Nan had never had children. Perhaps she was trying to be kind, but taking on too much. On the other hand, Nan wasn't the sort to fade at the first hurdle.

Billy staggered out of the shelter. His jacket and trousers were rumpled and his sleeves halfway up his arms. He yawned noisily.

'I've had good news,' she told him excitedly. 'Nan Barnes is going to take care of Lucky.'

Billy stretched his long arms. 'Well, as it happens I've got a bit of good news meself.' He sat down beside her, rubbing his knuckles in his eyes.

Connie frowned. 'Like what?'

'I've got a job. A proper one.'

'But you're still at school.'

'I ain't been for ages.'

'What!'

'They think Mum evacuated me. I told my teacher I was going to Wales.'

'Oh, Billy, you didn't. What if they check up?'

'They won't. Half the schools are closing because there's no kids left on the island.' He gave her a nudge. 'Come on, give us a smile.'

'You worry me.'

'What's to worry about? I'll be making a nice few bob with this job. I'll tell Mum as soon as I get me first pay packet.'

'What is this job, then?' she asked suspiciously.

'Roofing. A bloke I know needs a lad to help him. We're collecting all the tiles that get blown down and putting them back on other houses. It's a doddle really, up and down ladders all day and driving around in Taffy's lorry.'

'Taffy who?'

'Taffy Jones. He's a cockney Welshman.'

Connie couldn't help laughing. 'Oh, Billy, trust you.'

He grinned as he sprang to his feet. 'Now, I gotta sit on the lav and have a fag before Mum comes back.'

Was roofing a proper job? Connie wondered as the

bathroom window shot open and a lot of coughing followed. At least it wasn't roaming the streets or worse, Connie decided as she lifted Lucky into her arms.

This was the best part of her day. When he opened his beautiful eyes and looked into hers – and smiled in recognition.

Nan regaled her that evening with all Lucky's antics, recorded down to the last teaspoon of strained veg. He could suck his toes, almost turn a circle on his tummy. She and Lofty had bathed him in the tin tub and dried him on the towel in front of the open fire.

Connie's mouth was watering. Not for food. She wasn't hungry. But the thought of bathing Lucky's little pink body, trickling the water over his bald head and dressing him in some of the fresh clothes that Pat had given her, was a sweet torment. How she longed to care for him herself, she thought, as she sat in one of Nan's large armchairs set either side of the blacked-out window.

It was a pleasant room, if cluttered, unlike her own home, not a cushion out of place. Nan and Lofty cared little for the appearance of their nest. The sideboard was overflowing and the old upright piano was in use as a clothes horse. But the room was easy on the eye and restful, as though the turmoil of the outside world had not yet reached in.

Connie listened to Nan's hearty laughter and saw the twinkle of a smile that Lucky gave her as he rested in her arms, all clean and scrubbed. Connie ached to take part in all these baby developments. Work had been miserable! Mr Burns had kept his staff's nose to the grindstone all day. Even Len had been out of sorts after a terrible night with his mother, who had refused to leave her warm bed when the warning went. He had been forced to stay up all night, as the bombs exploded around their ears. Ada had not seen Wally, either, and was pining for her boyfriend. The atmosphere at work had been sombre now that the raids looked set to continue.

'Here we go again!' Nan exclaimed when the siren wailed. 'Lofty! Where are you? Get this girl and baby home quick!'

Nan handed Lucky over. Connie wrapped him in his shawl, all thumbs as Lofty appeared. They ran together along the street and the sky grew dark against the searchlights.

Her mother and father were just leaving the house. 'Constance, are you coming with us?'

'No, I'll wait for Billy in the Anderson.'

'I don't know how you can—'

Ebbie gripped his wife's arm. 'Come along, Olive. Connie, take care of yourself, love.'

'Your dinner's in the oven,' Olive cried as Ebbie dragged her on. 'It's still warm.'

Connie rushed through to the kitchen. Balancing the baby in one arm, her dinner in the other she rushed out to the Anderson. Having forgotten to bring the milk with her, she laid the baby in the cart and rushed back in again. A few minutes later, back in the Anderson, she was too scared to move as the bombs began to fall outside.

Her dinner went untouched and when Billy arrived she threw her arms around him.

'Oh, Billy, thank goodness you turned up.'

'What's the matter? Has Hitler landed?' Billy teased as he secured the iron door and lit the Tilley lamp.

'I don't like it here on my own.'

'You've got Baldy.'

At that moment an explosion rocked the Anderson and Lucky began to scream. Connie lifted him from the cart and held him tight. 'What can I do to comfort him?' she asked helplessly.

For once, Billy didn't come up with an answer. 'I don't know about babies,' he said lamely.

Connie was beginning to think she didn't either.

Vic Champion inspected his face in the washhouse mirror. He groaned. He'd had practically no sleep in two nights and it showed. His jaw was covered in sharp, dark bristle, there were bags under his eyes and his thick, dark hair needed a good wash. As did the rest of his body, but with just a pitcher of water available he would have to be careful. He'd brought two big jugfuls from the standpipe this morning on his way home from night duty. Gran would certainly need one of them for her household chores and he always left her a spare, just in case the water was off for the day.

It was an irony he looked so rough, he thought as he rubbed his face with the penny-sized fragment of soap that he kept aside for shaving. Saturday had arrived, the day he had been looking forward to all week. The day he had intended to make a good impression!

Removing his greatcoat, he flipped his braces from his shoulders and unbuttoned his shirt. Pouring the freezing water into the enamel bowl, he bathed himself the best he could, then proceeded to shave. The cutthroat razor, freshly honed against the pummy stone, sliced off the stubborn beard and at last a smile formed on his face. That was better. He felt human at last.

After throwing the dirty water into the lavatory, he poured the remainder from the jug into the bowl. This time he washed his hair with the same tablet of soap, whistling as he did so. He was relieved to complete another daunting night standing in as an unofficial ARP warden. The noise of the bombs and the Mudchute ack-ack still resounded in his ears. As did the cries of the unfortunate victims he had worked to save from their ruined homes. Against his will, pictures flashed up in his mind. The distress, the blood and broken bones and, in some cases, the horror of a lingering death. He had worked desperately to free one man and his wife in the ruin of their home. She was dead, but the man was still clinging to her hand. The doctor had arrived and had known at once his lower limbs were crushed for ever. Even before the doctor had begun to amputate, the man was dead.

Vic blinked his eyes at the memory. He was twenty, young and able, but he had seen enough in one week for a lifetime. Did he still feel the way he had on that day in May when Operation Dynamo had begun? The whole island had turned out to salute the flotillas of small boats as they sailed down the Thames to France. Rescuing the

Allied forces stranded at Dunkirk had been no mean feat. His heart had been heavy with yearning to help as he'd made his way over the bridge and turned left before the donkey field opposite the Seaman's Mission and the Dock House pub, to stand at Pier Head. He had been filled with patriotic pride at the awesome sight. Our boys were being slaughtered on the beaches of France and every man who owned a vessel was turning out to help. He'd felt the same way in July and August when the Spitfires had protected London and the coasts with such tenacity against the Luftwaffe. All he'd wanted to do was to be up there with them, shooting the enemy down before they could create more carnage. But instead he'd been sitting safely behind an office desk in his reserved occupation at the Port of London Authority. He'd told his boss he was determined to join up. He was still waiting for his papers, still hoping to prove that he was prepared to fight for king and country.

But after this week, he felt sick to his stomach. So much death and destruction. And he hadn't even set foot out of England! Did he really have the guts to be a warrior, to look a man in the eye and shoot him? Did he have the courage to risk his life and, if necessary, sacrifice it?

'Vic? Breakfast, son.'

Gran's voice rocketed out of the back door. Vic quickly dried his hair on the ancient towel full of darns. He fingered the wet locks across his scalp and plastered the weight flat with the palm of his hand. He glanced in the mirror once more and saw someone he at last recognized.

The kitchen was warm, filled with the smell of frying bacon. 'Blimey, where did you find a porker?' Vic asked his Gran, who stood at the stove.

'Less said the better on that score,' Gran muttered, tapping the side of her nose. Her beady eyes looked up at Vic with mirth. He grinned, stretching his muscular arms above his head. 'Never quiz a woman about her coupons, eh?' he chuckled.

She pushed him out of her way. 'Now, you might look like Rudolph Valentino standing there half naked, but you can't sit down undressed to breakfast in this house. Lower the rack and put on a clean shirt. There's one ironed already.'

Vic did as he was told. 'Where would I be without you, Gran?'

'Oh, don't give me any of that flannel,' she cried. 'Hurry up, your bacon's getting cold.'

'It's not out of the pan yet.'

'It will be by the time you get your arse on the chair.'

Enjoying the familiar banter, Vic removed the pristine white collarless shirt from the wooden slats and raised the rack to the ceiling again. When he was dressed, he sat down in front of two fat slices of crispy bacon, one egg and two thick wedges of bread spread with lard. A cup of tea stood beside his plate and a round of toast as back-up.

Gran sat beside him, her small, plump figure lost in the folds of her black garments. He had never known her to wear any other colour. Woollen jumpers, long skirts, headscarves, gloves and coats, all as black as night.

'Go on,' Vic urged, lifting the plate of toast towards her, 'indulge yourself. Have a slice.'

'No thanks, cock, I prefer me Bemax. The tin says it's gas proof!' Gran chuckled as she tilted her spoon into the chipped china bowl.

'That stuff'll put hairs on your chest, you know,' Vic teased as he attacked his cooked breakfast.

'Shut up and eat up, you saucy sod,' Gran replied gamely.

He would have preferred to see her eat a good breakfast once in a while. But she wouldn't hear of it, no matter how hard he nagged. Relishing the feel of the perfectly cooked hot food sliding down into his empty stomach, he had to admit the sustenance made him a whole man again.

Vic thought, as he did every day, that he couldn't have had a happier life. He was grateful to Gran for the gift of it. If it hadn't been for her, he'd be an orphanage kid and so would Pat. None of their relatives had stepped forward when their parents had died. Had it not been for Gran, they wouldn't have known what life or love was about. Vic worshipped the old woman who sat beside him now. And he knew the feeling was returned.

They talked for a while, discussing the raid last night and how Pat and her husband Laurie had converted the cellar of their house in Manchester Road into a nice little sitting room. And how even Dorrie was getting used to the explosions and how Gran slept on the put-u-up next to Dorrie's camp bed and caught a draught down her neck. Vic related some of the events of his warden's rounds but not all. Though he could see by her eyes roving his face that his Gran was well aware of the horrors that had passed.

'Now,' said Gran as she scooped the last puddle in her bowl to her dry, wrinkled lips, 'where are you taking your girl today?'

Vic almost dropped his knife. One thing about Gran that he wasn't too struck on was her second sight, as she termed it. She'd had the knack all her life, coming out with things that even he or Pat didn't know were about to happen. She read the tealeaves and could give an answer to a problem or foretell the future. And she didn't ask you whether you wanted to know it or not. Out it came, like this morning, when he hadn't even finished his tea, and he knew that once the tealeaves were strewn out before him he'd be hot at the back of his neck, wondering what she was about to say.

'What are you on about?' he demanded, playing for time.

'You're meeting a lady, aren't you?'

Vic blushed as he tried to swallow his bacon. 'You're an old witch you are.'

'No, that was deduction, boy,' she clarified swiftly. 'You washed and shaved and put on a clean shirt without an argument. You've got a smile on your mug as wide as Greenwich Reach, and that means only one thing.'

Vic relaxed a little, though not for long.

Gran bent forward. 'But I can tell you something more, lad, and this isn't guesswork. She's special, this one. She's got good lights. The only problem being there's other lights around her I don't like. Mucky stuff.'

This time Vic did drop his knife. It clattered on his plate and he almost choked. He took a long swig of tea. Before he'd finished swallowing Gran was pointing her bony finger. 'Tip your cup and turn three times.'

'Do I have to?'

'Gave you the best china, didn't I?'

Groaning, he tipped and the tealeaves swam over the saucer in rocky little piles. To Vic it looked a mess. But he knew that to Gran it was probably the meaning of life.

She took a sharp, wheezy gulp of breath. Her eyes went wide until Vic could see their whites, then slowly she relaxed and her eyelids fluttered. 'Well now, that's a to-do, that is, a real to-do.'

'What do you mean?'

'I'm sorry to say she has trouble ahead.'

Vic sighed inwardly. It wasn't fair. He'd hardly got back to knowing Connie yet. He'd been sweet on her at school and too shy to do anything about it. She wasn't giggly or mouthy like the other girls. She'd had these amazing blue eyes that filled her face and warmed him up the moment he looked in them. Her hair was all wavy right down her back, like a field of corn in the wind. And now Gran was telling him about troubles and mucky stuff, just what he didn't want to hear.

'Gran, you know I don't understand all this stuff,' Vic protested miserably. He wanted to enjoy today with Connie. In fact, he wanted to enjoy a lot more time with her if given the chance. It wouldn't be so bad in a reserved job if he had Connie as his girl.

'I've told you before, son,' Gran said patiently. 'We all have lights. Around us, shimmering like a second skin. You can tell if a person's not well, or what troubles they're in—'

'Yeah yeah, I know that, Gran. But it's only you that see them. How should I know what Connie's got—'

'So it *is* Connie Marsh?'

Vic rolled his eyes. 'It's nothing serious,' he insisted, but Gran was already shaking her head.

'It's dead serious, lad, you mark my words. Your lights are an identical match, like rainbows you both are, like the sun and the rain, they need each other.' She shook the saucer gently. 'And there's something else too.'

'I don't want to know,' Vic groaned, pushing back his chair.

Gran was silent then and reached out to grasp his hand. Her fingers were shaking as she squeezed his knuckles. 'There's an envelope on its way. Brown it is. Same as the mucky lights.'

'A letter's nothing to worry about,' Vic joked, clasping the frail hand tightly between his own. 'There might be money in it.'

'No, it's not money.' Gran frowned as she indicated a little pile of tealeaves that bore an uncanny resemblance to the shape of the British Isles. 'Britain see? The old woman sits on her pig. Scotland, the rider, Wales, the pig's head. Over here, the east and the beast's bum.'

Vic gave a little shudder as he shifted uncomfortably. 'Yeah, I remember me geography, Gran, though I can't say it was taught like that.'

'Well in my day it was – now concentrate. I don't like the pig's head. My advice to you is sit astride the animal and take fate into your own hands.'

He laughed nervously. 'Can I go now?'

'Remember what I said.'

'Righto, Gran,' he said quickly and stood up. 'And just to put you out of your misery, yes, I am seeing Connie, that is, if I can find any trousers to put on.'

Gran waved her hand. 'They're hanging over your chair upstairs. Oh, and don't go up West today. I'd stay local if I was you.'

'Why's that?'

Gran looked up. 'Me water's telling me they'll be over soon.'

Vic didn't stop to ask any more. He wanted to see Connie more than he wanted to listen to any more forecasts about the future.

Chapter Five

'Vic, this is Mum and Dad.' Connie knew she was stating the obvious but was too embarrassed to stop as the family lined up in order to be introduced. 'And this is Kevin and Sylvie – and Billy.'

If it hadn't been for the bus being late when she'd left Dalton's, she would have been safely outside the house now and waiting on the corner with Lucky as arranged.

Vic was standing in the middle of the front room, nodding and smiling at the full complement of the Marsh family. Even Billy's presence was a rarity; Saturday mornings he usually vanished before anyone was up.

'Pleased to meet you all,' Vic said several times again, beaming another smile as he looked slightly confused at the effusive greeting.

'And we're pleased to meet you – again – son.' Ebbie winked at Connie as she held a freshly changed Lucky across her hip. 'Used to watch you playing football when you were knee high, but I don't expect you remember me.'

'I do as a matter of fact, Mr Marsh. It was a long time ago, but I know your face.'

Vic was relieved of his coat and a tin of Jacob's Assorted Biscuits was found and offered swiftly past the noses of the family, to linger in front of the visitor. Vic sat on the couch, drinking more tea than Connie suspected he had ever drunk in his life before.

She was relieved when all the questions were over and they were on their way out to the car. 'Sorry you had to knock for me,' Connie apologized as they climbed in. 'I was late getting Lucky ready otherwise I'd have been on the corner waiting.'

'When you weren't there,' Vic said as he started the engine, 'I thought you'd changed your mind.'

'I wouldn't have done that.' She gestured to Lucky, who she had dressed in Dorrie's rompers, a blue bonnet and a blue coat that Nan had picked up from the market. 'As you can see, I didn't go to the Welfare people. Do you mind if he comes with us?'

Vic winked at the baby. 'Course I don't. He looks grand now he's washed up. Look at them big eyes. Same as yours. As blue as a clear blue sky.'

Connie blushed. 'Yes, they were dark at first, but now they've changed.'

'Did your Mum have him whilst you were at work?'

'No, I had an unexpected offer of help from our neighbour, Nan Barnes. She's wonderful, bless her heart, but does go on a bit. I don't like to be rude so by the time I left her house and got back home today it was almost two o'clock. I didn't even have time to change.'

'You look lovely.'

Connie grinned. 'I'm still in my working clothes.' She

hadn't had time to put on a dress, or pin her hair up.

He glanced at her. 'Well, you still look lovely. The pair of you do.' He looked back at the road. 'I've checked all the missing lists, by the way. No one's reported a missing girl and her baby, not a whisper.'

'But she must have an identity and so must he.'

'If anything turns up, you'll be the first to know.'

Connie didn't like to admit she was in no hurry for the baby to be claimed. Instead, she wound her fingers through his and looked into his eyes. It was very strange that he had her colour eyes. She wondered what colour his hair would be when it grew.

'I intended to drive up to town,' Vic said thoughtfully. 'But I'm undecided now.'

'Because I brought Lucky, you mean?' Connie asked worriedly.

'No, it was something Gran said, not that I should take her seriously, but once she makes these predictions it's hard to ignore them.'

'Predictions?' Connie repeated curiously.

He paused for a moment. 'I feel a bit of a twerp, really, repeating what seems like a load of cobblers. But this morning Gran knew about me taking you out.'

Connie looked confused. 'Did you tell her?'

Vic's dark eyebrows raised. 'Never said a word.'

'How did she know, then?'

He drew the car into the gutter and pulled on the handbrake. Switching off the engine, he turned in his seat, lifting his shoulders in a shrug. 'She said it was deduction, but she also reads the tealeaves. Now don't ask me how it works, 'cos I don't know. It's something I've grown up with from a kid and makes me a bit uncomfortable really. I always try to get out of it.'

Connie was fascinated. 'Why is that?'

'I suppose because she's not often wrong.'

'Does she tell you bad things, then?'

'Oh no.' He shrugged, drumming his fingers on the steering wheel. 'It's not bad or anything, but you get a sort of warning and you're obliged to take notice of it, whether you like it or not. Anyway, one of the things she went on about was not to go up West today, stay local, as she reckons we might get a raid.'

'What, in daylight?'

He nodded. 'I shouldn't take no notice really. I don't know why I'm hesitating.'

Connie nodded thoughtfully. 'Well, perhaps we could just go up to Cox Street? See if they've put out the stalls.'

Vic rubbed his jaw. 'Are you sure?'

'Of course. I like a bit of mystery.' She giggled.

Vic grinned as he glanced at her. 'I'll have to polish up on my mysterious skills, then.'

'You're doing quite well as it is.' Connie gazed into his beautiful eyes, so dark and dreamy, with little orange flecks in the centre of the brown that she hadn't noticed before. His smiling lips were full and smooth and set in the middle of a strong, square jaw that seemed to be just the right shape for his long, aquiline nose. He dressed so nicely too, the collar of his overcoat turned up, his shirt and tie just showing beneath, even driving gloves on the dashboard, though she hadn't seen him wearing them.

'So . . .' he said, taking a deep swallow, 'the market it is.' He stretched across to take Lucky's tiny hand in his big fingers. His palm covered the back of her hand briefly and their eyes met. Never before had she felt like this. Now she actually knew the meaning of the words weak at the knees, and the world for one breathtaking moment seemed to stand still. He gazed deeply into her eyes and very slowly leaned towards her. 'Connie, I—'

'What's all this?' a deep voice boomed through the open window. Connie saw a policeman standing there. 'We don't want no argey bargey in broad daylight, do we? Plenty of time for all that sort of stuff in the blackout.' He gave a little grin. 'Now, 'oppit!'

Looking embarrassed, Vic started the car again quickly. He drove off, the engine revving noisily over their suppressed laughter.

Everyone seemed to be defying the Luftwaffe to turn up. A fruit and veg barrow with a notice inscribed 'Hitler's bombs can't beat us' hanging from its canvas awning was surrounded by women opening their purses and shopping bags. People bustled to and fro as if it was quite normal to step over girders and deep craters. A piano had been pushed into the open and an old lady was sitting in front of it, bashing away at the keys. All the kids had gathered round and were singing whilst people carried furniture and possessions from the remains of one house into another. Even the demolished buildings were part of the scenery now. The islanders were out in force, searching for replacements for their losses, or simply to cheer themselves up.

Vic took Lucky in his arms as they strolled down the street. Connie noted the curious glances cast their way. What were people thinking, she wondered? What would it be like to have a husband and child of her own?

'Gran used to bring me and Pat here to the market, get us out of the way like, when Mum was ill and needed a bit of peace,' Vic said as they walked. 'She knew everyone. We'd tag along, playing with other kids, and help to bring back what she bought. Mostly it was fruit and veg and a bit of meat, all dead cheap.'

'How long ago was that?'

'I must have been six or seven and Pat a year younger. We lived up Poplar in two rooms then, but when Dad died of TB we came to stay with Gran. Mum lasted two years without him. Gran said she just wasted away. I don't remember much, but what I do remember, though, is Mum's smile. It was lovely, like a ray of sunshine.'

Connie felt sad. She was so lucky to have a family. 'Have you had your call-up papers yet?'

'Would you miss me if I went away?'

'I'd hardly notice.' She shrugged, then smiled. 'Well maybe I would – a bit.'

'A bit will do for now.'

'Why do you want to join up when you've got a reserved job?'

He transferred Lucky to his other arm, nestling the baby comfortably as he spoke. 'I've always wanted to do something that would make Mum and Dad proud of me. Even though I know they're not here to appreciate it. But I believe they're somewhere, that two lovely people like

80

them couldn't just disappear, never to be heard of again. Do you reckon I'm daft, thinking like that?'

Connie smiled. 'No, I don't.'

'Dad was ill from a kid. He had this shadow on his lung and got turned down for the navy. Gran said he always wanted to go to sea. He had ambition but he never lived to achieve his dreams.' He frowned down at her. 'What are your dreams, Connie?'

A week ago it would have been a good career with prospects, a dream that she had pursued since starting at Dalton's in the typing pool and working her way up to Mr Burns's shipping office. But now her aspirations seemed to have taken a back seat. 'Ada and me are the only ones left from our class at school that are single. Everyone else is married with kids, most of them living in the same houses as their relations, so hard up they've not got a penny to spare.' Connie looked up at him. 'Mum keeps on at me to settle down, as she calls it. But I don't want to rush into a marriage I'll regret as soon as the novelty wears off. I want – well, I want too much, she says. Apparently I've got exaggerated ideas of me own importance. She maintains she's managed on a shoestring and was happy enough, so why shouldn't I? But I know one thing, I don't want to be poor all my life.'

'Not many girls think like you,' he said quietly. 'All they want is a ring on their finger.' He steered her towards a stall full of china, brass and other strange objects. 'Come on, Miss Independence. Let's have a look, shall we?'

Connie wondered if he was secretly laughing at her. High faluting ideas was what Mum said her dreams were.

But she'd worked hard at school and even harder at Dalton's to get where she was. One day she could even be a secretary to the boss; it wasn't out of the question. She glanced at Vic and Lucky out of the corner of her eye and sighed. What did she really want out of life?

At the front of the stall stood a pile of thumbed *Woman's Own* and *Home Notes* magazines, all priced at a bargain halfpenny each. Propped against these was a child's Mickey Mouse gas mask, next to this a tea service, the cups, saucers and plates all chipped but painted in a nice floral pattern.

'Decent bit of china that,' the stallholder yelled. 'Get yer 'ubbie to treat you to it.'

Connie went red. She didn't look at Vic. 'Why is it so badly chipped?' she asked quickly to mask her embarrassment.

'Shrapnel. Took the full blast.'

'Oh.' Connie dug in a box of ornaments. She was still flustered that the stallholder had called Vic her hubbie. Had he heard the comment? It made her feel very strange, especially as only a moment ago she'd been Dalton's top career woman!

On the top of the box was a rude novelty toilet roll holder proclaiming 'S(h)it down with Goering and Use Hess Paper for Mess Paper!' She replaced it quickly.

Next to this was a stained chamber pot on top of which was propped a notice. 'Marmet pram for sale. Ask Mrs Pritchard'.

'A pram sounds just the job,' Vic said over her shoulder. 'He'll be too heavy to carry around soon.'

Connie was still staring at it. 'But a pram would cost a lot.'

'Hold Lucky a moment and I'll find Mrs Pritchard.' Vic handed over the baby.

'I've got my wages with me,' Connie called after him, her heart already dropping at the fact that most of it was already spent. After giving her mother the housekeeping, keeping some aside for Lucky's food and clothes and a little for herself, the remaining amount wouldn't be enough to pay for a pram.

Vic disappeared behind the stall. Connie lost sight of him then and went on to the next stall. Perhaps the pram was already sold!

Very soon she felt a tap on her back. Vic was grinning from ear to ear. He was rocking a large pram with a faded red hood and maroon apron. There was a large dent in the chassis and the wheels were three times the size of those on Billy's cart. A little blue elephant lay on the frilly pillow inside.

Connie's jaw dropped. 'Where did that come from?'

'Mrs Pritchard. She was over on the pie and mash and the pram was full of junk. She took it all out and the deal was done. Try it for size.'

Gently she lay Lucky inside, placing the elephant beside him. 'It's a perfect fit.'

'There's a harness too.'

'What a find!'

'Let's try to put it in the boot of the car.'

'I must pay Mrs Pritchard first.'

He took hold of her hands and placed them firmly on

the pram. Giving her a little push, he moved her forward. 'This one's on me – and no arguments now.'

Connie would have preferred to pay for the pram, even if it meant owing Mum the housekeeping. After all, Lucky wasn't Vic's responsibility. But she sensed he would be upset if she argued. She looked up at him. 'Thank you,' she said simply and he nodded.

'You're welcome.'

By the time they returned to Kettle Street it was almost four o'clock. Vic struggled to lift the pram from the boot where he had tied it with a rope. They had driven very carefully back, avoiding the potholes. Now, as he lowered it to the pavement, Connie lay Lucky in again, his soft crying denoting an appetite brewing.

'Come and meet Nan,' Connie suggested, knowing Nan would have the bottle at her fingertips.

'All right. But I won't stop. I've got firewatching tonight.'

Nan opened the door. She put her hands over her mouth. 'A pram!'

'This is Vic.' Connie smiled. 'He bought it at the market.'

'Lofty! Get yourself out here. We've got visitors.'

Lofty appeared in his shirtsleeves, a newspaper in hand. 'Blimey, a bath on wheels.' He grinned. 'Which end does the water come from?'

All four of them struggled to lift it over the step and into the passage. Connie pushed it into the front room. She hadn't realized it would take up so much space but Nan seemed delighted.

'Put it here by the chairs, love. I'll fetch his bottle. It's all ready.' Nan went out and Lofty rocked the pram.

'Sturdy bit of machinery this. I'll make a shelf to fit between them wheels.'

'Are you sure you want it here?' Connie asked, not knowing what she would do if he said no. But he shook his head, tapping the newspaper on the apron as he inspected the new addition.

'A jar of jam is just what she wanted.'

'I'll buy some covers for it next week.'

Lofty straightened his back. 'So you're the lad who helped our Connie rescue the baby? We've heard all about you. Now you'll stay to tea, I'm sure.'

'I've got to get back,' Vic said as Nan returned with the bottle. 'I'm on duty at five and I have to see Gran's all right before I go. There wasn't a raid today after all,' he added, glancing at Connie, 'but she was a bit worried.'

'Another time then,' Nan said. 'Now, I'll feed the boy whilst you see your young man off, Connie.'

'So I'm your young man, am I?' Vic asked as they walked out to the car.

'I never told them that,' Connie replied, blushing. 'Nan just assumed—'

'I wish I was,' he interrupted, moving a little closer. He took her hand. 'I wish a lot of things, Connie. And I think you know what they are. Can I see you again?'

'I'd like that.'

'When? Tomorrow?'

'I have to help Mum with the chores on Sundays.'

85

He looked disappointed. 'I'll have to wait till next Saturday, then?'

'Well, you could drop in anytime – if you're passing.'

He gazed deep into her eyes. 'Oh, I'll be passing all right.' He paused, squeezing her fingers, then slowly let them go. 'Goodbye, I suppose.'

'Goodbye – and thanks!'

She watched him drive off, her heart missing a beat as the car disappeared round the corner.

'Nice boy that,' Nan said when she went back in.

Connie sighed as she sat down. 'I know.'

'Reminds me of when I met lover boy here. Though you'd never believe it to look at him now, but he was a right good-looker. Romanced me good and proper he did, brought me flowers an' all.' She pushed Lofty's feet from the stool and brushed off the dirt. 'Now all he thinks about is his grub.'

'And lovely grub it is too,' Lofty mumbled from behind his raised newspaper.

'Talking of which I've saved a nice piece of bread pudding for you, love,' Nan said. 'Here, I've winded the child, but there's still some left in the bottle.'

Connie was daydreaming as she took Lucky and cuddled him in the big, comfy armchair. The fire in the grate was just embers now and the room was very warm. As Lucky sucked contentedly, gazing up at her with his big blue eyes, her mind wandered back to Vic and the way his hand had rested lightly on her waist as they'd strolled through the market. Had he heard when the stall-holder called him her hubbie?

'That poor old geezer popped his clogs you know,' Lofty said suddenly as he scrutinized the middle pages of the *Gazette*.

'What did you say?' Connie came back to reality with a start.

'A pawn shop was broke into up Stepney last Saturday. A gang pulled this job just as the first raid started. They shot the old boy in cold blood. Defenceless he was. Had a gun but it never worked. Was trying to scare them off.'

'He . . . he died you mean?'

'Yesterday, in the 'orspital.' Lofty rattled the newspaper angrily. 'The heartless sods want locking up and the key chucking away.'

The lunchtime drinkers of the Rose and Crown were all staring at Billy, who lay flat on his back, gasping. His jaw felt twice its normal size. Straw and sawdust spattered his bare chest and his filthy feet poked from the ends of his muddy trousers. A wave of sickness rolled slowly over in his stomach. He hadn't seen the blow coming. The Fat Man, his opponent and padded with lard, had landed a good one. Billy began to regret the glass of ale that he'd drunk from sheer bravado. If he'd had his senses about him when he stepped into the ring, he would have ducked in good time. He wasn't a drinker, didn't like the stuff, but all the blokes had been egging him on.

'Come on, lad, up you get.'

Billy felt the tip of Taffy's boot tickle his thigh. Conquering the urge to throw up, he climbed unsteadily to his feet. The heckling was loud, every man there hoping to see seven bells knocked out of the young whippersnapper.

'You'll get your second wind,' shouted Taffy in his ear as he pushed Billy forward. 'I've got a few quid on you, son. Don't let me down.'

Billy wiped his filthy hands across his swollen mouth. What had he let himself in for? He'd had no idea that you really – actually – got hurt in this game.

'You said he was a pushover,' Billy muttered.

'He's all wind. Just skip round and stay out of trouble. He'll soon run out of puff.'

As Billy blinked the sweat from his eyes, he wished he hadn't boasted he was handy with his fists. Taffy's sideline of setting up pub fights had momentarily dazzled him. He should have stuck to the roofing.

'You a scrapper, then?' Taffy had asked in surprise.

Billy'd nodded arrogantly. 'What's the money like?'

'Not bad, boyo, but you look a bit undersized to me.'

'See these?' Billy had raised his fists and punched air. 'So quick you'd miss 'em if you blinked.'

'Don't look up to much to me.'

Taffy's words echoed inside Billy's head as he wobbled precariously, trying to focus the three blurred faces of his opponent.

'Go on, lad, move!' he heard Taffy scream.

Billy's last thought before he crashed into the human wall of blubber was that not even Taffy's lorry would be able to knock this jelly flat.

'Missed,' growled the Fat Man as he gripped Billy's thin body between bulbous arms. Besides being slowly crushed to death, Billy was humiliated. He'd been smacked silly, knocked down and laughed at. He had to think of something or his roofing job would be just a distant memory.

'All right, I give in, mate, I'll go down,' he wheezed into the ugly mug. A trickle of oxygen squeezed into his lungs. The massive biceps relaxed. An instant later Billy's teeth were fastened over a thick, fleshy ear lobe.

Fatty's screams echoed round the pub yard. Billy tasted blood and revelled in it. He spat out the severed body part. The roar from the crowd was the last thing he remembered as he was flattened by a ton of ferocious flesh.

Connie jumped up from the bench as Billy stumbled into the Anderson. 'Oh!' she gasped at the sight of his swollen face. 'Billy, what's happened?'

'I walked into a door,' he said, trying to laugh.

'Your eye's all black.'

'Let me sit down.'

Stepping around the cart in which Lucky was fast asleep, Connie poured water from the jug into the pudding basin. The shelter was now equipped with enough supplies to get them through the difficult nights. Mum had donated old crockery and a first-aid tin. Dad had made a cupboard for food and Lucky's things. She opened the first-aid tin and took out the cotton wool.

Gently she bathed her brother's eye. She used a dab of tincture of iodine, a smear of Burnol cream and two of the dressings from the Emergoplast pack.

'Well, I'm waiting,' she said unsympathetically when she'd finished. 'What have you done now?'

'Sit down,' he said with a lisp from his swollen mouth. 'I can explain.'

'You always can.' She sat stiffly on the bench and folded her arms.

'I was in a fight.'

'I can see that.'

'No, sis, not an ordinary fight. A proper one, like you see at pubs, with counted rounds and all. My boss, Taffy Jones, set it up at the Rose and Crown. It's his sideline.'

Once more her jaw dropped. 'But what do you know about fighting?'

'Nothing. But I'm going to learn. Taffy says he'll teach me. This is just the beginning of what could be a very lucrative career. I could even be a proper boxer at the end of it.'

'I thought you wanted to be a roofer.'

'I'm doing that as well.'

'Is it legal?'

'What, fighting? Course it is. I don't say that the betting is kosher, but I don't have nothing to do with all that. I just get ten per cent of the purse.'

'What purse?'

'It's what they call a fighter's wage when it's all added up.'

Connie didn't know what to say. Billy's bright ideas always sounded wonderful. She didn't want to throw cold water on his enthusiasm, but would this idea be any different from all the others that had failed?

'Connie, I've got a paddy on me and I've never known what to do with it. Now I can use me fists for a purpose. It was amazing. All these blokes came round afterwards and patted me on the back, said I had what it took to be a real scrapper, that all I needed was a bit of building up.'

'But Billy—'

'Look what I got.' He dug into his pocket. 'Three quid, Connie, look! A genuine, honest to goodness three quid for doing sod all.' He thrust a pound note into her hand. 'Here's that three bob I owe you, with interest. Buy Lucky something nice from Uncle Billy.'

She tried to give it back again. 'I don't want this. Take it back.'

He shook his head firmly. 'That's me good deed for the day.'

'But you earned it.'

Billy took her by the shoulders. 'I don't intend to get clobbered like this again, Con, that's a mug's game. I'm gonna learn proper how to fight. Taffy's teaching me.'

Connie closed her eyes. 'Oh, Billy! I give up.'

He laughed aloud. 'Don't do that, gel. Things have turned out all right, haven't they?'

She gazed at him sadly. 'Not for the old man in Stepney, they didn't. He was shot and died.'

Billy's bloodshot eyes gazed out from their swollen sockets. 'What do you mean?'

'Lofty was reading the *Gazette* tonight. That gun never worked, so it must have been Reg that was doing the shooting.'

Billy looked as though he didn't believe her. 'Christ,

91

Con, I swear I never knew about any guns. I just went along with it all.'

'Have you met up with them since?' Connie demanded. Was he really as shocked as he looked or was this just another act?

'No. Course I haven't.'

'Do you intend to?'

'What do you think?'

'To be honest, Billy, I don't know. I'm frightened you'll get into trouble again.'

'Didn't I give you my promise I'm a changed man?'

'Yes,' Connie said on a whisper, wanting to believe him. 'It was such a shock hearing what Lofty read out.'

'Did the paper give a description of anyone?'

'No, I don't think so, otherwise Lofty would have said.'

'And nothing about the car?'

'No.'

'Then I might be in the clear.'

'Except that one man is dead when he shouldn't be.'

He dragged his hands through his hair. 'If I could turn the clock back I would. But as there's nothing I can do about it now, I'll just have to live with it, won't I?'

Connie knew that Billy had a good heart or else he wouldn't show remorse like this. And he was right. There was nothing they could do to change the past. But what did the future hold for her brother? If she advised him to resist what sounded like yet another dodgy deal, he would only go and do it anyway. Nagging him would make him more determined than ever.

Connie sighed and went to the cupboard. She had hidden five Woodbines and a box of matches behind the tin of tea. She gave them to her brother. To her surprise he laid them down on the bench. Then he put his arms around her, sniffing noisily into her ear. 'You're my best mate, Con.'

'Please do something sensible for once. Find a job that won't get you into trouble.'

'Trouble finds me, Con. Wherever I am, it seeks me out.'

'Don't say that. You're frightening me again.'

'I frighten meself, sis. But it's the truth.'

The explosions began, softly at first then gradually drawing closer. What a crazy world they were living in!

Chapter Six

On Sunday, according to Gran's prediction although one day late, the Luftwaffe arrived in daylight. Connie was feeding Lucky and quickly put his bottle away.

'Billy's not home,' her father shouted as they prepared to leave for the shelter. 'Come with us, Connie.'

'He'll turn up. He knows I don't like being on my own.'

Her mother was tearful and although Connie kissed her quickly goodbye, Olive gazed at the baby in her arms with anxious eyes. 'The poor little mite should be evacuated somewhere safe.'

'We're used to the Anderson now, Mum. Don't worry about us.'

'Well, you're old enough to decide for yourself, but don't forget you're taking responsibility for another life now.'

Connie watched her parents join the small crowd of neighbours leaving Kettle Street for the public shelters. Was her mother right about Lucky? She held him close, receiving one of his lovely smiles as he looked up at her.

She would never forgive herself if anything happened to him.

Ten minutes later Billy joined her in the Anderson. 'Sorry I left it a bit late. Kept out the way so as Mum didn't see me face.'

'You can't stay out of the way for ever.'

'No, but I'll look better tomorrow. If she asks, I'll say I fell off a roof.'

'Are the bruises still painful?' Connie asked.

'Nah. Only my lips when I move 'em.'

'You'd better stop talking then,' she grinned as they laughed beside each other on the bench.

The Luftwaffe didn't let up all night. She managed to doze but jumped awake each time the bombs dropped close. Her nerves felt frayed and the next morning even her 'quiet time' with Lucky at dawn failed to revive her spirits.

After leaving him with Nan, she made her way tiredly to work. A Green Goddess was blocking the end of the street. She could hear the lumps of masonry falling as the firemen hosed the smouldering building. The water spilled through the rafters on to the flames in the heart of the ruin.

'What happened to the Parkers?' Connie asked one of the firemen.

'We dug 'em out from the Anderson. Took 'em down the Sally Army for breakfast.'

'Was anyone hurt?'

'No, but the poor sods were in shock.'

'What will happen to them now?'

'Well, they can't come back here, can they?'

Connie hadn't known the newly arrived family very well, only old Mrs Parker, who had died six months ago and had been a resident for years. Her son, his wife and three daughters from the east coast had come to live in her house. They'd had a lorry to move in all their furniture and Lofty and Dad had gone along to help them. Connie stared at the charred remains of the Parkers' new home. Nothing to say it was once a house, just embers.

She walked on in a subdued mood. All along the roads one by one the houses were being picked off. Perhaps she should give some serious thought to what her mother had said about Lucky. What would she do if something happened to him?

'What a terrible night!' Ada yawned that morning as they sat on their stools and tried to concentrate on work. 'A bomb landed just over the back of us. Our next door neighbours came home to find all their windows gone and their karzy blown right away. The top of our chimney landed in their yard. Me Dad's fed up with bits falling off the house. So Mum says she's going to evacuate the girls.'

'But she didn't want to let them go last year.' Connie was getting worried. Everyone was talking of evacuation again.

'Yeah, well, nothing really happened in the Phoney War, did it? But after last night, she's changed her mind. 'Specially as Dad's being transferred to another port. Millwall docks have been damaged so bad that it's disrupted all the trade.'

'But you'll all be split up.' Connie was shocked.

Ada nodded miserably. 'It's what's happening to everyone. Some poor souls who are bombed out have nowhere to go except public buildings or churches or the Sally Army. Mum says it's best to leave before it comes to that.'

'But where will they go?'

'Dunno. You just have to go where you're sent.'

'What about you, Ada? Would you leave the island?'

'I wouldn't without Wally!' Ada cried, drawing Mr Burns's attention.

'All right over there, girls?'

'Yes, Mr Burns.'

'What are you going to do then?' Connie whispered a little later.

'Find digs, I suppose.'

Connie felt sad for her friend and although they managed a few laughs in the canteen, things didn't seem the same. That night, Connie was thinking about the Freemans as she sat in the light of the candle, holding Lucky tightly. Would Mum allow Ada to come and live here? But Mum was already upset about Lucky's presence in the house. Connie knew she couldn't ask for yet another waif and stray to be taken in.

The bombing began and Billy didn't show up. The vibration seemed to jar all her bones even though Dad had placed more sandbags over the roof. Lucky began to cry and she rolled little balls of cotton wool into his ears, covering his head with two bonnets and then a blanket. She cuddled him tight.

By ten o'clock, they were still alone. Where was Billy? Had he got into trouble with this new brainwave of his? She was very frightened. The candle flickered and a judder went through the ground. The next second an explosion knocked them off the bench. They fell on the hard floor. Dust tumbled from the ceiling and the shelf crashed down. With her eyes tightly closed, she covered Lucky with her body. Was this it? Was this the end? Noise roared all around them.

'Keep us safe, please,' she prayed between little sobs. She was too scared to move.

'Connie!' A voice was calling. She cried to call back but nothing came out. She could hear someone banging at the shelter door.

'It's me, Vic. I'm digging you out. The door's blocked with sandbags.'

'Vic?' She scrambled to her knees. The door finally swung open. 'Oh, Vic!'

He rushed in and grabbed them. 'Oh thank God you're safe!'

'There was a terrible bang.'

'It was in the next road. But when I saw the smoke I thought it was Kettle Street.'

'Oh, Vic,' she sobbed as he held her tight.

'Are you both okay?'

'Yes, but I fell on top of him.' They both looked into the shawl. A dirty little face gazed up at them. She pressed him against her chest as he began to cry. Automatically she rocked him. 'It's a wonder he isn't squashed and deaf.'

'That was very close.'

'I know. But why are you here?'

'I bumped into Billy today on my way home from work. He said he had to go across the water with this new boss of his and didn't know if he'd get back before nightfall. I intended to be here earlier but I had to report in first and it was bedlam. I just couldn't get away.' He held her face in his hands. 'Connie, I was so worried about you being on your own.'

'You're here now, that's all that matters.'

Gently he stroked her cheeks with his thumbs. 'I won't let anything happen to you, sweetheart – to either of you.'

He had called her sweetheart! Her heart fluttered as he hugged her. 'Come on, sit on the bench.' He righted the seat and helped her to get comfortable.

'Have the planes gone?'

'For the moment. But they'll be back again.'

'I don't want to be on my own.'

He put his arm around her. 'You won't have to. I'll stay until morning.'

'Oh, I wish I was braver.' She rested her head on his shoulder. 'I get so scared.'

'Just like everyone else,' he soothed, stoking her head. 'And you are brave. Very brave indeed. Now, Lucky seems to have gone off. Why don't you close your eyes.'

'I don't want to let go of him.'

'All right. I'll put my arms round you both.'

And they were the last words she remembered before sleep claimed her.

When she woke, she was lying on the bench where Billy usually slept. A blanket was draped across her. The Tilley lamp was on and Vic was slumped in the corner, snoring softly. His arms were folded across his chest, his long legs stretched out in front. Lucky was asleep in his cart. He was getting used to the bombs. And so, it seemed, was she.

Connie's heart tightened with joy. Vic had called her sweetheart!

The following week the BBC broadcast that already over one hundred and eighty-five enemy planes had been shot down and the raids were expected to continue. Connie saw pictures in the newspaper of a changed Oxford Street. Peter Robinson's department store and John Lewis's both had their ornate facades ripped away, almost every window shattered. It was reported that Londoners now enjoyed less than four hours sleep at night, a fact to which Connie herself could testify. She was only half awake at work and sometimes found herself dozing on her stool. Not that she hadn't noticed Mr Burns stifling a yawn, as he removed his spectacles and cleaned the lenses methodically. Ada, once a self-confessed night bird, now replenished her make-up so frequently that her eyes resembled a panda's. Even Len's jokes about his mother were fewer. But life continued in a haphazard way and Connie was relieved to discover that Lucky was none the worse for his nocturnal trials.

Nan's joy was the pram in which she wheeled Lucky

out, either to the shops or the park. Connie couldn't wait for the weekends, when it was her turn. Vic had taken to meeting her after work on Saturdays. They would dare to stroll out, rarely using the car. Petrol was scarce. Few private vehicles used the roads.

'I've been thinking,' Vic mused one late September Saturday as they pushed the pram to Island Gardens and sat down on the bench by the big domed entrance to the foot tunnel. 'It's odd that no one has claimed him. Do you think his mother took lodgings in Haverick Street quite recently?'

'It would explain why the neighbours didn't know her.'

They were silent for a moment as they gazed out across the Thames. They could see Greenwich clearly, the shape of the Wren buildings and, on top of the hill, the Royal Observatory. The scene was majestic and peaceful.

'Have you given any more thought as to what you're going to do if no one comes forward?' Vic asked after a while.

Connie felt a flutter of fear. Was he hinting, like Mum, that Lucky was too much for her? 'I don't like the thought of him being sent to an orphanage.'

'A baby is a big tie for a young girl.'

'I know.'

'You're very fond of him, aren't you?'

'Yes, I am.' Panic filled her. Was he going to make her choose between them, she wondered? She looked into his eyes. 'But I can't expect you to feel the same.'

Her heart stood still. She knew if she lost Vic, she

would be devastated. Could she give up Lucky if he asked her to?

He took her hands and held them, a small frown pleating the inch between his eyebrows. 'At school, Connie, I was always bashing a ball around, showing off, trying to make you notice me. Looking back I cringe to think of how I behaved. Well, now I've got a second chance and, believe me, I'm not going to throw it away. The way you've taken Lucky under your wing only makes me respect you more. You're a beautiful girl and I haven't a clue what you see in me, but I hope to God you go on seeing it.'

Connie felt as if a bright, warm light had filled her. So this was what it was like to feel as though you were the luckiest, happiest person to walk the planet!

'Oh, Vic, you've said some lovely things.'

'I mean them.'

'Do you think the authorities would make me give him up?'

He paused for a moment before he spoke. 'Why should they? You're providing him with a good home, something a lot of kids haven't got in wartime.'

'I'd like to register him properly, you see. There's lots of things he'll need, such as orange juice and cod liver oil, and something will have to be done about getting an identity.'

'Sounds like a visit to Poplar and the town hall. I'll drive you up, if you like. And whilst we're on the subject of kids, Pat has been on at me to ask you over. You can meet Doris again and Laurie, Pat's husband.'

Connie felt very flattered. 'I'd like that.'

'Good. Well now, it's almost teatime.'

'Are you on duty tonight?'

'Yes and I'll try to call by. Make sure Billy's put in an appearance.'

Connie wasn't certain if he used Billy as an excuse or if he took the opportunity whenever he could to see her. But she didn't care why he called, only that he did.

'Mum told me to ask you if you'd like some tea. She queued for some nice sausages yesterday.'

'I don't need asking twice.' Vic grinned.

It was heaven just being by his side, with his arm around her, Connie thought as they strolled home. And now Lucky was sitting up in the pram he looked a real little boy. Under his bonnet there was a soft and downy patch of fair hair poking through. She thought with pride how this ugly little duckling was turning into a beautiful swan. She felt so proud of him.

How lucky could a girl get?

Billy sat in Taffy Jones's house in Poplar High Road, staring at a big shaggy dog that had just cocked its leg on the fender and ambled lazily off. The puddle it left was quickly splashed by the foot of one of a dozen children filling Taffy's front room.

Over the mantel, under which lay the neglected ashes of a fire, hung a large, crumpled poster. The illustration was of a young fighter, mildly representative of Taffy, with one front tooth missing as he posed, smiling, at the photographer. The muscular arms and proud naked chest were definitely no longer evident on Taffy's present-day physique. Billy cast his eyes to Taffy, sprawled in an armchair, lost under a corpulent belly and sagging breasts. Round circles of sweat formed in his armpits and discoloured his shirt. The face, though, was definitely that of Taffy – at least two decades ago.

'See, son, I was the pride of the valleys,' Taffy hastened to explain as he looked reverently up at the display. 'Put all the bastards down in under four, never an exception. Got meself a real reputation, boyo.'

Taffy, who normally spoke as cockney as the next East Ender, now lapsed into a strange concoction of accents. Billy tried to decipher it as endless streams of children ran wildly in and out of the room. They were filthy, shoeless and noisy, tripping over the assortment of winged fowl that strutted across the bare lino. A large black fluffy cat appeared, swiped a paw at the birds, and seated itself on Taffy's knees.

'I was just sixteen then, with the world at me feet,' Taffy continued. 'And if it hadn't been for the leg, I'd have gone on to great things.'

'What happened to your leg?' Billy looked down at his employer's stained brown trousers. Other than never having seen Taffy in any others, they seemed unremarkable.

'I've an inch off the right one, so I have.'

'You'd never notice.'

'Birth defect,' Taffy said in a conspiratorial whisper. 'Gives you a disadvantage as you grow. And I was still growing then. Lovely lad I was too. Potential was there.

105

But swinging an inch off target, you begins to make mistakes. By the time I was twenty it was all over. See that there, the Cardiff Cup? The big one to the left? That was my best trophy. A beauty, ain't she?'

Billy nodded vigorously, although he couldn't quite distinguish the model Taffy was referring to. There were at least a dozen battered and misshapen cups, surrounded by a plethora of beribboned badges, war medals and a large three-legged horse tipped on its side, all arranged on the shelves of a glass case the panes of which were broken or splintered. Billy didn't know if its contents were silver or gold, or even precious, but like the children there were many.

'Now, listen to me, son,' said Taffy, dispatching the cat. 'You're young and you've got ambition and I reckon we can make something of you. But the thing is, you can't win all your fights by biting off your opponent's ear.'

'I never won the fight,' Billy reminded him as he tried not to inhale the smell of cat pee on his chair. 'I got thrashed.'

'Yes, you did.'

'I had to do something.'

'If you play your cards right next time, you'll keep out of the way, wear your opponent out, as most of them round here are all show. Three rounds in and they couldn't walk up a hill without a crutch.'

'So there's gonna be a next time?' Billy asked eagerly.

Taffy wrinkled his brow. 'You got to learn, lad. You got to use your noddle, *think*. Keep that trap of yours shut, not waste your breath on insults.'

'I was angry.'

'Make your anger work for you. Be crafty, sly like. Look out for your opportunity. Come under their punches and catch them off guard. Now come with me.'

Taffy led him through a dark corridor and out into daylight. The rear yard contained a shed. Taffy slid the bolt, beckoning Billy after him. 'Now, this, laddo, is me sanctum of sanctums,' he announced as they stepped in.

Billy stared round in surprise. Hanging from the roof was a leather punch bag. Pictures of muscular young fighters, all with their fists raised, were pinned on the wooden walls.

'Top left is Teddy Baldock, Bantamweight Champion of the World, 1927,' Taffy explained. 'Defeated Archie Bell, bottom right, at the Albert Hall.'

'Was he from round here?'

'Local lad from Poplar no less.'

'Champion of the world . . .' Billy breathed incredulously.

'His fight went down in the history books,' Taffy continued. 'Took more than fifty buses to carry his supporters to Kensington Gore for the event. See that bag there?' Taffy puffed out his chest. 'It was strung up in the yard of the Dock House pub. There was just enough room for a boxing ring and a row of chairs either side. Wag Bennett, Ernie Jarvis, the Softleys, Tom Cherry and young Baldock, they all gave it a right bashing in their time.'

Billy reached out to touch the hallowed leather. He

looked up at the big photograph in front of him. 'That's Joe Louis! I seen his picture in the paper.'

'Aye, the Brown Bomber,' Taffy sighed. 'Did you know his right cross is as lethal as his left hook? That one of his punches only has to travel six inches to rearrange an opponent's features?'

Billy was flabbergasted. 'He ain't from the island is he?'

'Course he's not. But I had the photograph signed, see – had it sent over from America special like. *To Taffy, mitts up!* What an honour! Do you know, he risked his crown against Schmeling the Hun in '38? Louis scored a KO in the first round. Schmeling didn't even see it coming.' He nudged Billy's arm softly. 'Now, if you can pull one out of the bag like that, then we'll all be happy.'

'Yeah, but I got pulverized, didn't I?' Billy digressed on a wave of serious doubt.

'That's experience for you, son. They all started at the bottom of the ladder. Take Tammy Jarvis, another local boy. He was your weight and just as green. Then one day he upped and went to America. Won his fight and came home with a Stetson on his bonce. Bought a greengrocer's in Westferry with his earnings. Now, what do you think of that?'

Billy was awestruck. He was looking at seriously famous fighters, who had amounted to something in their lives. America! That's where he wanted to go too. He'd make amends for what he'd done in the past. One day he would amount to something.

Once more he looked up at the photograph of the

Brown Bomber. Joe Louis had come up the hard way, just like him. Billy smiled to himself. Lady Luck was with him now.

He could feel it in his bones.

Chapter Seven

It was early in October when Connie noticed the stranger. She was walking briskly to work, her mind on what had happened the previous day – her visit to the council offices with Vic – when the man stepped across the road, pausing to light a cigarette as he examined the remains of a ruined house.

She lost sight of him as she joined the small groups of women she met every morning, hurrying to the dock factories and warehouses. He caught her attention again the following day, reading a newspaper as he stood on the corner of Kettle Street, the brim of his hat pulled over his eyes.

The next time she saw him was a week later, outside Dalton's gates. Once inside the factory grounds she looked back, but he'd disappeared. As she entered the shipping department, Ada came hurrying towards her. 'The wharf outside our office had a hole blown in it,' she explained hurriedly. 'We're being moved along to the next office. Mr Burns told me to find as many boxes as I could to put our paperwork in. There's some in the cupboards downstairs.'

'I'll hang up my coat,' Connie said at once. 'How bad is the damage?'

'There's glass and dust everywhere and a gale blowing in off the river. It's bloody freezing. Mind, it's October now, so I suppose it's to be expected. Lucky for us, the office next door hasn't been used for months, not since the fruit boats stopped coming. You'd think those U-boats would have better things to do than sink a load of flamin' bananas.'

'Well, I expect we'll have to clear the mess up, won't we?'

'Len asked a couple of the young boys on the shop floor to help us.' She gave Connie a little push. 'I'll come with you to the cloakroom.'

'Ada, have you seen a bloke in a mac and trilby hanging around the gates lately?' Connie asked her friend as they hurried down the staircase and into the small room provided for the female office staff.

'No, why?'

'I've noticed this man, once on the corner of Kettle Street, another time in Westferry Road and now outside Dalton's.'

'There's lots of strangers about,' Ada conceded as she scrutinized her make-up in the small square of chipped mirror above the hand basin. 'What with the demolition and rescue squads and blokes tearing up railings for the war effort.'

'Yes, but he wasn't a workman.'

'Might be a snoop! The papers say spies aren't only in Whitehall, but could be anyone on the street.' She turned quickly to Connie. 'What with Mr Burns putting me on weigh-ins, I haven't had a chance to ask if you went to the council about Lucky.'

Connie nodded as she combed her hair, adjusting the grip on the side of her head that held back her tumble of curls. They were all over the place this morning as she hadn't had a chance to pin up her hair. She'd slept late after a noisy night and climbed out of the hammock in a daze. By the time she'd washed in the house and got Lucky ready for Nan's, she hadn't even had time for breakfast. 'I went to the Public Health Department for Maternity and Child Welfare who said normally a certificate from the doctor or midwife attending the birth had to be sent in to get coupons, but of course we don't know anything about his beginnings.'

'Did Vic go with you?'

Connie nodded. 'I wasn't half glad he did too. We had to go to all these departments and then back to our doctor to ask for a letter to confirm that I was a suitable person to care for a baby.'

'Course you are, can't they see that?'

'Well, I could be anyone, couldn't I? Dr Deakin asked me a lot of questions about how I would manage. I told him about Nan and Lofty taking care of Lucky in the day. He also hinted that there shouldn't be much opposition as the government are trying to accommodate over 400,000 city kids already. And there's still thousands more in the pipeline to evacuate. I'll probably be classed as a war nanny.'

'What's that?'

'Someone who cares for non-evacuee children.' Connie replaced her comb in her bag and snapped it shut. 'But when we went back to the council offices, this clerk put the wind up me. He said I should think very carefully about taking on the responsibility of a baby. He said evacuation was the course of action to take.'

'Bloody cheek!' Ada cried. 'What's it got to do with him?'

'Vic reminded him that only last month the *City of Benares* evacuation ship was torpedoed on its way to Canada. Only thirteen out of the ninety kids survived. He asked this chap to put it in writing that Lucky would be guaranteed survival after being removed from my safe keeping.'

'Good for him.'

'Then we were sent to see a Mrs Burton, who turned out to be really nice. After we'd been through the story again, she said the government don't like moving bereaved children from the area too quickly as it's caused a lot of mix-ups. Lucky's dad might turn up or a relative even. As long as I can prove I'm assisting the war effort, there won't be any objections, for a while anyway.'

'What a lot of red tape just to do a good deed,' Ada grumbled as they opened the stock cupboard and took out the boxes. 'Talking of which, did you hear that when Buckingham Palace got hit last month, the queen is reported to have said she was glad they were bombed because she can now look the East End in the face.' Ada's eyebrows shot up. 'So I wonder who's forking out for a red carpet to be laid when she arrives?' she added cynically.

Connie giggled. 'It'd probably disappear down a crater never to be seen again.'

Laughing, they made their way back to the office. A gust of wind from the river almost blew them off their feet as they entered. All the glass was gone from the tall windows and the stools and chairs were knocked over. The surfaces normally crammed with papers, pens and envelopes were bare.

It was the first time they had seen Mr Burns in a tizzy. He was covered in the white dust falling from the ceiling and treading carefully over the shattered glass.

'Mr B. makes a good Father Christmas, don't he?' Ada spluttered behind her box.

Connie had to agree. Even this disaster had a funny side to it.

The following Saturday Connie rushed home from work. Vic was taking her to Pat's house. She washed her hair and pinned it carefully up on one side of her head above her ear. The other side fell loose in blond waves. Normally she didn't use rouge but this time she added a discreet glow to her pale cheeks. Unlike Ada, whose obsession was make-up, Connie favoured a natural complexion. She put on a dark blue dress, old but stylish, and tightened a thin black belt around her slim waist.

Vic whistled through his teeth when he saw her. Then, turning round, he held his hand to his brow, gazing along the street. 'Who's the lucky man who's going to take out this beautiful woman?' he teased her.

'I wanted to make a good impression,' she admitted.

'Last time I saw Pat and your gran I was covered in dust from under the stairs.'

'Shall I wait in the car?'

'Come in if you like. Everyone's out.'

Vic sat in the front room whilst Connie got Lucky dressed in fresh white rompers, one of Doris's matinée coats and a blue woollen bonnet to match his little blue elephant. Connie lifted him into her arms from the cot that Lofty had found on his travels. She was so proud of Lucky and eager to show him off to Pat and Gran.

When she returned downstairs, Vic took Lucky in his arms. 'What are you feeding him on, steak? And what's that, a tooth?'

'There's one coming on the top too.'

'You'd better get ready with the bubble and squeak then and a nice bit of roast beef.'

They were laughing together as they left the house. But as Vic opened the car door for her, Connie caught sight of a figure up by the ruins of the Coles' house. She was certain it was the man in the raincoat.

When she was settled in her seat and Lucky placed safely on her lap, she turned round to look through the rear window. The figure had gone.

Pat and Laurie Grant's flat in Manchester Road was one of many terraces that ran in a straight line, except for the casualties of war, all the way up to the Queens. It had huge big windows, three big bedrooms, a scullery and kitchen. The large sitting room was filled with Laurie's books and Pat's embroideries. Pat's friendly, broad-shouldered husband was a stevedore in the docks and Connie liked him at once.

The men were left to look after the children as the women gathered in the kitchen. Gran sliced a large green apple and indicated a chair. 'Sit down, ducks, and help me with the pudding.'

'What are you making?'

'Apple pie without the pastry.'

Laughing, Pat turned round from the sink. She looked very smart in a lemon-coloured twinset and black skirt protected by a gingham apron. Her dark hair was pulled up at the back and two kiss-curls made up her fringe. 'It's apples mixed with condensed milk and some of Doris's orange juice, with a square of chocolate thrown in and whipped together. I had a few nuts left over and made it crunchy. Bake for five minutes and you won't notice the missing pastry, or at least that's the idea.'

'Whip this up for me, will you?' Gran pushed the basin towards Connie. 'Now, tell us how you got on with the little boy.'

Connie stirred the mixture with a fork, aware that Gran's dark eyes were fixed intently on her. 'Did Vic say that we went to the Welfare about him?'

Pat said he had, but Gran asked her to go over it again, which Connie willingly did. When she came to the end of the story, repeating more or less word for word what she had told Ada, the mixture was ready for baking.

'So he can stay with you temporarily?' Pat asked as she slid the basin in the big oven and took out a delicious-smelling savoury dish.

'Yes, until his dad turns up.'

'And what does your mum think of that?' asked Gran bluntly.

'I think she'd prefer him to be evacuated.'

Gran wiped a cloth over the table. 'She's thinking of his safety, no doubt. And of her daughter, who's not a lady of leisure, but a hard-working girl having to rough it in an Anderson.'

Connie looked into Gran's eyes. 'I know Mum's concerned for me, but firewatching and volunteer work is just as dangerous.'

'And if his dad comes back, he won't have far to look,' Pat added quickly.

'Yes, exactly.' Connie nodded.

Pat winked at Connie. 'And if you want my opinion, that baby took to you the very first night he laid eyes on you.'

Gran smiled, but Connie wasn't convinced that she agreed with the situation. Pat slid a knife into the centre of the golden-brown baked potato and allowed a trickle of rich sauce and steam to ooze out. 'It's lentils, some onions and herbs with the potato and a little fat mixed with stock and a few more vegetables,' she told Connie. 'Not much of a substitute for meat, but it is quite tasty. You need loads of gravy to absorb the lentils. Now, I'm sure the boys and the children are hungry. Let's eat shall we?'

When they were seated at the big drawleaf table, the laughter and chatter was in full swing, despite the brief moment of tension in the kitchen. If Gran had any reservations about Connie – and a baby – being suitable for her grandson, then she had kept them to herself.

Vic met Connie's eyes across the table and she blushed. Pat grinned, her dark eyes twinkling as she offered second helpings. There was very little left when the meal was over, and there were satisfied sighs all round. The afternoon ended with a game of snap, with Doris the clear winner. When it was time to go, Connie presented her gifts. A bar of Nestlé chocolate for Doris, a jar of Chivers strawberry jam for Pat, a tin of Three Nuns tobacco for Laurie and a quarter-pound of tea for Gran. She had swapped all these at work for a bottle of Evening In Paris.

'Come again soon,' Pat said when it was time to leave. Laurie gave her a hug and Gran kissed her goodbye.

There were no lights to be seen on their journey home. They were silent while Vic negotiated the dark roads, and Kettle Street was deserted as Connie got out of the car.

Vic bent to kiss Lucky's cheek. Then gently he covered her mouth with his lips. 'Take care of yourself, sweetheart,' he whispered.

'You too.'

'I don't want to leave you.'

She didn't want him to go either. It had been a wonderful day. She watched him walk back to the car. Then when she could no longer see the moving shape, she went indoors, reliving the wonderful time she had spent with his family.

It was a misty morning in November and Gran was queuing outside the butcher's on East Ferry Road, wondering if, after buying the piece of mutton she'd saved her coupons for, she'd have enough energy left to cross the road to the chemist's and haggle for a bottle of Sloan's Liniment. There would no doubt be an array of coughs and sneezes to avoid in that particular shop, so perhaps she shouldn't trouble and take an aspirin instead to cure the rheumatics. Her mind was debating this problem as the queue moved forward with excruciating slowness. She knew most of the faces and had already indulged in small talk, but the wait seemed endless this morning.

'I reckon Winnie's got himself elected in the nick of time,' Albert Cross threw over his shoulder. 'We need a strong leader. Paper says them U-boats are being made by the dozens, like toys, to set loose on us. Our neighbour's lad was lost in the Atlantic last month. We were too slow on the uptake to spot Jerry's merchant ships were men-of-war. Hoodwinked they was, the paper said, and there's rumours going round that Jerry's got new battleships, small but lethal like, could sink half our fleet without drawing breath. It's not Britannia that's ruling the waves no more, if you ask me.'

'Chamberlain let us down bad,' said Eve Beale next to him, shaking her head slowly. 'Winnie's got a mouth on him but he's still wet behind the ears.'

'Rubbish!' another voice chimed up. 'Churchill knows what he's doing. Battle of Britain proved it.'

'Our airforce was what beat 'em, not Whitehall,' Albert Cross disagreed angrily.

Gran's attention returned to the present as the usual arguments broke out, and she felt the stir of unease inside her. Eighteen was young indeed. But then she knew of boys as young as fifteen running away from home to join up. It was all excitement and thrills to them, so many unemployed and without an aim in life. The war had made heroes of some and victims of others. She didn't want Vic to be either one of those, though she knew as certainly as the nose on her face, his time was due. She had *seen* it and now there was no turning back.

Gran felt her purse drop from her hands. She gave a little cry. How careless she was getting. Her mind was not what it used to be. She wasn't concentrating. Her mind was always three steps ahead. With an effort she reached down to the pavement where her purse had landed. Thankfully, still buttoned tightly. Her hand was just a few inches away when she was beaten to it.

Long, smooth fingers closed over it. 'You don't want to lose this now, do you?'

She recoiled slightly at the voice, but caught herself from showing it as she straightened her back. The face was shadowed by the brim of a trilby hat.

Gran felt another deep wave of anxiety. Her purse was her most valued possession. The idea that she had lost her grip and dropped it was sin enough. But worse was the fact that she did not feel inclined to retrieve it.

'What you waiting for, gel?' Albert Cross laughed. 'He ain't gonna fill it for you, is he?'

Eve Beale nudged her arm. 'You feeling all right, Gran?'

The purse remained in the outstretched hand. She looked into the man's eyes. Not a colour exactly, not brown or blue or even grey, but nearer to murky.

'It ain't gonna bite you,' Eve chuckled.

Gran took her purse and the man smiled. 'My pleasure,' he said and strode unhurriedly away.

Eve nudged her again. 'That's not like you, Gran, chucking your money away.'

Gran gulped a breath and nodded. 'Just a bit short of puff that's all.'

'You're nearly there now!'

But Gran's thoughts were elsewhere.

There was always one rotten apple in the barrel and she had met him today.

Vic made his way home from the warden's post in the early morning light. He walked slowly, inhaling the smoke from his cigarette. The raiders had flown, back to Germany and safety. Would the families of these pilots be waiting anxiously, wondering as he was, what mankind would bring upon itself next? Berlin, Hamburg and Munich had been hammered relentlessly by our bombers. How many innocent people had died in the process? London, Birmingham, Coventry, Southampton, Sheffield, Glasgow, Manchester had been targeted in return. The fires were still burning over English and German cities alike. And now with the Battle of the Atlantic there were countless losses at sea.

Vic looked up at the dawning sky. He watched the twinkle of the last stars. The same stars would be shining over all the countries of the world. Three weeks to the day to Christmas. Peace on earth and goodwill to all men. Hah! The poor souls he'd pulled out of that base-ment a few hours ago wouldn't be celebrating. No pints in the pub on Christmas Eve or a knees-up round the joanna. Yesterday they had been going about their busi-ness, wondering where the next penny was coming from for presents, saying sod it, who cares, we're alive aren't we? Then, today, those worries were immaterial. Men and women lived by the hour now.

He walked on, more briskly now, turning up the collar of his coat. He passed the remains of the burning build-ings and memories tormented him. He needed a couple of hours solid kip to shake off this mood.

But sleep wouldn't come. He lay in bed, staring at the ceiling. He could still hear the wounded, still feel the desperate grip of fingers on his arm. The blood that cov-ered him from the ruptured artery and a look of surprise at the end – that look in a man's eye – knowing it was the end – there was no tomorrow.

At seven, he rose and washed, rubbing away at his skin as if the memories were ingrained there. What was wrong with him? He'd held it together so far. Why this, now? He stretched out his bare arms. His hands were shaking. There was a feeling in the pit of his stomach, driving upwards like a cannon ball under his breastbone. He was sweating, his whole body shaking now.

Fear! It gripped his throat, tightening the knots in his shoulders, scything through his stomach muscles. He shook his head, his wet hair flinging out the beads of moisture.

'Boy?'

He swung round. 'Gran!'

She moved towards him, a small figure in black.

'What are you doing back?' he said, embarrassed at the tremor in his voice. Then his blood ran cold. 'It . . . it's not our Pat, is it?'

She shook her head slowly. 'No,' she said quietly. 'I left their place early. Got a breath of fresh air on me way home. Pat's not working today so she don't need me for the littl'un. Anyway, wanted to see you before you left. Don't like you going off on an empty stomach.'

He relaxed a little, wiping the sweat from his brow. The last few weeks Gran had been looking after Doris whilst Pat went to work at the shoe shop. In her absence he'd sworn he ate a regular breakfast. But most mornings he couldn't face it now.

'I'll put on the stove.'

He sat down at the table, pulling his hands over his eyes. 'Not this morning, Gran.'

'Ain't you well?'

'I'm fine,' he assured her. 'Just a cuppa will do this morning. I ate with the blokes earlier. Spoiled my appetite.'

'You make a rotten liar, boy.'

He sighed. 'I can't get away with nothin', can I?'

She smiled, an expression on her face that reminded him of when he'd been up to mischief as a kid, covering his misdeeds with a lot of baloney. He only had to meet her eyes and she'd see right through him, quirking up an eyebrow that made him shut his gob as swift as he'd opened it.

He heard the kettle go on, but not the frying pan and he was mildly surprised that he wasn't about to be force fed. He listened to all the familiar sounds that he had listened to all his life, knowing move for move what she was doing: the splutter of gas, the catch of a match, the water boiling and the comfort of familiar human breath. Somehow all this helped his anxiety and slowly the sweat dried on his skin.

She brought him a mug and placed the big brown teapot on the table and pulled the cozy over it.

'Drink your tea, son.'

Vic nodded, content to be in his oasis of calm and familiarity before he left for work. He was going to call for Connie and drive her to Dalton's, so making him even later to the PLA offices. But he didn't care this morning. He couldn't wait to see her.

Chapter Eight

The group of ragged young carollers were huddled by the barrow, stealing warmth from the glowing brazier. Good King Wenceslas had been done to death, but no one cared. The East End was making the most of a few hours of aerial silence before another night's bombardment. Connie touched Ada's arm. 'Those poor kids must be frozen.'

Ada grinned. 'Not too frozen to risk nicking a couple of chestnuts while the bloke is serving.'

Connie turned a blind eye to the little boy, who was wafer thin and didn't have a coat, just a big, holed jumper, his knees under his short trousers bright red with the cold. He stuffed the hot chestnuts in his pockets with alarming speed. She threw a sixpence and some coppers into the hat on the ground. 'Merry Christmas,' she called as Ada reluctantly dug in her purse for a contribution.

It was the week before Christmas and no one knew if they'd eat their Christmas dinner hot or cold or even if they'd eat one at all this year. But Connie was determined to enjoy her afternoon with her friend, their one and only shopping trip for presents. The Food Minister had announced extra rations for the nation and the market was still the best place to look for bargains.

'Just like old times.' Connie smiled as they walked arm in arm.

'Like when we was kids,' Ada agreed, a wistful note in her voice, 'without a care in the world, only where the next sweet was coming from.' She sighed contentedly. 'It was nice of your mum to have Lucky today and give us an hour by ourselves. What's Vic up to this afternoon?'

'He's driving Gran to Poplar for her Christmas shopping. What about Wally?'

'Oh, he's not doing much, just mending a puncture on his bike.' Ada frowned. 'Do you want a surprise?'

Connie stopped dead. 'What?'

'Wally's sister has offered to share her room with me.'

'Oh, Ada, I'm so glad.'

'I hope we'll get on. Jean's all right, but she's only just left school.'

Connie giggled. 'You're only nineteen yourself.'

'Yes, but you know what we were like at fifteen, real nosy little cows. I don't want her following me and Wally round everywhere spying on us.'

'You'll have to watch out when you're canoodling, then.'

Ada rolled her eyes. 'I'll just have to behave meself.'

Connie laughed again. 'You must be in love!'

'Yeah, either that or crackers.'

'You do love Wally don't you?' Connie asked as they came to stand by a stall decorated with holly.

'Mmm,' Ada replied hesitantly. She looked very pretty, Connie thought, in her best green coat with a little fur-trimmed collar that complemented her auburn hair. But there was something in her expression that made Connie wonder.

'You don't sound all that certain.' Connie knew Ada was a fun-loving girl and she'd had lots of boyfriends before Wally. 'Are you sure about settling down?'

'Course I am,' Ada retorted sharply. 'But what I want is to live with Wally in our own place and all that.'

'I'm sure living with the Wipples will only last a short while,' Connie replied diplomatically, though by the look on Ada's face she thought there was more to the matter than Ada was letting on. 'When is your mum leaving?'

Ada looked upset. 'After Christmas.'

'What will happen to your house?'

'Dunno. I expect the landlord will rent it out again.'

Connie squeezed her friend's arm. 'Well at least you'll be with your Wally.'

Ada didn't reply. Instead she pointed to a notice on a veg stall announcing *Oranges from Musso's Lake*. Everyone knew that this meant fruit that had been smuggled across the Mediterranean under Mussolini's nose. 'I'll buy some of those for Mrs Wipple.'

Connie nodded and moved on to the next stall. She was left with a feeling that Ada was unhappy, which was not surprising in the circumstances. As she examined some of the bottling jars, which would make a suitable gift for her mother, Connie wondered what she would do in Ada's position. She hoped she would never have to make such a choice.

'I bought apples instead,' Ada told her a few minutes later as she came to stand beside Connie. 'I wanted to get bananas too as no more are going to be imported, but they'd go black before Christmas.'

'There's some chocolate over there.' Connie nodded across the road. 'I spotted some Kit Kats and some of that lovely Barker and Dobson fruit and nut. But the stall-holder had it hidden, so it's probably a bit iffy.'

'Just up my street. See you in a minute.'

Connie went back to searching for her own gifts. She bought the set of pickling jars for her mum and four packets of Senior Service, one each for Kevin, Billy, her dad and Lofty. For Nan she bought a book on knitting patterns and a lace hanky for Sylvie with the letter S embroidered in the corner. She still had to buy Ada's present and something appropriate for Len. She always gave him socks, but this year she would be lucky to find an inexpensive pair unless they were second-hand.

She was about to pick up a copy of *Illustrated* when someone else beat her to it. The photo-filled magazine was just what Ada was interested in and older copies in good condition were scarce. Connie's eyes lifted to the person who now held it.

The man gazed back at her. Connie froze. This time he wasn't dressed in a raincoat, but a light-coloured suit. He smiled, but it was a cold, unnerving smile, hardening his thin features.

'Watch where yer stepping, gel! You've trod on me toe,' a woman complained behind her.

'Oh, I'm sorry!' Connie moved quickly sideways. When she looked back at the stall he was gone. She was certain it was the same person who had stood on the corner of Kettle Street and outside Dalton's.

A hand landed on her arm and she jumped. 'Blimey, your nerves are in a bad state,' Ada giggled.

Connie gulped. 'Oh, it's you, Ada.'

'Who did you think it was?'

'I was thinking what to buy.' She didn't know whether to tell Ada or not.

'Put your things in my basket if you like,' Ada suggested before Connie could speak. 'There's plenty of room on top of the chocolate. You were right, it was knocked off.'

Connie tipped her shopping into the big straw bag and they moved across the crowded street. Her eyes swept left and right, searching for the unmistakable figure.

'Tea's on me,' Ada said as she pulled Connie towards the tea stall. 'You're quiet.'

'Am I?' Connie hesitated as Ada passed her a mug of tea. 'Actually, I thought I saw that man again.'

'What man?'

'The one I told you about at Dalton's. He was looking at the magazines.'

'Are you sure it was him?'

'Positive. He had a suit on this time but it was definitely him.'

Ada fluttered her long black lashes. 'You've got an

admirer by the sound of it.' She went on to tell her about one of the married girls at work rumoured to have taken a lover after her husband had been called up. Connie tried to pay attention but all the time she felt as though eyes were watching her – and waiting.

It was Christmas Eve and the country was holding its breath. Would the Luftwaffe make a Christmas visit or abstain? Connie and Ada were sitting on their stools in the new office, looking out of the window at the unusually quiet waterway. If Connie moved close to the glass she could see the silhouettes of the cranes and derricks dotting the waterline, towering over the barges below, berthed along the wharves for the Christmas break. The light and shadow was constantly changing. Sometimes a blazing sunset glowed off the water. Sometimes, as now, a silver-grey mist shifted slyly with the ebb of the tide.

The river Thames, the gateway to the world! And it had all passed in front of her eyes, thousands of tons of cargo constantly on the move. She had seen the small ships and the big ones, the ants amongst the giants, the busy, stinking coal and timber barges, the slow-moving ferries and brave little tugs, the watermen's rowboats and the limping casualties of a long, weather-beaten journey. As a child she had even witnessed the last of the clippers and three- and four-masted schooners that had sailed from China to London with tea and silk and spices in their holds. She had been fascinated by the billowy canvas, the complicated rigging and the ominous foredeck gun ports. She had listened to the stories of the men that had manned those vessels. Tough seafarers, ready to fight their passage and defend their cargo against pirates. But in those days their weapons had been cutlass, pistol and cannon. What would they think of a modern day aircraft, or the sound of ack-ack?

Connie sighed, her chin resting on her hands. So much history! And now there was more in the making. Would Hitler ever set foot on these shores?

'Mr B. is stringing it out tonight,' Ada whispered noisily, bringing Connie sharply back to the present.

Connie looked over her shoulder to where Ada was frowning. Mr Burns was assiduously checking the last of the accounts.

'And we haven't been busy either,' Connie agreed.

All the staff of the shipping office were looking forward to being dismissed. As usual on Christmas Eve, they would hurry to the canteen, make merry for an hour, then scramble as the hooter blasted.

'Happy Christmas, Ada – Connie! Enjoy your holiday and we'll see you back safe and sound on Friday,' said Mr Burns at last, slapping his ledger closed. He walked over to hand them their Christmas cards.

'Thank you, Mr Burns,' the girls chorused.

They opened their envelopes and were shocked to discover that their boss had deviated from tradition. Fat-breasted red robins and seasonal greetings had been exchanged for texts.

'Little drops of water,' purred Ada, attempting not to laugh, 'little grains of sand, lots and lots of buckets standing close at hand. Yards and yards of hosepipe ready in the hall, that's the stuff to search for, when the incendiaries fall!'

Connie had to look away as Ada almost choked. 'Wh . . . what does yours say?' she spluttered.

'When lengthy is the butcher's queue,' Connie began, aware that Mr Burns, who had returned to his desk, was awaiting their reaction. 'And joints and sausages few—' Connie had to stop as Ada slapped her hand over her mouth. She tried again. 'We say whilst facing fearful odds, it's in the lap of all the gods, what we shall have for Christmas dinner!'

Ada made a choking sound. She buried her red face in her handkerchief. Connie replaced the card in the envelope and smiled at her boss, who was now looking at them expectantly. 'Thank you, Mr Burns, lovely cards.'

'A pleasure, Connie.'

'Thank you, Mr Burns,' croaked Ada, about to burst.

'Well, off you go, girls. And as the cards indicate, keep your wits about you.'

'We will.'

Connie and Ada fled to the cloakroom. For a good ten minutes they wiped the tears from their eyes. Connie splashed cold water on her face and Ada sat on the lavatory, wiping the trail of black mascara from her cheeks.

'Hosepipes!' Connie gasped, her sides aching.

'Sausages!' Ada screamed.

By the time they had composed themselves and arrived at the canteen, Len was waiting for them. 'Thought you two were never coming!'

'Did you get a card from Mr Burns?' they asked at once.

Len grinned as he stood his offering of VP wine on one of the tables. 'Yes and very appropriate it was too. A lengthy discourse on the merits of first aid in the workplace.'

The girls were in fits of laughter again and by the time some of the other staff came to sit with them, a knees-up had started. The men were singing 'Pack Up Your Troubles' and 'It's A Long Way to Tipperary' and the canteen staff, relieved to be released from the hot kitchen, had launched into a repertoire all of their own.

'What are you doing for Christmas?' Connie asked Len, who was pouring a second round into their chipped and slightly brown canteen cups.

'It's the Lake District this year,' he replied in a dramatically posh voice. 'One of them hotels on the edge of the water, a three-course dinner and cocktails afterwards on the veranda. Or is it before?'

'You're joking?' cried Ada, pink cheeked with a mixture of Whitbread, VP and envy.

'Course I am,' Len chuckled. 'Can you really see Mother sitting in her sparklers and fur, chatting sweetly to a dinner companion? No, I don't think so. In fact it'll be more like spam and mash if I have to cook, because Mother wouldn't know the difference anyway. She doesn't even know what day of the week it is.'

'How is she . . . er . . . healthwise?' Connie asked tactfully.

'Dangerous,' Len growled as he knocked back his drink. 'She smokes like a trooper and drops her dog ends alight all over the place. The gas was on for ten minutes the other night before I discovered what the smell was.'

'Has she seen the doctor?'

'Yes, and he's still recovering.'

Once more the laughter flowed, though Connie knew Len made light of what must be a worsening situation at home. He'd never married although he wasn't bad looking. But what woman was going to fall into his arms with an eccentric mother-in-law to contend with? Connie gave him his present, a book on gardening as she knew he had a little veggie patch and was keen on growing his own. He kissed her cheek warmly and poured her another drink which she eventually passed to Ada.

When the hooter went there was a great cheer. The hugs and kisses were abundant at the gates, and pressing a powder puff wrapped in brown paper into Ada's hand, Connie said, 'Don't open it till tomorrow.'

'Thanks, Con. Here's yours. It's not much but I had to save up for the housekeeping to give Wally's mum.'

Connie took the small square parcel, also wrapped in brown paper. They embraced then went their separate ways. Despite the cold she had a warm glow inside her. Instead of catching a bus, which she had taken to doing lately, she decided to walk home and breathe in the air. There were no brightly lit windows to look into or displays of festivities and the gaping holes where houses had once stood were a constant reminder of the Blitz. Even so, it was almost Christmas!

Connie was deep in thought about what she was going to wear tomorrow when she noticed the footsteps. They seemed to be keeping in time with her strides. She told herself not to be silly, that she was a bit squiffy on Len's VP. But as she turned the corner, a figure drew up beside her. The man raised his hat politely. 'Tucker is my name, dear. Gilbert H. Tucker. Got time for a quick word, have you?'

Connie stepped back. 'Why are you following me?'

'I'm looking for information, that's all.'

'Such as?' Connie was frightened but she wasn't going to show it.

'It's about a young girl, just turned twenty, small, dark, not bad looking. Her name was Rita. Ring any bells?'

'No. What makes you think I know her?'

'This might jog your memory.' He reached inside his raincoat, took out a wallet and slid a crumpled photograph from inside. 'Course, she's a few years younger there. It was took before the war.'

Connie was forced to look at the photograph. It was almost dark, but there was light enough from the moon to see. The young girl had long, dark hair framing her face and a fringe cut straight across her forehead. Her heart raced as she saw the wide, sad eyes.

'Ring any bells?'

'I . . . I don't know.'

He replaced the photograph in his wallet. 'She was my daughter.'

'Your *daughter*?' Connie repeated slowly.

'Surprise you does it? What did she tell you about me? Well, you don't want to believe all you hear. My Rita didn't have no call to boast. She weren't married, you know. Had the kid and never knew who the father was. Matter of fact, I could tell you a thing or two 'bout her that'd make your hair curl.'

'I don't want to know.' Connie backed away. 'Please stop following me.'

He gripped her arm. 'I just want the answers to a few questions.'

'Let go of me.'

'Just as soon as you tell me what Rita told you before she died. I know it was you that found her and the kid. A woman in Haverick Street told me. Said a bloke had been round asking questions and left his address and yours.'

'If the woman told you all that then you should know that the girl I found was in no condition to speak.'

'She must have said something.'

Connie pulled her arm away. 'Why don't you go to the police if you want to find out more? Look, there's a constable on his bike.'

He let her go as the policeman cycled towards them. 'No time to talk now,' he muttered. 'But I'll be back again.'

Connie watched him hurry off as the policeman cycled past. Was he really the dead girl's father and therefore Lucky's grandad? He had shown no sign of grief that his daughter was dead. If he wanted information, why hadn't he just knocked on her door and asked her?

All the way home, she thought about Gilbert Tucker. Would he follow her again. What should she do?

Connie turned into Kettle Street, looking behind her as she did so. No one was in sight. People were preparing for the holiday, making certain their blackout precautions were securely in place. She felt a little shiver go through her. Who could she confide in?

Christmas Day was going to be celebrated despite the Blitz. Billy had brought home a chicken and no one asked where from. Connie and her mother were plucking the fowl between them and preparing a Christmas pudding so small it needed twice as much as the normal amount of custard.

'We'll eat at one o'clock prompt,' Olive shouted as Billy, Kevin and Ebbie went down to Lofty's for a drink. 'So don't be late, or else.'

'On the dot,' they all chorused.

'Let's set the table,' Olive decided as Connie lifted Lucky from his cart in the kitchen and took him to the front room. On her way past the window she glanced out. The street seemed to be empty. Placing Lucky in the armchair, she wedged him with cushions and kissed his head. His hair was soft and honey coloured, with a bald patch at the back.

Connie sighed heavily. He was such a lovely child. Could that unpleasant man really be his grandfather? Connie began to set the table, her eyes darting to the window.

The men arrived back and were all smiles as the food was piled in front of them; carrots, potatoes and gravy overwhelming the meat. Lucky sat in his cart and was fed, grinding his two tiny teeth in the process.

The presents were distributed after the King's Speech.

Connie was delighted with hers. Two scented tablets of soap from Ada, a cardigan in pale grey wool knitted by her mother, a blouse from Nan that looked almost new with a Peter Pan collar, and chocolates from her brothers. She was touched by the unexpected gift from the family for Lucky. A bonnet knitted in blue wool with matching bootees and mittens and a red pig money box into which everyone had dropped their pennies.

By six o'clock the skies were still clear. Everyone was hoping they had escaped a raid. 'Billy, I want to talk to you,' Connie whispered as they helped Olive with tea. 'Come upstairs when I put Lucky to bed.'

Later, Connie told him all that had happened, from the first day she'd seen the stranger to last night. 'He claims he's Lucky's grandfather,' she ended worriedly. 'And wanted to know what the girl – who he said was his daughter – had told me before she died.'

'That's a funny thing to say,' Billy agreed.

'It was a very strange meeting.'

'Do you think he'll try it on again?'

'I don't know.'

'There's a lot of funny people about. He might be trying his luck for some reason.'

Connie nodded slowly. 'He gave me the creeps.'

Billy put his arm around her shoulders. 'If he shows up again, tell me. I'll have a word in his ear. Now, come on downstairs and stop worrying. It's Christmas after all.'

It was just before eight when there was a loud knock. 'I'll get it!' Connie ran to the front door.

'Merry Christmas!' Vic looked so handsome he took her breath away. He was wearing a dark-coloured jacket with wide lapels and large patch pockets. His flannel trousers had turn-ups and the sporty green wool sweater with a V-neck revealed the glimmer of a crisp, cream-coloured shirt. She had waited all day to see him and was beginning to think he wasn't coming.

'Merry Christmas.' She gave a little shiver as he bent to kiss her.

He lifted Gran's shopping basket. 'Christmas comes but once a year and this year is very special.'

'Don't keep Vic on the doorstep,' Olive called from the front room. 'It's still the blackout even though it's Christmas.'

Vic spoke softly as she closed the door. 'I missed you today.'

'What did you do?'

'I took Gran over to Pat's for dinner. They all send their love. Asked us to go over tonight, but I said I was coming here.'

'Do you mind?'

'Course not. I'm with you, and that's all that matters. Added to which, it looks like Jerry is taking the night off too.'

The room was warm and inviting as they walked in. There was no Christmas tree, but the paper decorations were strung up and the fire was blazing. There was a smell of baked apples that Olive had prepared for supper.

'Merry Christmas, son.' Ebbie rose from his armchair to shake Vic's hand.

Olive looked up from her place on the couch. 'It's nice to see you, dear.' She patted the spot beside her. 'Come and warm yourself. Constance will make the tea. I was hoping the boys would be here too, but they've both gone out seeing as there doesn't seem to be a raid.'

Connie prepared the tray in record time. When she returned, the presents from Gran's basket had been distributed. Her mother was wearing a smooth paisley scarf around her neck and her father was investigating a tool set.

'Yours are on the table, dear,' Olive said as she helped everyone to tea.

Connie sat by the fire and opened the tin of Saturday Assortment that Gran had sent her. Next was Pat and Laurie's gift, a pair of earrings that looked like tiny glittering half moons. Vic's present was a pair of luxurious silk stockings that had Connie blushing.

'They're beautiful!'

He lifted a parcel from the table and handed it carefully to her. 'I made it myself. For the lad.'

Connie unwrapped the brown paper carefully. Everyone gasped as a beautiful red and blue wooden train appeared with a big black shiny funnel. 'Did you really make it yourself?'

'Will it do?'

'I've never seen such a lovely toy.'

'Look, there's even a cord to pull it with,' Ebbie noted.

Olive took the train and inspected it. After a moment, she looked up. 'It reminds me of when the boys were young. They had wooden soldiers like this, painted in lovely colours, and Kevin and Billy used to spend hours playing with them, building imaginary castles and forts . . . do you remember, Ebbie?' She glanced at her husband. 'It seemed such a long time ago . . . until tonight . . . and all those memories have come flooding back . . .' She gave a little sniff. 'You know, Vic, I was so worried over Constance. She's an independent young woman and we don't always see eye to eye. But I have to admit –' Olive's voice wobbled – 'she's looked after that baby as if it was her own. The fact that you have come into her life and you seem to like the little lad too – well, it's a blessing, it really is.'

Ebbie cleared his throat loudly. 'Anyone for a tipple?'

'A beer would do fine,' Vic accepted quickly.

'Righto.' Ebbie nodded. 'And a nice port and lemon for the girls.'

Connie glanced at Vic, who gave her a big grin. She felt a warm glow of contentment inside her. Even that awful man Gilbert Tucker wasn't going to spoil her perfect Christmas night.

Chapter Nine

It was the 29th of December and Billy's fifteenth birthday. Although the Luftwaffe had returned on the 27th, the following evening the skies were silent and everyone hoped this evening would be the same. With the presents opened, Ebbie was planning to take his sons for a beer, even though they couldn't officially drink in a pub. But it was an unwritten rule that landlords turned a blind eye in wartime.

They were preparing to leave when the siren wailed. Connie looked at her mother, who closed her eyes and sighed. Kevin made a hasty escape to be with Sylvie and Ebbie disappeared to collect the bedding for the public shelter.

'I'm sorry, Billy,' Olive said as she hurriedly put on her coat. 'You'll have to celebrate another day.'

Connie could see he was disappointed. Once more the family separated and Connie hurried with Lucky into the yard, expecting her brother to follow.

'Con, would you mind if I went over to a pal's?' he said as he stood at the door of the Anderson. 'It is me birthday after all.'

Connie had grown to rely on Billy's company and she didn't want to be on her own. 'You will come back soon, won't you?'

'Course I will. I'll light the lamp then shut you in tight, okay?'

Connie nodded. 'Billy?'

'What?'

'Happy birthday.' She gave him a big smile.

'Thanks, Con.'

The door of the shelter closed. She sat on the bench and cuddled Lucky tightly. Perhaps Vic would call by again? The explosions grew nearer. They sounded louder tonight but she was by herself and listening for every bump. The minutes passed by and Billy didn't return. The shelter shook and trembled as though it was made of paper. There were no lulls in the bombing, just a continual pounding of the earth. Suddenly a bang so loud erupted close by that her ears popped; the Tilley lamp fell over and a gust of wind blew open the door. Lucky was torn from her arms by an invisible force. A second later there was total darkness.

'Drink this,' a voice was urging her. 'Small sips, sweetheart.'

She swallowed the brandy and coughed. 'Where am I? What happened? Where's Lucky?'

Vic replaced the hip flask in his pocket. 'He's safe in the house. Now, sit up slowly, I want to check you're all right.'

'Is Lucky hurt? Is he crying?'

146

'No, he's not hurt at all. The cart was in one piece so I took him in and laid him in it.' Vic grasped her shoulders. 'It's you I'm worried about.'

She looked around her. The Anderson seemed to have disappeared. She was lying in the open air and the yard was full of twisted metal. She felt very dizzy.

Vic peered into her face. His eyes were full of concern. 'Oh, Connie, I was in the next street when it happened. I thought it was your house that took the blast.'

She held on to his shoulders. 'Whose was it?'

'Next door, I'm afraid.'

'Oh, no!' Connie looked into the next yard. There was a yellow glow where the Spinks' house had once stood. The roof had collapsed and gleaming tongues of fire were licking against the rafters.

'Your mum told me they go to their church to take shelter. Is that right?'

Connie nodded. 'Yes, they do. I just hope they didn't change their minds tonight.'

'There's nothing left of the house or its contents, I'm afraid.' He ran his hand down her arms and turned her wrists. 'Nothing amiss there. Can you move your legs? The bench was across them when I found you.'

She wiggled her toes inside her shoes. She bent her knees and nodded.

'I'll help you up.'

With his arm around her she climbed to her feet. Slowly they walked to the house. He helped her into the kitchen and sat her on the chair. Lucky was in his cart on the floor. Miraculously Billy's invention had survived the

147

blast. 'Oh, Lucky,' she sobbed, a lump in her throat. 'I couldn't hold on to you.'

Vic lifted him from the cart and laid him in her arms. To her astonishment he was fast asleep. 'He's none the worse for wear. When I found you, he was still wrapped in his shawl and only crying a bit.'

She rocked him gently. 'I can't believe we escaped. I just hope the Spinks' are all right. They never went in their Anderson. Like Mum, they hated it. They always went to their church.'

'I'm sure they'll be all right.'

'It will be an awful shock when they see their house, or what's left of it.'

'Talking of which, there's damage upstairs above your room. The roof's caved in where the Spinks' house was joined to yours. I just had a quick look to make sure no one was up there. I'm afraid you won't be able to sleep there for a while.'

'Oh, Vic, why was it so bad tonight?'

He drew up a chair and put his arm around her. 'They came at low tide and bombed all our water mains. Must have been planned thoroughly as they knew where to hit. The blokes on the engines ran out of water, which was what Jerry intended.' He brushed back her hair and she took a shaky breath.

'Lucky and me were so lucky tonight.'

Vic nodded. 'He certainly deserves his name.'

It was light and Connie was sitting on the couch. The events of the night had left her shocked and dazed. When

Kevin and Billy arrived home, Vic had gone to report in. Connie wasn't going into work. She and Lucky could have died last night. It had made her realize what was important. And at this moment it certainly wasn't Dalton's.

Kettle Street had suffered two more losses. Number thirty-five, the Spinks' house, where it was confirmed the couple were safe. They had taken shelter at church. But number ninety-seven had suffered a direct hit. Ken and Kitty Wilmot and their seven-year-old son Derrick had been killed by a high-velocity bomb. It was the force of these two bombs that had demolished the Marshes' Anderson. The news of the Wilmots' deaths had come as a terrible blow. The rescue services had been working to retrieve their bodies since first light and the area was now cordoned off. A silence had settled outside.

'You warmed up yet, Con?' Kevin asked as he dropped the poker in the grate. 'Vic said you was a block of ice when he found you.'

'I don't remember much. Only the explosion and a gust of wind blowing Lucky out of my arms. The next thing I knew Vic was there.'

'I shouldn't have left you,' Billy said unhappily. 'Trust Jerry to pick my birthday to set fire to London. They dropped parachute mines on the water mains, then followed with fire bombs knowing we'd be made short of water. I was waiting for a lull to get back here. But the bombing just went on and on.'

Kevin nodded. 'I heard from one of the firemen that the exhaust pipes of the fire engines were red hot because of the pressure of pumping. In the end it was the boats that got their pumps going and strung the hoses across the mudflats. They were going like stink all through the night at the bridges and docks. Trouble was the incendiaries kept starting fires in different places. As soon as our blokes arrived at one, another started. Dunno what the City looks like today. A lot worse than us, I should think.'

'Taffy told me the streets around Saint Paul's are worst,' Billy agreed. 'The Guildhall went up like cardboard and the bell of Saint Bride's melted.'

Connie stood up. Her legs were still shaking. She lay Lucky in the pram by the window and looked out. People were walking around with dazed expressions, dust and ash was still falling from the sky.

At that moment Olive and Ebbie rushed in. Olive hugged her children, tears spilling from her eyes.

'What happened to the Spinks?' she sobbed.

'They were at church,' Kevin told them. 'Mr Shutler said the Salvation Army have given them a bed for tonight and tomorrow they're going to relatives.'

'Thank God they're safe. But they'll never be able to come home, will they?'

'We heard the Wilmots were killed,' Ebbie said quietly.

'Those poor, poor people,' Olive wailed.

'Like the Spinks' house, it caught a direct hit. The one next door was damaged too.'

Olive sank down on the couch. 'Is our house damaged?'

'There's a hole in the roof over Connie's room,' Kevin

explained as he sat beside his mother. 'But it's not too bad really, considering.'

Olive burst into tears. 'We'll never see the Wilmots walk down the street again.'

Ebbie brought out the sherry left over from Christmas. He poured five measures into mugs and gave them out.

'How big is the hole?' Ebbie asked his son.

'Big enough to see the sky.'

'There must be a lot of mess,' Connie said anxiously.

'Me and Kev will see to all that,' Billy volunteered. 'But you won't be able to kip there o' course.'

'Bring down the mattress and the cot and we'll clean them up,' Olive said, gulping her sherry. 'You can use the front room till the roof's mended.'

Billy stood up. 'I'll borrow a roof tarpaulin from Taffy to keep out the weather.' He grinned at his father. 'You'll be able to make use of that nice new toolbox you got for Christmas, Dad.'

No one commented until Olive took another swallow of sherry and remarked, 'Just as soon as he's worked out how to open it.'

On New Year's day, Vic took Connie for a drive. The mood at home was sombre. After the Wilmots' deaths and the Spinks' evacuation, everyone felt vulnerable.

There was little traffic, but plenty of activity. People were salvaging what was left from the ruins; wardrobes, chests of drawers, tables and chairs, beds, birdcages, anything that could be moved was moved. The devastation hadn't stopped people burrowing, hammering and digging. The fire brigade's hoses still lay on the streets as if to hint at more to come. Clouds of dust rose up like walls. Horses pulled carts piled high with debris.

Queen Victoria Street was impassable. Prince's Street now had a large crater in the middle of the road. The Houses of Parliament had been damaged. Masonry still toppled from the beautiful ornate windows. There were warnings of unexploded bombs and dangers to the pedestrian, but no one took any notice. Life had to go on.

'I feel blessed when I see all this,' Connie sighed as she rested back in her seat. 'We might have a hole in the roof but it's nothing to what some people have had.'

'It's making everyone stronger,' Vic answered firmly as he swerved to avoid another hole in the road. 'We'll never give in. Winnie's right. We'll never surrender.'

'No, but there is a cost.'

'It's war, Connie. If we were prepared to live under a dictatorship, we'd have been trounced centuries ago.' He pulled the car into the curb and switched off the engine. They were by the Embankment. The river looked a misty grey. The sun broke through the clouds and sparkled off the water.

'Sweetheart, I've got something to tell you.'

Connie felt her heart miss a beat. 'What is it?'

'I've been called up.'

Connie stared at him. She hadn't really believed it would happen. 'You won't go, will you?'

'I have to.'

'But you had a reserved job.'

'And anyone can fill it. I know it's hard for you to

understand. But fighting for my country is fighting for us. I'm coming back, I promise you. You mean the world to me and now I've found you I never want to let you go.'

'Then don't,' she begged. 'Please stay.'

He pulled her close, wrapping his arms around her. 'You don't mean that,' he murmured. 'Do you?'

She pushed her face into his coat to hide her tears. His smell was so familiar, his voice, his laughter, his touch. She couldn't bear to think of being without him. At this moment she didn't know if she had the courage to let him go.

He lifted her chin. 'Let's get engaged, Connie.'

'But you're going away.'

'It will give me strength to know you're waiting.'

For a moment she didn't trust herself to answer. The most wonderful thing in the world was happening to her. The man she loved was asking her to be his wife. Yet the future was so uncertain. If he went away to fight, would he ever return? She had seen other women waiting for letters that never arrived. There were wives at work whose husbands were missing and they were still waiting, praying for a miracle, dreading the arrival of a telegram.

'I want to say yes.' She looked into his dark gaze. 'But I'm scared.'

'So am I.' He nodded. 'But you're my brave little damsel and I'm your knight in shining armour. There's no dragons we can't slay together.' He pushed his hand in his pocket and brought out a small red box.

'This is for you.'

153

Connie lifted the lid. She gasped. A bright blue jewel glinted in the morning light. 'It's a ring!'

'The colour of your eyes, see? Sapphire.' He slipped it on her finger.

'It's the loveliest ring I've ever seen.'

He took her hand and squeezed it. 'So the answer is yes?'

She nodded. 'But what about Mum and Dad?'

'I'll have to ask for their daughter's hand in marriage, won't I?' He grinned as he lifted one eyebrow. 'Think they'll say yes?'

Connie smiled as she thought of her parents' faces when Vic broke the news. A regular bloke was all they had ever wanted for her. And now Connie had to agree, it was all she wanted for herself.

Chapter Ten

'Where the flippin' heck are we?' Vic muttered as he and his fellow conscripts disembarked from the bus. Pushing back his ruffled dark hair with the palm of his hand and being vaguely aware that the stubble on his chin needed swift attention after the long journey from Paddington to North Wales, he nudged the arm of the young man standing next to him.

Both men squinted up at the ornamental archway emblazoned with the words 'HMS *Glendower*'. Beneath this was the not so carefully hidden greeting, 'Welcome Campers.'

'Strike a light!' exclaimed the tall, fair-haired young man with freckles scattered across the bridge of his nose.

Vic dropped his kit bag and eased his stiff shoulders back and forth. 'Don't count your chickens. Here comes the gaffer.' He stood to what he thought resembled attention as the uniformed officer strode towards the straggling bunch of young men who had tumbled wearily from the naval bus. The barked orders had them scurrying towards the camp's reception area. Here they were counted, re-checked and assaulted by a blast of tannoy. 'All men who arrived on this morning's bus report to the clothing store at the double.'

'Struth,' muttered George as he stamped his cold feet, 'I thought the first thing they'd do is put food in our stomachs.'

'Yeah,' grinned Vic as they were frog-marched along to the clothing depot. 'But then you can't have everything On His Majesty's Service.'

George laughed loudly, only to be stopped in his tracks by the thrust of a giant hand.

'What's so funny, son?' bellowed the officer, causing George to stumble backwards.

'Nothing – nothing.'

'Nothing – *what*, you ignoramus!'

'Sir, nothing, *sir*,' George mumbled.

'Blimey, don't you know anything, lad? It's Chief Petty Officer sir! – got it?'

Vic stood with his eyes in front of him not daring to look sideways as George was made to eat humble pie in front of the assembled. When they were marching again, George groaned. 'I've gone off camping already.'

Vic smiled ruefully, wondering what Connie would make of all this. His emotions were divided between the desperate miss of her and the simple desire to get through his first day in the service of his country. At least he had made a friend in George Mullen.

All thoughts of home vanished as they approached a counter staffed by a long line of Wrens.

'Females!' croaked George. 'I'm not letting that big one take my trouser size.'

'You'll be lucky to get a smile,' Vic remarked as each rookie sailor was solemnly kitted out with his uniform.

'I've got thoroughbred legs,' George complained as they were hurried on without the appearance of a tape measure. 'I like my trousers to fit. I don't want a tight crutch or short bottoms.'

Vic grinned as he heaved a khaki bag over his shoulder that felt like the weight of an anchor. The two men were loaded with the last of their gear: a piece of grey canvas with brass eyelets, two sizes of mess rope and two rough woollen blankets.

'What's this for?' George asked curiously as lastly an ink pad and rubber stamp dropped on top of his kit.

'What do you think, you fairy?' demanded the Chief Petty Officer appearing from nowhere. 'That is to mark your name on your kit bag, this is your 'ammock and these little things are the ropes to 'ang it up with. Now, unless you have any more questions, sonny, get your arse out of this shed and into those clothes in double quick time.'

Once again Vic avoided eye contact with his superior and breathed a sigh of relief at his escape as the contingent of men were marched back to their freezing cold quarters.

'Home from home,' George remarked as the four inmates of billet 219, now stripped bare with just enough floor space to swing a cat, selected their corners.

Vic took hold of the piece of canvas that was to be his bed for the next three months and began to assemble its construction. His first day could have been worse. He was billeted with George and two others, Tommy Drew and Sammy Kite, all three good blokes. But what was worrying him was what they had discovered from some of the other lads. HMS *Glendower* was a land training base for naval gunners; some of the men had brothers or friends stationed here, all serving on the country's merchant ships. It was common knowledge that a merchant ship was fitted with toy guns, whilst the escorts did all the work. In Vic's books he had a whole lot of fighting in front of him. Hiding behind the skirts of a Royal Naval battleship was not his idea of fighting a war.

'What do you think of my missus then?' George pushed a photo under Vic's nose.

He studied the smiling, wholesome-looking lass. 'Very nice, too.'

'Bit of all right, isn't she? What about yours?'

'We're not wed yet.'

'Why not?'

'There wasn't time. We only got engaged six weeks ago.'

'Well, if it was down to me I'd get that ring on quick,' George advised, holding up his piece of canvas to the light and turning it upside down. 'You might be away a long time. A long, long time if you know what I mean.'

Without comment Vic took hold of George's equipment and folded it into shape then strung it from wall to wall.

'Thanks, mate. You're good at this lark. Where are you from?'

'The Isle of Dogs.'

'It's all dock work there, isn't it?'

'More or less.'

'I'm a Bermondsey lad myself. Work for the council on lorries. I don't know one end of a boat from the other. I wanna get in and out of this war as quick as I can. After all, there's no career prospects on a merchant ship is there?'

'I don't intend to board one,' Vic said as he assembled his own kit.

George leaned against the wall, a curious expression on his face. 'So what are your plans, if you don't mind me asking?' He produced a packet of squashed Woodbines. 'A nice cosy touch in the officer's mess, catering for the top brass? I've heard it can be done, if you've got what it takes.'

Vic laughed as he stopped working, sucked in the smoke, then balanced his cigarette on the window shelf. 'The truth is, Georgie boy, I've no desire to spend the war licking some petty officer's boots.'

'Right, so you're going over the fence, is that it?' He laughed at his joke.

Vic looked at him steadily. 'No. I'm putting in for training.'

'As what?'

'Anything with a stripe.'

'You mean an *officer's* course?' George looked surprised.

'What's wrong with that?'

'Dunno.' George shrugged, gulping in smoke. 'It just seems a bit ambitious for blokes likes us.'

Vic stared into George's light brown eyes and smiled. 'What exactly are blokes like us? What makes you and me any different from the loudmouth who gave you stick this morning?'

George looked embarrassed. 'Well, I had to take it, didn't I? This is our first day.'

'Same as he had to take it once. He was just the same as you and me, wet behind the ears, with two left feet. He pisses just the same, eats and drinks just the same. All that's happened is he's climbed the ladder of success. And in the long run, an armful of stripes is a far better bet than getting wiped out before you've even started the fight.'

George squashed his dog end with his boot. 'I just don't see myself as a leader of men.'

Vic clasped a hand to his friend's shoulder. 'It's the same as the playground, George. Stand up to the bullies and when you see a chance, go for it. There's opportunities here, all we've got to do is grab them.'

'Blimey,' George gasped, 'you've got it all sussed.'

Vic shook his head slowly. 'Not a bit of it. But I have got a life, George, and I intend to live it.'

Gran was in the front parlour, waiting for Connie. She had made the tea as usual of a Saturday afternoon, reserving her butter and sugar rations for today so they could have a little treat, a good helping of jam on the bread and a generous spoonful of sugar in the tea. A quarter of a pint of milk was reserved for Lucky and a baked rice pudding. This routine was the highlight of her week since her grandson had been called up.

Pulling the curtain to one side, she peered along East Ferry Road and searched for the tall, slim figure pushing a large pram. She hadn't realized just how much she looked forward to seeing Connie. The young woman made her feel closer to Vic.

Gran returned to her armchair. She was worried for the young couple. Not just the war, but those murky lights. Gran sighed. She felt too tired to work it all out. She only wanted to sleep these days. With an effort she propped herself up in the cushioned chair, looking around the parlour walls. They were crammed with photographs. Husband Maurice, killed in the first war, and so like Vic, handsome and dark eyed. Mother and Father, both Quakers, standing erect, side by side. Brothers and sisters now dead or mislaid, in a world that she had no desire to search now that she was old. Photographs of her only son, Freddie, and his wife Josephine, always in her heart. Freddie taken by a cruel, unrelenting disease, a curse of the poor. She shuddered as she thought of how she had nursed him through the TB. Josie had given up after his death, literally, just wasted away. How could their young lives have ended so cruelly? It was only the kids, Vic and Pat, who had kept her sane afterwards. All legs and arms they were, like little fawns, tiny orphaned innocents . . .

'Gran . . . Gran?'

The soft calling broke into her dreams. The faces that filled her mind, replicas of those on the walls, slowly faded. Gran opened her eyes to see a fresh young face, full of vitality, staring down at her.

'Connie, ducks! I must've drifted off.'

'Don't get up. I'll make the tea.'

'Where's the lad?'

'He's out the back, asleep in the pram. Now, rest a while longer.'

If this was getting old, Gran didn't care for it. She was used to being independent. It came as a shock to find yourself addressed as a child, though she knew Connie meant well.

When the girl returned, they sat at the table as the sun broke in through the window. Connie poured and Gran watched as her lovely hair fell over her shoulders, waves of spun silk, curling against her pale cheek. As delicate as her long, graceful fingers on the china. What a beauty this girl was, both inside and out!

'Gran? One sugar or two?'

'Not for me, love. You go ahead.'

'You spoil us on Saturdays.'

'Why not, if you're good enough to visit?'

'Gran, you're my family, least you feel like it now. Fact is, I can't remember being without you, or Pat and Laurie and Doris. It's just like you've been around for ever.' Connie smiled reflectively as she spread the jam evenly over the bread. 'I don't half miss him, you know.'

'I know you do.'

They finished the buttered bread and when Lucky woke Gran fed him the rice pudding as he sat on her lap. She was beginning to think of this little boy as Connie's, but then did that mean he was Vic's also? It was a strange arrangement but she admired the girl. What would happen in the future? Would the father turn up? It would break her heart of course if Lucky were to be taken away now.

Gran put the disturbing notions out of her mind as she wiped Lucky's little mouth and tickled him under his chin. He had such an infectious laugh and dazzling blue eyes.

'I reckon he'll be walking soon. Crawls everywhere if he gets the opportunity,' Connie said proudly.

Gran lowered him carefully to the floor between her feet. She gave him the box of toys to play with, amongst them his wooden train that Vic had made. She looked up at Connie. 'When you've finished your tea, I've a surprise for you.'

Connie's eyes widened. 'What?'

'Take the dirties away first and stand the fireguard in front of the fire, will you, for the child.'

Connie lifted the square mesh frame in front of the glowing coals and asked breathlessly, 'Is it to do with Vic?'

'Hurry up and I'll tell you.' She watched Connie run out of the room with the china. Then, as she ruffled Lucky's blond head, she thought of the surprise that she'd had herself yesterday. A heavy sisal bag had been returned to her from the navy. Inside, she found her grandson's civilian clothes. On searching the bag thoroughly she had discovered two sheets of folded paper hidden in a flap. One was addressed to her, the other to Connie. She was eager to see the girl's face when she read it.

★

Connie paused, the words coming a little unsteadily as emotion caused her to stop reading.

Gran was grateful that Vic had not worried this young woman with graver news. Instead he'd written words that could only lift her spirit rather than crush it.

'Sweetheart, I'm bunked with three good chaps, George being a Bermondsey lad, Sammy Kite from the sticks and Tommy Drew a city boy. Now, promise me you'll take care of yourself and Laughing Boy? I look forward to my first leave, though when and where it will be I have no idea. Keep safe for me, and to you and Lucky, my deepest affection and love. Yours as always, Vic.'

Gran watched Connie fold the sheet of lined paper into its creases and take a shuddering breath. 'Oh, Gran, I want to see him. Do you think he'll get leave soon?'

'I don't know the answer to that. But he'll move heaven and earth to arrange it.'

Connie searched Gran's face. 'Read the leaves? P'raps they'd tell us something.'

Gran felt her ribs creak as she leaned forward to stretch her arm across Lucky's head. She patted Connie's cheek, skin as soft as a baby's. 'I see lots of good things for you without them leaves, and I promise to read them when the time is right. To be honest with you, love, I've got a bugger of a back this afternoon and I thought I might get myself over to Pat's so's I can have a lie down.'

'I'll walk over with you.' Connie jumped to her feet.

'No, ta. Jerry won't be long in arriving. You'd never get home in time.'

Reluctantly Connie agreed. She took the baby into the passage and put him in the pram. Gran pulled herself up from the chair and walked out to the hall-stand, lifting her coat and slipping it on.

'See you both next week, then?'

Connie held her in a tight embrace. 'Wouldn't miss it for the world.'

'Say hello to your mum for me.'

Connie pushed the pram out and bounced it down the three steps. Gran waved goodbye, watching her progress down the road. Then when it was safe to go back inside, she removed her coat and re-hung it on the hall-stand. She had no intention of going to Pat's, it was Vic's letter to her that she wished to analyse again.

Quietly she resumed her position in the chair by the fire and took out the letter from her apron pocket.

'Dear Gran, I'll write again very soon, but it will be an official letter, not under the counter like this one. I want you to know something important. You were right about that porker's head. I've fetched up in North Wales, dead on target for DEMS ships, that is, training as a gunner for the merchant fleet. But remembering what you told me about taking fate in my own hands, I've put in for an interview with my CO. I had to stretch the truth and say as how I passed exams at school. Lucky my job was with the PLA as I've got a bit of experience under my belt and can beef it all up. My plans for a commission could all fall through if they rumble me, so didn't want to tell Con what I'm after. Let's hope it all works out, eh? I miss your cooking. Don't think I'll bother with Butlins after this.

All my love, your devoted grandson, Vic. P.S. Look out for Con for me, the brown lights and all. xx'

Gran drew her handkerchief from her sleeve and blew her nose. She read the letter once more. When she had finished, she looked up at Freddie standing so tall by Josie. Her voice trembled as she whispered, 'Give him a bit of help, son. What you couldn't do for him down here, then see to it up there.'

Then she closed her eyes and let her head rest back on the cushion, the note falling from her tightly clenched fingers and into her lap.

It was an early May morning when Connie walked into the office and for the second time found her workplace non-existent. The damage from the raid on Saturday night was extensive. Not only were the windows shattered, but the floor was holed and very dangerous. This time, there was no sweeping up by the staff or gathering of important papers. Connie saw at once it was too risky even to tread around the outer floorboards that remained. The warehousemen below were trying to secure the floor joints that had literally snapped in two and a great deal of argument was going on over which was the best way to do it.

Mr Burns and Len English, Ada and Connie all stood at the top of the stairs, watching the workmen scurrying here and there, until finally Mr Burns ordered his staff to the canteen whilst he made alternative arrangements.

The canteen, however, had been damaged too, though not so severely. The large south-facing window was still intact, but the two smaller ones were being boarded up and the preparation of food had been cancelled.

'Is there a cup of rosie going?' Len shouted to one of the girls as they stood in the dishevelled room.

'Sorry, Len. And we ain't got no water.'

'Might as well go home,' Len sighed as he pushed his way through the fallen tables and chairs to a free corner. He brushed the plaster from one of the seats along the wall, then righted two chairs. 'Come on, girls, let's have a smoke.'

They took no persuading as the three of them sat around a dusty table and Len brought out his roll-ups. 'I'm only surprised the damage isn't worse,' he commented, flinging an arm over the back of his chair. 'We're still up and running. Which is more than can be said for the House of Commons. I heard on the radio that one of the chambers is just rubble now and the square tower of Westminster Abbey went up in smoke. Saint Paul's took another hit too, but by all accounts it's still standing. They reckon it was tit for tat with what we did to Berlin.'

Ada stubbed out her cigarette. 'I'm sick of all this dust. You eat it, drink it, breathe it. I was coughing all last night in the shelter and didn't get a wink. What with that and Wally's dad going on about that Rudolf Hess parachuting from his plane up in Scotland and Mrs Wipple complaining about cheese being rationed to ten ounces a week, my head was well and truly done in.'

Connie pulled her coat round her, shivering as the breeze whistled though a shattered pane of glass. 'I wonder where we'll be put now.'

They were all silent for a moment until Ada giggled. 'Well, I hope we get a few nice-looking blokes to help us clear up the mess.'

Len feigned shock. 'You're already spoken for!'

'Nearly but not quite.' Ada touched her hair. 'I'm still officially single.'

Len's eyes widened comically. 'Is that so, Miss Freeman?'

'Oh yes it is, Mr English.'

Connie smiled as the pair acted the fools, relieving the tension of the Monday morning that had brought with it yet another wave of disaster.

'Anyway, let's look on the bright side,' Len suggested as he took a last drag on his cigarette. 'Mr Burns said we might get our old office back.'

'This time, I bags the stool by the window,' Ada cried. 'I want to look at the river. It makes me feel like everything is back to normal.'

'Talking of normal,' Len mused, 'I might unlock Mother from the cupboard tonight.'

'Get away with you!' Ada screeched. 'She's not locked up, is she?'

Len kept a straight face. 'I've lost the key to the handcuffs, though.'

Ada giggled, nudging his arm. 'I wish my Wally had a few laughs up his sleeve. He used to be such a giggle. These days he's a right old misery guts. Ever since he was told he had flat feet and wasn't eligible for the call-up. And when those five incendiary bombs fell on Maconochie's where he works, in February, it was the highlight of his life. He ain't stopped talking about it since.'

'At least he's safe,' Connie reminded her friend.

'Yeah, course.' Ada glanced at Len. 'Go on, tell us about your mum, again. I feel like I want to laugh until I cry, if you know what I mean.'

Connie listened as Len obliged. But under his humour she sensed a thread of desperation, and it was what Ada didn't say about her life that worried Connie. War brought out the best and worst in everyone. People's lives changed in ways that no one would have ever dreamed of. Ada's family were now settled in Kent and urging her to join them. Was Ada considering going? Was her great love affair with Wally over? Len made jokes about his mother, but sometimes Connie felt he wanted to be taken seriously. Dealing with an eccentric mother must be exhausting.

'I'd offer you a fag for your thoughts but I suspect they're priceless.'

Connie looked up. Len and Ada were staring at her. Len shook his head. 'I'm gonna call you the Mona Lisa from now on. You've always got a smile on your face these days.'

Ada giggled as she threaded her arm through Len's. 'Well, she's got something to smile about, hasn't she? Her Vic's due for leave any day now.'

Connie's heart somersaulted. Vic's letter had arrived last week. He was coming home! After five long months away she would be holding him close once more.

Chapter Eleven

Connie jumped off the bus in Westferry Road. It was a lovely May evening, but the country was in shock. HMS *Hood*, Britain's beloved flagship, had been sunk by the German battleship *Bismarck*. It was thought that only a handful of her 1,421 crew had been saved. Everyone had listened to the radio reports trickling in and disbelievingly read the newspapers. At work, voices had been hushed and incredulous as the tragedy became clear. Connie's thoughts were with Vic, who had not written since his last letter saying he hoped to get leave. Where was he? Would he come home soon? Did the disastrous events that had unfolded at sea reflect in his life?

Nan, with Lucky astride her hip, opened the door to Connie. 'Hello, love. Come in and sit down.'

Connie kissed them both, taking the child into her arms. 'Hello, mischief, have you been a good boy?'

Lucky gurgled and offered her his blue elephant. Connie squeezed him tight, then looked at Nan. 'Where's Lofty?'

'In the backyard, nailing up the broken fence. He'll be in soon. Sit yourself down.'

Connie took Lucky into the front room and, moving aside the usual clutter from the couch, she sank down with a sigh. 'I'm glad to be finished today. Everyone had their chins on the floor with such depressing news.'

'The nation's grieving, love,' Nan agreed, sitting beside her. 'I was up the shops this morning and they was all talking about Kathleen Walker's sister, that lives up Poplar. Her husband was serving on the *Hood*, just boarded at the last refit.'

'Oh, Nan. I don't know what I'd do if something like that happened to Vic.' Connie hugged Lucky against her, trying to tell herself she was strong. But since the terrible news she wasn't so certain any more. Now she was engaged to be married and the reality of what she had done had come home to her. She was worrying herself silly over Vic's safety. And as far as she knew, he hadn't even left England yet!

'You'd do like all the rest,' Nan said steadily, 'and keep hoping. That's what keeps us afloat. Hope in the future.'

Connie knew that Nan was trying to bolster her spirits. But Lofty was only out in the backyard, repairing a fence and within calling distance. Then she felt ashamed of herself. If he wasn't too old Lofty would have volunteered for the front line too. And Nan would have risen to the occasion, just like she always did.

'Now, would you like a bit of tea with us?' Nan asked, straightening the ties of her pinny. 'I've got a nice pot of stew on the go.'

Connie smiled gratefully. 'No thanks, Nan. I'd better

get home. Mum's still anticipating a raid tonight even though we haven't had one in almost two weeks.'

'Let's hope Jerry has his hands full.' Nan nodded as they walked to the front door. 'If Adolf's got his panzers on their way to Moscow, as they say he has, then it will take the strain off us. Nevertheless, my heart goes out to those poor souls he's turned his attention on.'

Connie nodded sadly. 'Thanks for having Lucky, Nan.'

'You don't have to thank me, it's a pleasure.' She put a hand on Connie's arm. 'Any news from the Welfare?'

'They allocated me the extra coupons for Lucky, so I'm officially a war nanny.'

Nan smiled, showing her large front teeth. 'Had another letter from Vic?'

'Yes, but no date for his leave. I'm beginning to think that him coming home is just wishful thinking.'

'He'll turn up, ducks. Now, give my love to your mum. I've not seen her in a couple of days, so tell her I'll call later in the week.'

Bidding Nan goodbye Connie made her way home. Lucky blew bubbles and made noises in his own baby language. She loved this time of the day. Cuddling and playing with him seemed to draw her closer to Vic. The memory of Gilbert Tucker was receding fast.

She kissed Lucky's blond head as she stood in the evening sunlight outside the house. She didn't want to go in. Spring had arrived. The nightly bombing had ceased after nine long months of continuous raids. A neighbour from down the road, Mrs Baines, and her two children strolled by. They called out hello and Mr Haskins from number ninety-one passed, raising his cap. Groups of young children played hopscotch again.

A young man walked towards her whistling. He was tall and dark, like Vic. As he grew closer she saw it was Ben Shutler, from six doors up.

'All right, Con?' he cried, and she smiled.

'And you, Ben?'

'Got me call-up at last,' he said, pausing briefly at the gate. 'Can't wait to get going.'

'Your mum will miss you,' Connie said sadly.

'Yeah, but when I come home on leave it'll be a pat on the back,' Ben joked as he walked on, 'instead of a flea in me ear for being a dirty stopout.'

Connie watched him saunter off. Ben had been a handful to his mum and dad and was known as being a bit of spiv by the local residents. But he didn't lack courage and had been waiting eagerly for his call-up papers. Watching him swagger down the road, Connie's heart tugged. So many young men sent to war, including her Vic. Oh, when would she see him again?

The evening was quiet and skies remained clear except for the barrage balloons swaying above like huge metallic clouds. The residents of Kettle Street gossiped on doorsteps and the kids dared to stay out longer.

Connie went indoors. The house was empty. She knew that her parents had gone for a walk to Island Gardens. Billy spent his evenings in Taffy's shed for what he called his fitness instruction. By day he helped Taffy on the roofs. He won more of his fights than he lost and had kept his promise to stay out of trouble. The nights when they were cooped up in the Anderson seemed a long way away.

Much later, when Lucky was asleep, Connie went out into the yard. She sat down on the bench that she and Billy had spent so many hours sitting on in the Blitz. Dad had filled in the hole with the debris from the shelter and laid earth on top. A few brave weeds were working their way up to the light.

A soft wind blew her hair lightly around her shoulders. The smell of the river was back again, unpolluted by the odour of cordite. The evening stretched long and lonely before her. Kevin and Sylvie had asked her to go to the pictures. Mum and Dad would have looked after Lucky, but she didn't want to play gooseberry. Connie envied Sylvie not having to worry about Kevin going in the forces. His engineering job at the factory making components for radar was a reserved occupation.

If only Vic would come home. She would marry him tomorrow! Not having a big wedding didn't matter. She just wanted to be his wife. Five months apart had made her realize how much she loved him.

She looked up at the beautiful spring sky now going dusky. The gulls were screeching over clouds tinged with a delicate, rosy hue. It was a true English evening. There was even a blackbird on the soil, digging away with its yellow beak. Connie lifted her face to the warm breeze and sighed.

Suddenly a pair of hands slipped over her eyes. 'Guess who?'

She couldn't breathe or speak.

'Blow me down, that's the quietest I've ever heard my girl.'

Then Connie was in his arms, her heart beating so wildly she was afraid it would burst. Tears of joy trickled down her cheeks and sobs of delight filled her throat.

'Oh, Vic! Oh, Vic, I don't believe it.'

'You'd better.' He kissed her passionately. 'There, does that help?'

She nodded. 'I was thinking of you and you appeared . . .'

'Oh, sweetheart, I've missed you so much!'

She pressed her lips hard against his. 'Say that again.'

'I've missed you so much—'

'No.' She lifted her mouth, whispering softly, 'just say sweetheart.'

He held her face between his hands. 'Sweetheart,' he whispered huskily, 'my own dear sweetheart.'

She trembled in his arms. 'I nearly faint when you call me that.'

A twinkle came into his eyes. 'That's what all damsels do just before getting saved. They faint into a pair of strong arms and get taken off on horseback.'

She was laughing and wiping away the tears. 'Oh, just look at your uniform!' She inspected the slim-fitting dark blue tunic and flared trousers that moulded his body. He looked taller than ever and, yes, a little older, though she couldn't quite see why. His lovely dark eyes had a new expression that made her feel both proud and sad at the same time.

'How long have you got?'

'Till the end of the week.'

'Is that all?'

'I'm lucky to have got that.' He lifted her chin. 'There's so much I've got to tell you and so much I want to know.'

'Come inside. Are you hungry?'

'Not for food.' He kissed her again and her head swam with joy.

'Have you seen Gran yet?' she asked as he took her hand and they walked into the house.

'No. I came straight here. Where is everyone?'

'Out, making the most of the quiet. We haven't had a raid recently, though the last one was terrible. A lot of the city was demolished, even the House of Commons was hit. But with the news about Russia, people are saying it might be the end of the Blitz.' She pulled him along to the front room. They gazed into Lucky's cot. 'Do you think he's grown?' she whispered, watching Vic's face as he gazed at the sleeping child.

'You know, he looks the spit of you.'

'Yes, he does,' Connie admitted, a little embarrassed. 'Let's sit down and talk.'

In hushed whispers and holding hands, they tried to catch up on the news. Vic traced the shape of her ring with his finger.

'Anything about Lucky?' he asked.

'No.' She wasn't going to mention Gilbert Tucker. She didn't want to spoil a lovely evening.

'Let me look at you.' He took her face between his hands and kissed her long and hard. 'You're more beautiful than ever.'

Connie didn't want the kissing or the loving to stop. Her body cried out for him. She felt as though she had been starved for a year.

'We're home!' Olive's call made them jump apart. Connie sighed. Whenever would they find time to themselves?

Her parents followed by Kevin and Sylvie tumbled into the room and swept Vic into their warm embrace.

The next day Connie asked Mr Burns if she could take time off. In view of the circumstances, he agreed. When the hooter went at five thirty, she flew down the stairs and hurried towards the gates, Ada running beside her. Vic was waiting in his uniform. All the girls were staring at him. Connie felt very proud.

Ada nudged her arm. 'What an eyeful he makes, Con.'

'I can't believe he's home.'

'I'd never have come to work today if it was me.'

'I didn't want to let Mr Burns down. He's very good to let me go at such short notice. And now I've got Lucky I need my job.'

'Hello, Ada.' Vic bent to kiss her cheek.

'How's the navy, Vic?'

He grinned. 'I've got to find a ship first.'

Connie looked up at her handsome fiancé. He was so good looking! She wanted to hug and kiss him all the time.

'Right, we'd better be off,' he said, grabbing Connie's hand. 'I don't have the car any more, so it's Shanks's pony I'm afraid.'

Ada winked. 'Enjoy yourselves.'

'We will.'

They walked hand in hand and Connie felt she could burst with pride. People they passed looked in admiration at the tall young man beside her.

'What would you like to do?' he asked as they made their way home. 'We could push Lucky out in the pram. Don't think there's any chance of a raid, do you?'

'Hope not,' Connie agreed as she felt the exhilaration flow through her veins. 'It would be nice to be by ourselves.' She felt her cheeks go pink.

Vic looked down at her, his gaze intense. 'I was hoping you'd say that.'

'I could ask Mum and Dad to babysit.'

He nodded thoughtfully. 'Gran's staying the night at Pat's. The house is empty.'

Connie looked into his eyes. They didn't need words. They could read each other's minds.

At Nan's, Lucky was in the tin bath. Vic pushed a toy boat on the surface. They all shrieked with laughter as Lucky's fat hands hit the water and splashed them. After supper it was Nan who suggested they leave him with her for the evening.

'He'll go off in the pram with a bit of rocking. Why don't you two go to the cinema or somewhere nice? In fact, if it's late, you can collect him in the morning.'

An hour later they found themselves in Gran's parlour. Lying on cushions in front of a blazing fire, Vic kissed her again and again. Connie kissed him back, needing his hands to touch her, arouse her.

'I want you so much,' she groaned as he undid the buttons of her blouse. His lips covered her in tiny kisses only stopping when he looked into her eyes. 'Connie, if we go on—'

'I don't want you to stop.'

'Are you sure?'

She nodded, placing his hands on her naked breasts. 'Feel what you're doing to me.'

'I want you, my darling, so much.'

'And I want you. Make love to me. Make me remember this evening for ever.'

He took her into his arms and adored her; she had never imagined such bliss could fill a human heart.

'Connie, I've something to tell you.' The firelight flickered on their naked bodies. The smoke from his cigarette curled up into the air as his fingers played lightly on her skin.

She rolled against him, nestling her head on his shoulder. 'I don't want to know it.'

He smiled as he rubbed his chin against her forehead. 'I've been posted to Chatham.'

'What's that?'

'It's a big naval barracks. From there we'll be sent to our ships.'

She sat up. 'When will I see you again?'

He pulled her against him, his hand brushing the soft blond curls from her eyes. 'I can't tell you that, I'm afraid.'

'But how will I know where you are?'

'Or that either. Everything is secret. Even we don't know what's ahead of us.'

Connie looked into his eyes, frightened now. How could she bear the sacrifice they had to make for their country? 'I hate this war,' she said fiercely. 'I hate it with all my heart.'

'We're fighting for freedom, darling.'

'I know. But it's such a heavy price to pay.'

'I promise I'll come back.'

She knew he was trying to reassure her and she wanted to believe him. 'Make love to me,' she whispered. 'I don't want to think about tomorrow. I just want you – now – this moment.'

Taking her in his arms, he kissed her, and sinking back into the cushions they shut out the world and all the worries of tomorrow.

Connie's memories of the two short days they spent together were the happiest of her life. The Blitz really did appear to be over, but in another corner of the world the Russians had been caught unprepared by the German onslaught. There was also news of another ferocious Atlantic battle. The British naval fleet had avenged HMS *Hood* by sinking *Bismarck*. Germany's pride had been destroyed with a vengeance that had even the British people gasping aloud. Pursued relentlessly by every available British ship and aircraft, she had been cornered and sunk, so avenging the death of *Hood*.

'Were there any survivors?' Olive asked the night before Vic was due to return to Chatham. Ebbie was reading from the newspaper and Vic and Connie were sitting side by side on the couch, listening solemnly to the report.

Ebbie shook his head, his eyes not lifting. 'A thousand plus crew there were. Most of them are presumed to have perished, sent to the bottom with their ship.'

'She was a doomed vessel,' Vic said quietly. 'Even if she was Germany's newest and fastest, it didn't make any difference to our High Command. The morale of our fleet depended upon a kill.'

'It's terrible.' Connie shuddered, thinking of the wives and mothers who, like those of the *Hood*'s crew, would never see their men again. 'All those lives lost on both sides.'

Olive put down her knitting and stared at the cot where Lucky was asleep. 'It's for his future and all our children's future that we're fighting. Even I can see the sense in that.'

'And we'd do well to keep the fact in mind.' Ebbie nodded as he lowered the newspaper to his lap. 'The Luftwaffe has a sting in its tail. They might have let up on us a bit but they're bombing other towns now, going through the bloody Baedeker guidebook, if you please! Who would have ever thought of that?'

The room went silent. Connie felt Vic squeeze her hand. It was their last night together and she wanted to have him all to herself, to be made love to. She didn't want to talk about war and all the killing. But, despite her need to distance herself from grim realities, it seemed only right they share some time with the two families.

Vic stretched his long legs. 'Well, I won't keep you all up too late.'

Again silence as Ebbie rose and came forward to take

hold of his hand. He pressed it hard in a firm grip. 'It won't be long before we see you again, son, I'm sure. Until then, good luck and keep out of trouble.'

Vic grinned. 'You bet I will.'

'Look after yourself now, Victor.' Olive embraced the young man, lifting her hand to pat his cheek.

Outside, the sky was dark blue, crammed with stars and a bright silver moon. Hand in hand they strolled down the deserted street. There was so much she still wanted to say, with no time left to say it in. She knew he felt the same, as they made their steps shorter and slower and her aching heart felt as though it was painfully filling her chest. She tried to brush away the tears surreptitiously, but he saw her and caught her hand. Bringing her against him, they clung together.

After a long time, he whispered, 'Oh, Connie, I love you so much.'

'And I love you.'

'Look after yourself while I'm away.'

'I hate goodbyes.'

'I'll come home. Believe that, won't you?'

'I'll try to.'

He bent his head and kissed her, bringing back in a flash all the wonderful hours she had spent in his arms, memories that would help to sustain her in the lonely days ahead.

'Be brave, sweetheart.'

'I don't want you to go.'

'Neither do I.'

He took her shoulders and cleared his throat roughly

as though he was about to speak. But then he let her go and she watched him stride away, out of her life once more.

Connie felt sick with love and grief. Half of her world was missing. She wouldn't truly live again until he was safe in her arms once more.

Chapter Twelve

Lucky turned his first approximate 'birthday' in June. Connie and Nan made a cake, celebrating what everyone hoped was the end of the nightly bombing. Whilst the all clear persisted, Billy enlisted the help of Taffy to replace the corner of roof that was missing. Tiles and rafters were nailed back and the office at work was once again habitable. Life was getting back to normal, Connie reflected one warm August morning, as she walked to work. Even Ted Jackson, the postman, was looking more cheerful as he hopped off his bike to hand her a letter.

'One for you, Connie!'

'Thanks, Ted.' Her heart turned over as she glanced at the naval postmark.

Tucking the letter in her pocket, she resisted the temptation to open it just yet. She'd wait until she could savour every word and maybe – oh, please God – he'd say when he was coming home again.

It wasn't until she was sitting on the wharf wall with Ada in their dinner break that Connie found time to read it. 'I promised myself I wasn't going to get upset,'

Connie said when she came to the end of the single page, 'but he doesn't say when he's coming home or where he is or anything like that. It's like eating an ice-cream without any flavour.'

Ada grinned. 'Yeah, but the lovey dovey bits are nice, ain't they?'

Connie nodded, but she had been hoping dearly there would be a clue to his whereabouts or a small hint as to his next leave.

'Wally don't know one end of a pen from the other,' Ada continued to grumble. 'Your Vic's got a real way with words.'

Connie immediately felt guilty. She had so much to be grateful for. Her family and friends had survived the Blitz and her job at Dalton's was still safe. She even had her own room back, where she and Lucky could sleep in peace each night. But without knowing when she was going to hold Vic in her arms again, there was a huge gap in her life.

'The thing is, Wally's never written me a letter or said anything like Vic says to you.'

'He might if he went away somewhere.'

'Sometimes I wish he would.'

'You don't mean that.'

Ada didn't reply, just chewed on her lip. Then suddenly she lifted her hands and slapped them down in her lap. 'Oh, life is just so boring, Con. We never do anything, just sit in or go out for a walk and that's only if he's not tired. What a laugh, eh? Usually it's the woman who is knackered or has a headache, but oh no, not in Wally's case. He has more headaches lately than mum ever did and that's saying something. We used to go to the pictures and sit in the back row, but we don't even do that now. And the last blooming time we went we had to take bloody Jean with us.'

Connie knew that Wally's sister had become a nuisance; not only had Ada to share a room with her, but the couple were continually pestered by Jean's demands to go out with them.

'Ada, don't you miss your own family?'

'Course I do. My sisters especially. Jean is nothing like them. She's spoiled and selfish and a right little madam.'

'What about Wally's mum and dad?'

'Well, they're not bad really. Just a bit straight-laced. They go to church on Sundays and I have to go with them to keep the peace. But my heart's not in it and neither was Wally's once. As I said, life is just so boring seeing each other every day, doing the same thing over and over again, never getting any time alone. Even when we do – you know – *enjoy* ourselves, it's over and done with in seconds.'

Connie had noticed lines of discontentment forming around Ada's mouth. Her auburn hair was neglected and now she didn't even bother to wear make-up. She didn't laugh much either, not like she used to. Not so long ago they had sat in this very spot, giggling and making each other laugh until the tears ran down their cheeks. What had happened to the happy girl she had once known?

'Oh, I don't mean to complain,' Ada continued tiredly. 'But I want a bit of what you've got. When Vic went back after his leave, you'd changed. I could see it in your eyes, that special glow. It was like that for me and Wally once. We could spend ages mucking about and just having a laugh as well as enjoying a bit of the other. Now it's as if he's taking me and our future for granted. To be honest, the last thing I want to do is live with his mum and dad and sister for the rest of my life, though sometimes I think Wally would be quite happy to. If he was away like Vic at least he'd want to be on his own with me when he came home.'

Connie thought how strange life was. She would do anything to have Vic here in the flesh, whilst Ada would prefer to have Wally at war. It seemed more romantic to her that way, but it wasn't. 'Ada, you don't know how lucky you are to have Wally safe. I don't know where Vic is or where he's going. Or even if he's on board ship and in the middle of a battle. Churchill might be sticking up his two fingers and telling us all that the V sign is the symbol of the unconquerable, but it don't help my heart much every time I hear of a ship sunk.'

Ada looked repentant. 'Yeah, you must feel rotten.'

An idea formed in Connie's mind. 'Look, Billy's got a big fight next month. He asked me to go and see it, but he knows I'm not keen to watch. If it's excitement you want, why don't you and Wally go?'

'I've never seen a bare-knuckle fight before,' Ada said excitedly.

'Well, here's your chance.'

'I'll ask Wally. It would certainly make a change.'

Connie dug her sandwiches out of her bag and,

unwrapping the brown paper bag, offered them to her friend. 'Spam, spam or more spam.' She grinned.

Ada considered, then, pushing her own brown parcel aside, raised her plucked eyebrows. 'I'll have spam if it's all right with you. Beats the living daylights out of dripping.'

Both girls laughed and Connie began to feel hopeful. Perhaps a night out on the tiles would bring Ada and Wally together again.

Billy's fight was big island news. The event was arranged to take place at the Queens, Millwall. Ada had been looking forward to it for weeks, but at the eleventh hour, her hopes were dashed.

'We had a row,' Ada sniffed when she turned up on the doorstep alone. 'He's not coming. But I'll still go.'

'What, on your own?'

'No, with you.'

'Ada, you know how I feel about watching fights.'

'Yeah, but it will only be this once. We can't let Billy down.'

Connie suspected Ada wasn't concerned with Billy's feelings. It was her own she was more worried about, and the fact that she was angry with Wally.

'What about Lucky?'

'Ask your mum and dad to look after him.'

Connie was wishing she had never got involved in Ada's love life. The trouble was, she didn't want to let Billy down and Ada knew it.

A quarter of an hour later, they were on their way to the Queens. 'What was the row about?' Connie asked.

'I called Jean a nosy cow and told her to eff off.'

'Why did you do that?'

'I found her going through my things.'

'What was she looking for?'

'She said she needed stockings that wasn't laddered. As I've got a few pairs in my drawer she took it on herself to look whilst I was at work. I said she had to ask first. She said why should she, as it was her house I was living in. I told her I didn't care what flaming house it was, and then the balloon went up. Naturally, Wally took her side.'

'Oh dear.'

'Well, he can lump it. I'm going to enjoy myself tonight. What time does the fight start?'

'Seven o'clock. So Billy said.'

'Good. I fancy a drink.'

'The Queens is rough, Ada,' Connie warned. 'Not many women go there. It's all dockers.'

'I don't care where I drink,' Ada retorted sharply. 'It's my one and only night off from misery guts.'

Connie wished for the hundredth time that evening that she'd never opened her mouth about the forthcoming event. She had guessed from the second Ada appeared on her own, she was looking for trouble. All dollied up in a summer dress and high heels with her make-up carefully applied for the first time in months, she looked very pretty. No wonder Wally was sulking.

The Queens, as expected, was noisy and crowded. Connie's heart sank as they hovered on the doorstep. Waves of stale beer wafted out along with the saucy comments. Ada giggled, returning smiles from the men, one in particular, Connie noticed. He was tall and dark, with a dangerous smile, just the type Ada was attracted to.

'Ada, let's wait on the pavement till seven.'

'Why? I want to go in.'

'Only because that bloke smiled at you.'

'It was just a smile.'

'You don't know him and he looks—'

'A bit of all right,' Ada supplied, fluttering her eyelashes.

Before Connie could reply a man wearing a red, white and blue waistcoat approached them. 'Hello, Connie, it's me, Taffy.' He smiled.

Connie had only seen him wearing cap and dungarees before as he climbed the ladder to help Billy mend the hole in the roof. Now he looked smart with his hair smoothed across his head.

Connie was about to introduce Ada when Taffy grinned. 'You're mate's done a bunk over to the bar.'

Connie looked round. Ada was standing at the bar flirting with the stranger.

'Want me to go after her?'

Connie sighed. 'Not in the mood she's in. She'll find us if she wants us.'

'Oh well, Billy will be pleased to see you anyway.'

Connie stuck to Taffy's heels as they walked into the back room. From here they entered a passage and were halted at the end by a huge man with no hair and tattoos on his arms.

'Open up, you daft bugger,' Taffy ordered.

'Who's this?' the man demanded, nodding at Connie.

'She's family. Now let us in.'

'Who was he?' Connie asked as they walked through.

'The pub's muscle. Need it to keep out the riff-raff.'

Connie hoped there wasn't going to be any trouble. Thirty or forty people were assembled around a square patch of sawdust in the pub's backyard. Billy was standing by a bale of straw, swinging punches in the air and trying for all the world to look dangerous. Naked above the waist he wore baggy trousers that were rolled up to his knees. With an arrogant swagger he sauntered towards Taffy and raised his hands above his head. Smiling at Connie, he gave her a confident wink.

She forced herself to smile back, then gasped as she saw his opponent, a mountain of a man with muscular arms, a hairy chest and bright red hair. He snarled at Billy and spat noisily on the ground.

For the first two rounds, Connie listened to Taffy urging Billy to protect himself from the the Ginger Giant. But Billy was using his mouth more than his feet.

'Go on, Billy, move your arse!' Taffy threw back his head in exasperation. The Giant was living up to his reputation as a hard nut to crack.

Billy was trapped in a corner. His breathing was heavy, his thin chest bathed in sweat. Connie could see by the red welts on his cheeks that he was losing his temper, but unable to vent it on the bigger, stronger man.

A loud cheer went up as Billy landed a blow. He hurled himself at the enemy but was punched in the groin. A slap to the head followed and Billy was down.

'That's not fair!' Connie cried, only to see Billy kicked

as he tried to stand up. She turned to Taffy. 'Did you see what he did?'

Taffy shrugged and turned his attention back to the fight. Connie listened to the boos and cheers echoing through the pub's backyard as the Giant set about Billy once more.

'The man he's fighting is twice Billy's size,' Connie complained, as a tiny man wearing a cloth cap signalled the round was over.

'But he's got a weakness,' Taffy whispered out of the side of his mouth.

'What's that?'

'A glass jaw.'

Connie didn't stop to ask what it meant. 'Does Billy know that?'

'Course he does. We sussed this fight out between us, got all the moves in place.'

'What's happening then?'

'The Giant deliberately verballed him before the fight, made Billy lose his temper. It's an old trick and a good one. You need to stay cool in the ring, keep your wits about you and dance.'

'Your boy can't fight his own shadow,' a man shouted to Taffy. 'I want me money back.'

Connie wondered if everyone in the yard was blind to the fact that it was an unfair fight. Billy had been kicked when he was down and even if the bigger man did have a weakness, Billy hadn't been able to get close enough to find it. Even she could see the match was not equal.

The bell rang and Billy stumbled back to his corner. Connie rushed up to him. 'Billy, what's wrong?'

He tried to smile. His lips were so swollen it came out like a grimace. 'Where's Ada and Wally?'

'You'll have to put up with me. Billy, why are you letting him hit you like that?'

'I lost me rag,' Billy muttered as he spat blood from his mouth. 'And he took advantage.'

'Taffy says he's got a glass jaw.'

Billy's bruised eyebrows rose. 'Blimey, the girl knows what she's on about.'

'Don't let him make you angry. And – *dance* – whatever that is.'

Billy laughed again. 'Yes, ma'am.' He stood up. When the bell rang he bounced lightly forward and dodged the swing of a massive fist.

Connie went back to Taffy. 'I don't think I can watch much more.'

'Whatever you said is having an effect.'

Billy was ducking and diving. Connie held her breath as he landed a punch on the Giant's nose. A roar of delight erupted from the crowd.

'Credit where credit's due,' Taffy breathed in her ear. 'Billy can give punishment as well as take it.'

'You weren't saying that five minutes ago.'

'Five minutes ago I was thinking of going in there meself.' Taffy grinned at her. 'He's just broke the bugger's nose.'

'I thought it was his jaw that was suspect?'

Taffy shrugged. 'Nose, jaw, eyes – what does it matter? He's down and that's all that matters.'

Connie felt sick at the sight of so much blood covering the sawdust. A thick red stream flowed between the Giant's fingers as he rolled on the ground in pain. The crowd were jumping up and down, calling Billy's name. Two men hoisted him on their shoulders. Battered, bruised and bloody, he was hailed the winner.

Connie stared up at her little brother. He threw her a kiss. She couldn't help jumping up and down too.

Connie stood with her hands on her hips, outside the Queens. 'You missed Billy's fight.'

'I know,' Ada said repentantly. 'And I'm sorry.'

'You don't look sorry at all. You look—' Connie forgot her annoyance as she stared into her friend's excited face. Her smile was soft and her skin flushed. The old twinkle was back in her eyes.

'Connie, it was my only chance to have some fun. Oh, I ain't had such a nice time in ages.'

They began to walk home and Connie sighed. 'Go on then, tell me all about it.'

'No, tell me about Billy first.'

'He won.'

Ada smiled. 'You must be ever so proud.'

'Yes, but I've had enough fighting to last me a lifetime.'

'Well, he won and that's the main thing. Now, shall I tell you what I've been up to?'

Connie knew that Ada had lost interest in what she had to say. Her friend had something more important on her mind and Connie had the sinking feeling she knew what it was. 'Whatever you've done I hope you remembered you have a boyfriend already.'

Even in the dusk, Connie saw Ada blush. 'It was just fun, that's all. This bloke called Freddie Smith bought me a gin and lime. He said would I like a quick one and I said yes. I just couldn't help myself. He had these lovely blue eyes that made me go shivery all over.'

'Oh, Ada. What would Wally say?'

'He won't know, will he?' Ada shrugged indifferently.

'Are you seeing this Freddie again?'

'Course not.'

Connie glanced out of the corner of her eye at Ada, who tossed back her head and hummed a little tune, swaying her hips as they went. She guessed Ada wasn't telling the truth. It was on her lips to question her more, when she thought better of it. In this case, ignorance might be bliss.

'Connie?'

'What?'

'Are you angry with me?'

Connie smiled. 'I'd be a rich woman, Ada Freeman, if I had a penny for the times you ask me that.'

They laughed then, just like the old days, as they strolled in the soft evening, their voices echoing along the streets. The island air smelled tangy, with the whiff of beer coming from the pubs on every street corner. Underlying it all was the river's saltiness, the water's scent that seeped into the heart of the night and seemed to stretch up to the full yellow moon.

'It's a lovely evening,' Ada breathed, squeezing Connie's arm as her voice trembled softly. 'I wish we didn't have to go home. I could stay out all night.'

'You used to once,' Connie reminded her friend dryly.

'Yeah,' Ada agreed wistfully. 'A lifetime ago.'

With full military honours the two British sailors were buried at sea from the hangar deck. The conditions were calm after yesterday's sortie. Town-class light cruiser HMS *Oxford* rocked gently on the surface of the blue Mediterranean water. Both coffins slipped silently away, leaving no trace behind.

Vic swallowed hard as he beat down the shock and grief for his brother at arms. Sammy Kite had boarded *Oxford* with Georgie at Rosyth. They were the only three to have come through from Glendower. Sammy was too young to die and would be sadly missed.

As the naval officers and their ratings began to sing 'Abide With Me', Vic closed his eyes in respect. Next to him stood George Mullen, also with head bowed. This was the first loss they had encountered and it had devastated them.

Vic guessed that more of the same lay ahead before they reached safe harbour. For the three cruisers that were part of a convoy bound for Malta, the going was tough. Battleships *Rodney* and *Prince of Wales* were to join them, part of a vast force of British naval ships, as they encountered the enemy, in this case the Italians. But after the last vitriolic attack the mood of optimism had faded.

The last foray with the Italian torpedo bombers had claimed Sammy's life and injured another five. All the crew were shaken, but Captain Chamberlain had shown no weakness, and that was the way his men needed it to be. Chamberlain was a good captain, a role model. One day, Vic told himself each morning as he climbed out of his hammock, he would lead men too. His first wavy gold band was a dream no longer. He was going to get something good out of this bloody war if it—

A droll smile touched his lips. No, he wasn't going to die. At least, not yet.

'Action stations! Action stations!'

The alarm sounded, men scattered everywhere.

'Here we go again!' Georgie exclaimed as two aircraft appeared on the horizon, their low drone coming closer. Gunfire cracked across their heads. Vic threw himself down as a plane dived, bullets carving water and metal alike. He dragged himself to the side and looked over the bow. A deadly arrow of white below the surface missed *Oxford* by inches. Heart in mouth he jumped to his feet and ran past 'A' turret. Above him the six-inch gun was already in operation. The noise was deafening him.

'They're reforming,' someone shouted. 'Get your arse into action, mate. They mean business.'

Vic ran to the forward funnel. He wondered if Georgie was ahead of him. The vessel's small folded-wing Walrus aircraft were stationed dead centre of the ship. They were the spine, the backbone of *Oxford*, over-looked by the crane that was used to recover aircraft when they misjudged their landing and fell into the sea. But the crane was also a marker for enemy pilots.

How long before *Ark Royal*'s Swordfish torpedo bombers arrived? Our lads would give those bastards a run for their money. The evening was clear and perfect for a scrap. Vic felt a sudden prickle of excitement. Then, to his dismay, heard a loud explosion.

'Direct hit!' Georgie shouted, poking his head out from behind the four-inch gun turret. Vic swivelled on his heel. To the east, a tail of black smoke crawled ominously into the air.

'Who is it? Can you see?'

'One of our chicks,' Georgie yelled. 'Going up like a bonfire.'

Vic felt his legs go weak. A merchant ship on its way to the bottom. He thought of the mighty *Hood* and *Bismarck*, and of the men who had already been lost and were lying on the ocean bed. Then he pulled himself together, in time to notice the moving cloud on the horizon. It was dissolving into countless small specks.

The Italians were returning.

They were flying in from the sun!

Chapter Thirteen

August 1942

Connie made her way carefully along the platform. It was crowded with couples, some embracing, some laughing, some crying. The GIs were in town, creating a new kind of excitement. Since the Japanese attack on the American fleet in Pearl Harbour last year, tailored uniforms and smooth accents abounded. The Yanks were an everyday sight now, since December '41, all part and parcel of the Allied force.

British soldiers, sailors and airmen mingled with their new comrades. Girlfriends, wives and children were swept into their loved ones' arms, ecstatically happy or filled with confusion. So many emotions, hopes and dreams poured into one brief, blissful reunion.

Connie heard the guard blow his whistle. The train began to move slowly out of Paddington, as though reluctant to leave. Where was Vic? His letter was in her bag, The day, time and place were engraved in her mind. She knew every word by heart.

Someone bumped into her. She stumbled sideways

and was grabbed by two big hands. 'Jeez, little lady, I almost knocked you off your feet!'

Connie looked up into the friendly face of the GI. 'I'm all right,' she told him a little unsteadily, then smiling shyly added, 'You can let go of me now.'

Looking embarrassed, he put her back on her feet. 'Heck, my apologies, ma'am. Did I hurt you?'

'No, I'm fine – really, I am.'

'You're so – well – kinda delicate looking – if you don't mind me saying.'

Connie blushed as she straightened her jacket and the blue-eyed stranger continued to stare at her. Her costume was new, well, nearly new from the market. A lilac two-piece as slim as a pencil, flattering her tiny waist with its nipped-in pleats. Ada had been with her when she bought it and found a matching felt hat in almost the same shade, with an upswept brim and a purple petersham ribbon trim. Connie had splashed out on accessories: second-hand but well-preserved high-heeled shoes and a dark leather bag with rouleau handles. The outfit had cost over three pounds but she hadn't needed coupons, always a plus when you shopped at Cox Street. Now she decided by the attention it was drawing, the investment was worth every penny.

'Are you sure I didn't hurt you?' His blue eyes were dazzling under his silver crew-cut. The three upside down stripes indicated his rank, a sergeant.

'You didn't at all.'

He looked along the crowded platform. 'Can I – er – make up for my mistake and escort you somewhere?'

Connie went on her toes to glance round. 'I'm looking for my fiancé, actually. He was supposed to be on this train.'

The GI chuckled. 'So was half of the country, ma'am.'

'It's his first leave in ten months,' Connie said proudly. 'He's been promoted to lieutenant. I'm not sure I'll recognize him in his new uniform.'

'Well, he'll sure recognize you.'

She blushed again, then, glancing along the platform, she moved away. 'Well, I'd better go.'

He nodded. 'It was nice meeting you, as the English say.' He was still staring after her when she turned back, a head and shoulders above the crowd.

She felt flattered, but all she could think of was Vic. It was now three fifteen. He'd promised to meet her under the clock on the hour. What if his leave had been cancelled? Her spirits began to sink. She'd waited for this moment for so long.

'Connie! Connie!'

She turned, her heart racing. All she could see was a sea of faces. Had she been dreaming his call?

'Darling . . .' He emerged from the crowd and a pair of strong arms swept round her.

She buried her head in his shoulder, the hot tears squashed on her lashes. He lifted her face and kissed her, a long, hungry kiss that they had both been waiting for so long. 'You look so distinguished in your flat cap,' she gulped, 'and a lovely new jacket instead of the tunic. Oh, Vic, you've earned your wavy gold line! I'm so proud of you.'

'And by God, I'm proud of you.' He was drinking her in. 'The reason I'm late,' he whispered huskily as he pressed flowers into her hand.

'Oh, they're lovely.'

'Connie, I've missed you.'

She threw her arms around him. 'Me too.'

He held her tightly, a shudder going through him as he whispered in her hair, 'Let's get out of here.'

She nodded, reaching for his hand. 'Where shall we go?'

'Our place, the Embankment.'

He slid his hand around her waist as they hurried to the station exit. All around them, lovers were doing the same, trying to find a moment in time that was all theirs, with so much to tell and so little time to tell it in.

They jumped on a bus at Marble Arch. It was a beautiful afternoon as they strolled to Westminster and sat in Embankment Gardens. A hot August sun was dipping in the sky, turning the Thames to a molten gold. London was crammed with couples, strolling and laughing, or seated on the grass or benches, lost in their own worlds.

'I don't know where to start,' Connie sighed as she snuggled close to Vic, his arm laying lightly behind her on the bench. 'I had so much to tell you and now it's all gone out of my mind.'

'Tell me all the things I've only been able to imagine.'

She began with Lucky, describing his first steps and first words, his baby language and the little pearls that had appeared in his mouth one by one. She told him how the

Blitz had finally come to an end, though the raids continued randomly and other cities and towns were fiercely targeted. She described their Saturday afternoons with Gran and how she and Pat went to the market sometimes, and she made him laugh when she told him about Billy and his first big fight a year ago. She'd written all her news in her letters and felt as though she was repeating herself, but he didn't seem to mind as he sat beside her, looking so handsome in his new officer's uniform.

'You'd better stop me,' she sighed, 'or I'll go on for ever.'

He ran his thumb over her chin. 'Why should I want you to stop? Your voice is music to my ears.'

'All right then. Tell me you missed me.'

'I'd show you just how much if we were on our own.'

'Go on then,' she teased. 'I dare you.'

He inched forward, his eyes full of mischief, then taking her in his arms he hugged her. 'Oh, Con, I want you all to myself.'

'You've got me.'

'Where would you like to go?'

'Let's stay on this seat for ever.'

He kissed her slowly, the warmth of his body and his passionate lips making her dizzy with joy. She didn't care who saw them. London was full of couples in love doing exactly the same thing.

'You look so lovely, sweetheart,' he whispered hoarsely. 'There's not a girl I've seen who can hold a candle to you.'

She looked at him sideways. 'Just how many have you seen then?'

He chuckled softly. 'Where I've been lately the females wore big fur coats and snow boots. When we went ashore it was impossible to tell if they were young or old.'

Connie's face fell. 'I thought your ship was in the Mediterranean.'

'It was but at Malta we were ordered back to Scotland on the double.'

'What for?

'To make the run from Scapa Flow to Mermansk and Archangel. It's the route our supply convoys take to Russia. The Russians are desperate for supplies as Jerry's cut them off from all sides, so it's only us that are keeping them going.' He paused, pushing back his dark hair, and Connie realized how exhausted he looked.

'Is it dangerous?'

'It's bloody cold.' He grinned. 'So cold that the spray comes up from the bow and freezes mid air. If a ship ices up she goes top heavy and turns turtle. Half the time we're using steam hoses to disperse the ice.'

'Isn't there another way to Russia?'

'If there is, the British navy's not found it.'

'Were you seasick?'

He laughed. 'Not half. The *Oxford* is nine thousand tons in weight but she's bounced around like a ball on waves as big as mountains. On one trip all our depth charges and the rear six-inch gun turret were ripped up from the deck and washed overboard, just like that.'

'Thank God I didn't know. I'd have been worried to death. You never said in your letters.'

He trailed a finger down her cheek. 'Can't, can I? Everything is hush-hush.'

'I couldn't stand it if I didn't hear from you, even though you don't have much to say.'

He jerked an eyebrow. 'That's a back-handed compliment if ever I heard one.'

'I like the kisses you draw though.'

'Come here and let me give you a real one.'

Connie slipped her hands around his neck. How many times had she dreamed of this moment? 'Mr Burns let me have all this week off,' she whispered proudly. 'He knew I wasn't going to take no for an answer.'

'That's my girl.' He grinned, kissing the tip of her nose.

'Mum is cooking a slap-up dinner tonight and Pat and Laurie are taking us out to the pub. Your Gran said she'd babysit Doris and Lucky so we won't have to get back early. And Taffy, that's Billy's boss, has offered to drive us in his lorry if we want.'

'I wish I hadn't sold the car now. The first thing I do when the war is over is buy a new one.'

'The first thing I want to do this week,' Connie said impetuously, 'is get married.'

'What!'

'Well, why not? We can get a special licence. Lots of people do.' Her face fell as she stared at him. 'Have you changed your mind about marrying me?'

'Don't be daft, Con. You know I want to get married. But I want you to have a proper wedding.'

'I just want to be Mrs Victor Champion, that's all.'

He looked hard into her eyes. 'You might now, but in the years to come I don't want you regretting we never had the full works. The vicar, the dress, bridesmaids, the reception and the honeymoon. Now, isn't that dream worth waiting for?'

Connie bit down on her lip. 'So the answer's still no?'

He laughed softly, shaking his head. 'We have all our lives ahead of us.'

Why wouldn't he listen to her? The war might not be over for months – years, probably.

'Trust me, sweetheart.'

'It's Hitler I don't trust.'

'All the more reason not to let him spoil our plans.' He kissed her again, then whispered, 'Now, I've a surprise for you.'

She smiled reluctantly. 'Stop trying to change the subject.'

'There's a club up West called Valentino's. A pal of mine, Georgie Mullen's second cousin runs it – or he might be third – anyway, we've just got to give him the nod and we're dancing the night away.'

'Dancing!' Connie held her breath. 'I haven't danced in years! What would I wear?'

'What you're wearing now. You'll outshine every girl in the room.'

'Victor Champion, you can twist me round your little finger, I'm ashamed to say.'

'Is that so?' His dark eyes twinkled as he added softly, 'Tell me again when we're on our own.'

They sat a few seconds longer, drinking in the magic

of the moment. Then, holding hands, they stood up and turned to walk down the narrow stretch of Embankment that led towards home.

'Have you two made any plans yet for the future?' her mother asked one evening after a meal as they stood at the draining board, looking through the kitchen window at Ebbie and Vic sitting on the bench in the yard. With their feet up on the remains of the Anderson roof, the two men were enjoying a beer.

'I'd get married tomorrow, Mum,' Connie sighed as she continued to wash the dishes. 'But Vic is against it until the war is over.'

'Is the war his only reason?'

Connie laughed in surprise. 'What other one is there?'

Olive continued with the drying. 'It's not Lucky that's in the way, is it?'

Connie stiffened. 'What do you mean, "in the way"? You know how much Vic cares for him.'

'My point exactly.' Olive nodded. 'P'raps he doesn't want to get fond of the boy. What if Lucky's father is a prisoner of war somewhere? At the end of the last war, men turned up for years after. Some had been presumed dead and their families had given up hope. It could happen again. Have you thought of that?'

'I've thought of everything, Mum, until my brain aches,' Connie replied shortly, wondering why a nice evening had to be spoiled. 'No one knows when the war will end, or what will happen at the end of it. If Lucky is still with me then and no one's claimed him, we'll adopt. I know that's what Vic wants too.'

Her mother frowned. 'I'm not being picky, Constance, and I'm the first to admit that I didn't know how we were going to cope with a baby in the house. But now I wouldn't be without him and this is what worries me.'

'Oh, Mum, let me do the worrying, will you?' Seeing the distress in her mother's face, Connie dried her hands on the tea towel and drew the small, rigid figure towards her. 'What's brought all this on?'

Olive heaved a deep sigh. 'I suppose it's seeing you and Vic at the beginning of your lives. I start thinking of all the problems your dad and me had to get over in raising a family. It's just as you get older the fears get stronger, especially for your children. The uncanny thing is Lucky is you all over as a baby. The same wavy blond hair and blue eyes. His quick smile and happy personality. Sometimes I really believe he's my own grandchild.'

Connie held her mother's hands. 'If his mother hears you saying that, she'll be happy in heaven.'

'Oh, Constance, that poor girl. We don't even know who she was. It's like she was hardly here at all, and except for Lucky the world wouldn't know she'd been part of it.'

Connie nodded slowly. 'I think about her too. But what I remember most is the way she was desperate for me not just to find him, but look after him. I feel she'd been through a lot and I don't mean just the Blitz. It was in her eyes, that look, an expression I'll never forget.'

Olive's fingers went up to gently touch Connie's face. 'She was fortunate you came along that night and saved her little baby and took his guardianship so seriously. But I'm a mother, Constance, and you are my blood. So it's only natural I worry about you.' She expelled a weary sigh as she moved away and returned to the drying. 'You always was an independent child with a mind of your own.'

Connie was about to reply when Vic grinned at her through the window. The two men came laughing and joking through the kitchen door and put an end to Connie and Olive's heart-to-heart.

Taffy drove Connie and Vic up to town and dropped them outside the club. Valentino's illuminated sign was still in place despite the blackout. The V had fallen lopsidedly and the glass behind was secured with tape. But the door below looked as though it had just undergone a fresh lick of paint.

Inside the small foyer a tall man smoking a cigarette was standing by a pair of double doors. 'Reckon he's the gaffer,' Vic whispered to Connie. 'I'll be back in a blink.'

Connie waited, hoping no one would notice her in the shadows. She had been faced with the choice of wearing her old coat or going without one. But the manner of their transport had settled the question; riding bare shouldered in Ada's borrowed frock on the seat of Taffy's lorry didn't seem appropriate.

So Connie had opted for her coat, hoping she could dispose of it quickly once inside Valentino's. Noting the small cloakroom to the right no bigger than a large cupboard, she saw a young woman appear behind the narrow counter. Connie was tempted to go over before Vic returned, but to her relief he was back immediately.

'We're now life members,' he grinned, winking. 'Thanks to Georgie. Now, let me take your coat.' He slid it from her shoulders and Connie tried to hide her embarrassment as he handed it over. But the girl didn't seem to notice it was as old as the ark, and Vic whistled softly as he turned to admire her peach silk dress.

'You look wonderful, Con.'

'Do I?'

'Are you sure you want to be seen out with the likes of me?'

'Don't be daft.' She flushed.

'You're dazzling, honest. I've got to keep blinking to see where I'm going.' He took her hand and squeezed it.

'As long as you keep hold of me, I don't care.'

He bent and kissed her cheek softly, then guided her through the double doors. The air was filled with cigarette smoke, soft laughter and strong perfume. Couples sat at tables, all heads bent close under the soft, romantic lights. To the left was a bar with a man in a white waistcoat serving the drinks. Above the bar stretched a wide mirror reflecting the back of the bartender and his customers' faces. In the centre of the room was a miniature dance floor, at present unoccupied. The white piano beyond had no player, though there was an ashtray and a half-filled glass on top of it.

'Oh, Vic, it's so grand! I've only ever seen this sort of place in the films.'

He escorted her to a table and she glanced at the couples as they went. Some women wore ankle-length styles like herself and were partnered by clean-shaven men in dress suits. But there were also service uniforms like Vic's and a scattering of less formal frocks.

'Would you like a cocktail?' Vic asked as he pulled out her chair.

'I've never had one.'

'Well, it's time to try.'

'In that case, I'll say yes. But I don't really want anything but you,' she whispered as they snuggled together in the darkness. 'You're all that matters.' Love was the strangest thing. When it hit you, you had no defence. You were trapped in its spell.

'Two Manhattans, please.'

Connie realized the waitress was standing beside them, waiting for the order.

'I don't want to get tipsy,' Connie whispered when she'd gone, 'and embarrass myself.'

'I'll carry you if you fall over.'

She giggled. 'You might have to. The last time I had a drink was when Dad got out the sherry after the roof fell in.'

The piano player returned in his smart dark suit and bow tie. He smiled, looking into the faces of his audience. His hands began to flow over the keys. Connie held her breath as Vic's hand tightened over hers. The strains of the popular hit 'You Stepped Out of a Dream' began to fill the room. Connie felt the tears rush to her eyes. She was so happy. As she looked into Vic's face and found him looking back at her she wanted to pinch herself to make certain she wasn't dreaming.

'Let's dance,' he said, pulling her up.

Connie stood on shaky legs. But once on the floor he held her tightly against him. She closed her eyes and moved in time with the music, almost by instinct. As she nuzzled close to his chest she wondered what had happened to the old Connie. The single girl determined to resist love in pursuit of a better life. Her vision of the big manor, the lady of the house like she'd seen in the film *Rebecca*, the gardens that stretched down to the cliffs, with rose bushes and croquet lawns, was all her imagination. Now the only dream she had was to live the rest of her life with this man.

The melody changed to 'A Nightingale Sang in Berkeley Square'. They swayed slowly, Vic's hand pressed in the small of her back, his mouth touching the bare skin of her neck. When the tempo changed to 'You Must have Been a Beautiful Baby', he sang the words in her ear, whirling her round the floor and into the next medley of songs.

'To us, sweetheart. To our future,' Vic said breathlessly as they took their seats and lifted their glasses.

'Oh, Vic, I'm so happy. But I'm sad too. I don't want to go back to reality.'

'We'll always have tonight, darling.'

'Can we dance again?'

'All night, if you like. What do you want him to play?'

She lowered her glass. 'Can I chose?'

'Of course you can.'

'I'd like "Dancing in the Dark". Wouldn't it always remind us of tonight?'

'No sooner said than done.' She watched him weave between the chairs and tables, looking so tall and handsome in his new uniform as he made his way towards the piano. The pianist glanced up and nodded, spinning his fingers across the keys.

'Think of me whenever you hear this and your thoughts will reach me wherever I am,' he whispered as he held her tightly on the dance floor.

She lifted her face, committing every detail to memory. She was Cinderella tonight, with her prince. And all too soon they would be rushing out of the door, in their case not to the coach and six white horses to return to the castle, but to Taffy arriving in his lorry to drive them home.

Chapter Fourteen

Gran opened the front door and searched the cloudy skies. The raids now had nothing like the intensity of the Blitz, and it was a relief. But the Luftwaffe visits were still unpredictable. The warning siren was as disturbing as ever, though all she could hear was the sound of Barker Brown's old nag, clip-clopping along the main road. The rag-and-bone man was off to an early start. The inclement September weather, a gusty wind and continuous rainfall, had him encouraging the horse faster before a downpour.

There was a lot to be said for the old-fashioned methods of transport, Gran thought to herself as she tied on her scarf and buttoned up her coat. A horse and cart made a friendly noise, unlike these new-fangled motor cars, frightening the daylights out of unsuspecting pedestrians. Vic had convinced her to ride in his car once or twice, but she wasn't impressed. You couldn't put your foot down and stop it when you wanted, like a bicycle. And as for all that pulling and pushing of levers, well – what a game! No, she was quite satisfied to take her morning stroll to the shops – even in the rain – by Shanks's pony.

Once fully attired, Gran set off. Her umbrella blew sideways once or twice, but she held on grimly. Gran was an all-weather veteran. She prided herself on her resilience to the elements.

'Hope yer wearing your long johns,' a voice said beside her as she waited on the pavement to cross the street.

'Oh, it's you, Albie.' She smiled at her next-door-but-one neighbour, Albert Cross. 'And no, in answer to your question, I ain't got me flannel drawers on yet.'

Albie's wizened face wrinkled into a grin. 'Come on, let me take you across the road, before you fall over that bloody umbrella.'

Gran held out her elbow and Albie grabbed it. 'Which way you going?'

'Down the butcher's.'

'Me too. I'll keep you company.'

It was a conversation they enjoyed regularly, old friends from a different generation, still around to tell the tale of a previous existence. Gran liked Albie. He'd been a costermonger in his time, starting off in Cox Street as a barrow boy. She had known his wife, Elsie, a dressmaker, who had died a decade ago of TB, leaving behind a heartbroken partner. Not that Albie had let on. His pride wouldn't allow it.

'Still can't get used to all these missing houses,' Albie complained as they walked. 'Went by the old Star pram and mangle factory the other day. Nothing left of it. Same with the Blackwall Mill and all those warehouses. Been there years they had. Snowdon Sons have moved out to Crawley I hear. As for the Clergy House of Saint John's, it's growing weeds as tall as trees.' He shook his head mournfully. 'And I daren't walk by the place where Bullivant's factory stood. To think of all those poor buggers sheltering there, a hundred by some estimates. All gonners that night in March last year. It still chokes me up something rotten.'

'I know,' agreed Gran soberly. 'I've only got to stroll down Roserton Street or Cleveland Terrace and see the gaps, and think of all the people I've known a lifetime, not there any more.'

'Yeah, I was born in Chipka Street, you know. Nothing left of the old home now. Still, I suppose there's not many who haven't lost someone or somewhere. Speaking of which, how's your Vic? Saw he was home last month. Waved to me as he passed, looking the cat's whiskers in that uniform of his.'

Gran nodded proudly. 'Been on the Arctic run to Russia.'

'Christ! Read about them convoys in the papers. Sitting ducks they are for the U-boats.'

'I daren't think about it, Albie.'

'No, course not.'

Gran stopped to get her breath back. She had been walking too fast as usual. Harris's the butcher's was on the next corner. There would be a queue, but she fancied a nice tasty bit of liver if she could get it.

'You all right, gel?'

'I'm not as young as some.'

'I was rushing to keep up with you.' Albie lifted the

219

collar of his raincoat. 'Fancy a cuppa in the café? My shout.'

Gran smiled a little wearily as she glanced across the road. 'It's rotten tea in there.'

'Yeah, but think of the riveting company you'll have. Worth a bit of poison for a laugh.'

Gran took her neighbour's arm and they crossed the road once more. The glass window of the café was drenched in condensation. She wasn't fussed about going in, but she was puffing like a dray. She must remember to take it slower in future.

The café was warm inside, if damp. Albie bought two teas and they sat a safe distance from the wet window and the puddles pooling on the lino. The two other customers were dockers, putting away plates of fried bread.

Gran examined her cup. She curled her lip. 'As I suspected, dishwater.'

Albie laughed. 'It's hot dishwater, though.'

They drank in silence and Gran felt the tea warm her insides, even if the taste was unrecognizable. Albie rattled his false teeth in pleasure and sat back on the wooden chair with a sigh. 'We should do this more often.'

Gran glanced at her companion. 'I've got better things to do than waste my time in here.'

'Such as?'

'Never you mind.'

'Don't you ever get lonely, Alice?'

Gran felt a funny little stir at the mention of her name.

Rarely was she called Alice. She had been known by all and sundry for years as Gran. Alice was part of ancient history. But then so was Albie.

'Why should I be?'

'Your grandson's at sea, that's why.'

'That doesn't make me lonely.' She regretted her sharp tone and said a little softer, 'Women are more resilient, got more stamina in their later years.'

'My Elsie hadn't.'

Gran sighed heavily. 'She was a good wife, Albert.'

He nodded, a quiver of a smile on his lips. 'Like your Maurice.'

Gran reached for her damp brolly. 'Well, this won't do.'

'Blimey, are we off already?'

'Needs must.'

He chuckled as he stood up. 'You didn't give me time to try out me courting tactics.'

Gran smiled ruefully as she gathered her bag and umbrella. 'You keep your tactics to yourself.'

As they approached the door, it opened and a man entered. Gran stood still as he rudely pushed past, and Albie muttered, 'Watch your step, chum!'

Gran turned slowly, her heart dipping as the man ignored them and pulled out a chair. He sank down on it, beginning to undo the buttons of his suit. Thin features, eyes set too close, an opportunist's face. Her eyesight wasn't up to scratch these days, but she was almost certain . . yes, she had seen him before. She couldn't forget lights like that. The dark, muddy brown . . .

Albie squared his shoulders. 'Bloody ignorant, some people.'

Gran pulled him with her through the door and into the fresh air. The rain was coming down harder.

Albie stared at her, his brow furrowed. 'Don't forget to put yer brolly up.'

Gran nodded, though she wasn't for once concerned about a few drops of water. It was those lights that had upset her. Just like the ones round Connie.

'I'm glad you've called, I've got something to tell you,' Pat said as she showed Connie into the front room. A fire was burning and there were toys scattered on the rug in front of it. 'Laurie's just gone to the park with Doris for an hour. Give me your coats and Lucky can play with her toys.'

When Lucky was settled, Pat sat next to Connie. 'We've just had some bad news. Laurie received his call-up this morning.'

'I thought Laurie's security job at Kenward's was safe.'

'The firm is cutting down on staff and moving out to Rayleigh. Laurie wasn't asked to go with them. Not that I'd want him to go away, but if it meant him not having to join up, I would have agreed.'

'When has he got to go?'

'Next week.'

'That's a bit short notice.'

'They're recruiting all and sundry now.' She looked down at Lucky. 'We're trying to make the best of it for Doris's sake.'

'What have you told her?'

'Just that Daddy is going away for a while but will be home soon.'

'I'm really sorry, Pat.'

'Can't be helped I suppose,' sighed Pat, trying to be cheerful as she pushed her thick brown hair from her face. 'Anyway, that's enough of our troubles. How are you?'

'All right – well, I was until this afternoon. I've just been round to Gran's and she wasn't her usual self. I wondered if you knew why. Is it because of Laurie, do you think?'

Pat frowned. 'She doesn't know yet. When you say upset, do you mean ill?'

'No, at least I don't think so.' Connie was bewildered. 'She told me she'd read her cup and there was a big exclamation mark in it. She didn't know who it was for, but thought she would tell me to be on the safe side. She did seem worried, though, kept asking funny questions, like had anything queer happened lately?'

'And has it?'

'Nothing out of the ordinary.'

Pat sank to the floor and waggled the little dog's tail. Lucky gurgled and perched his fat bottom on her knees. 'I'll be seeing her tomorrow, so don't worry.'

'Will you tell her about Laurie's call-up?'

Pat nodded and Connie put her hand on her shoulder. 'It's no consolation, but I'll be around to help you.'

Pat smiled sadly as she looked up. 'I know you will.'

'You'll miss him something rotten.'

Pat's eyes filled with tears. 'Especially with the baby coming.'

'What!' Connie gasped.

'The doctor confirmed it yesterday.'

Connie hugged her friend. 'Congratulations, Pat, to you both. And I'll say it again – I'll be here for you, and the baby.'

Pat's cheeks grew wet and she took out her hanky.

Lucky came up to her. 'Auntie Pat crying.'

'No, ducks, I'm laughing,' Pat assured him, giving him a big smile. 'Now, how would you like a drink of orange juice? Hold my hand and I'll take you out to the kitchen. I'll make Mummy a nice cup of tea too.' Pat glanced at Connie and smiled through her tears. 'I think Gran got it all wrong, don't you? That exclamation mark was definitely for us, not you.'

Connie nodded her agreement as they left the room. She was sad to hear that Laurie would soon be conscripted, especially as Pat was expecting. But selfishly she couldn't help feeling a sense of relief that Gran's reading was not meant for her.

Billy was on top of the world. Another notch on his belt. His opponent was being dragged to his corner. Blood streamed down his chin, his flabby body spent. Several of his front teeth were lost in the sawdust, but no one was going to look for them. It was the victor of the grudge match, not the loser, who drew the crowd's adoration.

Billy raised his fists above his head and gave Winnie's

two-fingered salute. He was victorious! The men beneath him roared in approval. Two years ago in this very yard they had given him the thumbs down. He remembered that first thrashing as if it was yesterday. Could still taste the humiliation as he'd grovelled on the ground, wondering if a tram had hit him. He'd only clawed back a grudging respect when he bit off a chunk from the Fat Man's ear. Now the crowd at the Rose and Crown worshipped him.

Billy revelled in the limelight. What a brilliant right jab! The man's teeth had met with a crack, his tongue in between them. He'd still been screaming when Billy had dealt a low punch that would see him walking with a stoop for a week. There was no coming back from that and Billy knew it.

'You done it, Billy my lad,' Taffy shouted at him. 'They love you. You're the champ!'

Billy was high as a kite. He had never felt so good. 'I can beat 'em all, Taff. Every last one of them.'

'You can, boyo, indeed you can.'

'I'm gonna celebrate, buy a few beers.'

Taffy took his arm and pushed him to the stable door. Inside smelled of horse dung and ale. 'Celebrate tomorrow, Billy. When you've calmed down.'

'But me mates are waiting.'

Taffy pushed him on a barrel. He flung a towel in his face. 'They're not mates, Billy boy, they're leeches.'

'Just give me my share,' Billy demanded, standing up. 'I earned it fair and square.'

'If I do, it'll be gone by the morning.'

'Leave off, Taff, you're not me father.'

'I'm not trying to be, lad. I'm just looking out for your business interests. You gotta remember you're only as good as your last fight.'

Billy threw the towel aside. 'All I seem to get from you these days are scraps with fat gits.'

Taffy looked insulted. 'I'll ignore that, Billy, owing to your excitement.'

'I want to box, Taff. You promised.' Billy felt as if he was about to explode. Why couldn't Taffy see the talent in front of him? He knew for certain he could box at the British Legion if only Taffy would pull his finger out.'

'We'll talk about it soon, lad.'

Billy grabbed his shirt and pushed past Taffy.

'Where are you going?'

'To drown my sorrows.' Billy strode out to his friends. They cheered when they saw him and followed him into the pub. Billy ordered drinks all round, assuaging his pride, but not the anger that was smouldering inside him.

'Name your poison, chum.'

Billy was in the Rose and Crown, his head reeling pleasantly. 'I'll have another pint if you insist.'

'Good fight,' said Freddie Smith, signalling the barman for two more ales.

'Yeah, for me it was anyway.'

'Get that down you.'

Billy took a hefty gulp. He was getting his revenge on

Taffy and enjoying his freedom. He was skint, but the barman knew the fight would cover his slate. At least Freddie had the decency to buy a round, and, to Billy's surprise, was telling him all the things he wanted to hear.

After all, who did Taffy think he was? In reality he was a failed Welsh lightweight turned cockney roofer. He hadn't thrown a punch in years. Well, bollocks to Taffy. This last fight had proved a big point. Billy was ready to box. If winning his last six fights on the trot wasn't experience, he didn't know what was.

And his opinion on the subject had been confirmed many times over this evening. All his mates were of one mind. He could knock spots off any fist fighter this side of the river. Why wouldn't Taffy see sense?

'You were a right hard case today,' said Freddie, looking at Billy in admiration. 'The other bloke made twice of you, but you wore him down.'

'That was me plan.' Billy nodded, gulping his ale.

'Then you landed those crafty jabs. It was a shock to the other geezer. Could see it in his eyes.'

Billy stood tall as a chum on the other side of the bar gave him the thumbs up. Another patted him on the back. 'I'm quick on my feet and stay out of range. That's where they all go wrong, see? They think one wallop and I'll be on the floor. But I fool them all.'

'Anyone can see that,' his companion agreed. 'You've got a career ahead of you.'

'I know.' Billy frowned in consternation. 'That is if I can get Taffy to set me up with gloves.'

'You want to box?'

For the first time Billy really studied the man standing beside him. He was dressed in a suit and tie, unlike the majority of dockers and stevedores who drank in the pub. 'Yeah, that's the plan, anyway.'

'Well, a nice little southpaw like you should go places.'

Billy looked surprised. 'You reckon I'm a south-paw?'

'With a right hook like that, what else? Take it from me, I should know. I'm in the management line myself.'

Billy's eyes opened wider. 'No kidding?'

'Remember Joe Wallace, the middleweight from Lancashire, and Archie Johns, flyweight, from across the border? Little Willie Faulkner from Skegness?' He glanced at Billy sideways. 'Course you've probably not heard of them. A bit before your time.'

Billy racked his brains. 'Was they really your boys?'

'They were, but they've all done so well they've pissed off to the States now.'

'America!' Billy yelped, spilling his drink. 'That's where I'm headed.'

'Not surprised,' Freddie agreed casually. 'You're wasted here.' He held up his hands apologetically. 'No offence to Taffy – but pub yards? Do me a favour, they're carve-ups.'

Billy swallowed hard. This was someone in the business who he could respect. Freddie signalled the barman for top-ups. When their glasses were filled he turned to Billy and frowned. 'How much is Taffy's rake-off?'

Billy considered this. 'I get five pounds if I win or not.'

'Yes, but how much does he get?'

'Dunno. Never asked.'

Freddie nodded slowly, leaning his elbows on the bar. 'Taffy is probably pocketing four times as much as you.' He tapped the side of his nose. 'Keep it under your hat, of course.'

Billy tried to do his sums. He'd never thought about Taffy's earnings, just as long as he was getting his. Four times five was . . . Billy frowned, his brain working overtime. About twenty, wasn't it? Blimey, enough, anyway. And it was him, Billy, who was doing all the work!

'See what I mean?' The blue eyes narrowed.

'Yeah, I do.'

'So ask yourself this. Why would Taffy want to change things? You wouldn't get much for a three-rounder with gloves. You'd start right at the bottom again, to prove yourself like.'

'Would I?' Billy hadn't thought of that either.

'Your man is on to an earner with the pub larks. He's not planning to see the back of it, is he? You're an unlicensed fighter, so the bookie loves you, chum. But as a rookie boxer you'd be earning peanuts.'

Suddenly it all fell into place. All Billy's protests to Taffy to let him box, all useless as he wouldn't be making them any money.

Billy's shoulders slumped. He pushed his hands down in his trouser pockets and tried to think straight. Freddie smacked his lips. 'I've got to go, son.' He gave Billy a pat on the shoulder. Then, turning, he pushed his way through the evening drinkers and disappeared.

Billy tried to use his befuddled brain. What was he to do? He felt he was sliding into a pit he'd never be able to climb out of. He stared around him. At the unflattering décor and the dirty tables, the shabby clientele, his mates. He was champ all right, but of what? All in all, he had nothing and was nothing and would go on being nothing unless . . .

He fought his way through the crowd, deaf to the flattery that an hour ago he was thriving on. The street was dark, the blackout still well in force. He looked to his left and saw Freddie just turning the corner.

'Freddie, wait!' Billy caught him up. 'Will you take me on?'

'I don't know about that, son.'

'Why?'

'Dunno that it'd pay me—'

'I'd take what you give me, I just want to box. To prove meself to everyone. All I need is a chance.'

Freddie looked at him, then, leaning casually against the wall and ignoring the blackout, drew out a packet of cigarettes. Lighting up, he nodded thoughtfully. 'We'll have another little chat sometime.'

'When?'

'Dunno. Tomorrow night maybe.'

'Where?'

Freddie shrugged, blowing smoke into the night air. 'Here.'

Billy watched him saunter away. He was filled with hope, yet was he being disloyal to Taffy? Well, he hadn't done anything yet. And if Taffy wanted to keep him, then he'd have to match what Freddie could do.

Chapter Fifteen

'Five bob says our office is first for the chop,' Len English muttered to Connie as they joined the queue in the corridor outside Mr Dalton's rooms. 'They've got to make cuts with business going downhill like it has.'

'The government might step in,' Connie posed. 'And take us over for the war effort.'

'They could have their own people,' Len speculated as they moved forward. 'We might prove expendable.'

'No one's expendable in war. Everyone has to do something,' Connie whispered as they entered the large outer office that was usually strictly off limits to the staff and reserved for Mr Dalton's sole use. In front of them were rows of wooden chairs placed neatly in front of a small raised platform.

'Blimey, this looks official,' Len muttered as they filed in and sat down.

'I've never been in here before.' Ada looked cautiously around the room as the thirty or so other clerical workers and members of the typing pool joined them. Rumours had abounded as scarcity of petrol had crippled

Dalton's transport services. The import and exportation of food, vegetables and household goods had sunk to an all time low as the war had intensified. Government inspectors had visited the shop floor; Dalton's, it was said, was ripe for requisitioning.

'The ball-bearings factory up the road needs staff,' Ada whispered suspiciously. 'But if they think I'd work in one of them factories, they can think again. My fingernails would chip something rotten and I couldn't stand the noise of those machines! Bang, crash in your ears all the time.' She frowned across Len, who was sitting between them. 'Anyway, I'm a trained shorthand typist like you, Con. Why should we work on a shop floor?'

'Because you'll have to, if that's what the government wants,' Len intervened. 'You don't get a choice, Ada. None of us do.'

'Well, I'd rather piss off somewhere else,' Ada said indignantly. 'Sign up for the Land Army even.'

'Can't see you looking after pigs when you can't even stand the smell of fish in the canteen.' Len smiled ruefully. 'And, anyway, what about Wally?'

Ada shrugged carelessly. 'What about him? He don't even notice me around most of the time. And to tell you the truth, sharing a stable with a horse would be an improvement on living with his sister. At least horses don't criticize and keep telling you how lucky you are to have a roof over your head. And they don't pinch your clothes or spy on you, either! When I complain to Wally all he does is tell me to stop nagging and make the best of things. It would teach him a lesson if I left.'

Connie knew things between Ada and Wally were at an all time low. But would she really consider joining the Land Army just for spite?

'Shh, ladies.' Len jerked his head as Mr Burns and Mr Layman, the workforce manager, entered the room and ascended the platform. Mr Dalton, leaning heavily on his stick, followed at a snail's pace, aided by his secretary, Miss Cummings.

What changes, Connie wondered, were in store for the employees of this once lucrative, but now ailing family firm? The bells of victory had been ringing over Britain for the last two days, the first time since the threat of invasion in 1939. General Montgomery had won the battle of El Alamein. Germany's Afrika Korps had been plundered in the deserts of North Africa. The British had reason to celebrate and had been doing so for longer than twenty-four hours. But here at Dalton's everyone was waiting anxiously for bad news.

Connie stared unseeingly through the tall windows at the dense grey morning beyond. The weather reflected the mood inside, air heavy with mist from the river as it rolled over the glass. This was the way the river worked, unpredictable in its nature, as was the war.

What would happen if she lost her job? Where would she go? What would she do? She had imagined the rest of her life spent here at Dalton's, moving steadily up the ladder of success, one day to be sitting where Miss Cummings was now.

Connie sighed softly. Once the picture had been clear in her mind. She had been prepared to sacrifice marriage in her attempt to rise above poverty. But then the war, and Lucky, had come along. Now, unlike Ada, she didn't care what work she did. Lucky came before everything.

A stiff clearing of throat brought Connie back to earth. 'Good morning,' Mr Dalton said shakily as he rose to his feet with the aid of his stick. A stooped, aged figure in an old-fashioned pinstriped suit, he was rarely seen on the premises now. 'This, unfortunately, is a duty I am reluctant to perform. But one that I must undertake to ensure that our business survives through the continuing conflict.'

Heads turned and anxious looks were exchanged. The room remained silent as the old man continued. 'I am afraid we can no longer rely on our import business or our transportation departments for revenue. Therefore – drastic changes need to be made.' After sipping from a glass of water handed to him by Miss Cummings, he pulled out a white handkerchief from his pocket and pressed it against his brow. 'I am, however, relieved to say that, with our new management, we shall suffer no specific change to the numbers of workforce.'

An audible sigh ran through the room. 'What does he mean, new management?' whispered Len, glancing at Connie. But before she could reply Mr Dalton continued.

'Our company has been selected to assist the war

effort, the details of which are rather – er – complicated. Therefore, I shall sit and listen with interest to the information provided by our new directors, the – er – United States Army.' Mr Dalton sank down wearily on his chair.

'What does he mean the United States Army?' someone whispered behind them. 'The old boy's going barmy.'

Soon everyone was talking at once, until with a rush of air the door flew open and two tall American servicemen strode in. One ascended the platform, the other seated himself in the front row.

'Major Abraham T. Barker at your service,' shouted the American soldier standing to attention on the platform. Everyone jumped as he added, 'Here as representative of the United States of America, her people and government!'

Silence descended.

Mr Dalton nodded uncertainly. 'Please continue, Major Barker.'

'Absolutely, sir!' The major cleared his throat and looked around. 'Folks, first let me say how glad we are to be here in your country. It's our intention to assist you in the winning of this war. Our men are fully briefed as to the pain you have suffered since '39 and we come with respect and admiration, knowing that nothing can replace the loss of your possessions and, in some cases, loved ones. But we must look to the future and from this day on add our strength to yours. Guess you've noticed plenty of our uniforms around London lately? Well, you'll be seeing them right up close now, on these fine premises of yours. Whilst you continue to do your jobs, we'll do ours. Now, have we any questions?'

No one moved a muscle or spoke. Connie was sitting, as everyone else was, in shock. No one knew if this was good or bad news. They all stared up at the smartly dressed major, who was waiting expectantly.

'Go on, Len, ask a question.' Ada nudged his elbow.

'Why don't you?'

''Cos you say things better.'

Len turned to Connie. 'Have you any questions, Con?'

She nodded. 'Ask if our jobs stay the same.'

Len stood up and spoke in a quiet voice. 'Do you mean we still continue to do our clerical work?'

'Yes, sir, that's exactly what I mean.'

'But,' replied Len bewilderedly, 'as everyone knows, our warehouses are almost empty.'

Major Barker smiled an all-American smile. 'Have no fear, sir, once Uncle Sam takes over, they'll be overflowing.'

'But what with?'

'Weapons, sir. Your country's armoury!'

There was an audible gasp. Len steadied himself on the chair in front. 'You mean guns, tanks, that sort of thing?'

'That sort of thing,' agreed the major.

Len stood with his mouth open, until Ada pulled him down on his chair. 'That's good news, isn't it?'

Len blinked. 'I don't know.'

'We'll keep our jobs won't we?'

'To give you a clearer idea,' the major continued before Len could reply, 'Sergeant Clint Hershey here will tell you more.'

The army officer in the front row stood up and took the major's place. 'Pleased to meet you all,' he said in a soft drawl as he removed his cap to reveal a smooth blond crew cut beneath. 'It'll be my job to see that all goes smoothly and I'll be around to help you folk in any way I can. Your books will be kept just the same, only it'll be navy and army stuff you'll be entering, 'stead of domestic goods.'

'But you can't load tanks on boats like you can vegetable and fruit,' someone observed in the back row.

'Yessir, you can,' the sergeant replied politely. 'That's what we're here for. To install our new system, get your show on the road. We have a new way of loading called roll-on, roll-off. Fork-lift trucks and pallets are used to shift heavy equipment as easily as you would a sack of potatoes. They enable us to stack warehouses higher, fill ships quicker and move weapons faster.'

Connie wasn't listening as the sergeant continued to explain how Dalton's was going to become one of the country's fastest shippers to the front lines of conflict. Instead, she was staring incredulously into the handsome face of the soldier who had bumped into her on Paddington station that day in summer, when she had been searching for Vic.

★

Sergeant Clint Hershey was sitting in an army vehicle parked just inside the gates of Dalton's. When he saw Connie and Ada he jumped out and hurried towards them.

'Hi there, again!'

Connie felt Ada grab her arm. 'He's talking to you, Con.'

Connie was embarrassed as the sergeant removed his cap and smiled broadly. 'Didn't think I'd be so lucky as to meet you again.' He held her eyes with his magnetic blue gaze, then put out his hand.

Politely she took it. 'Hello, er, Sergeant . . .'

'Clint, ma'am. Just plain Clint.'

'And I'm Ada Freeman, Connie's best friend. We work together in the offices.' Ada smiled sweetly as she held out her hand and the sergeant grasped it. 'Connie didn't tell me she knew you.'

'I don't,' Connie said as Ada turned to look at her accusingly. 'We bumped into each other at Paddington station, that's all.'

'I'd never forget a face like yours,' Clint Hershey said as he transferred his attention back to Connie. 'When I saw you today, sitting there, I thought gee-whiz, there's the little lady that I almost ran over. Do you know, you were the first real person, other than ticket collectors, that I had a real conversation with in England?'

Connie smiled awkwardly. 'No, I didn't realize that.'

'Did you find your fiancé?' he asked quietly.

'Yes, I did. He wasn't far away.'

'I've no doubt about that, ma'am.'

Ada leaned forward. 'Fancy that, bumping into Connie again. Who would have believed it?'

'Sure is one hellava coincidence,' he agreed, smiling at Connie. 'You sure brightened my first day in England.'

Connie smiled uncertainly. 'Well, we'd better be going.'

'Let me give you ladies a ride home in the truck.'

'Oh, no – thank you.' Connie pulled Ada's arm discreetly. 'We haven't far to walk.'

But Ada stood where she was. 'Oh, Con, you can't say no. I live farther away than you do. And look at the weather.'

Sergeant Clint Hershey lifted his big hands. 'It's no trouble, ma'am. Gasoline and time are no problem for the US army. And that weather sure looks thick.'

Connie didn't want to be unfriendly, but she didn't want to give him any encouragement either. If he was going to be working at Dalton's it meant she might see him frequently and she didn't want to start a habit she would later regret.

'No, really,' she declined again. 'I'd prefer to walk.'

This time he nodded, but the disappointment was clear in his eyes. 'Another time maybe.' He turned and strode back to his truck.

'What did you do that for?' Ada demanded as she followed Connie out of the gate. 'The poor bugger was only being friendly.'

'You could have gone if you wanted to.'

241

'And what would I have looked like, climbing in that thing on my own?' Ada marched angrily beside her. They walked in silence until they turned the corner and then Ada burst out, 'You can be a right snobby cow sometimes.'

Connie stopped dead. 'I wasn't being snobby. I just didn't want to start something that would be difficult to stop.'

'It was just a lift he was offering.'

'And what if he was there tomorrow night and the night after?'

Ada shrugged. 'So what? I wouldn't say no.'

'I know you wouldn't, Ada. That's exactly the trouble. You've got a really good catch in Wally yet you're always flirting with other blokes.'

Ada's face paled. 'It's none of your business what I do with blokes. And ain't you the pot calling the kettle black! You never told me about Sergeant bloody Clint whats-hisname did you?'

'There was nothing to tell.'

Ada laughed scornfully. 'Pull the other one. He could-n't keep his eyes off you.'

It was Connie's turn to look angry. 'Nonsense, Ada. I don't even know him.'

'Well, he seems to know you.'

Connie knew they were heading for a serious dis-agreement. 'Look, I'm not going to stand here arguing. As you said, what you do is your own business.'

Ada looked so annoyed the ends of her hair were trembling. She spluttered something that Connie couldn't understand then turned away, swinging her hips aggressively under her red coat.

Connie was on the point of calling her back when she changed her mind. Perhaps they both needed to cool off. They were two opposites, which was the attraction of their friendship, but if they ever fell out, which was rare, it was never long before they were speaking again.

Connie began to walk home. Her conscience was already pricking. Ada was unhappy. At the start of the Blitz she had been in love with Wally, refusing to leave London without him. Now, as their affair had cooled, her mood was unpredictable. Wally had been good for her, and whilst she was with him Ada had been content. Was Jean, Wally's sister, the cause of all the trouble? Living with Wally's family couldn't be easy, especially as they were church going, which Ada wasn't. Connie wished she had spent more time with her friend lately. Their lives had been so busy and talking over problems had been pushed to the background.

Connie walked faster. She couldn't wait to hold Lucky in her arms. All her worries disappeared when he cuddled her tight. He drew her closer to Vic and eased the ache in her heart. Life dealt out so many twists and turns. If only Ada and Wally knew what they could have together, they would be afraid of losing it.

The days came and went and Ada continued to ignore her. They sat at different tables in the canteen and Len told them both they were silly cows. But as November came to a close, Connie wondered if their friendship would ever recover. She'd tried many times to break the ice but Ada would have none of it.

Clint Hershey did not sit in his truck at the gate again, though Connie saw him often in the warehouse. The army equipment that arrived in the American ships had to be registered on entry to the country. Connie and Ada took it in turns to complete inventories. Clint Hershey was polite and courteous, as were all the American servicemen who gradually populated Dalton's along with their English colleagues. She always noted his tall figure and blond head, six inches above everyone else. To her relief, he never singled her out.

The Christmas spirit was revived at Dalton's as the smooth transition of management took place. Connie, like every other member of staff, was relieved still to have her job.

On the first Saturday of December, Ted Jackson met her on the way to work.

'One for you, Connie,' he called, jumping off his bike to hand her a letter. 'Been a while, ain't it?'

She took it gratefully. 'October, Ted.'

He gave her a wink and hopped back on his bike. 'Keep your chin up, girl.'

Connie's heart was hammering as she slid the letter into her bag. She would wait until she had finished work to read it. As Ada wasn't walking home with her, she'd be able to read it over and over again, savouring its contents. Two months was a long time not to hear from Vic, although she had gone as long as three without a letter.

'You look like the cat who found the cream.' Len grinned, as, after hanging up her coat, she took her place by the window.

'I've heard from Vic.'

'What did he say?'

Connie smiled as she opened her ledger. 'I'm saving it to read till after work.'

Len placed a handful of invoices in front of her. 'Don't ask me what these are. Mr Burns don't know either. It's all engineering stuff with newfangled names. Just copy out what you see there.'

'It's like another language.' Connie glanced at the strange invoices. 'Bit of a change from tea and coffee.'

'Mr Burns wants them completed for ten o'clock and then Ada will have to take them downstairs. Talking of which, where is she?'

Connie glanced at the empty stool. 'I don't know.'

'You two still not speaking?'

'I would if she spoke to me.'

'You can cut the air in here with a knife, you know. Even old Burnsy has noticed it.'

Connie looked across to their manager's seat, as yet unoccupied. 'I've tried to make friends, but she cuts me dead.'

'What's the row over?'

'Nothing really, just something silly. When she comes in today, I'll make a special effort.'

'Good girl. Well, I'll leave you to it.'

Connie realized that it would probably end up with her apologizing, as usual. But if that was what it took, then she would. After this little spat, though, she would never again refer to Ada's relationship with Wally, even if Ada commented on it herself.

But by one o'clock, Ada hadn't arrived. Mr Burns appeared at Connie's side, a deep frown on his face. 'Miss Marsh, do you know what's happened to Miss Freeman?'

'No, I'm afraid I don't.'

'Was she feeling ill yesterday?'

Connie turned red as she recalled their cold behaviour towards one another. 'I don't know, Mr Burns. She didn't say.'

He hesitated and Connie knew that he wanted to ask her what was wrong between them. But, being the reserved man he was, he gave an abrupt nod and walked away.

'Where could she be?' Len asked as he joined her on their way out of the office.

'I don't know,' Connie replied anxiously. 'I'm worried, Len.'

'She doesn't usually have time off without saying.'

'No.' Connie stood undecidedly at the foot of the staircase. 'I've got to go and fetch Lucky now, but I could put him in the pram and walk over to Blackwall after.'

'It's a long way, Con, in this fog.'

She bit her lip as she nodded, having decided earlier that it was too foggy to walk to Gran's this afternoon.

If it didn't clear, she would stay home in the warm. Lucky had been chesty last week and the fog would only aggravate it.

'Tell you what, I'll go on my bike tomorrow,' Len said as he pulled up the collar of his navy blue coat.

'What about your mum?'

'I'll lock her in the cupboard again.' He laughed. 'Or get Mrs Next Door to come and sit with her. She won't mind on a Sunday. It gets her out of her old man's way when he comes back from the pub.'

'Oh, thanks, Len. I feel awful that we quarrelled now.'

'It's not your fault. She's probably got a cold what with this weather and all.' He patted her arm. 'Go on and read your letter now.'

Connie nodded slowly. 'Bye, Len. Oh, and if you see her, tell her I send my love, won't you?' She paused. 'And that I miss her.'

Len grinned at they walked out of the gate. 'I'll tell her.'

Connie watched him stride off, his head down against the swirling mists. She was in half a mind to catch a bus, but she wanted to read her letter. Once she had Lucky in her arms, there would be no time to digest the details until after he was in bed tonight.

Connie slid the letter from her bag and made her way round to the wharf. The river lapped against the stone and the smell was potent. A cold, ripe aroma of salt and smoking chimneys, and the water itself was grey and murky. She sat where she always sat with Ada, on the wall, and opened her letter. Vic's bold handwriting gave her butterflies.

Eagerly her eyes went to the top right-hand corner of the page expecting to see what she always saw. 'Care of the Fleet Mail Office, Great Britain'. But she took a shocked breath as she read, 'Care of the Fleet Mail Office, New York.'

'Sweetheart, we sailed in September on the *Queen Mary* herself. What a ship she is! Arrived in New York at 30 breathtaking knots! The Americans are wonderful people. We have been billeted on 6th Avenue at the Barbizon Plaza, a famous hotel! All of us are still in shock at the warm hospitality. As to our mission, it's still hush-hush, but I can tell you that we'll be part of the "Big Push" against the Axis. Are you well and taking care of yourself and Lucky? How is the family? I have written to Gran and Pat. Christmas will be very lonely without you in my arms. As ever, you have my love and all my thoughts. P.S. Keep writing (even if you don't hear from me).'

'Oh, Vic, I miss you.' She read the letter again. What was it like in New York? The hotel sounded very grand. Was his mission dangerous? Were the American women as glamorous as the GI's in England? She felt a wave of dismay as she thought of Vic wearing his officer's uniform. He was so tall and handsome he would stand out from the crowd.

Miserably, Connie turned the corner of Kettle Street. Sixth Avenue and the Barbizon Plaza! Names that she had only ever read about in papers and magazines. She was relieved that the British sailors were so warmly regarded. But she was also a little jealous.

A movement ahead caught her eye. The fog was yellow now. Out of the centre of it walked a lone figure.

'Hello, love,' said the man, as he pulled up his collar. 'I've been waiting for you.'

Connie stood still. The chill that came over her nothing to do with the weather as Gilbert Tucker approached.

Chapter Sixteen

'Wh . . . what do you want?'

'A little chat, that's all.'

Just then the door of number eighteen opened. Two tall figures hurried out. 'Connie, is that you, love?' Nan made her way slowly towards them. 'Can't see a foot in front of me in this muck. Lofty was just coming to look for you.' She stopped when she saw Connie was not alone. 'Oh, you've got company.'

'Pleased to meet you.' Gilbert Tucker touched the brim of his hat. 'I'm er – a friend of this young lady.'

Nan stood looking puzzled. She pulled her coat around her and frowned. Connie was silent. She didn't know what to say to Nan. Where had this man sprung from after all this time?

'You'd better bring yourselves in sharpish,' Lofty shouted from the doorstep as the fog thickened. 'No sense gossiping out there.'

Nan peered into the stranger's face. 'If you're a friend of Connie's then you're welcome to take shelter with us for a bit.'

Gilbert Tucker accepted quickly. 'I'm much obliged.'

Reluctantly Connie followed. 'Hello, sunshine!' She smiled as Lucky ran along the hall and into her arms.

'Con-Con,' he gurgled, burrowing his face in her hair.

'I'll put the kettle on,' Lofty said once they were all in the front room. As he left the room he touched Connie's elbow. 'We was worried about you, love, seeing the time. I was just going to put me coat on and walk to the end of the street, see if I could see you.'

'I'm sorry I was late,' Connie apologized. 'I had a letter from Vic and stopped to read it on the way.'

'Well, you're safe and that's what matters.'

Connie sat stiffly on one of the dining chairs. She watched Gilbert Tucker remove his hat and make himself comfortable in front of the fire. 'I don't want to put you to any trouble,' he said meekly, smiling at Nan.

'No trouble. A friend of Connie's is a friend of ours. I'll see what Lofty's doing in the kitchen.'

'So this is my grandson,' he muttered when they were alone. He reclined back in the chair, staring at Lucky.

'How do I know you are who you say you are?' Connie asked suspiciously.

'I showed you the photo of Rita, didn't I? Look, I'll show you again.' He took out his wallet. 'See?'

'It just shows a young girl, that's all. You could have found it anywhere.'

'Trusting sort, ain't you?'

'Do you have her birth certificate, or Lucky's?'

He laughed. 'I don't even have my own, love. I lost

252

them all in the bombing.' He smiled curiously. 'Is that what you call him – Lucky?'

Connie nodded slowly as Lucky wriggled in her arms and slid to the floor. Looking cautiously at the older man, he picked up his toy train and began to play with it.

'He's a good-looking kid. Got nice hair. Very nice hair.'

'What to do you want, Mr Tucker?'

'Just to see my family, that's all.'

'If you wanted to see him so badly why did you disappear for two years?'

He shrugged. 'I was trying my luck up north. In my line of business you move about, see, where the trade is. With the war an' all, there's not a lot going for a bloke of my age. I won't see fifty again.'

'What work do you do?'

'Pubs now, but it was hotels. Good ones an' all. Doorman up West I was, had all the clobber, white gloves and topper, and the tips alone could have kept body and soul together. Now, o' course, they want the young ones, the good-lookers and quick on their feet when the bombs drop.'

Connie observed him as he leaned close to the fire. He must have been a smart man in his day and he still wore a suit and tie. But he didn't look quite as smart as when she saw him last. What could he want with Lucky? Was he really who he said he was? If so, he had every right to see his grandson. But without proof, he could be anyone.

'There now, here's a nice hot cup of rosie,' Nan said as she entered the room holding a tray full of mugs; tea for the adults and orange juice for Lucky.

Gilbert Tucker rubbed his hands together. He drank the offered tea down in big gulps, as hot as it was.

'Well now, Mr –?' Lofty prompted. 'I didn't catch your name?'

'Tucker. Gilbert Tucker.'

Nan folded her arms slowly. 'So how do you know our Connie, then?'

He looked slyly at Connie. 'We got a mutual acquaintance, haven't we?'

Connie turned to Nan and Lofty. 'Mr Tucker claims to be the father of Lucky's mum.'

Nan's jaw dropped. 'What!'

'She was my girl all right,' Gilbert Tucker added quickly. 'Her name was Rita.'

'Your daughter?' Lofty and Nan spluttered together.

'She was all I had left in the world after my dear wife died. But Vera's death upset her and she ran away from home.'

'How old was she?'

'Fifteen.'

'Didn't you try to find her?'

Gilbert Tucker nodded indignantly. 'Course I did. And it was the shock of my life when I discovered what she was up to.' He lowered his voice. 'I know a tart – excuse my language – when I see one. And there was my own daughter, mixing with 'em up in the city as if they was best friends. I tried to get her to come home to Mile End, but all she wanted was money.'

'Did you give her any?'

'Course I did. My poor Vera must have turned in her grave listening to some of the things our daughter come out with. I lost track of her until the Blitz, when she wrote telling me she was pregnant, didn't know who the father was and wanted to get rid of it. All I can say is, looking at the boy now, thank God she didn't.'

Connie, Nan and Lofty stared at the man, who had tears in his eyes. They were silent until Nan said slowly, as though she didn't understand what she had just heard, 'So your daughter was definitely that poor girl – the one that Connie tried to help, who died in Haverick Road? Is that what you're saying?'

Gilbert Tucker nodded. 'Which makes this little lad my grandson, and the only member of my family that I've got left to turn to.' He stood up and got out a grubby handkerchief. 'Well, I'd better not wear out my welcome.'

Nan gave him his coat and hat.

He bent down to Lucky. 'Goodnight, son. Your old grandad is happy now he's found you.'

'Did you believe him?' Nan asked Connie when he had gone.

'I don't know, Nan. What do you think?'

'Search me, love. He sounded genuine enough.'

Connie rinsed out the mugs and placed them on the wooden drainer. 'When I first met him he said he could tell me a few things about Rita that would make my hair curl. Now, what kind of a father would say that about his daughter, even if she was doing what he said she was doing?'

'Not a very nice one,' Nan agreed. 'How long ago was this?'

'Two years.'

'But why didn't you tell us then?'

'I didn't want to upset everyone. I know it's no excuse but I hoped he'd go away.'

Nan dried up the last mug and placed it in the cupboard beside the others. 'I can't see why he'd make such a claim if he wasn't Lucky's grandfather. What can he hope to gain? He seems to know a lot about this girl. Did you recognize her in the photo?'

Connie shrugged. 'I thought it might be her, but I couldn't tell for sure.'

'He'll have to prove it with more than a photograph.'

'What shall I do if he wants to come round home? Mum doesn't know about him yet.'

'You'll have to tell her. Let's go and see what Lofty thinks.'

'Could smell the drink on him,' Lofty said as he lifted Lucky on to his knee. 'P'raps he's just a lonely old sod looking for company.'

'Can't help feeling a bit sorry,' admitted Nan as they sat there.

'Yeah,' agreed Lofty. 'The war's crippled people in different ways.'

Nan straightened the arm covers on the recently vacated chair. 'We won't make any assumptions till we know the truth. He seems harmless enough. And in his state he can't even look after himself, let alone a kiddie. Probably disappear again in a few days like he did before.'

But as Connie put on Lucky's little red siren suit, she felt worried. Alarm bells were ringing inside her head. And, unlike two years ago, she wasn't going to ignore them.

The following afternoon, she told her parents. Olive was upset. The questions came fast and thick, and by the time Connie had finished trying to answer them Olive had developed a headache.

'Why didn't you tell us two years ago?' she demanded, pink in the face. 'I can hardly believe you kept the man a secret. What would we have said to him if he'd knocked on our door?'

'I'm sorry,' Connie said miserably. 'I didn't want to worry you.'

'That's not the point,' her father grumbled. 'He says he's the boy's grandfather.'

'We don't know that he is.'

'What reason has he got to lie?'

'I don't know, Dad.' Connie was tired of trying to give explanations when she didn't even know them herself. She realized that this was why she had wanted to keep Gilbert Tucker's existence to herself. His presence was disruptive and her parents hadn't even met him yet. Also, his story put Rita in a bad light. That was, if she was called Rita. It made no difference to Connie what she had done or been. She was still the mother of Lucky and had given her life to save him. If Gilbert Tucker had shown remorse at her death, she might have softened towards him. But the tears he had shed when telling his story had seemed to be for himself and for his lonely situation. What would Rita say now if she was sitting here and could tell her story?

As Olive took out her hanky and blew her nose, there was a knock at the door. Connie went to answer it. Len's thin face was pale and he was breathing hard. 'Len, what are you doing here?'

'I've just been over to Ada's.'

'Oh, I'd almost forgotten!' With all that had been going on, Ada's absence from work had escaped her mind. 'Come in.' She opened the door wider, expecting him to enter.

'No, I've got to get back to Mum. But I thought I'd let you know first.'

'Let me know what?' Her heart sank at the tone of his voice.

'Ada's left.'

Connie stared blankly. 'Left what?'

'Wally's house. She's gone away.'

Connie shook her head. 'She wouldn't do that!'

'Well she has.' Len shivered in the damp, misty afternoon that once again threatened fog. 'Some of her clothes have gone, her shoes and personal things. She must have taken them on Saturday morning when the Wipples was all out.'

'I can't believe it,' Connie gasped. 'Where would she go?'

258

'Must have had somewhere in mind.' Len shrugged.

Connie's eyes filled with tears. 'Oh, Len, I wish I hadn't rowed with her.'

'It wasn't your fault. Something's been up for ages.'

'Oh, please come in!' Connie didn't want him to rush off. Perhaps there was something he wasn't telling her.

'I can't. I'm on me bike. And Mrs Next Door won't wait for ever.'

Connie nodded sadly. 'See you in the morning, then.'

'I'll have to tell Mr Burns if she don't show up. Lord only knows what he'll say. Just as we're getting busy again too.'

Connie watched him pedal off, head down, his long back bent. She stared into the thickening mist sightlessly. She couldn't believe that Ada had thrown in her job. They had worked together at Dalton's since leaving school, survived the Blitz and begun a new chapter with the Americans taking over. If only they hadn't quarrelled!

'Con-Con play,' Lucky gurgled as he tugged her hand. She closed the front door and lifted him into her arms. Burying her face in his soft hair she hugged him tight.

'Con-Con's coming,' she sniffed, wondering where her friend was and when she would see her again.

That night Connie woke suddenly from a deep sleep. Something in the house had disturbed her. Careful not to make a noise, she climbed out of bed and listened. Lucky was fast asleep in his cot, the wooden bars of which were now missing in order for him to climb in and out. His toys were gathered neatly in the corner, and though the room was cold it was watertight after the repairs that Taffy and Billy had done.

Pulling on her dressing-gown she trod softly out of her room and stood at the top of the stairs. Both her brothers were heavy sleepers and left their door ajar. Mum and Dad's was always closed, but tonight a crack of light showed in the hall below. As the blackout was still in force, she could see it clearly.

Halfway down the stairs she identified a tap running. Quickly she made her way to the bathroom and pushed open the door.

'Billy?' Her brother was bending over the basin. More than bending. He seemed to have fallen across it.

'Shh, Con. Shut the door.'

She closed it quietly. 'Billy, it's half past three in the morn—' Her mouth fell open as he looked round. 'Oh my God, Billy! What have you done to yourself?'

His face was as large as a football, swollen and bleeding. 'Shh. I don't want Mum and Dad to see this.'

'What happened?' She went up to him. 'No, don't speak, sit down on the chair instead.' Quickly she opened the cupboard and took out the box of clean rags. Tearing one in half she soaked it in water. 'This is going to hurt, but sit still.'

In silence she bathed the hard scabs around his mouth and the cut above his eye that warranted more than bathing. 'Billy, who did this to you?'

'I didn't duck quick enough.'

'That wasn't what I asked.'

Billy grunted as she wiped his swollen mouth. 'My opponent was more than I could handle tonight, that's all. I suppose it had to happen one day.' He tried to laugh. 'I can't win 'em all, can I?'

'What did Taffy say?'

Billy shrugged, then groaned. 'Christ, me chest hurts.'

'Is it your ribs?'

'Yeah, I think so.'

Connie undid the buttons of his shirt. 'Oh, Billy, you're black and blue all over. Who did this to you? Whatever was in Taffy's mind to set you up with such an animal?'

Billy pushed her gently away. 'I'll be all right tomorrow.'

'No you won't. You need a doctor now.'

'I'll go tomorrow.'

'I'll come with you then.'

He held on to her gently. 'No, Con, thanks all the same. I ain't lost the use of me gob yet.'

She looked into his bloodshot eyes. 'Billy, is there something you're not telling me?'

'Course not. I just got a hiding for once. Serves me right. I was getting too big for me boots, like Mum always said I was. Look, the best thing you can do for me is forget this ever happened. I'll go see the quack tomorrow and by the end of the week I'll be my 'andsome self again. Now, give us another once over for good measure, eh?'

Connie washed out the rag and bathed his face again.

She didn't know where to start. It was a mess. Why had Taffy allowed this to happen?

Connie went back to the cupboard and took out the small black bottle of iodine kept for emergencies beside the bandages and bandettes. 'This will hurt,' she warned him.

'Ouch,' he yelped as she dabbed it on. 'Go easy, Con.'

She did the best she could and when she was done Billy stood up. 'Thanks, Con. Will you do me one more favour?'

She pulled her dressing-gown round her. Even before he spoke she knew it was something she wouldn't like.

'Stuff a few clothes in a bag for me will you?'

'Why? You're not going out again!'

He reached for her hand. 'Look, Con, I'm going to kip at a mate's. Don't make a fuss, there's a good girl. No sense in giving Mum a fright tomorrow, is there?' He gripped her tightly. 'Remember my first fight? I got walloped rotten then, but in a week I was right as rain.'

'You said then you'd never let it happen again.'

'I know. This was just a one-off.'

Connie shook her head hopelessly. 'Billy, I was beginning to think everything was turning out all right.'

'It is, worry guts. Now, just nip up and get me a pair of trousers and shirt will you? They're over my chair.'

Against her better judgement Connie did as he asked. She didn't know what was going on, but if she argued with him all night, he wasn't going to tell her. And he was right about Mum. Seeing Billy so battered in the morning, she was likely to have one of her turns. It had been a bad day all round.

Connie crept into the boys' bedroom and felt for the chair. She could hear Kevin snoring loudly. Gathering Billy's clothes she tiptoed out and took them to the bathroom.

'Ta, sis. Now, let me out quietly and go back to bed. In the morning you've not seen nothing, all right?'

'When will you be back?'

'Dunno. I'll catch Kev at the factory and tell him to tell Mum I'm training for the next fight.'

Connie walked to the front door and opened it. Billy bent to kiss her cheek as the cold, damp air rushed in. She watched him hobble away and wanted to run after him and drag him back. 'Oh, Billy, take care of yourself,' she whispered as he melted like a ghost into the night.

Gran came to the door as soon as she heard Connie. 'Hello, ducks, how are you? And my lovely boy?' She bent down and drew Lucky into her arms. 'Where's your pram gone?'

'We caught a bus to Island Gardens, then walked.' Connie's cheeks were flushed with cold as she stepped into the warmth of the old house. 'It wasn't foggy this afternoon, so we made the most of the weather.'

'Come on in. I'll put the kettle on.'

'Look who's here!' Connie smiled as they walked into the front room. Pat pushed herself up from the chair and the two women embraced. 'How's the little one?' Connie asked, laying her hand lightly on Pat's round stomach. 'Any movement yet?'

'Not much.' Pat shrugged. 'Not like Doris. Hello, darling.' She held out her hand to Lucky. 'Come and give Auntie Pat a cuddle.'

When the children were sitting on the floor playing, Connie hung their coats and gas masks on the peg behind the door. She sat beside Pat. 'Heard anything from Laurie?'

'His battalion is in training up near Wanstead somewhere. He says he's at last found out which end of a rifle shoots.' She laughed sadly. 'I just hope he points it in the right direction. You know Laurie, his face always in a book. He was never one for anything mechanical.'

'He made a nice job of the cellar, though,' Connie recalled. 'At least you all had a place to go in the Blitz.'

Pat smiled thoughtfully. 'Yes, bless his heart. We never had to endure the shelters like some.'

'I don't suppose he can say much about where he is,' Connie said, wondering if it was the pregnancy or the miss of Laurie that was giving her shadows around the eyes.

'Only that he's training and assures me he's not in the thick of anything more dangerous than the Three Nuns baccy I send him.'

'At least you can write back and tell him all the news.'

'Well, I'm not sure I can, really.' Pat pushed back her dark hair and adjusted her maternity smock. 'I had to give up work last week.'

'Well, you are five and a half months, aren't you?'

'I'd hoped to go on longer. But the doctor said I should stop as I was spotting a bit of blood.'

Connie looked concerned. 'Was it often?'

'Once or twice it happened.'

'Oh, Pat, you'll have to take it easy. From now on me and Lucky will come over on Saturdays and do your shopping and whatever housework there is.'

Pat smiled faintly. 'Thanks, Con.'

'I'll catch the bus like I did today and we'll be over by two o'clock. I'll call at Gran's after.'

'The thing is, I don't know how long I'll be able to stay at the flat.'

'What do you mean?'

'Without my wage, I can't really afford to keep such a large place on. We could've managed on Laurie's wage, but it's just army pay now.'

'But where will you go?'

'Gran's offered to put us up.'

'Oh, Pat, you'll miss your lovely flat. You and Laurie worked so hard to make it nice.'

'Beggars can't be choosers. I'm lucky to have Gran.'

'What will you do with your furniture?'

'There's only the dresser and table that are really worth anything.'

'What about Laurie's books and your embroideries?'

'I'll ask the coal man to take them on his cart. He'll do it for a couple of bob.'

'When are you thinking of leaving?'

'Before Christmas. We could have stayed till after,

but it will be better for Doris to be settled.'

Just then Gran brought in the tea. 'Did Pat tell you her news?'

'Yes, it's a shame she has to leave the flat. But at least she'll be with you, Gran.'

'She can have her old room back and Vic's is empty too. There's plenty of space.' Gran set the tea on the table and lowered a china cup to each saucer. She gave the two children a mug of orange juice each, then sat on the couch. 'I'll let you pour, Connie. Don't use the strainer, because I'll read our cups.'

With all that had gone wrong this week Connie wasn't so sure she wanted to know the future. But Pat was eager to drink hers and, after twisting the cup three times in the saucer, she gave the dregs to Gran.

The old lady frowned as she examined the evidence. Then, looking up at Pat, she shrugged lightly. 'There's nothing there I can't tell you that you don't know. A move is forecast, but you don't need the leaves to tell you that.'

Pat pouted. 'Nothing else?'

'Not today.' Gran looked at Connie, her dark eyes piercing in her brown, wrinkled face. 'Someone has come into your life and someone has gone out,' she said as she stared at the contents of the saucer. 'There's two figures here, male and female, and upside down. In other words, passing.'

'As usual, Gran, you aren't far from the truth.' Connie took a breath and began to tell them the story of Gilbert Tucker and how he had first appeared in her life, followed by Ada's mysterious departure from Dalton's.

'One in and one out,' Gran nodded. 'The leaves never lie.'

Sometimes, Connie mused, she wished they did.

Chapter Seventeen

Gran studied the two young women sitting in her front room. Separated from their men and fending for themselves was no easy task in a world of rationing, blackouts and the threat of invasion. It was a miracle they had reared two youngsters and survived the Blitz.

Playing on the floor was Doris, who, at four years old, was a pretty little thing with curly dark hair like Pat's and Laurie's friendly, open features. Lucky, poor little mite, was as blond as Doris was dark, his blue eyes the same shade and shape as Connie's. The children complemented each other perfectly, Doris a natural born leader, Lucky content to hang on to her every word. They were playing Mummies and Daddies and had forgotten the adults. She was putting Lucky to bed and instructing him to go to sleep, assuring him they were safe in the cellar, protected from the bombs. The little boy was curled under the table obediently.

They had been through so much. And now Pat had to leave her beloved home. The old saying was true. The poor grew poorer, although, in all honesty, she had no real insight of the rich. But if they were worth their salt, they'd be on the island, campaigning for the rights of the common man, like Pat and Laurie, not helping themselves to the cream of society.

Gran had seen all the do-gooders arrive in a blaze of light and blow out faster than a fart. Lloyd George and his coalition. Baldwin and MacDonald in and out of power like cuckoos in a clock. All prepared to speak on behalf of the poor, just as long as they weren't one of them. And now Churchill – a giant in war, but a leader in peace? Who could tell? The island had seen them come and go and fared none the better for all their talk.

'Gran?' Connie's voice roused her.

She blinked sharply. 'Are you going?

'Yes, it's late.'

'This man, Gilbert Tucker, will he show up again?'

'I've got a feeling he will.'

'Watch out for yourself, love.'

'Time for me to go too.' Pat struggled to get out of the chair.

Connie helped her up. 'I'll walk you to the bus stop.'

Gran dressed Lucky in his red siren suit and Doris in her blue winter coat and muffler. Pat picked up her shopping bag and the gas masks and Connie took each child by the hand. 'See you next week, Gran, a little later, as I'm calling at Pat's first.'

'No rush, love. I'll have the kettle on.'

They kissed her goodbye and she watched them walk out into the dark afternoon. Gran closed the door and went back to the front room. Sitting down in the chair, she thought about Gilbert Tucker. There was no doubt in her mind she had seen him for herself, once when she was at the shops and then in the café with Albie. He was the child's relative she had no doubt of it. The lights matched and always would until Lucky was free.

Nature could be cruel at times. She didn't understand the workings of the universe, but it was so. She was getting older sadly, but none the wiser!

It was a murky December morning when the new girl started at Dalton's. Jenny Beam wore sensible shoes and pinned her mouse-coloured hair into a bun.

'She doesn't say boo to a goose,' Len confided to Connie as they made their way up to the office. 'But she comes with excellent references. Mr Burns is very pleased. Especially as we've struggled in Ada's absence.'

'I miss Ada,' Connie agreed as they ascended the stairs to the office. 'I wonder why she left.'

'At Christmas, too,' Len agreed in a mystified tone. 'She was the life and soul of the canteen party.'

'For weeks before it she'd drag me round the market looking for something to wear. I haven't had the heart to go shopping without her.' She paused as they stood outside the office. 'Len, I'm going to give the party a miss this year.'

'But I'll be there.'

'Even so . . .'

Len lifted his eyes. 'Women! I just don't understand them.'

'That's why you're still single.' Connie grinned.

He pushed open the door. 'Look there's Jenny, in already. Must have been here at the crack of dawn.'

Connie studied the unfamiliar figure perched on Ada's tall stool. One hand rested demurely on her long plaid skirt, the other was busy turning the page of the ledger in front of her.

Len heaved a sigh as he walked over. 'Hello, Jenny.'

Connie had never seen someone blush so deeply. 'Oh, er, good morning, Mr English.'

'This is Connie and she'll show you the ropes.'

Jenny smiled nervously. 'Hello.'

'Pleased to meet you, Jenny.' Connie gave her a big smile.

In the absence of further comment, Len coughed. 'Well, I'll leave you two to it.'

Connie sat on her stool. 'Have you done this sort of work before, Jenny?' she asked in a friendly fashion.

'Yes,' came the slight nod. 'At Masterson's.'

'The oil blenders? Didn't they move out to Essex recently?'

'Yes.'

Connie waited for more, but nothing was forthcoming. 'Well, I'm sure you'll like it here. Everyone's very nice. All the girls from the typing pool and other offices meet in the canteen at one o'clock. I'll introduce you, if you like.'

'Thank you.'

'Did you find the cloakrooms all right this morning?'

'Yes.'

Connie nodded slowly. It was, she could tell, going to

be an uphill struggle. Ada never let you get a word in edgeways. She'd make a joke of anything when she was on form – Connie stopped herself there. If she was honest, Ada hadn't been on form for weeks, months even. More often than not she'd bitten off someone's head before the day was out.

Connie glanced at the little figure beside her. Who was to say, underneath those thick spectacles and pink hamster cheeks, there mightn't be another Ada waiting to get out? But, as Jenny silently studied the book in front of her with deep concentration, Connie doubted it.

It was half past four when the office door opened. Clint Hershey's tall figure appeared. The sergeant's blue gaze swept towards her and with a soft smile he removed his cap. Then, striding past her, he approached Mr Burns.

Connie strained her neck to see what was happening. The next moment Len was following Clint Hershey from the room, a worried look on his face. Under normal circumstances, Connie and Ada would have begun whispering furtively as they speculated on what could have happened. But Jenny had her nose in the ledger, her pen going at top speed as she wrote, unaware of the interruption.

Ten minutes later Len returned. Mr Burns's eyebrows rose higher and higher as Len talked to him.

'Connie, something awful's happened,' Len gasped as he came towards her. 'Mother must have escaped from Mrs Next Door. She's downstairs, saying she's lost her way to the theatre and needs to change into her costume.'

'You mean she's here at Dalton's?' Connie gasped.

'Yes. She was wandering around the warehouse when Sergeant Hershey found her. He managed to persuade her into the W.C. Now she won't come out.'

'Why didn't he just bring her up here?'

'Because she hasn't got hardly anything on.' Len was so upset he could hardly speak. 'Just her underwear.'

'Oh dear, she must be frozen,' Connie gasped.

'You haven't got any spare clothes at work, have you?'

'No, but there's an old coat hanging in the cloakroom. It's been there years and doesn't belong to anyone.'

'Could you come and help us? Mr Burns has given his permission.'

Connie slipped off her stool immediately. 'There's a bit of an emergency downstairs, Jenny. Will you be all right on your own?'

The girl nodded silently.

'Thanks, just put my books away if I'm not back, would you? I'll stay late tomorrow to finish my work.'

Sergeant Hershey was standing beside the green wooden door of the outside lavatory. 'Gee, Len, she says she won't come out till her costume's arrived.'

'This will have to do,' Len stammered as he pushed Connie forward.

Clint smiled. 'Okay, we'll give it a go.' He opened the door slightly. 'Okay, ma'am, uh . . . Miss Betty Grable is here with your costume.'

The door opened slowly. A tall woman wearing a long silk petticoat and very old, discoloured slippers smiled graciously at them.

'How nice it is to meet you, Miss Grable.' Mrs English smiled. 'Do come in.'

Connie heard Len groan beside her. She stepped inside the dark, damp-smelling toilet. An audible sigh of relief came from the two men as Connie closed the door behind her.

Once dressed in the ownerless coat, Len's mother finally consented to being driven home in Clint's 'limousine'. Connie sat beside her in the rear seat of the truck as the elderly woman recalled the past in glowing terms. Len made several attempts to quieten her but all to no avail.

'You will come in,' she insisted when they arrived at the tiny terraced house in Cubitt Town. 'We'll have cocktails.'

Both Connie and Clint accepted and Len made tea in the absence of alcohol but was clearly distraught at his mother's eccentric behaviour.

'I think you'd better escape while you can,' he whispered as they sat in the small modestly furnished front room. 'Thank you both for your trouble.'

'No trouble,' Clint assured him as they listened with one ear to his mother's ramblings. 'She's a great gal,' he added kindly.

'You know none of it's true,' he said sadly when at last they left. 'Mother worked in a cinema for years. It was her whole life. Now she seems to think she's a film star. As you know our neighbour comes in to keep an eye on her in the day. It's not usually a problem as Mother doesn't like going out. Which was why I was so shocked at her appearance at work this afternoon.' He walked out with them to the truck. 'I'll bring the coat in tomorrow, Con.'

'Was it the Blitz that made her like it?' Clint asked as he drove Connie home.

'No, but it made her worse.'

'Isn't there somewhere she could go?' He frowned through the truck's dirty window. 'I mean like a hotel for retired actresses, that kinda thing?'

Connie smiled softly. 'Do you have them in America?'

'Honey, we have *everything* in America.' He grinned.

They drove on in silence until Connie said quietly, 'Thank you for helping Len's mother today.'

He laughed. 'You mean I shut her in the rest room!'

Connie nodded. 'She thought you were Douglas Fairbanks.'

He roared with laughter. 'First time I've been called that.'

'And I've not been called Betty Grable before.'

'You sure do look like her.'

Connie laughed to cover her embarrassment. 'I think I've had enough of Hollywood for one day. Could you turn down the next street, please?'

'Sure.'

'It's number eighteen, just there.'

He pulled up at the kerb. 'Is that your house?'

'No, I live at number thirty-three with my parents and two brothers. Our neighbours Nan and Lofty take care of Lucky when I'm at work.'

Clint Hershey frowned. 'Lucky? Is that a dog?'

Connie laughed. 'No, he's a little boy.'

'Yours?' he asked in surprise.

276

'No, not mine. He was orphaned in the Blitz. I've cared for him ever since.'

'Gee, that's swell.' He rested his arm across the wheel. 'Connie – can I call you Connie?'

'If you want.'

'You know, I'm real sorry if I upset you before.'

'I didn't want to give you the wrong impression, that's all,' Connie replied quickly. 'If you see what I mean.'

'Understood. But I hope we can be friends.'

'I hope so too.'

He nodded to the house. 'There's a little boy waiting for you.'

Connie turned round. 'That's Lucky,' she said proudly.

'Looks just like you.'

'It's a coincidence isn't it?' She pushed open the door. 'Thanks for the lift.'

'Any time.'

'Who was that?' Nan asked as she hovered on the doorstep, holding Lucky's hand.

'Douglas Fairbanks, would you believe?' Connie lifted Lucky into her arms as he waved to the smiling sergeant.

Nan nodded sagely. 'Now, would that be senior or junior?'

Connie smiled to herself as the truck roared off. It was nice being told she was like Betty Grable even though she knew it was flattery!

That night, Connie was washing the kitchen floor when Olive appeared. 'Oh, Constance, you shouldn't be doing that after a hard day's work.'

'It gives me something to do.'

'Why don't you come and listen to the radio with Dad and me?'

Connie leaned back on her heels. 'I'll be in when I've finished this.'

Her mother paused. 'Was it good news from Vic?'

'What do you mean?'

'I left a letter on your bed this morning. Didn't you see it?'

'No.' She dropped the rag. 'Lucky must have knocked it off.'

Her mother pulled her up. 'Well, you'd better go and find it, hadn't you?'

Connie took the stairs two at a time. Lucky lay fast asleep in his cot, his breathing soft and gentle. Connie found the letter on the floor. 'Oh, darling!' she gasped as she hurried downstairs to read it.

A letter before Christmas! Was there a card inside, or just a few lines? She didn't care, as long as it was from him.

Unfolding the blue sheet of paper she began to read. The smile slowly disappeared from her face as she read it over again and again.

'Connie, whatever is wrong?' her mother gasped when she walked into the kitchen. 'It's not bad news is it?'

'No, I suppose not.'

'What does that mean?'

Connie couldn't stop a tear escaping. Irritably she brushed it away. 'He's staying at a hotel, a really wonderful one. Last night there was a dance to welcome the

British navy.' Connie recalled what Clint had said about the Americans having everything. She wondered if that included beautiful dance partners.

Olive sat down beside her. 'What's wrong with that?'

'I thought he'd be missing me.'

'And *that*'s what's upset you.'

'I couldn't think of enjoying myself without him. I even told Len I wasn't going to the Christmas party. I didn't know my fiancé was going to be dancing the night away.' Connie looked miserable. 'Oh, Mum, I've got this ache inside me and it won't stop.'

'You're lonely, love,' her mother said gently. 'And if you're not careful a bit of green-eye will creep in and make it much worse.'

'I can't help it.'

'That's no excuse,' her mother said sharply. 'You've got a good man in Victor Champion, a man who could have stayed home and played it safe. But his conscience wouldn't let him and off he went to war. You should be relieved he's fetched up in America for a while. I expect he's not telling you about the dangerous part and is just trying to put your mind at rest.'

'Well he hasn't. I'm dead worried now.'

Her mother sniffed noisily. 'Constance, I've worried all my life and look where it's got me. A bundle of nerves. And, yes, I've been jealous too, though I wouldn't admit it to your father's face.'

Connie looked surprised. 'You've never told me that before.'

'I'm not too old to forget what jealousy feels like.'

Connie looked down at the letter and Vic's bold writing. She knew she was being unreasonable and imagining things that hadn't happened. Vic would be faithful, she was sure of that. But she still couldn't stop feeling this way.

Olive stood up. 'Now let's have a nice cup of tea and listen to the radio.'

But Connie didn't want a cup of tea or to listen to the radio. All she could think of was Vic.

In bed that night, she gave way to tears. She didn't know what a swanky hotel like the Barbizon Plaza on 6th Avenue looked like, or the women inside it, but imagining was bad enough.

'Come to the party tonight,' Len said when Connie told him about Vic on Saturday morning.

'No, I don't want to.'

'You're being daft now.'

'Mum said that.'

'Well, she's right. When did you last go out?'

Connie shrugged. 'With Vic, in August.'

'And now it's Christmas!' Len wagged his finger in her face. 'You might as well be a nun. You should try and break the habit.'

Connie glanced at her friend. They burst out laughing. Len could always bring a smile to her face, just like Ada.

'Listen, Con, odds on Jenny won't say a word, and she don't dance either. I'll be sitting there all night like a blooming great wallflower!'

Connie knew that Jenny hadn't mixed with any of the staff, despite all hers and Len's encouragement. To cap it all, yesterday she had informed them she didn't drink or dance and was quite content to sit and 'watch' at the Christmas party.

'Come,' Len urged mischievously. 'For my sake. It'll be the only bit of life I'll see over Christmas.'

Eventually he talked Connie round. That afternoon Pat suggested she borrow her pearl grey dress with the sunray pleated skirt. It wasn't as frivolous as the little peach number she'd borrowed from Ada, but it was her size and quite tasteful. She washed her hair and let it fall in waves on her shoulders. By the time she was ready to catch the bus, there was a big smile on Olive's face.

'Have a good time,' she told her daughter. 'And enjoy yourself.'

Connie caught the bus feeling nervous. She hadn't been out of an evening for a long time. But as soon as she arrived at Dalton's, she felt better. Everyone was looking forward to the evening, as they hurried in groups up the stairs to the canteen. Laughter and insults abounded. There were no raids to worry about, at least not like the Blitz. And it was an opportunity to eat, drink and make merry.

Connie stood at the canteen door, looking for Len. She hoped nothing had happened to stop him from coming. The room looked very festive, nothing of course like the Barbizon Plaza, all glass and marble and shining surfaces, apparently. But the bare, scuffed boards of the canteen floor were now cleared for dancing. Someone

281

had strung paper chains across the ugly blackout material of the windows and the upright piano was standing as usual at Christmas, beside Ted Lavender's ancient drum set. Queenie Wright, the canteen manageress, had pinned bunches of genuine mistletoe to the ceiling, already gaining much attention. The black market refreshment was said to be hidden in the kitchen, under lock and key.

'You've got that look on your face again,' a voice muttered beside her. Len, dressed smartly in a dark blue suit and tie, was frowning at her. 'You're not about to do a bunk, are you?'

Connie grinned. 'Course not.'

'If you hadn't turned up, I'd have done one myself.' He steered her towards the serving hatch. 'Now, what's your fancy?'

'Port, please. Don't suppose they've got any lemon.'

Len ordered the drinks. 'I bought one for Jenny too,' he whispered from the corner of his mouth as they looked for her. 'There she is, by the piano. At least the noise will drown the silence.'

'Thank you, Mr English, but I never drink,' Jenny refused politely as he placed the glass of shandy in front of her.

'It's Len,' he reminded her again as they sat down. 'And shandy's not really a drink, it's mostly lemonade.'

Jenny braced her plump shoulders. She was dressed as usual, in a dark skirt and a sensible blouse to match. 'I don't like lemonade either.'

'What do you like then?'

'Water or tea, Mr En— I mean, Len.'

'I'm drinking port, Jenny,' Connie said, holding up her glass. 'It's very nice, a lady's drink. Would you like a sip?'

'No thank you.'

Connie met Len's gaze and stifled a grin. She breathed a sigh of relief when Elsie Drinkwater took her seat at the piano. Placing her pint of frothy ale on its splintered top, she nodded to her burly son, Norman, the accordion player. Ted Lavender joined them and banged heavily on his drums. Soon no one could hear themselves think.

By nine o'clock Connie was breathless. Neither she nor Len had missed a dance, in an attempt to avoid Jenny's silent gaze. In this way, Connie had enjoyed herself thoroughly and didn't feel the least bit guilty either. Trevor Black had commented on her hair and Bob Cummings had told her how well she danced. Len, too, looked as if he was feeling more his old self, having danced with every available female. When at last they collapsed on their seats, even Jenny's flat smile didn't seem to bother them.

'Are you enjoying yourself, Jenny?' Connie asked as the band took a breather.

'Yes, thank you.'

'Would you like more water?'

'No, I've still got some left.'

Silence ensued until Elsie bawled at the top of her voice. 'Let's put our hands together, boys and girls, for two very talented lads from the United States of America!'

There was a slow, mystified applause as a young GI took his place at the piano, the other seating himself on a stool.

'It's Clint!' Len whispered hoarsely. 'He never said he played the trumpet. Now that's a dark horse for you, if ever I saw one.'

No one danced, spoke or attempted to eat as the duo played. The only trumpet player Connie had seen before was a man at the Queens on Variety Night who'd struggled his way through the National Anthem. Clint was playing music like she'd never heard before. At first she didn't know if she liked it, but half an hour later, like everyone else in the room, she was demanding more. Couples began dancing and Len pulled her up. No one wanted the music to stop. Once more, the two musicians finished to huge applause.

'Bloody brilliant!' Len roared at the top of his voice as Elsie, Norman and Ted returned to their instruments.

Clint laid his trumpet on the piano and walked over to their table. 'Mind if I take a seat?' he asked, and everyone made space.

'That was amazing,' Len said. 'What was the first number called?'

'"Body and Soul",' the young GI told them.

'What kind of music is it?'

'Jazz,' he explained. 'Did you like it?'

'Not half. Where did you learn to play like that?' Len asked excitedly.

'My old man,' Clint explained.

'He's a musician?' Connie asked.

Clint smiled softly into her eyes. 'He was, till he died. Taught me to play as a kid. I still do a little jamming at Jimmy Ryan's on 52nd Street. You know it?' he asked curiously.

'No, but I know the Barbizon Plaza,' she burst out before she could stop herself. 'My fiancé Vic is staying there with the British navy.'

Clint looked impressed. 'Then he'll be having a swell time, you can be sure. Some of your English boys were arriving when I left. We're sending them back with these lil' ol' boats that open up at the front.'

Connie didn't know what he meant and wasn't able to ask, as Len began to talk about the music. Soon Clint was explaining that it was jazz he liked to play. 'Though Bop and Swing are all the go Stateside,' he ended, taking a gulp of the beer he had brought with him.

Connie blushed as he smiled at her.

'You're a very good player.' Jenny nodded, speaking suddenly. 'I love to hear the trumpet. Especially when it's played so well.'

'Than you, ma'am.' Clint gave her a big white smile. 'I'm real pleased to hear you say that.'

Elsie, Norman and Ted started to play. Connie decided that at the next available opportunity she would ask him more about those lil' ol' boats that opened up at the front.

Chapter Eighteen

It was the last waltz and Clint asked Connie to dance. 'You dance real well, Connie,' he said as he took her in his arms and placed his cheek against her head. 'Makes me forget about home for a while. New York is such a great place to be at Christmas. You get the full works, snow, Santa, and you'd go crazy for the shops.'

'Have you lived there long?' she asked, pressing slightly away.

'All my life, till Mom died. Me and my kid sister, Janey, went to live out of state, with relatives. But pretty soon we got sent back to Pop.' He breathed softly into her hair. 'With him being on the road and playing all over the country, Janey and me learned pretty fast to look after ourselves. She's married now, moved out west.'

'But you stayed in New York?'

'Had this day job in construction so's I could play the clubs with Pops at night. Then he got ill and died five years back. I signed up after Pearl Harbour; gee, those Japs sure turned our country around. God alone knows what you Londoners have suffered.'

'What you said about those small ships,' she asked,

taking her opportunity. 'Do you really think Vic could be involved with them?'

He nodded. 'Yes, I do. The NY dockyards are building them in their hundreds so's they're ready for Roosevelt and Churchill's plans to invade Europe. It's guys like Vic who are sailing them back across the pond and risking their necks against the subs.'

Connie shivered. She wished she hadn't asked now. What had the world turned into when it sent so many young men to war with the threat of death looming over them at every moment?

When the music ended, Clint looked down at her. 'I've sure had a swell time, Connie.' Politely, he held out his arm and guided her back to the table.

Jenny and Len were preparing to leave and Clint lifted Connie's coat from the back of the chair.

'It's mighty cold out there. Can I give you folks a lift home?'

Len and Jenny nodded but Connie hesitated.

Clint chuckled softly when he saw her waver. 'Don't tell me, you'd prefer to walk.'

'No, she bloody wouldn't,' Len said before she could reply. 'Not at this time of night. If you're offering, Clint, then all of us are accepting.'

The sergeant collected his instrument and they all made their way downstairs. Connie sat with Len in the back of the truck and Jenny took the passenger seat.

Len nudged her arm gently. 'Good night after all, wasn't it?'

In the darkness, she gazed up at the clear, star-studded

sky. For once it was cold and frosty, a typical winter's night. The fog that had made everywhere so damp and dreary had lifted and the spirit of Christmas was in the air.

She thought of Vic and wondered if he was in the middle of a sub-infested ocean. After what Clint had said, she hoped he was still at the Barbizon Plaza. She would rather have him safe than in the thick of action, even if it did mean him dancing with the most glamorous women in New York!

This Christmas, three of the people she loved most were missing. Billy had never moved back home and only made occasional visits. Mum had gone spare at first, but no amount of her nagging had brought him back and finally she'd given up. Vic was fighting a war, the end of which seemed nowhere in sight. Wherever Ada was, Connie hoped she was happy. Their quarrel had been over nothing at all. She just wished she could see Ada and make amends.

The fog and the blackout made it dangerous to travel and Christmas week arrived low key. On the Saturday she had arranged to help Pat with her move, but Lucky was sick. Reluctantly she had to cancel and Kevin and Sylvie went in her place. By Christmas Day, Lucky was worse. On Boxing Day, he was running a fever and Kevin cycled round for Dr Deakin.

'Plenty to drink,' the doctor advised after he'd given Lucky a thorough examination. 'Keep him warm, but try to get the fever down. I'll call again tomorrow. We'll watch him carefully. If he's not better, I'm afraid he'll have to go to hospital.'

Connie spent a sleepless night. She bathed Lucky's face in cool water, but his cheeks were burning. The following day the doctor returned. 'His temperature's down, but I'm still not happy.'

Once more Connie didn't sleep. On Tuesday morning the rash appeared.

'Measles,' the doctor confirmed. He patted Lucky's arm gently and pulled up his sheet. 'You're over the worst now, young man.'

Connie applied calamine lotion to the rash and both she and Lucky slept that night.

'Where did Christmas go this year?' Ebbie complained on Wednesday morning as he wearily opened his paper and yawned loudly.

Connie studied her father. She wondered if living with a small child in their midst was the cause of his fatigue. She was beginning to feel an imposition. Her mother had volunteered to have Lucky when Connie went back to work. Lofty hadn't had measles and it was dangerous for a grown-up to catch. Connie hadn't considered the likelihood of things like infectious diseases. What would be next on the list? she wondered, as New Year's Eve arrived. She longed to talk to Ada, to have a laugh about their worries. Where was she? Why had she gone off without saying goodbye?

That night Lucky's breathing returned to normal. She wondered what the future would hold as one year ended and a new one began. Where was Vic? Suddenly the picture of Gilbert Tucker sprang to mind. Was he really Lucky's grandfather?

As her lids grew heavy, she said a prayer for the millions of people in turmoil. She was so lucky to have her family alive and well. The stories of atrocities towards the Jews were in every newspaper. German cities were now being bombed in retaliation and innocent men, women and children were dying, just as they had in Britain. The Russians had suffered terrible tragedy, as had all the countries of Europe, whilst Japan had turned a new page of the war at Pearl Harbour. Who could say when it all would end?

She missed Vic so much. She had to believe he would return. As she closed her eyes, she saw his face. His dark eyes looked down on her, his smile filled her with warmth and longing.

In sleep he drew her into his arms. His lips touched her face and she heard him whisper that he loved her.

In January, the Luftwaffe got its second wind. A school was flattened, killing forty-four children outright. Connie was afraid to leave Lucky. The raids were on the increase again.

A month or so later, the warning went. In the panic to get down the Tube 173 lives were lost. Then rumours of a new and more deadly Nazi weapon began to circulate. Everyone feared the worst. Even Jenny at work took time to join in the discussion.

What was it that Hitler had planned for them? In March, the RAF dropped 900 tons of bombs on Berlin. The British pilots reported they could still see the fires 200 miles away. A big part of Dusseldorf was laid waste.

In the Battle of the Ruhr, the sheet of orange flame from the explosions below shot 1000 feet into the air.

A letter arrived from Vic one Friday. Connie read it as she sat on the wall after work. 'I don't know when you'll receive this, sweetheart, I hope in time for your birthday. I wish I could be with you on your twenty-first. How is everyone? And Lucky? Grown I expect. I want to walk with you to Island Gardens and sit on the bench. I imagine it every night. We took freedom for granted, but never again. Remember, freedom is what we're fighting for. I'll be with you in thought on the 3rd April. Sorry this is short and I can't say much. You know why. Deepest love as always, and remember me. Your Vic.'

Connie was staring at the letter, when someone tapped her shoulder.

'Are you Connie?'

'Yes.'

'I'm Albie Cross, Gran's friend.'

Connie jumped off the wall. 'What's wrong?'

'It's Pat. She's having the baby.'

'But she's not due for three weeks!'

'Can you come?'

They hurried to the gate, only seeing the truck as they turned into the street. Clint waved through the open window. She grabbed the old man's arm and pulled him with her. This time it was Connie who asked Clint for his help.

'How is she?' Connie asked the doctor as she scrambled out from the truck. 'Has she had the baby?'

Doctor Deakin nodded. 'I'm sending round the mid-wife.'

'Is Pat all right?'

'Yes, but there were complications,' was all he said as he climbed into his little black car. 'Gran will explain.'

Connie ran back to the truck. 'Thanks for the lift, Clint.'

'Has she had the baby?'

'Yes, but the doctor said she had complications.'

'Do you want me to come in with you?'

She hesitated. 'I don't know how long I'm going to be. But it would help if you could tell Nan and Lofty what's happened. I'll be late home tonight.'

He nodded and started the engine. 'Can I call back for you?'

'No, I'll catch the bus.'

'Take care, Connie.' The truck roared off.

Albie was still standing on the pavement. 'Tell Alice to shout if she wants me.'

'Thanks, Albie.' Connie hurried up the steps. The house was quiet, too quiet. The door to Pat's room was closed but Vic's was open. A crib stood beside his empty bed. She could hear movement from the kitchen, but made a detour to the baby. A little red face surrounded by thick black hair poked out above the white covers. He looked perfect.

'Hello, ducks,' Gran said softly as Connie entered the kitchen. 'Thanks for coming.'

'Where's Doris?'

'I sent her next door to Eve Beale.' Connie sat down at

the table and waited for Gran to continue. 'The baby isn't quite right.'

'He looks fine . . .'

Gran shook her head before Connie finished. 'His foot is misshapen. No one knows why. Doctor said most likely he was growing like it inside her.'

'Will he be able to walk?' Connie asked quickly.

Gran sighed heavily. 'At the moment it's just a stub that turns inward. And, as if that's not bad enough for the poor girl, Dr Deakin says this is the end of her child-bearing days.'

'Oh, Gran, poor Pat.'

A small sound echoed and they both stood up. 'That's the baby,' Gran said hurriedly. 'He must be hungry again. Go and talk to Pat and cheer her up. The birth took it out of her. She fed him, then fell asleep as we cleaned her up. Must be feeling rotten about now, especially with what the doc told her.'

Connie hurried towards Pat's closed door. Without Laurie, she was going to need all the support she could get and by hook or by crook that was what she was going to get if it cost Connie every last ounce of strength she had.

It was third of April and a warm, sunny Saturday. The skies were clear when Connie left for work.

'Happy birthday, Con,' Len said, pressing an envelope into her hand.

'Happy birthday,' Jenny added pleasantly. She held out a small packet. 'It's not much, I'm afraid.'

Connie opened them both. A card depicting a bowl of red roses from Len and Jenny's gift, a white lacy hand-kerchief with a pink '21' embroidered in the corner.

'It's lovely, Jenny.'

'I wish I was twenty-one again,' Len said ruefully.

'Just start counting backwards.' Connie grinned.

'Are you celebrating tonight?'

'Mum is making a cake.' Connie nodded. 'Though it might be made out of cardboard.'

'Yeah, well, it's the thought that counts.'

'Happy birthday, Connie.' Mr Burns handed her a card.

'Thank you, Mr Burns.'

'Enjoy it while you may. Youth doesn't last for ever.' Connie glanced at Len, who was smothering a chuckle, and even Jenny smiled as they studied it.

'Don't forget to put out this birthday card for salvage!' it warned under the heading of 'Happy 21st Birthday'.

The girls of the typing pool and canteen had clubbed together for a small bunch of flowers. She had three more cards from the other offices and several from the girls in the packing department.

Connie left at one o'clock, wondering if Clint would be sitting in his truck by the gates. But the yard was empty. As usual she hurried, intending to catch the bus to Gran's and be home in time for tea. Kevin and Sylvie had promised to be there. And Olive had asked Nan and Lofty to come as well. Connie would have liked a party, it was her twenty-first after all, but no one had suggested it.

When she arrived at Nan's, Lucky was busy playing with his train. She thought of Vic as she helped him push it over the lino. Her twenty-first and the man she loved could be anywhere in the world by now. Still, at least his letter had arrived in time.

'Going out anywhere tonight?' Nan enquired as she brought in Lucky's coat and threaded his arms through the sleeves.

'No, Mum's made a cake though. You coming along to share it?'

'Wouldn't miss it for the world.'

Connie held Lucky's hand as they walked to the door. 'See you later, then.'

'Yes – oh, and happy birthday, love.'

'Thanks, Nan.'

Olive and Ebbie were out when she got in. 'Well, it looks as though it's just you and me.' She smiled as she gathered Lucky in her arms. 'We'll catch the bus over to Gran's, shall we?'

'Gran's!' Lucky exclaimed excitedly.

Connie gave him a big kiss. 'We'll see Doris and baby Lawrence too.'

They set off and caught the bus at the end of the road. She hoped Pat was feeling better. She hadn't set foot in the street since the birth of the baby. It would be lovely if they could celebrate her birthday by walking up the road with the pram and the two kids. They could even stop for a drink at the café. But when they arrived at Pat's, Laurie was home.

He put his arms around Connie and hugged her.

There were tears in his eyes. 'It's good to see you, girl. And Lucky, blimey, haven't you grown?' He patted Lucky's cheek. 'You're a handsome lad, you are, chum.'

'Have you got leave, Laurie?' Connie asked as she hung their coats and gas masks on the hall-stand.

He nodded. 'Two days. But it's better than nothing. I've been trying to get a smile out of Pat, but she's not her old self. We always wanted a big family and now it seems that's never going to happen. For me it's not such a big thing, as Pat and the kids we've got is enough for me. But for a woman as young as Pat, it's a bitter pill to swallow.'

'It's early days yet, Laurie, she needs time to recover her health.'

He nodded. 'Yes, course. Maybe she'll cheer up when she sees you.'

They went into the front room, where Gran was sitting with little Lawrence in her arms. He was bawling louder than the kettle whistling in the kitchen and Doris was in tears. Pat looked distressed as she tried to comfort her little girl.

'None of us had any sleep last night,' she complained to Connie. 'I don't know if he's in pain with his foot or if he's just hungry.'

'Has he been fed?'

'Yes, just this minute.'

Laurie shook his head. 'You're worrying too much, love.'

'I can't help it,' Pat replied on the verge of tears. 'You don't understand. You're away all the time.'

Connie took the baby from Gran, who retreated out

to the kitchen. 'Why don't you and Laurie take Doris out for a walk?' Connie suggested as she rocked Lawrence. 'It's a lovely afternoon. The fresh air will do you good.'

Ten minutes later Connie had rocked Lawrence off to sleep in the pram. Gran was taking forty winks in her bedroom and the house was quiet again.

Connie turned her attention to the pile of nappies and dirty rompers in a basket by the boiler. She would have them hanging on the rack all smelling nice by the time Pat and Laurie returned. No one had remembered it was her birthday, though. But did it matter?

Connie couldn't help feeling a little neglected as she rolled up her sleeves and began the washing.

When she got home at five o'clock, her mother had made a real cake. The sponge had two small candles stuck in the top and a paper fringe tied around it. A carrot had been diced up to read, 'Happy 21st'.

'It's lovely, Mum,' Connie said as her mother lowered the plate to the front room table.

'Happy birthday, Constance.' Her mum and dad kissed her, then sat down.

''Appy, 'appy,' warbled Lucky, climbing on to the chair and poking his finger in the sponge.

'What time are Nan and Lofty coming?' Connie asked, taking Lucky on her lap.

'We said we'd go down to them,' her father replied stiffly.

'Oh.'

Her mother stood up. 'Let's go and spruce ourselves

up, dear,' Olive suggested to Connie. 'Put on something nice. It is your twenty-first after all.'

Yes, but it doesn't feel much like it, Connie thought as they went upstairs.

'You two look nice,' her father greeted them when they returned.

Lucky flung his arms around her. 'Con-Con, birfday!' He pushed his head through the folds of her soft blue summer dress and pulled her round and round, making them laugh.

At six o'clock they all walked down to number eighteen. 'Anyone home?' Ebbie called as he pushed open Nan's front door.

No one replied. They all stood in the hall, gazing at the closed front-room door.

'We might as well go in,' Olive said. 'Open the door, dear.'

Connie turned the handle. 'Happy twenty-first!' everyone shouted as a multitude surged forward to greet them.

The presents were piled on the sideboard: a pair of woollen gloves for winter, a game of Lexicon with a damaged top. A Handy Wartime Guide for the woman at home, a copy of *Sew and Save*. One tin of Bemax, one of Bournville, a packet of blackout playing cards, a set of blouse patterns, a jar of Nelson strawberry preserve, Potato Pete's recipe book, a pair of lovely silk stockings and a half-pound box of Cadbury's Milk Tray. There were more gifts unopened at the back, awaiting investigation.

Connie looked around. How had so many people fitted into one room? All her friends, family and some of the neighbours were there. She hadn't suspected a thing. The cry of 'Happy twenty-first!' was still in her ears.

Len and Jenny, Gran, Pat, Laurie and the children – all of them had managed to keep the secret today. Kevin and Sylvie, Taffy and even Clint, the Shutlers from down the road and Nan and Lofty. Baby Lawrence was asleep in Lucky's pram, positioned carefully under the stairs. Doris and Lucky entertained themselves as usual with the toys.

Mrs Shutler opened the piano lid and began to play. Taffy pushed his way over to Connie. 'Sorry to see Billy ain't here.'

'Me too.' Connie nodded as she folded up the paper from her presents and tucked it to one side. 'We haven't seen much of him lately.'

'Me neither.'

Connie was surprised. 'Why not?'

'He's gone with someone else.'

'You mean, roofing?'

'That and fighting. Or, as he calls it, boxing. Don't let on to your mother. But there was nothing I could do to change his mind. Wouldn't wait till he was ready. Palled up with this joker to get himself gloves. I hope he knows what he's doing.'

'Now I'm worried, Taff. He was injured badly last time he fought.'

Taffy shook his head. 'Don't know anything about that.'

Connie had known something was wrong. What was Billy doing, leaving Taffy? They were a good team and Billy was on the straight and narrow.

'Anyway,' Taffy winked, 'don't let it spoil yer day, gel. Happy birthday.'

The evening wore on, but Connie was disappointed that Billy hadn't shown up. Kevin hadn't been able to find him. No one knew where he was. After what Taffy had told her, she was worried.

'That sure is a pretty headscarf,' a deep voice rumbled beside her.

Clint's blue eyes were bright and his tailored uniform made him stand out in the room full of shabby English clothes.

'It's from Billy. He brought it to work and gave it to Len to give me.'

'Where is he tonight?'

'I don't know.'

'He'll show up.'

Connie wished she was as certain as Clint that he would. She felt the soft silk between her fingers. It was a quality headscarf covered in a beautiful oriental design. She inhaled its fragrant aroma. Was he really able to afford a gift like this?

'Billy's a good kid,' Clint said quietly. 'He's just young and impressionable.'

'That's what worries me.'

'Is your fiancé still in New York?'

'He wrote but didn't say where he was.'

Clint nodded thoughtfully. 'The Red Army broke

through at Leningrad this year and the Allies are heading for Italy. I'd guess he's on his way back to Europe.'

Connie's spirits lifted. Perhaps Vic would get leave. Even if it was only twenty-four hours, how wonderful that would be. Clint was pouring himself a beer when Olive appeared from the kitchen. 'Connie, you've got visitors.'

'Who is it?' Connie followed her mother out.

'It's that man, Gilbert Tucker.'

'How did he find us?'

'He heard all the noise and came looking.' She glanced sideways. 'There's a woman with him. Says they're going to be married.'

Connie wondered what Gilbert Tucker was up to now.

Chapter Nineteen

'This is Sybil, my fiancée.' Gilbert Tucker pushed his lady friend forward.

The woman seemed very timid. She held out a limp, gloved hand. Connie judged her to be about forty, but she could have been younger as her plain dark hair and grey coat made her look older.

Connie didn't know what to say. The woman was looking at her with a nervous expression.

'I've been to the authorities,' Gilbert Tucker said. 'It won't be long before I can prove who I am. I'm going to get everything done legal before we get married. We don't want any misunderstandings.'

The small woman looked up at him. 'When are we taking Sydney?' she whispered vaguely.

'Who is Sydney?' Connie said, alarmed.

'Sydney is what the boy will be called,' Gilbert Tucker answered sharply, 'when he comes to live with us.'

Connie caught her breath. 'What do you mean?'

'That's what we're here for now, to look him over. See if he's – suitable.'

'Suitable? What for? What's this all about?'

Ebbie took hold of her shoulders. 'Calm down, now, love. Don't get yourself upset.'

'How can I calm down, Dad? You heard what he said.'

Ebbie frowned at their unwelcome guests. 'You'll have to come back another day when we can all sit down and discuss this properly.'

'There's nothing to discuss as far as I'm concerned. But have it your way,' Gilbert Tucker said in a nasty tone as he took hold of the woman's arm. 'Next time we meet, you'll all have to cooperate whether you like it or not.'

He pushed by Ted Jackson and Ben Shutler, dragging the woman after him as he marched through the open front door.

Connie was shaking. Did he mean what he said about Lucky living with them?

'It's late, Constance, you should try to get some sleep.' Olive locked the back door of the kitchen and pulled up the collar of her dressing-gown. She turned to her husband. 'Ebbie, I'll see you upstairs. Don't stay up too long. It's past midnight now.'

'All right, love.'

Everyone had gone home from Nan's, with Clint and Taffy giving lifts. Connie had put on a brave face as she'd said goodbye to everyone, but at the end of it all nothing could change the fact that if Gilbert Tucker was who he said he was, then Lucky was his kith and kin.

She looked enviously at little Lawrence asleep in his mother's arms, with Doris holding Laurie's hand as they

304

walked up the garden path to Clint's truck. Her heart ached for the child she had lost.

After Olive had gone to bed, Connie sat in the front room with her father. He rolled a pinch of Empire Shag, licked the edge of the paper and lit up. Letting out a stream of smoke, he sighed heavily.

'Odds on a relative had to turn up one day.'

'But it's not fair, Dad, I love Lucky. And they don't even know him.'

'Blood is thicker than water.'

'Why is it?' Connie demanded, suddenly angry that her own father didn't understand. 'Gilbert Tucker's not a nice person.'

'But what does he want saddle himself with a youngster for then, if he's not genuine? He must have an interest in the boy.'

Connie fought back the tears. 'Oh, Dad, what am I going to do?'

'There's nothing much you can do. Just wait and see what happens.'

She slipped her hand over her father's hard-working knuckles. 'Thank you again for such a lovely twenty-first.'

He gripped her hand tight. 'Sad it turned out so bad for you. We wanted it to be special.'

'I wish Gilbert Tucker would disappear again.'

He nodded, but she knew by the look on his face what he really felt. Both her parents had warned her from the start that Lucky was on borrowed time.

And now that time was running out.

★

Billy felt the sweat drip down his back, through his vest and into his shorts. He held his gloves up in front of his face, just like Freddie had instructed. But once he did that, his opponent came in low, sending his stomach through to bounce off his backbone. He felt sick and dizzy and his confidence was ebbing away.

The crowd assembled at Poplar Young Men's Sporting Club was booing loudly. They wanted their money's worth from this match. They were hoping to see the hot favourite and old pro Benny Bartlett, who was still as fit as a flea, give the young contender a good thrashing.

Billy couldn't believe such an old man was so good. He was losing his hair and had a face that had been hit so many times it looked like rubber. But Benny was dodging every jab and Billy was tiring in the effort to land one.

Billy held his gloves higher again. He tried to dance out of the way, but Benny stopped him with a lightning left hook. All Billy could do was fall back on the ropes. He shielded himself the best he could, but the crowd roared for more.

Benny Bartlett hammered in all he had. Billy's knees buckled. They'd gone four rounds with Billy chasing all the way. He lowered his gloves and took a breath. In the time it took to blink, a right jab caught his eyes. Blood spurted down his face, warm and thick.

Benny backed off, grinning, showing his gumshield. Billy swallowed as the jelly in his legs crept down to his ankles. What a pansy he'd look if he went down now. Freddie was sitting ringside, a cigar in his mouth. Billy knew what he had to do, only he just couldn't seem to do it. Nothing was working out; he had thought he was so much better than he was.

The belly punch came in like a hammer. Out of nowhere. He scissored up and hit the deck. It was all over, he knew, bar the shouting. He could barely raise his chin from the canvas. The last thing he remembered as he was counted out was catching sight of Freddie leaving his seat, with Ada not far behind him.

'Billy? Billy?'

He opened his eyes and through the slits saw a friendly face at last. 'Ada. Fancy seeing you here.'

'How do you feel?' She held a wet sponge on his forehead.

'How do I look?'

'Rotten.'

'Spoiled me good looks, has that bugger?' He managed a grin through swollen lips. The changing room smelled of leather and lineament and it reminded him of Taffy's shed. How long ago was that now? A lifetime, it felt like.

'You've got a dirty great cut under your eyebrow. It's stopped bleeding, but your eye's closing up.'

'How did I get here?'

'Two blokes dragged you back.'

'Oh, shit.'

'That's right, Billy, and you're in the middle of it.'

'I didn't see what was coming. Benny Bartlett moved round that ring like a two-year-old.'

Ada walked over to the small table with an enamel

bowl on the top of it. She squeezed out the sponge. Apart from a chair, a hook on the wall, a small cupboard and the long bench Billy was sitting on, there was nothing else in the room. Some of the pubs he had fought at had been better kitted out than this doss house.

Ada dug out a packet of Kensitas from her bag and lit up with a gold-coloured lighter.

'Nice bit of merry and bright you've got there,' Billy commented as she pushed the cigarette between his thick lips. The painful intake of breath made him gasp. 'Christ, I think my chest has caved in.'

'You'll survive.' She placed the cigarette on the edge of the bench and began to unlace his gloves.

'Where's Freddie?' he asked.

'Planning your next fight,' Ada said sarcastically, 'with a blind, one-armed cripple.'

Billy grinned. 'Go on with you, it wasn't that bad.'

'It was worse.'

'I wasn't on top form tonight that's true,' Billy admitted. 'Still, better luck next time. I had him on the hop more than once. I just gotta get the right moment to use the jab.'

Ada smiled, shaking her head slowly. 'I don't know why I'm wasting my breath.' She gazed incredulously into his eyes.

He had always fancied her, his sister's best pal, but it would have been more than his life was worth to admit it at the tender age of fourteen. She had lovely eyes, all big and done up with spidery lashes, and she smelled lovely. Her red hair was gorgeous and her close-fitting suit and nylons were the height of fashion. Freddie Smith was certainly keeping her in the style to which she wasn't accustomed.

Poor old Con, Billy thought as he sat there. She was so worried about her pal. He wished he could tell her Ada was living the life of Riley up the Commercial Road, installed in Freddie's flat with everything she could ever wish for. But Ada had sworn him to secrecy about her whereabouts. And Billy wouldn't have grassed anyway. He didn't want Connie – or Taffy, or that dimwit Wally – to come snooping round and spoil his plans to step right into Tammy Jarvis's shoes.

'You're not wasting your breath, Ada.' Billy grinned. 'I'm sitting here, listening to every lovely word.'

Ada smirked. 'You use that bloody mouth of yours better than you do your fists.'

'You know I like you, Ada.' He moved a little closer, grinning stupidly.

'Don't even think about it,' Ada warned, blowing smoke into his face. She gave his head a gentle pat.

'Aw, come on, I wasn't doing nothing.'

'But you was thinking it.'

'Then you must have been thinking about it an' all.'

She gave him one of her smouldering looks. 'How come you can be so mouthy after being mashed up like yesterday's potatoes?'

'This is just a one-off.' Billy shrugged. 'Freddie reckons I'm destined for the big time.'

Ada laughed outright. 'And you believed him?'

'Why shouldn't I?'

Ada ground out her cigarette. 'Sit forward,' she told him irritably, 'and I'll help you on with your shirt.'

'No, I can manage.' He grabbed her hand and looked into her eyes, serious now. 'You ain't answered my question, Ada. Why shouldn't I believe him?'

'If you don't know by now, then I'm not telling you.'

'Yes, you are.' He lifted her chin, slowly bringing her forward. He was going to kiss her, but at the last moment she stopped him.

'Don't let's make this more complicated that it already is,' she said, pulling her hand away. She looked under her lashes and into his eyes. 'You've gotta get out of this, Billy,' she whispered. 'I'm telling you this for your own good.'

'You've not told me nothing yet.'

She glanced round at the door. 'Let me ask you one question. Don't you think it's odd that Freddie's not here to give you a rollicking?'

Billy shrugged. 'He's waiting for me to come into form, that's all.'

Ada raised a finely pencilled eyebrow. 'Is that what he told you?'

'More or less.'

'Look, I don't want to hurt your pride, Billy, but he doesn't give a shit about your performance.'

'Oh, come off it Ada—'

'He doesn't. All he cares about is himself, and you're a mug if you don't listen to me.'

Billy was getting angry. 'If I'm such a mug, why did you shack up with Freddie, then? He's had more women than he's had hot di—' Billy halted as he saw the look of dejection on her face. He reached out and took her hands. 'Oh, Christ, Ada, I didn't mean to say that.'

'I know it's true.' She hung her head. 'I know what Freddie is.' She lifted her head slowly. Her eyes were heavy and sad. 'It's too late for me, Billy, but not for you. You can get out of this now before you're in too deep. All you have to do is walk away.'

'Walk away from what, Ada? I don't know what you're on about.'

She clutched his hands tight. 'All right, I'll spell it out. Freddie sets you up with fights you can't win. He tells you what you want to hear about building you up and making you a champ and he'll maybe even let you win one or two to keep you interested. But in the end you'll be taking the fall every time.'

Billy stared at her, his smile disappearing. 'You don't know what you're on about.'

'I do. Listen to me. Freddie is part of a syndicate. A lot of money rides on both the winners and losers. The payout is with the bookie and his associates, all big investors like Freddie who have stakes in the game. He'll let you go on for a few months, till you get really punch drunk and you can't think straight, let alone fight straight. Then he'll say, well, seeing as you need a bit of a break, only go on to the third or fourth round, then make it look good and take a dive.'

'What?' Billy cried, appalled. 'You're talking about a deliberate fix!'

Ada nodded slowly. 'The suggestion won't seem so

bad when your nose is broken and your eyes are swollen up permanently. In fact, the way Freddie will put it, you'll jump at the chance. The money will be good for a while, anyway, until Joe public doesn't want to see your brains on the canvas any more. Then, I'm afraid, it will all be over bar the crying.'

'How do you know all this?'

'I've got ears and eyes, haven't? I've learned a lot about villains in a very short while.'

'Why are you grassing him up, Ada? You're living with the bloke.'

'Because I care for you. You're my best mate's kid brother. I've known you all my life. You was better off with Taffy.'

'You mean I was better off with fat, drunk bastards who couldn't stop a punch coming if they saw it a mile off.'

'Go back to Taffy. He cares about you.'

Billy sank against the wall. Was he such a dope that he hadn't suspected something was up? Freddie must have singled him out at the Rose and Crown and known he was a sucker. He had wondered why Freddie had never had a go at him for losing. What an idiot he was to fall for it!

He could hardly look at her. 'You'd better go, Ada.'

She pulled his arm. 'Billy, I don't want to hurt your feelings. You'll make a really good boxer one day.'

'I'm fed up with hearing that.'

'Please—'

'Just go, gel.'

He stared down at the floor, the truth gradually sinking into his brain; he had wanted success so much that he had forgotten to be himself. He didn't know who he was now.

Other than Freddie Smith's patsy.

The door closed softly. He looked up. Ada had gone.

Vic got a thumbs-up from Georgie. His first mate was standing beside him in the corner of the pilot house, binoculars raised. Vic smiled, returning the gesture. Mission accomplished. All 185 soldiers of the Special Raiding Squadron were wading ashore.

'Marina d'Avola dead on target,' Georgie yelled above the gunfire. 'We've done it! They're on their way.'

'God speed them all,' Vic muttered as he leaped to the far side of the bridge. Puffs of silver light cut through the gloom, indicating enemy resistance as shown on the aerial photograph.

'It's the surf that's the danger,' Gerogie shouted, hurrying to join him. 'Look at it, will you! Filthy great mountains of the stuff.'

Vic wiped the grease and dirt from his eyes. He held his breath as he watched the men in the sea struggling to reach shore. Wave after wave rollercoasted over them. Some were fetched back in a tangle of debris. Others made it to the shoreline. There was no going back for any of them; they must advance, or die in the water.

Pieces of armoury crashed into the sides of the landing craft. The drone of aircraft grew louder. Enemy gunfire from the pill-boxes rattled into the water. Men disappeared silently.

'Somebody's bought it, poor sod.' Georgie nodded to the surf. A body was swept high on a wave, then was gone.

They watched, hoping for life, though they knew there was none. 'What state are we in?' Vic yelled as a fresh salvo from the beach landed close by.

'All present and correct, Skipper. But I wish we was on *Oxford*. By God I do. She'd show them a thing or two.'

Vic nodded, the urge to retaliate overpowering. But with seventy-five tons as opposed to 90,000, the most they could offer Jerry was a token blast from toy guns.

'Check all troops are despatched,' Vic shouted, signalling below, and Georgie nodded.

'Aye, Aye, sir!'

Vic watched him disappear below deck. He couldn't believe his luck to have come through with Georgie. When this little lot was over, they planned to build boats together, not demolish them.

A sudden rush of water lifted the little ship high. Vic clutched the conning tower rail. Darkness was settling swiftly. It didn't seem possible that out there a million Allied servicemen were converging on Sicily. He felt a swell of pride for the part his own small fleet had played.

If only he had been able to write to Connie . . .

A blistering scream echoed above his head. He ducked in time to see the underbelly of a plane. It soared low, throwing out a plume of metal grey smoke. He couldn't tell if it was one of ours or theirs, but the thud was sickening and the blaze of the sinking wreck lit up the sky.

Grief filled him. Friend or foe, they were fighting in service of their country. Tearing his eyes away he returned his attention to the shoreline. A burst of fire splattered starboard. The little ship rocked. A fountain of warm, wet sea – or was it oil? – cascaded over the bow. Stars lit up the water and fell like meteors. A crack astern and he reeled backwards.

The fall winded him. He lay there, staring up at the pilot house roof, now ripped to burning ribbons. The rails that he had been holding minutes ago were glistening, a molten red. The sky spread above, a silent, star-filled expanse far beyond the earthly violence. He lifted his head. Georgie was coming towards him. The whites of his eyes glowed. He was bareheaded, tousled gingery tufts sticking up like scorched bristles.

A small cone of smoke rose behind him. It was only when his knees buckled that the hole in his chest blew open. Vic held the burning, soft mass that once was his friend. He looked down in the darkness and cradled a smouldering bundle. Soon he couldn't tell what was flesh and what was bone, as the ship erupted, blowing him and the remains in his arms high into the air, and, finally, down deep into the cooling water.

Chapter Twenty

'Y̶ou all right, Connie?'

    'Yes, thanks.'

    Len looked at her in concern. 'You sure?'

'Just a bit tired that's all.'

'Well, only half an hour to go.'

Connie smiled, returning her attention to the ledger in front of her. She hadn't been able to concentrate all day. She had a sinking feeling in her stomach and it wouldn't go away.

'You do look a bit pale.' Jenny frowned at her. 'You haven't eaten something off in the canteen?'

'No, I didn't go up there today.'

'It might be the weather. Dad says we're in for a thunderstorm, but then he always says that when it's hot and sticky.'

Connie didn't bother to say what her problem was, and it had nothing to do with the weather. She had lain awake all Saturday night and half of Sunday night, her mind in turmoil over Lucky.

She missed Ada so much. She was the only one she could talk to who would understand. Even Nan and

Lofty, as much as they loved Lucky, had advised her that if Gilbert Tucker was who he said he was, there was nothing much to be done. As Lucky's grandfather he would have every right to claim his grandson.

When she had discussed her troubles with Gran, she was told what she didn't want to hear. 'The boy *is* linked to him,' Gran had warned. 'I wish I could say otherwise, but the lights never lie.'

'You think he's telling the truth and he is Lucky's grandfather?'

'I don't know about telling the truth,' Gran had puzzled. 'But you, Lucky and him have some connection.'

Connie sighed. There seemed no one who understood how she felt. Ada would have been up in arms on her behalf. She could hear Ada saying, 'Connie Marsh, you and me are going up the town hall right now and demanding your rights!' She smiled sadly as she heard Ada's voice in her head. She was always a good and loyal friend. Where was she now?

'Connie?' Jenny was standing beside her. 'The hooter's gone. Time to pack up.'

Slowly Connie put away her things and said goodnight to Len and Jenny. The feeling of apprehension was growing inside her. When would Gilbert Tucker turn up again? Connie closed her eyes in fear. She was working herself up into a state. Quickly she ducked into the cloakroom until the mad rush was over. She didn't feel like walking home with anyone. She wanted to be alone with her thoughts.

The late-July evening was mild and balmy when she walked into the big yard. The last few employees of

Dalton's were going through the gate. Connie stopped when she saw the truck. Although she saw Clint on the warehouse floor, they hadn't had much time to talk. The bonnet of the truck was raised and she recognized the lower half of Clint's body underneath.

'Hi there!'

'Hello, Clint.'

He grinned his white smile. 'At the speed you're going, my guess is you'd be home before I could mend the truck and offer you a lift.'

'Actually, I'm not going home straightaway,' she replied, nodding ahead. 'The weather's so nice I'm going for a stroll.'

He closed the bonnet on the truck with a bang. 'Now, I'm real tempted,' he said as he walked towards her, 'to ask if you want some company. But, gee, you'd probably only say yes because you're too polite to say no.'

'I'm only going to the Gardens, that's all.'

'The Gardens are fine with me.' He shrugged.

'I might not be very good company.'

He chuckled as he joined her and they walked through the gate. 'Okay, I'll just walk beside you – whistle a few tunes maybe – and take in the scenery.'

This brought a smile to her lips. 'There's not a lot of scenery to look at.'

'There's you.'

She gave him a frown, then, seeing the twinkle in his blue eyes, she laughed. 'How is life for you at Dalton's, lately? You're always busy when I come down to the weigh-ins.'

'Things are moving quickly in Europe.'

Connie nodded. 'The letter I had from Vic last week said he was leaving the United States and would be in Europe by the time I received it.'

'Then I guess he won't be home on leave.'

'No.' Suddenly the tears filled her eyes. She couldn't trust herself to speak, so she stared straight ahead, trying to disguise her unhappiness.

'I guess I just put my great boot in it.'

'Not really. It's just everything seems to have come at once. I've got things on my mind and I'm trying to work them out.'

He lifted his big palms. 'What are friends for? Just fire ahead.'

'You won't understand.'

'Try me.'

Connie looked up at him. 'Do you ever take no for an answer?'

'Not in your case.'

Connie sighed again. 'I give up.'

'Great. Now hang on to this arm, honey, and tell me all about it.'

'So you're pretty sure this old guy is Lucky's grandfather?'

Connie sighed. 'Pretty sure.' They had been sitting on the bench in Island Gardens for nearly an hour. Once he had persuaded her to tell him the whole story, she had been unable to stop. She had described the last three years in detail beginning from when she found Lucky to the moment Gilbert Tucker arrived at Nan's.

'Why didn't you go to the police about this creep?' he asked.

Her voice was husky. 'What could they do? He only followed me, not hit me over the head or tried to steal my bag.'

'What would you do if he was the little guy's relative?'

'I don't know.' Tears filled her eyes. 'I love Lucky so much, I don't want to lose him. At the same time I want him to be with his family. But what if his family isn't very nice?'

Clint reached out for her hand. 'Hey, there, I understand. Love makes you blind and yet it makes you brave; it makes you confused and yet you never see more clearly in all your life.'

Connie looked up at him, shocked. 'Yes, that's exactly how I feel. How did you know?'

He squeezed her fingers. 'You're not the only one to experience that powerful drug.'

'But what can I do if he is Lucky's grandfather?' she wailed again, gazing into his eyes for an answer.

'If he provides no proof that he is, there's no way he can take Lucky from you. Leastways, that's the way it would work at home.'

'But,' spluttered Connie, 'Gran sees these lights around people, you see. And Lucky and me and Gilbert Tucker all have the same lights. So if Lucky turns out to be his grandson—'

'Hey!' Clint interrupted with a rueful smile. 'You don't believe in all that hocus-pocus, do you?'

Connie shrugged. 'I don't know.'

'Well, let's say Gran is right and Lucky is the guy's grandson. He brings along proof – demands to take the kid – what are you going to do about it?'

'That's what I'm trying to work out.' She felt her lips tremble. 'I can't bear the thought of losing him. But how can I keep him?'

Clint took both her hands in his as he turned to look in her face. 'One of the first things you learn in the army is that all great battles have contingency plans. Have something tucked up your sleeve to distract the enemy.'

'What does that mean?'

'If it was me, I'd go to the authorities, beat him to it. Tell them everything and holler like crazy that you want to keep Lucky.'

Connie smiled. 'You sound like Ada.'

'Well, what can you lose?'

'Nothing, I suppose.'

Suddenly Connie remembered the lady who had helped her and Vic when they went to the Welfare department. 'I do know someone at the Welfare, a Mrs Burton.'

'Why not give it a try?'

Connie looked at the handsome young man sitting beside her. 'Thank you,' she said quietly.

'Connie . . .' She felt the warmth and strength of his hand over hers, the suppleness of his fingers. She remembered the way they had moved over the trumpet keys and made such beautiful music. In the soft summer's evening, her heart raced. He was going to kiss her.

She jumped up.

'Connie, you know I'd do anything for you, don't you?' he said, trying to pull her back down.

'Clint, I'm leaving now.'

He looked dismayed but he let her go. 'I should've kept my big mouth shut.' He stood up. 'No hard feelings?'

She shrugged. 'No, but I told you to begin with, we could only be friends.'

'That's all I want if you say so.'

They walked, slightly apart, to the road and said rather embarrassed goodbyes.

'I'm looking for a Mrs Burton.'

'Who?'

'Mrs Burton.' Connie hoped she'd remembered correctly as she stood in the office for Maternity and Child Welfare.

'There's no one here by that name.' The clerk looked suspiciously like the unpleasant young man that she had talked to three years ago.

'It was in October 1940 when I last spoke to her.' Connie looked over his shoulder to the door beyond. Through the opaque glass she could see someone moving. But she couldn't tell if it was male or female. 'I'd like to discuss a private matter with her.'

This was the wrong thing to say she discovered as the young man's mouth fell open. 'A private matter, you say? Then even if she did work here, this is not the place for personal discussions. We're a very busy department and all our staff are occupied.'

'I see,' Connie said disappointedly. She walked into

the corridor. The long hallway stretched on and on. There were offices on either side. Her spirits sank as she examined the headings on the doors. District boards of Works, Local Government Records, Parish Records – the departments were never ending.

She tried another office. 'I'm looking for a Mrs Burton.'

The answer was the same. No one here by that name.

Was her mission in vain? She had taken the Friday off especially and she only had one day to answer all her questions. Mr Burns had complained when she'd told him it was important. Finally he had agreed, reminding her that a morning would be deducted from her annual holiday.

Her footsteps echoed along the stone floors. When she saw a door marked Ladies' W.C. she went inside. Her cardigan, white blouse and navy blue skirt felt hot. She looked into the long mirror above the row of wash basins. Her hair had fallen across her eyes and there was a damp patch underneath it. She tried to brush it back but her fingers were slippery.

She ran the cold tap. Splashing some water over her face, she looked into the white basin, which was going rusty round the plughole. The water gurgled. She felt as though she was twisting and turning with it.

'Here you are, this might help, love.'

Connie blinked the water from her lashes. An older woman dressed in a green overall was holding out a towel.

'Thank you.' Connie dabbed her face with it.

'You can hang the clean one over the rail there and I'll take the dirty towel. You're not staff are you?'

'No,' Connie admitted.

'This is not really a public W.C.'

'Oh dear. I was just feeling so hot and sticky.'

'Don't mind me, love. Make yourself at home. I'm only the cleaning lady.'

'Do you know many people here?'

She laughed. 'I should do. I've only been working here man and boy for thirty years.'

'This lady was called Mrs Burton. She worked in the Department for Maternity and Welfare in 1940.'

'Peggy Burton, you mean?'

'I don't know if it was Peggy. But it could have been.'

'Well, that's the only one I know and she ain't here now.'

'She was so helpful.'

'Her son was killed in France and she didn't come back to work after that.'

'Oh dear.' Connie's hopes were dashed. 'I really need her advice again.'

'She was salt of the earth was Peggy, a real nice lady. This problem of yours – it is urgent, is it?'

'Oh yes, very.' Connie nodded. 'You see, since 1940 I've looked after a little boy whose mother was killed in the Blitz. His father never showed up and now a man is claiming to be his grandfather, not a very nice man either. He says he's bringing me proof of who he is, but I don't trust him. I was hoping Mrs Burton could give me some advice. I've no one else to turn to.'

The cleaning lady looked hard at her. Then, coming closer, she lowered her voice. 'In that case, I can tell you where Peggy is now.'

Connie's eyes lit up. 'Oh, yes please!'

'Peggy wanted to do something meaningful after her loss, so she started a soup kitchen at the Mission Hall just off Poplar High Street. You said you was desperate and I know Peggy would be first in line to offer her help. Tell her Pops sent you, all right?'

'You don't know what a favour you've done me.'

'Good luck, gel.'

Connie walked out of the building with a new spring in her step. Her journey hadn't been a waste of time after all.

The Mission Hall was now a soup kitchen for the distressed and homeless of the East End. The old building, in former days a chapel, was a hive of industry. In the main area where once the congregation had kneeled, volunteers served a bowl of hot soup to anyone incapacitated enough to warrant it. Four long wooden tables and the chapel's old pews were in full use when Connie arrived close to midday. Three women served the soup and bread, and the kitchen staff were hidden by a thin partition, the smell of cooking permeating to the wooden timbers above.

Connie imagined or estimated at least fifty people sat down to eat at one time. As soon as one got up to leave, another took their place. The queues were long, but orderly. Connie wondered which one of the women was

Peggy Burton. With their hair tied in turbans, and wearing pinafores, she didn't recognize any of them.

'Do you know if Peggy Burton is here today?' Connie asked one of the women.

'Yes, that's me.'

'Oh, thank goodness.' Connie hesitated. 'Pops, the cleaning lady at the council offices, sent me. I was very sorry to hear about your son.'

'Thank you,' Peggy said graciously. 'But who are you?'

'I'm Connie Marsh. I came to see you at the Welfare department after I found a baby boy in the Blitz. His mother had been killed in Haverick Road.'

'Oh yes, I remember you now, Connie. Did the father ever appear?'

'No. It's to do with this that I've come to see you.'

'I see. Well, as you can see we're very busy. But if you want to follow me as I work you're welcome. We're very short staffed and our washer-up, who is eighty-four, needs relieving.'

Connie soon found herself behind the partition where several women were juggling loaves and soup bowls and stirring two huge saucepans on a very ancient stove. In one corner there was a sink and draining board piled high with crockery.

'I'll take over now, Hilda,' Peggy said to the washer-up. The elderly lady stood only a few inches above the drainer. 'Go and make yourself a cup of tea and take it into my room.'

Hilda rolled down her sleeves and scuttled off. Peggy donned a pinafore from a hook by the sink and plunged her hands into the dirty water. 'Now how can I help?'

Connie stared at the mountain of china. 'Actually, I think it should be me asking you that.'

Peggy laughed. 'If you're serious, hang up your cardigan and bag on the hook there. These bowls have to be dried and taken to the tables, where they will soon be refilled. Any dirties you find, return them to me.'

In no time at all, Connie was drying the dishes, delivering them to the diners at the four large tables and hurrying back again. In the few moments she had to spare, she managed to tell Peggy her story.

'Come with me,' Peggy invited Connie after dinner was over. She showed her into the little room which served as the office. 'Lift those boxes up and sit down on the chair.'

Connie didn't know how all the women in the Mission Hall kept so cheerful. Peggy said they had been preparing from eight o'clock that morning. A task they repeated seven days a week.

Peggy sat behind a very old, narrow desk with lots of wooden engravings on the side. It looked like one a minister might read the sermon from. 'That's better. Now we can talk. It gets so busy here you can't hear yourself think.'

Connie rolled down her blouse sleeves. 'You do wonderful work.'

'You haven't seen us on a bad day.'

'What was this then?'

'Oh, a very satisfactory one actually. You turned up, didn't you? The Good Lord always provides.'

'I hope he does,' Connie sighed. 'There are so many people who need help.'

'The numbers have increased with people in transit from the bombing. We only offer food now, but during the Blitz we provided beds as well. So many found themselves homeless, without anywhere to go. The Mission never turned away anyone, I'm proud to say, even if they had to sleep on the pews outside in the backyard. Now it's just soup and bread, but some people stay here all day until we shut the doors at four o'clock.' She narrowed her gaze at Connie. 'Now, back to your little problem, my dear. I take it, Connie, you've grown fond of Lucky?'

'Yes,' Connie admitted. 'But I wouldn't want to rob him of his family. Yet Gilbert Tucker said some awful things about his daughter.'

'Not a very good start,' Peggy agreed.

'I wouldn't want Lucky to hear that kind of talk even if he is Rita's father. What I want to know is, can he take Lucky out of my hands?'

Peggy frowned. 'He'll have to make his case first.'

'Do I have any say in it?'

'You could consult a solicitor and take the case to court.'

'How much will that cost?'

'The expense would be substantial. Do you have any savings or funds available?'

Connie shook her head. 'Only what I earn at Dalton's.'

Peggy sat back thoughtfully. 'You see, Connie, you were fortunate that a lot of red tape was avoided when you applied for care of Lucky. Remember that the government evacuated most of the children in '39? Well, it was only because that plan was unsuccessful and many children were returned to London that homes were so badly needed. This and the fact that the child's father might be local was what stood you in good stead. But it was never meant as a permanent arrangement, as I'm sure you know.'

'But according to Gilbert Tucker, the father is unknown. Surely that gives me some rights as I've been looking after him for so long?'

Peggy was deep in thought. 'Do you know anything more about the mother – who he says is Rita?'

'Only what I've told you.'

'When is he coming back?'

'I don't know.'

Peggy nodded slowly. 'You must see that he brings an official who can make certain everything is done properly.'

Connie's shoulders sagged. 'I can't bear to think of Lucky in the wrong hands. Apart from my concern about him, the woman he was with didn't look capable of caring for a child. She was very strange.'

Peggy gave a little sigh. 'I wish I could help you, Connie.'

They sat in silence for a few seconds until they heard the women outside locking up. 'I must go,' Connie murmured.

Peggy wrinkled her brow. 'I hope it all works out for you,' she said as she joined Connie at the door.

Connie held out her hand. 'I do too, for Lucky's sake.'

Peggy clutched Connie's fingers. 'A greater power than any on earth will help Lucky, I'm sure of it.'

Connie left the Mission Hall, wanting desperately to believe that was true.

Chapter Twenty-One

It was August when the news came through that Allied warships were shelling the coasts of Italy; the Axis on Sicily had finally crumbled to British and American troops.

'Maybe you'll get a letter now,' Len suggested at work. They were sitting in the canteen and Len was enjoying a Woodbine.

'I hope so.' Connie had taken comfort from the other women at work whose men were fighting in Europe. Letters were far and few between.

'He might even get leave.'

'That's my dream, Len. I'm beginning to forget what he looks like.'

'You'll never do that.'

Connie smiled. 'No, I won't.' She paused as she set down her cup. 'How is your mum these days?'

Len rolled his eyes. 'Last week she was Joan Crawford. This week it's Dolores del Rio.'

Connie laughed. 'She's got good taste.'

'That's what Jenny says.'

'Jenny?'

Len nodded as he exhaled. He leaned forward and spoke in a whisper. 'If Ada was here she'd have rumbled us long ago.'

'You mean—?'

Len nodded slowly, his eyes twinkling. 'Keep it under your hat though.'

Connie couldn't believe it. 'You sly old fox. How long has this been going on?'

'Oh, a while.'

'But you hardly spoke to each other at the Christmas party.'

'We made up for it after.' Len chuckled at the expression on Connie's face. 'Don't look so shocked. Although, to be honest, no one is more surprised than me. With Mum an' all I'd lost hope of ever having a life of my own. Then, after work one day, Jenny comes up and asks after Mother. I make a joke of it, as usual, telling her how Mrs Next Door is sworn off the films for life, and then Jenny says, why doesn't she sit in for an hour at the weekend to give me a break?' Len raised his eyebrows. 'Well, I wasn't about to refuse, was I?'

'And that's how it started?'

'I thought she'd get tired of us, but she hasn't. Quite a little routine on a Sunday we've got going. Cooks a nice roast does our Jenny, even with rationing.'

'Oh, Len, you could knock me down with a feather.'

Len winked. 'Don't go letting on, now. I decided to tell you 'cos you'd be all for it, not like some of the others round here.'

'I won't tell a soul.' Connie giggled. 'Do I hear the distant sound of wedding bells?'

'You might,' grinned Len, stubbing out his cigarette. 'But I'm not rushing things. I know when I'm on to a good thing, and I don't want to spoil it, if you know what I mean.'

'Jenny's a lucky girl,' Connie said as they stood up. 'She's landed the best bloke here at Dalton's.'

Len blushed, a phenomenon Connie had never seen before, and they walked out of the canteen, smiling secretively. Connie felt happy there was romance in the air and that Len trusted her enough to confide his secret.

Len's news was still in her mind when she left work. She thought about it all the way home, laughing to herself at the thought of Jenny cooking a Sunday roast for Len and his mother. She could imagine Mrs English sitting down at the table in a feather boa and a sparkly tiara. If Jenny could take all the drama on board, and still manage to court Len, then she deserved a medal. It was surprising what people could do when in love. She had never seen Len look so happy. If she had not been so preoccupied with her own troubles, she would have noticed sooner. As Len had remarked, Ada would have spotted the affair a mile off!

Connie was smiling as she turned the corner of Kettle Street. The thought of Jenny and Mrs English was still amusing her as she pushed open Nan's unlatched front door. Expecting to hear Lucky's familiar call, 'Con-Con!', she paused in the hall.

'Hello, everyone! I'm home.'

But it was not Lucky who emerged from the front room, but her mother, with her hands clasped tightly together. Connie's smile faded as she looked into Olive's ashen face.

'Mum? What are you doing here?' Her dad appeared then and Lofty.

'What's the matter? Where's Lucky?'

'Come in the front room, love,' her dad said quietly.

'Dad, where's Lucky?' Her voice was high. She knew something had happened but why weren't they telling her? 'Is he ill? Has he had an accident?'

'No, nothing like that.'

Connie let herself be led into the front room. Nan was sitting in the chair, her eyes red with weeping. When she saw Connie, she tried to stand up, then sank down again. 'Oh, Connie, love, I'm so sorry. I didn't know what to do!'

Lofty patted his wife's shoulder. 'Now then, love. There was nothing we could do.'

'Sit down, Con,' said her father. 'It's bad news, I'm afraid.'

Connie felt her legs give way and she sank lifelessly on to the couch. 'Gilbert Tucker's been, hasn't he?'

Her mother sat beside her. 'He came this afternoon. A government official was with him.'

'Why didn't someone come for me at work?' Connie wailed.

'There was no time,' her dad replied quietly. 'Besides, it would have only been more painful for you. Nothing you could have said would've made any difference. They had the law on their side.'

Connie looked bewildered. 'What happened?'

'Gilbert Tucker is Lucky's grandad. They showed us the papers. It was all in black and white for us to see. You can't argue with the fact he's the boy's family.'

'That strange woman isn't though,' Connie sobbed. 'How can they take a little child from the ones who love him and give him to those who don't?'

'Now, Connie, that's not fair.' Ebbie's voice was reproving.

'Dad – you saw them when they came round. You heard what Gilbert Tucker said.'

'I did, but we couldn't have seemed very friendly either.'

Connie brushed away the hot tears. 'Why do you think Lucky's mum asked me to look after her baby?'

'Because the poor girl was dying, of course,' her mother answered.

'I don't think it was,' Connie said fiercely. 'I think she was frightened enough to ask a perfect stranger rather than take the chance of Gilbert Tucker finding him.'

Ebbie's face hardened. 'Connie, that's very far-fetched.'

'It's not, Dad. I know it in my heart.'

'I'll agree your heart is ruling your head,' Olive said, patting her hand. 'Be sensible now, dear. We've done everything to help you and Lucky and we know you're upset – and it hurt us just as much as it's hurting you. But shouldn't we be pleased, that one of Lucky's relatives was found after all this time?'

Ebbie sighed heavily. 'You're young yet and will raise a family of your own soon. You'll get over Lucky in time.'

But Connie knew she wouldn't. She ran out of the room and into the street. She could hear Olive calling after her but all she wanted was Lucky. Where was he now? Was he missing her? It was time for his tea, the best time of all, when they had fun before he went to bed.

She stopped at the gate of number thirty-three. She couldn't go in. Not without Lucky inside.

It was growing dark when Billy found her. She was leaning on the fence by the tunnel entrance in Island Gardens. She had walked for hours and though it was summer she felt chilled to the bone. She knew it was an inner chill that would stay with her for a long time to come.

'Connie?' Billy said quietly, standing beside her. 'Where've you been, gel?'

The view had been breathtaking as the sun had dipped over Greenwich. The sky was dusky now, almost dark. A few stars were out early and they twinkled between the clouds. 'I watched the sunset,' she said in an empty voice.

Billy drew her closer. 'I called in to see Mum and Dad. They're worried about you.'

She turned to stare at her brother. He looked much older now, scarred and puffy around the eyes and ears, as though time had weighed heavily on him. She felt a moment's sorrow, but her heart was aching too much with her own loss to feel his.

Connie stared back at the river, now a dark, inky shape curling eastward. The vessels that slipped up and down in the day were now in their berths. The hustle and bustle was over until daybreak. Somehow the night felt like a friend, disguising the hurt inside.

'I'm really sorry about Lucky,' Billy said softly.

'He didn't deserve what was done to him.'

'Neither did you.' He leaned close beside her. 'But you couldn't have done anything to stop it.'

She looked at him. 'I used to pretend he was my little boy. Even if I had kids of my own, I couldn't love him more.'

'I know that, Con.'

Her voice shook. 'I don't even know where he is.'

Billy put his arm around her shoulders. 'Maybe that's for the best.'

Connie hung her head. 'In my heart I knew Gilbert Tucker was his grandfather. Even Gran told me to be prepared, but I just wouldn't listen.'

Billy squeezed her shoulder. 'I'd give my right arm to bring him back for you.'

She smiled weakly. 'You'd be no good at fighting if you did.'

Billy was silent as he stood there. 'I never have been, to tell the truth.'

She turned slowly. 'What do you mean?'

'I'm no fighter, sis.'

'Billy, that's not true.'

'I'm quitting the fight game.'

'But what about America?'

339

He laughed. 'The only stars I'll ever see is on the end of a fist.'

'But boxing is your life, Billy.'

'Not any more. I'm joining up.'

'You can't! You're not eighteen.'

'I am in December. 'Sides, they're taking anyone they can get hold of. It's not just Germany we're up against. The army needs blokes to fight the Japs now.'

'Oh, Billy, please don't do it. I beg you not to. Mum wants you back home—'

'Me life's changed, Con. I've got to move on, don't you see?'

Connie felt she couldn't take any more bad news tonight. She hugged him close.

'Remember that night, Con?' he whispered into her hair. 'When we was down this way together, the first night of the Blitz? When you found Lucky?'

'How could I ever forget?'

'I didn't even hang around to help you. Same as I never went back to see if that old bloke was all right. I left him there, like I left you. I've never been able to get it out of my mind that I'm a coward, see?'

'That's daft, Billy.' She held him away from her, her big grown-up kid brother who was now twice her size. 'I've never stopped being proud of you, never.'

'It don't make any difference, Con, to the way I feel inside. You know what I think each time I get a wallop? I think, you deserve that, you gutless bugger. Taffy was right, I ain't got the balls for fighting, much less boxing. All I was cut out for was being a bit of a hellion and causing trouble.'

'Billy, you were young. You just made some mistakes like all of us.'

'I've got to do what my conscience tells me. You did a good thing that night and saved a life. As usual, I looked after number one.'

Connie held him tightly. 'I love you, Billy.'

'I know that.' He prised her gently away. 'You ready to go home now?'

She knew it wouldn't be easy, not with all Lucky's toys and clothes and his bed in her room. But she had to face them. Life had to go on.

Billy waited silently in the shadows of Narrow Street. It was a quarter to midnight and the moon was hidden in a cloudy sky. The streets of Limehouse were all blacked out. The building he had been watching, a terraced flat, showed no sign of life. But, then, he hadn't expected any. His knew his quarry would arrive any time now.

Sure enough, a car drew up. He recognized the shape of the two figures climbing out. Their voices travelled to him, though it was a windless night. Soon the man and woman entered a doorway. The crack of light was soon extinguished.

Billy stepped out into the deserted street.

He was sweating and licked the salt from his lips. The adrenaline burst through his veins. He stepped lightly to the door and listened. The raised voices continued up the stairway. He'd been up those stairs often enough himself and he'd never liked what he found at the top.

With his back against the wall he shifted noiselessly

into the building. At the top of the staircase he paused, looking left then right along the landing.

The door to the front room was ajar. The argument was in full swing, the man's voice raised, the woman's scared and pleading.

Ada came into view. The blow across her face was hard. She stumbled back, her red hair flying as she buckled and fell.

Billy crept lightly along the landing. Then booted the door.

Freddie Smith looked surprised. 'What the fuck do you want?'

'Call it a courtesy visit,' Billy said as he helped Ada to her feet. 'Courtesy to Ada.'

She recoiled from him. 'Christ, Billy, you shouldn't be here.'

'Go and wait downstairs.'

'But, Billy—'

'Do as I say.' He gave her a gentle push through the door.

'What the—' Freddie Smith began until he got a fist in his stomach and, choking, staggered backward.

'You set me up from the start.' Billy rubbed his knuckles happily. Why had he never felt like this in the ring? He'd have won every fight if he'd felt the hate he felt now.

'After this, you're brown bread, Billy Marsh. I'll be after your arse. There won't be nowhere you can hide.'

'I'm not even gonna try. It's just you and me tonight, or haven't you noticed?'

Freddie Smith laughed. 'You couldn't fight your way out of a brown paper bag.'

Billy nodded slowly. 'I couldn't agree more, pal. Wish I'd known that a year ago though, before you grabbed the chance to tuck me up. Still, now it's my turn to have a little fun. But before I do, I'll tell you this. You bother Ada or set foot on the island and I'm blowing the whistle on all them dodgy deals you've got carved out for yourself and your pals. Now, they ain't gonna like the taste of their own shite, are they? Not them boys, Freddie. You're gonna be carved into little slices and you know it.'

The big man standing in front of him froze. 'You wouldn't dare!'

'Try me.' Billy gazed into the other man's face, relishing his discomfort. Slowly he removed his jacket and the belt from his trousers. He didn't want the bastard complaining it was an unfair fight. No, Freddie Smith was going down tonight and this time the odds weren't stacked in his favour.

Billy had always wondered what the killer instinct felt like. Now he knew. This was one reckoning he was going to look back on with pride.

One fight he was definitely going to win.

'Billy, what have you done?' Ada was breathing rapidly as he hurried her along the street. She had been sitting at the bottom of the stairs when he found her, nursing her swollen cheek.

'What I should have done a long time ago.'

'He'll come after us.'

'No he won't.'

'Billy, I'm scared.'

'Listen, Ada. Freddie Smith is yesterday's news. Trust me.'

'But all my things are in the flat.'

'Have you got any money in your bag?'

'A bit. My emergency fund.'

'Well, this is an emergency. You can nip up the market and buy some other clothes tomorrow. Unless you want to go back there and mop him up off the floor.'

'He's not dead, is he?'

Billy pushed her into a doorway. 'Do you care if he is?' he demanded breathlessly.

'Oh, Gawd, Billy, don't frighten me any more than I am.'

'He's not dead, but he won't be walking a straight line for a while.'

Ada gave a terrified sob. 'I never meant for this to happen.'

'Do you love him?'

Her lips trembled. 'I thought I did once. But not any more.'

Billy felt a tightness relax in his chest. 'Ada, this is your chance to be free. I've seen you bashed around like a football and treated like a tart. Is that the kind of life you want for yourself?'

She began crying and Billy pulled her to him. He held her tight, wiping the tears from her cheeks with his thumbs.

'Oh, Billy, you ain't 'alf brave to do what you did.'

'I should've done it a long time ago.'

'Billy—'

'Shh.' He lifted her chin gently and kissed her. The tears ran in between their lips and into his mouth. He kissed her harder, the passion growing inside him.

'Billy, oh Billy!'

He ran his fingers up into her hair and felt the warmth of her, smelled the scent on her skin that made his body shudder. He was a fully grown man now, nigh on eighteen, yet his knees still trembled like they'd done at fourteen when he'd first ever fancied her. 'Come on,' he whispered, as he kissed her bruised cheek. 'We're going home.'

'I've not got a home to go to in case you'd forgotten.'

He slid his hand around her waist as he urged her forward. 'Despite me daft looks, I've got a very good memory indeed.'

Connie was staring at Lucky's little bed. In the darkness, she imagined him there, tucked under his eiderdown. She listened for the sounds of his breathing: the snuffles, the soft moans, the small arm flung sideways. And his voice when he came awake.

'Con-Con?'

'I'm here, darling.'

She would leap out of bed and hold him in her arms. Then she'd tell him a story, stroke his soft blond hair and he'd drift off to sleep again. Many times she wondered if he'd been dreaming of the night when she'd found him. What had happened in the hours before? Had Rita been frightened of the bombing? Had her intuition told her to hide her baby? Could Lucky, in his baby mind, recall any of this?

He'd had a proper name once. What was it? Would she ever see him again? The questions went on endlessly. Each morning she got up and went to work. Each night she came home, sat in the front room, sometimes with Mum and Dad, sometimes Kevin and Sylvie, occasionally Billy. The only change in routine was her fire-watching duties. Without Lucky to look after, she was now included in the fire-watching rota at Dalton's. London was by no means safe from attack. Everyone was still expected to do their duty.

Every night Connie climbed into bed and lay awake, no matter how tired she felt. The emptiness was growing inside her instead of disappearing. Lucky's train and all his toys were tucked under the bed. Nan said she had given the government official some of his clothes and his little blue elephant. But it was what Nan hadn't commented on that distressed her the most. Had he cried when he was taken away? He was a friendly child, but wary of strangers. In her mind, Connie imagined the worst. His eyes full of tears and his arms stretched out. She knew Nan didn't want to talk about it. Nor did her mum and dad. They said it was better to look forward rather than back. She knew they meant well, but she didn't want Lucky's memory to die. He had been part of all their lives. And he was still part of hers.

Tonight was no exception. Connie was more restless than ever. In three days' time, Lucky would have lived at number thirty-three Kettle Street for three years. He had grown into a beautiful, affectionate, happy toddler. Now she would never take him to school and help him to read and write. Even her worries about Vic were eclipsed by her loss. She didn't feel like Connie Marsh any more. She felt like an empty shell. Each day she went through the motions, but it was hard to act as though her world was normal.

Connie turned over and faced the wall. She closed her eyes, praying for sleep. She had been trying hard to keep them closed when she heard the front door open. A few moments later she heard the stairs creak. A light touch on her shoulder made her jump.

'Who's that?'

'Me, Billy.' He sat on her bed. In the darkness she couldn't see his smile but she knew he had one on his face. 'I've got something to tell you.'

'At this hour?' She sat up.

'I've got a person downstairs who wants to see you. She won't come up, 'cos she's frightened you'll tell her to sling her hook.'

Connie swallowed. 'What are you talking about, Billy Marsh?'

He leaned forward and his face caught the light. 'Put on your glad rags and follow me.'

Connie was out of bed in five seconds flat.

Chapter Twenty-Two

'Leave the light off, Con.'

Connie gasped. 'Ada? Is that you?'

'Who do you think it is, silly cow.'

'Now I know it's you.' She stepped forward in the darkness and the breath was almost knocked out of her as they collided.

'Oh, Connie!' Ada hugged her tight. For a moment they stood there, crying and laughing together.

'Keep it down, girls, if you don't want to wake everyone up,' Billy said behind them.

'That's the pot calling the kettle black,' Connie replied, gulping. 'You'd better close that door.'

'I'm off then. Goodnight, you two.'

Ada let go of Connie. 'Billy?' She moved in the darkness towards him. 'Thanks for tonight.'

'Just make sure you stick to your guns now.'

'I will. I'm never going back.'

'Going back where?' Connie whispered when they were alone. 'And why are we standing in the dark? The blackout's up, no one can see us outside.'

'It's what you can see inside that worries me,' Ada said

softly. 'If you switch the light on, be prepared for a shock.'

Connie put on the light. She took a sharp breath when she saw Ada's black eye.

'I warned you.' Ada put a hand over her cheek.

'What happened?' Connie groaned.

'There was a bit of a ding dong, and I got landed one. But Billy sorted it all out.'

'A ding dong? Who with?'

'Oh, Con, I've got so much to tell you. Let's sit down and I'll tell you everything.' Ada caught her arm and pulled her to the couch. 'I haven't half missed you.' They embraced and Connie inhaled Ada's scent. She sat back, a look of surprise on her face. 'I know where I smelled that before, it's on my scarf, the one Billy bought me at Christmas. I never washed it because the smell's so lovely.'

'I sprinkled a bit of me perfume on it,' Ada confessed. 'Billy asked me to choose a present for you, so I went up to John Lewis's and bought it 'specially.'

'Billy never let on about anything.'

'I made him promise not to.'

'But why? Where have you been all this time?'

'I shacked up with Freddie Smith, the bloke we saw in the pub that night we went to watch Billy. I lied to you about not seeing him again. We started going out and that was it.'

'Is he why you left Wally?'

'Yes and no. It was lots of things, really.'

'You could have written to me.'

'I was worried you'd try to talk me into coming back to Wally.'

Connie frowned in confusion. 'But we're best friends, have been since we were kids. I thought we shared everything. Didn't you think how worried I was about you?'

Ada hung her head. 'I knew you wouldn't approve, see. And, anyway, I didn't really have a plan. It just seemed exciting at the time to go off with Freddie and leave all my cares behind. Wally's sister was getting on me tits and his mum had started to nag. Freddie was all flattery, telling me I was wasting myself on a chump like Wally who couldn't even stand up to his own family. He was generous with money and bought me new clothes and perfume and anything I wanted really.' Look at this dress, for instance, it cost a lot.' She smoothed the skirt of her midnight blue dress under a little white bolero, then fingered the shimmering ivory pearls around her neck. Her red hair was still a lovely colour but her black eye was all shades of green and purple.

'Clothes and possessions aren't everything,' Connie said gently.

'I know, but they don't 'alf help. You know how vain I am about my appearance. I just can't help it.'

Connie's eyebrows shot up. 'So is a black eye the height of fashion by any chance?'

Ada giggled. 'Don't make me laugh, it hurts.'

'No, it's no laughing matter, that's obvious. Why did he hit you?'

Ada shrugged. 'When he has one over the eight he gets a bit short tempered.'

'In other words, he can't take his drink and lashes out at women.'

'I wouldn't put it like that.'

Connie looked at her friend helplessly. 'Ada, I simply don't understand. This isn't the Ada I once knew, who wouldn't have accepted such behaviour from any man. My God, if the situation was reversed and I was involved with a bully, you'd have gone up the wall.'

'I know, I know! I hate blokes that are handy with their fists on women. I despise them. But I'm ashamed to say I liked the lifestyle he provided. I was given things I never had in my life before. I never had to lift a finger. All I'd do all day was dust a few things in this nice flat we lived in, down Limehouse, or go out shopping up West. I saved up and sent Mum over twenty quid.'

'So you let a man beat you in exchange for money?'

'It wasn't like that,' Ada replied defensively. 'You might not believe this, but at first I thought it was true love.'

'You always do,' Connie reminded her friend gently. 'Wally was the reason you parted company with your family, remember? And stayed on the island while it was being bombed to smithereens.'

Ada nodded sadly. 'It all changed when I moved in with Saint Jean. If he'd taken me out a bit more I could have swallowed on a lot. But he was content to sit around like we was an old married couple.' Ada looked up under her long eyelashes, the right set being stuck down on her swollen cheek. 'You know me, Con. I like a bit of excitement in life.'

'So what happened to spoil this romantic interlude?' Connie asked ruefully.

'Your little brother, that's what.'

'Billy?'

Ada nodded. 'I knew what Freddie was doing to Billy and it made me sick. Freddie's a fixer, that means a bloke that makes things happen for the big syndicates who've got a lot of money riding on fixed contests. They've no interest in the fighter personally, only the result, which is decided before the match. Billy was set up to lose from the start. In the end, all Freddie's hopefuls turn into punch bags.'

Connie sighed as she began to understand. 'So that's why Billy has decided to give up boxing. Now it makes sense. But how did Billy find out the truth?'

'I told him. Though I might have thought twice if I'd known what Billy would do.' She touched her face cautiously, wincing as her fingers pressed on the swelling. 'When me and Freddie came home from this club, Billy was waiting and caught Freddie clobbering me. He gave Freddie the bashing of his life. I heard it all as I sat at the bottom of the stairs. Honest to God, Con, I was scared out of me wits.' Ada giggled. 'You should have seen your brother tonight, Con. He really stuck up for me. More than any bloke has ever done before.'

'Well, if I've Billy to thank for you being here, then that's all that matters. I was dead miserable when you left Dalton's. I blamed myself for the row we had over Clint. You were right. He's a really nice bloke who doesn't deserve the cold shoulder.'

Ada tried to look flirtatious with her one good eye. 'Is he still on the scene?'

Connie nodded. 'He even played the trumpet at the

Christmas party. You would have loved it. He can dance too.' She went a little pink.

Ada gasped. 'Are you telling me Vic's got competition?'

'Course not.'

'Where is Vic? Have you heard from him?'

'He's somewhere in Europe but I don't know where.'

'Oh, Con, you must have had a rotten time, what with—' She stopped as she slid her arm around Connie's shoulders. 'Billy told me about Lucky. I can't believe they would take him behind your back. Do you still miss him?'

'Of course I do.'

'Is there any chance of him coming back?'

'Not unless I had enough money to pay a solicitor. Even then, Gilbert Tucker has rights over me. I try not to think about Lucky but then I start worrying. Are they looking after him? Is he missing me? What if they can't understand what he says? What if he doesn't eat or gets ill? What if—'

'Now, now,' Ada soothed, squeezing Connie's hand. 'Kids are very resilient. I should know with me sisters. I used to look after them when I was younger and Mum worked. Don't you remember when she was ill with TB one year and had to go into a sanatorium? I was only fourteen and had to look after them. I couldn't go down the flicks with you on Saturday afternoons or anything. As for the girls, they bawled their eyes out for the first week, then got back to normal the next.'

'Are you saying Lucky won't miss me?'

'No, I'm saying he'll get accustomed to the change quicker than you will.' She sat forward and looked into Connie's face. 'What I'm worried about is the weight you've lost. You don't look up to much at all.'

'It is the middle of the night you know.'

'Talking of which, could I kip on your couch?' Ada asked hopefully.

Connie grinned. 'You can sleep in Lucky's bed if you like. It's small, but you can curl up on it.'

'Oh ta, Con.' Ada stifled a yawn. 'When we're in bed you can tell me all your news,' she whispered as they tip-toed out of the room.

But when Ada's head hit the pillow she was asleep in seconds. Connie lay awake, going over everything in her mind. There would be time enough tomorrow to catch up on their lives. Thank goodness it was Sunday.

'You're welcome to stay, Ada,' Olive said after breakfast the next morning. 'In fact, I'm glad of the company for Constance. She's not been herself since you, er . . .'

'Ran away,' Ada said, going pink.

'Thanks, Mrs Marsh. I'm really grateful. I feel awful about what I did. I didn't realize how much I'd hurt other people.'

Olive patted Ada's hand. 'How did you sleep on the cot bed?'

'Like a log.'

'I could always ask Nan for the loan of her put-u-up and leave it down here.'

'No ta, Mrs M., I like being with Con.'

Olive put on her hat and coat. 'Me and Dad are going up to Christ Church for morning service. It's not often we do, but there's special prayers being held for our boys in the front line. You're both welcome to join us if you want, but I should imagine you've a lot to talk over.'

They both nodded, and, as Kevin and Billy were out, they spent the next few hours gossiping in the front room. The news of Jenny and Len's affair came as a surprise to Ada, and she laughed loudly when Connie told her the story of Mrs English turning up at Dalton's in her underwear and wanted to know all the details of the missed Christmas party.

'I'd have enjoyed meself all right,' Ada sighed regretfully. 'Sounds like you did, even without your Vic.'

'He was in America, wasn't he?' Connie was loath to admit she was jealous, but equally reluctant to say she'd let her hair down on the dance floor with Clint. 'I wasn't going to make the same mistake twice and be thought of as a snob,' she added pointedly.

At this remark, Ada was silent as she curled her feet under her bottom on the couch. 'I wished I'd never called you that. It was a bad time for me what with Jean always on my back and Wally ignorant of my presence in his life. It's no excuse, I know, but when I look back on that time I get a real depressed feeling. Even worse than lately with Freddie.'

'Will you go and see Wally?'

Ada shook her head. 'I don't think he'd appreciate my appearance, do you? One day, though, I'll tell him I'm sorry.'

'He'd probably have you back. He was crackers over you once.'

Ada smiled. 'He's better off without me. I don't think I could ever have loved him if our relationship couldn't survive his family. I've been doing a lot of thinking and come to the conclusion I need someone strong to boss me round a bit.'

'What makes you say that?'

Ada considered this question carefully. 'Freddie is a womanizer, a liar and a cheat. But he's also good looking and charming when he wants to be. He knows how to treat a woman when he isn't pissed.'

Connie looked shocked. 'Are you considering going back to him, then?'

Ada grimaced. 'Not bloody likely I'm not.'

'What about Dalton's?' Connie asked. 'You could speak to Len and ask him to put in a word with Mr Burns for you.'

'I don't think I could work in an office again,' Ada admitted. 'At least I've had a chance to find out how much I hate being cooped up. The only good bit was you and Len and the other girls. I'll miss all that, but I won't miss the routine and boredom.'

'What will you do then?'

Ada drummed her fingers on her knee. 'I might join the WAAFS or the WVS.'

Connie laughed. 'I can't see you in a uniform.'

Ada looked offended. 'I always fancy blokes in them, so why not?' She threw back her red head. 'Anyway, I'm footloose and fancy free now. I can please meself.'

'Oh, Ada, you haven't changed!'

'I don't think I ever will, Con. I'm too selfish to share my life with someone else. Not like you and Vic. You two was made for each other. You're one of them couples that will walk off into the sunset holding hands, with the birds and the bees flying around their heads and romantic music playing in the background.'

'Is that what you think love is?' Connie asked as her fingers turned the slim gold band of her engagement ring.

'On the films it's always like that.'

'But films are made to make sense of people's lives,' Connie said as she tried to think of how to express her views. 'They always come to a satisfactory end, even if it's sad. But in reality life just goes on, taking you with it through all the ups and downs. And if you love someone enough, you hang on through it all.'

Ada looked sad. 'Do you think I should have hung on with Wally?'

'Only if you loved him.'

'Maybe I would have if I'd tried harder.'

Connie lifted her shoulders. 'I don't know what to say.'

Ada was silent until she giggled softly. 'Well, that definition of love certainly don't match up to mine.'

'And what's that?'

'To be honest, I only get as far as a bit of slap and tickle.'

They both collapsed into fits of laughter and were making so much noise they almost didn't hear the knock.

'Someone's at the front door.' Connie pulled herself

up, wiping the tears of laughter from her eyes as she went into the hall.

'Thank God you're in,' Pat gulped breathlessly, her cardigan open and her chest rising heavily under her frock. 'I dunno what I'd have done if you wasn't.'

Connie looked over her shoulder. 'Where are the kids?'

'I've left them with Eve Beale.'

Connie gently pulled her in. 'What's wrong.'

Pat leaned against the wall. Her brown hair was sweat laden and her eyes looked strangely bright. 'It's Gran. She got a telegram.' Pat licked her dry lips. 'I'm sorry to tell you this, Con, but it said that Vic is missing. I thought at first it might be Laurie – oh God, I nearly died. I only got a letter from him last week, too. Then when it said Vic's name I just couldn't believe it either.'

Connie stared into Pat's face. 'Vic is missing?' she repeated numbly.

'When Gran was reading it, she kind of, well, keeled over. It was awful. Terrible. She was lying on the floor and me and the kids were screaming and Albie rushed in and then Eve—'

Ada appeared from the front room. 'Hello, Pat. Did I hear Vic's name mentioned?'

Pat nodded. 'Gran got a telegram . . . it said he's gone missing.'

Connie felt the same sinking sensation she'd had on the day they took Lucky. 'What about Gran?' she asked in barely a whisper.

'I don't know – the doctor's come and she's in bed.' She began to sob.

'I'll get my coat and come with you.'

'Me too,' Ada said quickly. 'Can I borrow a skirt or something, Con? I've only got my blue dress.'

'Look in the wardrobe and take what you want.'

Ten minutes later they were all hurrying towards East Ferry Road.

Gran was trying to see where she was. She didn't recognize this place. Where was she? It was nice and light, no dark shadows or cobwebby ceilings. The thought reminded her that her own ceilings needed dusting and briefly she felt a wave of tiredness, an inner tiredness that she couldn't quite put her finger on. She used to have plenty of energy before the war. It was as if the enemy hadn't just dropped bombs, but sapped people's spirits, too. Even Albie said that lately he'd been nodding off over his pint at the Queens. Funny, she couldn't see Albie now, yet he was here a minute ago. Where was Pat and the kids? The house felt empty without them. But, then, this wasn't her house, was it?

She looked around again. Slowly, the light grew even brighter and a warm upliftment filled her. Like . . . like being young again. Yes, that was it! The sense of wonder when you looked up into an endless blue sky, or breathed in the change between seasons. Or when you paddled in the river mud and squeezed it between your toes. There was so much to discover when the tide went out.

Bobby was best at mudlarking. Her elder brother had the biggest feet in the family, with long, curling toes like the beak of bird. He used them to find treasures in the warm, black silt. There he was now, barefoot. Ribbons of black hair running wild down his shoulders. Trousers rolled up around his ankles, braces knotted, shirt patched and darned. Gran waved.

'Well, if it ain't me kid sister, Alice!' He slapped a muddy hand on her shoulder. 'Where've you been all this time?'

Gran shook her head. 'To be honest, I don't know where I've been.'

'Blimey, you lost yer memory, then?'

Gran studied him closely. 'Bobby, you don't look a day older than when you—' she stopped as her brother nodded.

'It was the current that did for me, gel. One minute I was swimming south towards Greenwich, the next I was on me way out to sea.'

Gran felt sad. 'We missed you. Especially Mother.'

Bobby nodded. 'She tanned my hide till I could barely walk when she found out what me and the other boys was doing. But a hiding never made no difference and I still went ahead and did it.'

'You should have listened to her, Bobby.'

'Yeah, but a dare was a dare, see? We all wanted to be first over. Course, I've swum the river hundreds of time since. Look, I'll show you.' Laughing, he ran into the grey, murky water.

Gran felt a moment's unease. 'Bobby, come back!' she called.

'It's all right, you can do anything you want to now.' He began to swim and something told Gran there was nothing to worry about any more.

She walked along the shore and saw a group of figures. Wasn't that Mother and Dad, her sisters and brothers, too?

A soldier, ramrod straight in his uniform, stepped out of their midst and strode towards her.

'Why, Alice.' He smiled, taking her hands. 'You're here!'

'Maurice?'

'I've been waiting for so long, my darling. We all have.'

Gran was perplexed. She was normally so punctual. 'I would have come sooner if I'd known the time.'

He gently touched her face. A feeling of great peace descended. The light was so beautiful, filling the figures surrounding her until they almost glowed. If she didn't know better, she would have said they were angels.

A young man appeared. He touched her shoulder. 'Mother?'

She squinted through the brightness. 'Freddie? Is it really you, son? Or am I dreaming?' A little flutter, like the tips of birds' wings, troubled her tummy. 'I can't see properly.'

'You will. Step forward. It's easy.'

Gran tried to but something held her back. 'What's wrong with me, Maurice?' She wanted to go towards the light not back into the dark from where she had started.

'There's something you still have to do,' he whispered.

'But what is it?' she cried. 'I've forgotten what it is.'

They all stood around her then, her family, her bloodline, bathed in a radiance that she yearned to be part of.

She had been seeing these lights all her life and didn't know what they were until now. What a discovery to make so late in life! She wouldn't have ever doubted if she'd known there really was a stairway to heaven.

As she thought of the word heaven, a great force gripped her. She was swept away, sucked into a vacuum, returned to the darkness again. She had so wanted to stay. Why couldn't she see or move? Why had the light faded and left her stranded like this?

A voice called her. She moved, a little clumsily, towards it. Then she felt the power of those who loved her, willing her on through the pain. And suddenly, with perfect clarity, she recalled exactly what she had returned for.

Dr Deakin took Connie aside. 'I've done all I can. She's very weak, but she's holding on, though for how long I can't say. In my opinion, it would be better for her to remain at home than be moved to hospital.'

'Isn't there something you can do?'

He smiled gently. 'If there was, I would have done it by now.'

Connie looked at the bed. Pat was sitting beside it holding Gran's hand. Gran looked very peaceful, but small, as if she had shrunk to half her size since yesterday.

'Can she hear us?' Connie asked.

The doctor nodded. 'Most certainly. She's drifting in and out of consciousness but she may not be able to respond clearly.' He took his case. 'I'll come immediately if you send for me, otherwise I'll call first thing in the morning.'

Connie saw him out. She returned to the kitchen, where Ada was making tea.

'What did he say?'

Connie told her.

Ada sat down with a sigh. 'What can we do to help?'

'Nothing, I don't think.'

'How's Pat?'

'She's taking it hard. I've left her to have a bit of time alone.'

'Course,' Ada said quietly, then looked at Connie. 'The telegram's in the front room. I saw it lying on the table.'

Connie nodded silently. She didn't want to go in there to read it.

'Want me to come with you?'

'No, it's all right.'

She went into the front room. It was as it always was, neat and tidy, smelling of lavender and ash. The only disturbance was the fireguard standing to one side of the grate, a brush and pan beside it. Gran must have been cleaning it when the telegram arrived.

An envelope lay on the table, a loose sheet of paper beside it. Connie seated herself on the dining chair. She stared at the odd-shaped letters that looked as if they'd been cut from the newspaper.

'Priority: Mrs Alice Champion.' Connie's heart raced as her eyes moved down the page. '. . .deeply regret to inform you . . . your grandson . . . Lieutenant Victor Champion . . . missing as a result of combined operations, Sicily 6–10 June 1943 STOP Any further information forwarded to you immediately STOP Pending receipt of written notification from the Admiralty STOP.'

She read it once more. 'Missing as a result of combined operations.' What did that mean? If someone went missing, where did they go?

Suddenly Pat rushed in, her eyes wide and staring. 'Gran's awake! She's trying to speak.'

They both ran into the bedroom. Pat stood as if in a dream, then began to sob. Connie sat on the edge of the bed. She took Gran's hand. It felt smaller than ever, as delicate as paper.

'Gran, it's me, Connie. Pat's here too.'

Gran's short, black eyelashes fluttered on her cheek. She mumbled and Connie leaned closer.

'I'm here, Gran. Pat and me are with you.'

Frail fingers tightened across her thumb. 'He's not on the other side, girl. I looked.'

'Looked for who, Gran?'

A smile flickered on her lips. Connie watched her facial expressions change, saw her skin soften over the round bone of her cheeks and smooth out across her forehead. She looked almost transparent, as though she was made of glass. 'I saw everyone else, Mother and Dad, Maurice and Freddie, too. Bobby was in the river, swimming the Reach . . .'

'That was a lovely dream.'

Gran's eyes flickered open. 'You've got lovely lights again, all pink and blue with a bit of orange and purple, exactly the way they should be.'

Connie squeezed the tiny hand tight. For a moment she thought Gran was going to speak, but her eyes closed. She looked serene and peaceful and when the last breath slipped from her lips Connie thought she was witness to the face of a young girl, at the beginning of life, not at the end of it.

'Gran?' Pat dropped to her knees beside the bed.

'She's at rest now, Pat. I know she is.' Connie reached out, pulling Pat against her to absorb the sobs.

Then despite the overcast sky outside it was as if the sun broke through the clouds and spilled a lustrous glow of golden lights across the bed.

Even Pat, in her deep distress, seemed to sense it. Her weeping ceased and the smell of the river's mud washed into the room. In the distance they heard children's voices and the echo of a ship's horn, making headway against the tide and ploughing out to the wide open spaces of the sea.

Chapter Twenty-Three

Gran was buried in East London Cemetery on a fine September morning. The burial plot was marked by a mossy green headstone bearing the names of her husband, Maurice, her son, Frederick, and his wife, Josephine. The cost of the interment was borne by Gran's thriftiness, an insurance she had maintained since her husband died in the war. Her friends and neighbours attended, most of whom had lived in East Ferry Road or somewhere close by for as long as they could remember. Alice Ethel Champion had lived sixty-eight years of a full and productive life and Connie knew that Gran would want her passing celebrated rather than mourned.

Albie Cross paid tribute to her at the graveside. 'Not a churchgoer, nor a do-gooder, nor a bible-basher. But to my mind there's not anyone in church of a Sunday that could hold a candle to Alice Champion.'

'She was generous to a fault,' Eve Beale agreed. 'And wasn't afraid to speak her mind. She was an honest woman and a brave one. I'm proud to have been called her friend. I know the only favour she'd ask of us now is to look out for the family she left behind.'

All heads turned to Pat, who stood lost in grief, her white face devoid of make-up under a small black hat. Connie carried Lawrence in her arms, whilst Doris held her mother's hand.

The gathering returned to East Ferry Road, where Connie and Ada had prepared the buffet. With shortages as they were, everyone donated rations. Gran's butcher provided the bacon and ham for the thin-cut sandwiches. The eggs came courtesy of her favoured stall at Cox Street market and cheese, tea and beer appeared from behind the counter of the Queens in Manchester Road.

Connie saw to it that no one was excluded, as Gran would have wished. As evening drew near, the gathering dispersed. Ada washed the kids' mucky faces and put them to bed.

When Connie joined her in the bedroom, Doris was already asleep. Ada was changing Lawrence's nappy.

'How's Pat?' she asked as Connie sat beside her on the bed.

'I think she wants to be alone,' Connie sighed. 'So I've left her doing the dishes.'

'What will she do without Gran, I wonder?'

Connie shrugged. 'There's a big gap in her life.'

'Has she got any money?'

'Gran left her some to tide her over and there's Laurie's army allowance.'

'Will the landlord let her stay?'

'If she can pay the rent, I don't see why not.'

Ada did up the last two buttons of Lawrence's nightgown. She placed him in Connie's arms. 'Take him. I know you're dying to have a cuddle.'

Connie rocked him gently. 'He's a lovely baby and never cries. Lucky was the same, a happy baby for all he'd been through.' She felt the tears prick behind her lids.

'You still miss him, don't you?'

'I just hope they love him as much as I do.'

Ada frowned as she gazed at Connie. 'I don't know how you've kept going, what with Lucky being taken away and Gran going on top of it, not to mention the telegram.' She reached across and pushed a stray lock of Connie's hair from her eyes. 'I'm worried about you, Con, about how calmly you're taking all this. I know it's good to be positive about Vic but you have to be realistic.'

Connie slowly turned to look at Ada. 'You think he's dead, don't you?'

'I never said that.'

Connie got up and laid the baby in his cot. 'You know, Ada, Gran said something funny just before she died and I've been trying to work it out.'

Ada joined her. 'What do you mean by funny?'

'Well, she said she'd seen all her family, Mother and Dad, her husband, who was called Maurice, Frederick, her son, and her brother, Bobby.'

'But they're dead,' Ada protested. 'She must have been delirious.'

'She wasn't,' Connie said slowly. 'She said quite clearly, "*He's* not on the other side. I looked."'

Ada shivered. 'Go on, frighten me some more.'

369

'I think it was Vic she was talking about.'

Ada rubbed her arms. 'Now I've got goose bumps.'

'I think instead of the seeing with the leaves, this time she had some kind of heavenly vision.'

'Well, you're entitled to believe what you like, but I haven't the stomach for all that.'

'Ada, I believe Gran was trying to say that Vic is somewhere in this world, not in the next. She "looked", she said. And she looked because she must have realized what was happening to her after she read that telegram and took ill.'

Ada wrinkled her nose. 'To be honest, Con, I can't stretch me imagination that far.'

'Nor could I, once. But Gran taught me that there's more to life than what you can see.'

'Hadn't we better go and see how Pat is?'

Connie looked at her friend. 'Yes, course.'

Together they bent over the cot to take one last look at Lawrence. His breath was even and he was snorting softly as he sucked his lips just like Lucky used to do. Connie's heart squeezed and a moment of yearning filled her. Then, quite suddenly, she thought she saw something move. A shadow in the corner, a breath of air through the window lifting the curtains, a light that spilled in from the moon as the sky darkened. But it happened so fast that when she looked again it was gone.

'What's the matter?' Ada asked nervously.

'Nothing.'

'You've put the wind up me tonight.' Ada grabbed her hand and pulled her to the door. As Connie was closing it, she thought she glimpsed the shadow again, close by the cot. She whispered under her breath, 'Goodnight, Gran.'

Billy closed the front door quietly. Standing outside the house he took one last look at the old homestead. He glanced up at number thirty-three, the battered red front door that needed a good paint, the blacked-out top window behind which Mum and Dad were still fast asleep and the smaller window, where Kev was in bed, snoring his head off. Well, for a start, he wouldn't miss that racket, would he? Not that he'd been at home much in his efforts to dodge Mum. She'd had fifty fits when he told her he was joining up. The sooner he was on the road the better.

An October chill freshened his skin. He liked the British weather and wasn't averse to the damp or the cold, or even the pea soupers. He would miss the early morning mists that rolled off the river, disbursing the scents he associated with childhood. The sweet and preserves factories were his favourite and their pungent ripeness could be smelled miles downstream. Not so much lately, of course, when the war had turned the factories into armament belchers.

The war – what would it be like? Blokes of sixteen and seventeen were lining up to fight the enemy when he'd been busy using his fists against his own countrymen. It was bloody ridiculous really.

Billy pulled back his shoulders and turned up the collar of his jacket. Sliding on his cap, he gave the old house a wink.

'Be seeing you, gel.'

As Billy made his way to Poplar, he wondered if he'd ever see the island again – if he'd ever see his family again! And Ada . . . now, there was a girl for you. The honest truth was he was sweet on her. Not that she'd look at him twice. All right, so they'd kissed that night in the front room, the way he'd never kissed a girl before in his life. And if he hadn't had it on his mind that the whole bloody house might come down and catch them at it, who knows what might have happened next? But he also knew that women like Ada needed a lot of upkeep, a big pot of honey to dip in and out of. Oh yes, Ada liked the good life. And what could he offer? Sod all, really.

Billy smiled regretfully at the memory of her lips and the soft curves of her body, the way just the smell of her made him get all hot and bothered. She only had to brush his arm or look at him with those big eyes and he was all port and brandy.

'How you doin' there, Billy?' Ted Jackson jumped off his bike as Billy strode on to Westferry Road.

'All right, Ted.'

'You're up early. What's the occasion, then? Someone's birthday?'

'No, I'm off to join up.'

Ted lowered his sack to the ground. 'You're too young, lad.'

'They're taking toddlers and pensioners these days,' Billy joked. 'Ain't you heard, we're liberating the Frenchies next.'

'Don't joke about France, boy,' Ted warned soberly.

'The invasion's on the cards. You don't want to be amongst that lot. Take a tip from me and string it out at home for as long as you can.'

'Not on your Nelly.' Billy puffed out his chest. 'I wanna do my bit.'

Ted shook his head mournfully. 'What does yer mother say to all this?'

'She ain't struck on the idea,' Billy admitted.

'I'll bet she's not.' Unexpectedly, Ted stepped forward. He clenched Billy's arm, then the other one. He only came up to Billy's shoulders and it felt a bit awkward, but then Billy returned the pressure gratefully. They stood this way for a few seconds until Ted coughed, picked up his postbag and reclaimed his bike. 'Good luck, son,' he said in a deep voice as he twirled the pedal with his foot and jumped on, raising his cap in salute. Billy watched him cycle down the road.

The importance of what he was doing suddenly registered. He was actually leaving home today and offering his life to his country. It wasn't a lark or a dare, or a way to make money or claim success. There was nothing in it for him, other than the possibility of extinction. Course, he might be a hero and win a medal!

At this thought Billy chuckled aloud and dug his hands deep into his pockets. He was going to say goodbye to Taffy first and make a long overdue apology. Taffy was a good sort and if he'd stuck with him he would have done all right. He might be fighting even now in the back of the Rose and Crown – and winning. Still, water under the bridge, as they say. Before he signed on the dotted line for king and country, he wanted to put his affairs in order.

Billy grinned. Hark at him! He had no intention of meeting his maker just yet. He was off to win a war, not lose it!

Peggy Burton gestured to the young man to enter the big, airy church hall. He was dressed as they all were, in Salvation Army handouts: overcoats that were too big or small, boots like boats, and scarves and socks knitted, unpicked for the next wearer and knitted yet again. His dusty brown hair was short, with threepenny-sized patches carved all over his skull. His features were blunting and his hands had a tremor; she recognized the shell shock even from where she stood. But it was the eyes that saddened her the most. Glazed, without any expression. She thought of David, her late son, and thanked God that he, at least, had not survived the trenches to become one of the walking dead.

'Have you eaten today?' she asked him gently as she led him to one of the benches.

He shook his head, wiping a thread of saliva from his unshaven chin.

'The soup's on. It's early yet, but I'll find you some.' She pressed him down on the bench, served him a generous helping of hot soup and a thick wedge of unbuttered bread. Then, together with her friend Eileen Williams, she continued in the arranging of the trestle tables and benches. In half an hour another fifty homeless would arrive, possibly more. On Sundays, a good day for striking the nation's conscience, they materialized from the woodwork. She hoped all the Sunday worshippers had heavy purses and retained a healthy portion for those outside the church doors as well as inside.

Two young women and their toddlers entered the dilapidated old building, now affectionately known as 'Peggy's'. Ginny Monk with her little girl, Kitty, and Fay Martin and her son, Joseph, were dedicated volunteers and Peggy welcomed them warmly. She led the children to the room beside the kitchen whilst their mothers found their aprons. For a few minutes Peggy sat and played, beating an old pot with a wooden spoon and throwing a ball to knock down some pegs. Very soon, a young girl joined her. Her long brown plaits fell either side of her head. She had a sweet face, but a pensive and worried frown stretched across her forehead.

Peggy held out her arms to the small boy at her side. 'Come here and give me a hug, dear.'

The tiny lad ran into her arms. She kissed him exuberantly on both cheeks as she had done the other children and then watched them settle down to play.

'Now, Grace, can I leave you to take care of these babies?'

The young girl smiled happily. 'Yes, Mrs Burton.'

'How is Mother today?'

The smile faded from Grace's lips. 'Poorly again.'

Peggy hesitated. 'Is she resting?'

Grace nodded, gazing down at her hands, anxiously rubbing the knuckle of her thumb.

Peggy sighed inwardly. From what she had discovered

Grace had a heavy load to bear at only fourteen: the care of her small brother and a mentally distressed parent. Over the past month, ever since Grace and the boy had wandered into the kitchen that Sunday morning, it was clear their home life was blighted by their mother's ill health. Peggy had enquired after the father, but Grace was evasive. The girl was certainly not undernourished and money did not seem to be an issue. She was articulate and polite and their clothes were clean. She had found Grace sitting at one of the tables one Sunday morning, the little boy nestled beside her. Peggy had fed them, though it was apparent neither was hungry. They had returned the following day and the next five days on the trot. When it became clear it was not the soup they had come for, but company, Peggy had taken decisive action.

'Have you any more brothers or sisters at home?' she'd asked Grace.

'I had a brother, but he died.'

'Shouldn't you be at school?' she'd persisted.

'I left,' Grace replied simply, 'to help Mum.'

'I see.'

'But she needs to rest now.'

'Is that why you're here?'

A nod for reply.

Peggy had decided that if the mother had any objections about her daughter helping in the kitchen, no doubt she would hear soon enough.

Now, as she watched Grace and her small charges, Peggy said a little prayer of thanks. The Almighty had sent someone along to help who needed help themselves.

Not in the way Peggy helped the poor, unkempt and ragged people of the street, but in another way, one which, she was certain, would become apparent in the fullness of the Lord's own time.

Meanwhile, Peggy turned her attention to her duties and headed for the kitchen and the two bursting sacks of potatoes that needed peeling for today's creatively cooked broth.

Connie was up early on Monday. Her internal alarm clock hadn't readjusted from her routine with Lucky. At five thirty each morning she was awake, her ears alert for his movements. Her heart always sank when she remembered he wasn't there. It was comforting to see Ada's curled form in his bed.

It was November and pitch black. She tiptoed downstairs and made herself a cup of tea in the kitchen. She always imagined what it would feel like to receive a letter from Vic. Or from the Admiralty saying he'd been found alive and well. Each week she wrote to him, using the same service address as she had always done. None so far had been returned.

Taking her tea into the front room she took her pad and pencil from the dresser. She had told him all about Lucky and poured out her heart over the past weeks. One very long letter had been entirely about Gran. She had broken the news as gently as she could. She told him that Gran's last words to her had given her hope.

When she had finished writing, she always held the letter in her hands and willed it to reach him wherever he was. By this time the light was breaking under the black-out and she was ready for work. On the way to Dalton's she posted her letter and had already begun to think about what she would say in the next one.

'You coming to the party on Saturday?' Len asked later that day as they sat in the canteen.

'You've got Jenny to keep you company.'

'I want you as well.'

Connie laughed. 'I'll bet Jenny doesn't.'

'Safety in numbers, Con.' He gave her a little grin. 'Honest, though, it won't seem the same without you.'

'Course it will.'

'What about Clint?' Len asked lightly.

'What about him?'

'You enjoyed yourself last year, dancing the night away.'

Connie shrugged. 'I wouldn't leave Ada, anyway. She's going on Sunday.'

'Why don't you bring her too?'

'Even Ada wouldn't have the courage to face all of Dalton's.'

'But I'd like to see her before she goes.'

Connie lifted her eyes. 'Come round to our house on Friday then.'

Len sat back in his chair, a look of resignation on his face. They drank their tea and Jenny joined them, bringing with her a large bowl of something gooey which she shyly shared with Len.

At half past five, Connie put on her raincoat and drew Billy's scarf, which still smelled of Ada, over her head.

She doubted it was raining, as November had been quite dry, but the mist from the river had a habit of crawling off the wharf and chasing everyone home. Sometimes she joined a few of the girls who were going her way. But if she worked later, it was a case of finding her own way. With the dark nights and the blackout still well in force, the island seemed to be cocooned in its own little world.

Tonight she was one of the last out from the offices. She had just entered the yard when she saw two figures standing outside the gates. Clint was unmistakable: tall and well built in his heavy army coat. The other, almost half his size, was Ada. They both turned to look at her as she approached.

'What are you two doing here?'

Ada was wearing a beige coat with a big collar that she had bought from Cox Street market. 'Waiting for you, that's what.'

Clint held his cap in his hand. His blond crew cut was shining even in the darkness. 'Hey there, Connie.'

She smiled. 'Hey there, yourself.'

He glanced at Ada. 'I found this young lady hiding outside the gates.'

Ada giggled. 'I was under your mum's feet so I came to meet you. Clint gave me the fright of my life when he tooted the horn.'

'Why were you hiding?'

'I'd be dead embarrassed, wouldn't I, if I saw Mr Burns or Len?' she admitted, peering over Connie's shoulder.

'Len was asking after you today. I told him to come round the house on Friday.'

379

Ada nodded eagerly. 'Oh, Con, that'd be nice.'

Connie looked at Clint. 'Are you going home for Christmas?'

'Not with the way things are in Europe.'

'Oh, you poor thing,' Ada said, glancing over her shoulder at Connie. 'What will you do with yourself at Christmas?'

'With luck, sink a few Jack Daniels if I can rustle me up a bottle or two.'

Ada sighed. 'If I was staying, I'd ask if you'd like to take me out on the town.'

'Why, that's real nice of you, ma'am, and I would have said yes, I sure would,' Clint chuckled.

'I've just had a wonderful idea!' Ada suddenly gasped. 'Why don't we *all* go out on Friday night? Your mum and dad, Ken and Sylvie and Len, too. Why don't we celebrate Christmas early?'

Connie didn't know what to say. What would her family think of the idea? 'Mum's still upset about Billy joining up,' Connie said doubtfully.

'I know, which is why she could do with a night out,' Ada decided confidently.

There was no time to answer, as Ada grabbed hold of their arms and dragged them towards the truck.

Chapter Twenty-Four

For the next half-hour they sat in the front room squeezed on to the couch, listening to Ada trying to persuade Olive into the idea. But eventually Olive pleaded a headache and went to bed. With a deep sigh, Ebbie folded the newspaper and tucked it under the cushion.

'I know you mean well, Ada, but Billy's departure was a shock for Olive. She'll get over it but it'll take time.'

'Sorry, Mr Marsh. I was only trying to cheer her up.'

'I know, love. It's not your fault.' He stood up and smiled as Clint rose to his feet, extending his hand.

'I sure hope she feels better soon, sir.'

'She will. Came at the wrong time, really, Billy going. But I don't see why us not coming should make any difference to you lot, 'specially with Ada leaving us on Sunday. You young people should go out and give her a good send-off.'

Ada glanced at Connie. 'What do you think, Con?'

'I'll have to ask the others first.'

Clint slid on his cap and stood up. 'Well, I'd better be going. Goodnight, folks.'

'Goodnight, son, and take care of yourself.'

Ada accompanied Connie and Clint into the hall. 'So Friday's on then?' she whispered excitedly.

'I don't know—' Connie began, but Ada threw her arms around her.

'Thanks, Connie. It'll be a wonderful send-off.' She glanced up at Clint. 'Can you bring your truck and we'll all squeeze in?'

'Sure will.'

Ada did a little dance, then ran lightly up the stairs. At the top of them she turned and blew a kiss from the palm of her hand.

'Don't come out, it's cold,' Clint told Connie as he put on his heavy coat.

'I wouldn't mind a breath of air. I'll walk you to the gate.' She reached up to the peg to lift her coat but his fingers were there before hers.

'Thank you,' she mumbled, opening the front door quickly.

'My pleasure.' The night air closed around them as they walked down the path.

'I get the feeling Ada hustled you a little today.' Clint smiled as they came to the gate.

'It was all a bit quick.' She nodded. 'You know Ada when she gets a bee in her bonnet. Still, it will be a good send-off, as she said.'

He stood quietly, then asked, 'Where would you like to go?'

Connie shrugged. 'To a pub, I suppose.'

'You mean for what you British call a knees-up?'

She grinned. 'Yes, that's what we call it.'

'Well, then, maybe Friday we can forget our troubles for a while.'

'I didn't know you had any.'

He laughed. 'Just being downright homesick, I guess. Now don't take me wrong. I'm so grateful for the friendship you Brits extend, but I still miss home.' He laid his hand gently on her arm. 'Though you, your family and friends make me remember what it's like to be part of a family. And, you know, I'd like to return the favour somehow. Even if it's only a shoulder to lean on when the going is tough. Just remember, I'm here whenever you want me.'

His breath curled into the misty air and a soft smile flickered on his full lips. Then he squeezed her hand gently and strode away to the truck.

Was that what she wanted right now – a shoulder to lean on? she asked herself as she went back inside. She shivered in the darkness. Dad had extinguished all the lights.

Connie smiled to herself as she went upstairs. She knew Ada would be waiting, all ears.

She wasn't wrong. She found her friend lying in Lucky's bed, pinning her hair into curlers. 'What did he say?' she asked eagerly, staring at Connie. 'Did he give you a cuddle?'

Connie grinned. 'Now that would be telling.'

'Oh, Con, don't keep me in suspense.'

'No, he was the perfect gentleman.'

Ada groaned. 'How bloody boring. Now if that was me—'

'He would have been lucky to escape with his boots still on.'

Ada roared with laughter, then clapped a hand over her mouth. 'It's not his boots I'm interested in,' she whispered, eyes dancing. 'He could have kept them on and we'd still have had fun.'

Laughing softly, Connie began to undress. It was nice having Ada around. Just like old times again.

All week Ada planned what to wear on Friday. On Thursday morning she walked up to Cox Street and bought two winter dresses, some underwear and a pair of dark blue shoes.

'It was the last of me money,' she admitted to Connie that evening as they were deciding what to put on. 'I've got five pounds left to give your mum and enough for the train fare on Sunday.'

'What are you going to do for work when you get to Kent?' Connie watched Ada turn up her nose in disgust at the bulge on the big toe of the second-hand shoes.

'Dunno. War work of some kind I expect.' Ada giggled. 'Look, the person that wore these must have had bunions as big as footballs.'

'Did you try them on when you bought them?'

'Yeah, but I was too busy eyeing up the bloke on the stall who looked like Humphrey Bogart.'

'You could stuff newspaper in them.'

'I don't like the dresses much either.'

'Why don't you wear that lovely blue one that Freddie Smith gave you, or is it bad memories?'

Ada frowned. 'If we was going somewhere nice I would. I'm really mad that I left all me nice stuff at Freddie's. Are Kev and Sylvie still coming?'

Connie nodded. 'And Len. He's bringing Jenny.'

'In that case, I will wear me blue.'

Connie smiled as Ada hurried off to prepare. Not that she need worry about being upstaged. No doubt Jenny would be dressed in her usual skirt and blouse and sensible shoes.

The truck arrived at half past six on Friday evening. Ada and Len embraced, throwing insults at one another immediately. To Connie's surprise Jenny looked beautiful in a soft green dress over which she wore a new and fashionable coat. Her brown hair was set free from restraint and bounced lightly on her shoulders.

'I'm pleased to meet you.' She smiled brightly at Ada.

'Likewise,' said Ada, fluttering her eyelashes.

Kevin and Sylvie sat in the back of the truck where the baggage was usually stowed. Connie noticed how pretty Sylvie looked too. She wore a dark coat and her hair was drawn up into a wave on one side. Every time she looked at Kevin, her big brown eyes sparkled. Kevin seemed to have grown taller and slimmer in his smart dark jacket and flannels.

Connie wore her lilac suit and wound Billy's scarf into the V-shaped neck. Like Ada, she felt a little overdressed, though as Clint drove them through the darkened streets no one had thought to ask where in particular they were going.

'We're at Aldgate, aren't we?' Ada suddenly cried.

Clint smiled. 'I'm taking you to a little club I know. Do you feel like listening to some great jazz?'

Everyone shouted yes! 'What, like you played at the party last year?' Len asked.

'You bet.'

Ada grabbed hold of Connie's arm. She whispered excitedly, 'Thank goodness I wore me dress!'

The Starlight was full of American servicemen and their English girlfriends. They sat at a table with crooked red lights right next to the dance floor. No one cared about the rather uncomfortable seating as couples crowded on to the small circle of floor below the stage.

Clint introduced them to his friends and told them about the four musicians who were playing that evening. 'The big guy is Ed Gorman, tenor sax. Next to him Jimmy Cutts on trumpet and Hal Farraday, who plays a mean clarinet.' He nodded to the man sitting at the black piano. 'That's Shooter. Gets his name from the way his fingers move over the keys, like shooting stars.'

'This is a bit different from the turns up at the Queens,' Len said admiringly. 'The beat really gets in your system.'

Clint smiled, flashing his white teeth. 'Some say it's an acquired taste, like oysters or caviar.'

'We'll try them next then.' Kevin nodded.

'You seem to know everyone in here,' Ada said as she sat squashed up to Clint's big body. 'Are you gonna play your trumpet tonight?'

'Maybe, honey.'

'Oooh, I love the way you say that.' They all laughed as Ada looked under her lashes. 'Can we dance?'

'I thought you'd never ask,' Clint said ruefully, taking her hand.

'What about you, Con?' Len asked politely.

'No, you two enjoy yourselves,' Connie said. 'I like listening to the music.'

She was content to sit and watch them as the memories flooded back of that wonderful night with Vic at Valentino's. It had felt so romantic as he had swirled her round the floor, his strong embrace making her feel so loved and cherished. Her thoughts drifted slowly to the passionate hours they had spent in each other's arms at Gran's. How tender he had been with her when they made love. Sometimes she wondered why she hadn't become pregnant. Their lovemaking had been so intense. She had willingly taken the risk and didn't regret one precious moment. At least she had those memories now to console her. Connie closed her eyes to prevent a tear from escaping.

'Connie, would you like to dance?'

Her eyes flew open. Clint was staring down at her. Ada collapsed on to her chair. 'Have a dance, Con. My feet are dropping off.'

'I don't know the steps.'

'You don't need to, just throw yourself about.' Ada giggled.

'Come on, Connie. Let your hair down.' Clint beckoned her with a big smile. 'Just one dance.'

Reluctantly she stood up. Clint took her hand and they made their way to the floor. The rhythm began to slow and the couples merged together.

'This is called "Body and Soul",' he smiled, taking her gently in his arms. 'Do you remember it?' He drew her against him. 'I played it at Dalton's party, the night I danced you off your feet?'

She nodded. 'Yes – I remember.'

His movements were easy to follow as he guided her round the floor. 'I don't know if this is the right time to mention it,' he said after a while, 'but I'm real sorry to hear about your fiancé.'

She hesitated. 'I suppose Len told you.'

He looked into her eyes. 'You know, a pal of mine by the name of Ricky Delahay was captured by the Japs at Guadalcanal in '42. His unit found his dog-tag three months later, buried in the mud. Half of it was shot away, and as our planes had flattened the area, it was assumed there were no survivors. In March this year a crazy man walked out of the jungle, straight into a marine corps. He turned out to be Ricky and they cleaned him up and shipped him home all in one solid piece.'

'Do you think there's others like him?'

'I sure do.'

'I won't give up hope.' Connie felt tears behind her eyes again. She didn't want to cry, but it was a relief to know that amazing things really did still happen.

'Don't cry, honey,' he whispered when he saw the tears in her eyes. 'I should have kept my big mouth shut.'

'I'm not sad,' she answered with a shaky smile, 'you've

just made me happy. At least happier than I have been in a long while.'

'Then swell,' he murmured and pressed her close as he tightened his hand over hers. 'If you're happy, then I'm happy too.'

She laid her head on his shoulder and discreetly smoothed her wet cheek. As her body relaxed, he pulled her a little closer and began to hum. His deep voice was husky in her ear as the top of her head rested against his jaw. She felt him draw in breath, so that automatically she inclined against him. Her body felt warm and tingly as slowly he turned his mouth into her hair and breathed against her scalp. 'Connie, you were wearing this suit the day we met, remember? You were such a tiny little thing, so beautiful that my heart stopped when I looked into your face.'

Connie felt her breath catch. Even her skin felt as though it was trembling as he increased the pressure of his hand against her waist. 'Something told me it wasn't the last time we'd meet. Do you know what that kinda feeling is like? Deep down in your gut, very deep down – it's real strange . . .'

His words were lost in a sudden burst of trumpet. The tempo changed and all the couples disengaged. She pulled away and he released her. 'Do you want to sit this one out?'

She nodded and he guided her back to the table. Ada was staring at them curiously.

'What was going on between you two?' she whispered as Clint made his way over to the piano.

'Nothing.' Connie felt her face redden as she sat down. 'We were only dancing.'

Ada lifted her eyes. 'Don't get all huffy.'

'I'm not.'

'He's a good dancer.' Ada nudged her arm. 'He's gonna play the trumpet. Look.'

Connie raised her eyes. Clint rested one muscled thigh on a tall stool and clicked his thumb and middle finger in time to the beat. His eyes were closed as he played, the beam of light above him pouring down on to his spiked silver hair. The intensity on his face was clear as he juggled the notes with such dexterity that people stood up to applaud.

'More!' Len shouted, jumping to his feet as Clint grinned, saluting to their table.

Clint held out his hand. 'Can I take a request from the good folks I came with?'

Connie didn't know any jazz and nor did the others. Then, gathering her courage, she stood up. 'I know it's not jazz, but can you play "Dancing In the Dark"?'

'Guess we can try.' Clint turned and talked to the rest of the musicians. The piano tinkled and Clint played a few notes before lowering his trumpet as the lights dimmed. Soon the music filled the room and Connie closed her eyes. She wasn't in the Starlight any longer but on the dance floor at Valentino's. Vic was holding her tight and she was overwhelmed with feelings that brought back every moment. When the music faded away, everyone was clapping. Connie swallowed on the lump in her throat and added her applause.

'They're bloody brilliant,' Len said, nudging her arm.

'Did you all have a good time?' Clint asked when he rejoined them. He looked Connie directly in the eye. Everyone said they had, as reluctantly they walked out to the foyer to find their coats.

'Would you like to do this again, sometime?' Clint asked Connie when they were alone for a few seconds.

'I dunno why I'm off to Kent,' Ada cried before Connie could answer. 'I'll be missing out on all the fun again.'

'You'll have fun wherever you are,' Clint told her, still looking at Connie as Ada linked her arms through theirs.

'I hope you're right, Clint. As long as I can drink the beer as well as picking bloody hops, I'll be all right.'

They left the Starlight laughing. But when they climbed into the truck Connie sat with Len and Jenny, leaving Ada to take the seat next to Clint. She was troubled by what had happened on the dance floor and the question he had asked her afterwards.

The only man she loved was Vic. When she'd heard 'Dancing In the Dark' it had brought back everything he meant to her. She thought Clint had understood that she wasn't interested in an affair. But now she wasn't certain.

Connie caught the bus into work the next morning. Although she hadn't drunk very much the previous night, just the one port and lemon, she slept in late, having fallen asleep at half past four in the morning. She'd tossed and turned, thinking back on all that had gone on. Her emotions were confused and she didn't like the feeling.

She knew her body craved love and affection. It would be easy to fall for a handsome man like Clint but her heart belonged to Vic and always would. Clint had even given her fresh hope by the story he had told her. But was that just a way of making her trust him?

When she arrived home the following afternoon, Ada couldn't stop talking about the wonderful time they'd had at the Starlight.

'I wish I was staying here now,' Ada confessed.

'Why don't you, then?'

'I can't disappoint Mum. She was really upset when I went off with Freddie. She never told Dad anything about it. He'd probably kill me if he knew the truth.'

'Is he still working up north?'

'Yes, but he travels to Kent once a month to see everyone. He's coming home for a family Christmas and I want to give him a big hug.'

'Well, Ada, for what it's worth I think you're doing the right thing going to live in Kent.'

'Why's that then?' Ada demanded.

'Because your family keeps you in line. Without them you were all over the place.'

Ada frowned. 'I can't live at home for ever. I'm an East Ender born and bred. I love the docks and the river. If it wasn't for my conscience pricking then I'd be staying put.'

Connie smiled. 'What conscience?'

'You mare!'

Connie laughed. 'What time are you leaving tomorrow?'

Ada's face went pink. 'Clint offered to take me up to Victoria in the truck. You will come, won't you?'

Connie shook her head. 'I'll say goodbye here if you don't mind.'

'But why?' Ada wailed.

'Stations are too much of a reminder of people coming home as well as going away.'

Ada's jaw dropped. 'Oh, Con, I'm sorry. I only ever think about what I want.'

'You understand, don't you?'

'Course I do.' She wrapped her arms around Connie. 'I'm gonna miss you so much.'

'Me too. Send me a card at Christmas, won't you?'

'Like one of old Burnsy's, eh? With something dopey written inside.'

They laughed and drew apart. Ada sat down on the bed. 'P'raps you could come up to Kent and stay for a couple of days?'

Connie nodded. 'P'raps I could.'

'Give my love to Billy when you see him. I miss the little sod.'

'I will.'

'Con?'

'What?'

'You're my best mate.'

When Clint arrived in the truck the next day, Ada was waiting on the doorstep. Her make-up was all in place and her case in hand. Ebbie, Olive, Kevin and Sylvie, Nan and Lofty were all there to say goodbye.

'I wish you were coming,' Clint said, looking disappointed when he discovered Connie wasn't travelling with them. 'Did you think over what I said about the Starlight? I'd sure like to take you there again.'

Before she could answer, Ada was hugging her hard. 'Bye, Connie.'

'Look after yourself.'

Ada giggled. 'Don't I always?'

When the truck drove away, Clint looked through the window and smiled at her. He was a handsome young GI who was lonely and a long way from home. And she was well aware, in view of what had happened at the Starlight, that he might be looking for more than friendship.

Chapter Twenty-Five

The champion of El Alamein, Britain's General Montgomery, and America's newly appointed General Dwight Eisenhower were the talk of every Christmas dinner table in Britain at the close of 1943. Between the two warlords, it was hoped that the full-scale invasion of Western Europe would drive the Nazis from occupied Italy.

In the Marsh household, over the thinly carved chicken, the celebrations had been modest. Although Sylvie sat beside Kevin this year, Billy's presence was missed. His letter, read out by Olive after the last helping of more-carrot-than-fruit Christmas pudding, was brief but in true Billy style. 'It's just been square bashing till now, but once our training's done,' he wrote enthusiastically, 'we'll be kitted up and moved out soon. I'll be home for a weekend's leave in the New Year. So, what about sinking a few pints, Dad and Kev? I'll be eighteen, old enough to buy a round or two. And a nice Sunday roast after, Mum? Connie, Ada, what about going to the flicks on Saturday night?'

Olive wept a little. 'He's not coming home for his birthday on the twenty-ninth.'

Ebbie laughed. 'Don't think the army cater for birth-days, love. Just thank your lucky stars he can make it at all.'

Olive tucked the letter in her apron pocket. Connie knew she would read it ten times over by the time she went to bed. After dinner they all sat round the fire and opened their presents. As Connie took the tray of tea into the front room afterwards, Kevin looked up at her. 'Connie, sit down a minute, Sylvie and me have an announcement to make.'

'What is it?' Olive asked as she clutched her cup tightly.

Kevin glanced at Sylvie. 'We want to tie the knot.'

The cup clattered into the saucer. 'What did you just say?'

'We want to get married. Her mum and dad have given us their blessing.' Kevin held Sylvie's hand.

'You've asked them already?'

'We had to, Mum.'

Olive stared at the two young people sitting on the couch. 'You mean – you're – you're – expecting!'

Sylvie burst into tears.

'Oh, Christ,' Ebbie muttered, glancing at his wife.

Connie put her arm around Sylvie. She was very upset and Connie patted her back gently. 'Don't cry, Sylvie. It'll be all right.'

Olive rose to her feet. 'How could you both be so irresponsible?'

Kevin went to his mother. He tried to put his arm around her but she shrugged him off. 'I'm sorry, Mum—'

'It's too late for apologies,' she broke in angrily. 'How are you going to manage? Where are you going to live? How do you propose to keep a family on your wage?'

'Lots of our friends are married,' Kevin protested. 'Why not us?'

'Because I expected something better of you, Kevin.' Olive's face was filled with disappointment. 'You've locked shackles on your ankles, young man, and you'll never lose them again.'

'Now, Mother.' Ebbie tried to calm his wife. 'What's done is done. We'll just have to make the best of it.'

'How do you make the best of nothing?' she retorted, her lips trembling. 'You've not got a penny saved between you.'

'It doesn't all boil down to money, Mum.'

'Doesn't it?' Olive's face tightened. 'So tell me, where are you going to live? Here?'

Kevin looked embarrassed. 'Billy's not here now so me and Sylvie thought we could use the bedroom.'

Olive looked shocked. 'There will be three of you very soon, plus your sister and me and Dad, and just because Billy's in the army it doesn't mean he won't want a bed to sleep on when he comes home. What do you propose he should do then? Sleep with the baby?' She turned her attention to Sylvie. 'And what do your parents have to say on the subject of accommodation?'

Sylvie flushed. 'We've only got two bedrooms.'

Olive looked back at her son. 'You don't know how disappointed I am in you, Kevin.' She turned and left the room.

They all sat in silence until Sylvie began to cry again softly. Kevin put his arm around her as she laid her head on his shoulder. Connie sighed. A baby in the family again. It was the most wonderful thing she could imagine. Once she might have agreed with her mother but after having Lucky in her life her ambition to become a career girl had vanished. All she wanted was to hold Lucky in her arms again. Where was he now? Was he loved and cherished? Did he miss her?

If only Sylvie knew how blessed she was!

Predictably, Christmas Day ended on a low note. Olive refused to resume the topic and turned on the radio as she began her knitting. Ebbie hid behind an old newspaper and finally Kevin walked Sylvie home.

When everyone was in bed, Connie sat by the embers of the fire. Christmas night and she was alone. She took out her pencil and paper and began to write in the soft glow of the room. The first letter was to the Admiralty. She requested that, as Vic's fiancée, she be informed of any developments in his case. The second letter was to Vic. She told him how much she missed him and that tomorrow, Boxing Day, she was going to spend with Pat and the children. When she had finished, she sealed both envelopes and addressed them.

The following day she walked over to Pat's. There was not a great selection in the larder and as there were no shops open Connie made bread and butter pudding accompanied by layers of spam. She cleaned the place from top to bottom, dragged in the tin bath and washed the children. Afterwards she played with them in front of the fire. Connie gave Lawrence a teddy bear for his cot and Doris a Hans Christian Andersen picture book. They sat reading after tea and it wasn't until eight o'clock that Connie finally took her leave.

Pat had been very quiet all day. What was going through her mind? she wondered as she walked back to Kettle Street. It was the first time that Connie had found the house and children in a neglected state. And even though Laurie's Christmas letter had arrived, Pat had seemed oddly detached.

Connie knew there was something wrong but she didn't know what. She would call again soon and try to find out.

Peggy Burton finally closed the doors of the Mile End soup kitchen. She let out a long sigh. Her feet were aching to the point of screaming. It was four o'clock on a Friday, the last Friday of 1943. She had fed and watered the world, it felt like, and now all she needed was to spoil herself with a cup of tea and feet up beside her husband as the New Year dawned.

She removed her apron and went into the small room. All the decks were clear thanks to Eileen, Ginny and Fay, who had gone home. Only Grace and her brother remained on the premises.

She watched the young girl and little boy as they played together on the floor. More bruises on the girl's arms, though she had pulled down her sleeves now. Peggy's suspicions were growing by the day. But, alas, now she had to send them home.

'Grace, it's time to go, dear.'

The young girl nodded but the boy didn't look up. He seemed to be in a world of his own, though he liked playing with the other small children.

'Grace?'

'Yes, Mrs Burton?'

'How is your mother?' As eager as Peggy was to go home to her nice warm fire and somewhat neglected husband, her instinct told her that her work wasn't yet finished.

'Resting.'

Ah! That word again. What did resting really mean? Peggy sat down on one of the wooden chairs and patted the seat beside her. Grace walked slowly over and lowered her tiny bottom, tucked her black patent shoes underneath her and sat contentedly.

'Well, now, before you go, shall I see if there's a biscuit or two left?' Peggy asked.

'Yes please!'

The little boy looked up eagerly. Peggy knew how bright he really was. She'd wondered if his hearing was at fault when often he refused to respond. So she'd made her own investigations, rattling spoons to his right and left, and caught his attention immediately. No, the child was neither deaf nor dim. On the contrary, this child was as healthy as the next.

Peggy smiled and stood up. In the New Year she would make more enquiries regarding this curious pair. It was strange the mother had never arrived to see where her children were going each day. And where did those marks on Grace's arms come from? Or, possibly, from whom?

The mild, unseasonable January confused everyone. But just in case Jack Frost arrived Connie wore warm woollen gloves, a scarf and a heavy coat as she left work and went straight to Pat's. All the chimneys were belching smoke. There was talk again of a new and deadly weapon that Germany was testing out. The rumours circulated every so often; people still did their stint of fire-watching or Home Guard duties, but with all the talk of the European invasion nerves were on edge at what would happen next.

When Connie arrived at Pat's, a man dressed in a dark coat stood on the doorstep. Pat was staring out from her dark-rimmed eyes, trying to console a screaming Lawrence.

'This is unacceptable, I'm afraid,' he was shouting above the baby's cries. 'The matter must be settled at once.'

'I told you,' Pat pleaded tearfully, 'I'll pay you when I get a job. I haven't any money now.'

'What's the matter?' Connie asked anxiously as she ascended the steps.

He turned to frown at her. 'Who are you?'

'I'm Mrs Grant's brother's fiancée.'

'Do you live here?'

'No. Why?'

The man ignored her and turned back to Pat. 'I must insist on settlement or I shall have to refer the debt to our collectors. We have no wish to involve the bailiffs, but I'm afraid non-payment will result in just such an action.'

Doris appeared, tears splashing down her cheeks as she clung to Pat's skirt.

'I have my job to do,' the stranger continued, raising his voice over both screaming children.

'Does your job include frightening women and children?' Connie demanded as she took Lawrence, who smelled quite badly, into her arms.

A blood vessel seemed to swell in the man's neck. His red skin bulged over his collar. 'I can see I'm wasting my time.' With a glare at Pat, he moved down the steps. 'Good day to you.'

Pat sighed forlornly after he'd gone.

'What was all that about bailiffs?' Connie asked as she stepped into the cold, dark hall.

'I'm behind with the rent.'

'How much?'

'Ten pounds.'

'Has he called before?'

Pat nodded. 'I just can't seem to manage on Laurie's allowance and I'm too tired to even think about getting a job,' she admitted as Lawrence's cries rose to a crescendo. 'I feel exhausted.'

'Then why don't you go and rest,' Connie suggested as she took Doris's hand. 'I'll see to the kids.'

Without protest Pat walked wearily into the bedroom.

Connie ushered Doris into the kitchen and noticed at once that her dress was stained. Lawrence's romper was filthy and his nappy soaked.

'I'll change Lawrence,' she told Doris, helping the little girl on to a chair. 'And we'll make ourselves a nice cup of tea.'

'We ain't got none, Auntie Con,' Doris said.

'No tea?' Connie looked around. Dirty crocks abounded, the stove was unwashed and crusty with burned food. The place was freezing and a stale smell pervaded the room.

Connie looked in the larder. Apart from half a loaf and a rack of vegetables there was virtually nothing. She closed the door and turned back to Doris, who was looking up at her with expectant eyes.

'Are you hungry, Doris?'

'Yes, Auntie Con.'

'We'll go to the shops, shall we?'

'Mummy's got no money.'

'Did she tell you that?'

'No, she told the man. He was angry.' Doris sucked her lip. 'Mummy was crying.'

Connie bent down and balanced Lawrence on her knees. She took hold of Doris's cold hands. 'That's only because she's tired and needs a good, long sleep. We'll change Lawrence's nappy and make him comfortable, then put him in the pram and go down to buy some nice things to eat.'

Doris smiled. 'Can I have a gob-stopper?'

'Don't see why not.'

'Goodee!'

When Lawrence was dry and wrapped under his blankets in the pram, Connie helped Doris with her coat and scarf. Five minutes later she was skipping happily beside the pram and Lawrence was fast asleep, exhausted from all the crying he'd done

Connie used her own coupons at Mrs Gane's corner shop, filling up Gran's shopping basket. As they left the shop a car pulled up. The unpleasant man from the council stepped out. He was about to knock on a door when Connie pushed the pram towards him.

'Stop!' Connie called.

Once again she received a sneer. 'What is it?' He moved on to the pavement cautiously.

'I understand Mrs Grant owes you rent.'

'That's private business.'

'But you are the rent collector, aren't you?'

'I'm the council's department representative,' he corrected her pompously.

Connie reached into her handbag. She still hadn't opened her wage packet, and now shook out £3 17s 6d from the envelope, adding more coins from her purse. 'Here's five pounds towards what she owes.'

He took it suspiciously. 'What about the balance?'

'You'll get it.'

He looked at her doubtfully. 'I don't know what my superiors will say about this.'

'I should think you'll get promoted on the strength of this.' She pushed her purse back in her bag. 'Anyway, if the bailiffs put Pat and the kids on the street you won't get a brass farthing more.'

'There's no need to take that attitude,' he answered

nastily. 'We wouldn't evict someone unless it was absolutely necessary.'

'Well, you could have fooled me the way you went on at Pat today. Her health is poor after Gran's death and her husband is in the army, fighting for his country.' She deliberately looked him up and down.

'Am I to understand, Miss . . . er . . .'

'Marsh is the name.'

'That you, Miss Marsh, will stand as guarantor for repayment of the debt?'

'If that's how you want to put it, yes.'

He drew himself up to his full height. 'Then I'll take your address, please.'

Connie gave it. 'Now, if you'll write me a receipt?'

Reluctantly he brought out his little book, counted the money and wrote on the piece of paper. Connie took it and grabbing Doris's hand she pushed the pram away, her head held high.

'Is he gonna get cross with Mummy again?' Doris asked as they hurried on.

'No, love. No one's going to make Mummy cry again, I promise. Now, let's have a little walk to warm us up, then when we get home I'm going to make you a nice big dinner and we'll sit round the fire to eat it.'

Connie was thinking about what she had done. She had used up all of one week's wages. To economize she would have to walk to work and avoid the canteen and postpone any expenditure. She had five pounds in a jar at home, some of which she'd have to give to Mum. Had she been hasty in her promise to clear Pat's debt? But she just couldn't let Pat and the children be thrown out!

When they got back Connie shovelled the last remnants of coke into the fire. Then she cooked a meal: vegetable pie and mashed potatoes followed by a nourishing dried egg custard that both children ate swiftly. When this was done she took Pat in a cup of tea and helped her to dress.

'Go in the kitchen and sit by the stove,' she told her. 'I'll put the kids to bed.'

Connie washed and changed them and, when Lawrence was snoozing in his cot, she read Doris a story and kissed her goodnight.

Returning to the kitchen, she found Pat asleep in Gran's rocking chair. Her tea was untouched. Connie sat beside her and sighed. What was she to do with this sad little family?

Studying Pat's gaunt features as she lay in the chair, she knew there was only one decision to make.

And it was one that would solve everyone's problems.

Sunday dinner was over and Connie finished wiping up. She took off her apron and looked at Olive. The letter that had come from Billy yesterday saying his leave had been cancelled hadn't improved her mother's mood. Still, there was no going back now on what she had decided.

'Mum, I'd like to talk to you and Dad.'

Olive turned from the sink, an expression of alarm on her face. 'Oh, God, what is it now?'

'Nothing to worry about. It's to do with Pat and the kids.'

Olive sighed in relief. 'Thank the Good Lord. I'm living on my nerve ends these days wondering what's going to happen next in this family.'

'Can we go in the front room?'

Olive dried her hands on the towel. 'I'll just make tea.' The tray was set and brought in. Ebbie folded his Sunday newspaper as Olive poured the tea.

Connie sat beside her mother on the couch. She was ready for an outburst, which she hoped to calm with a bright idea that she'd had last night after coming home from Pat's.

'Well, Constance, what is it?'

Connie noted her mother hadn't picked up her cup and saucer. Her father was looking at her anxiously. She didn't want to upset either of them and she knew this would be difficult. But in the end it would be better for everyone.

'As I was saying, it's about Pat. She isn't managing on Laurie's pay.'

'But she gets all his soldier's allowance, doesn't she?' her father asked.

'His pay is only twenty-five shillings a week.'

'I thought Gran left her some.' Olive was looking worried now.

'She did, but it's gone.' Connie didn't say anything about the rent collector or having given him money.

'Can't she get her old job back?'

'She's still not very well.'

'What can we do to help?' Ebbie asked kindly.

Connie took a breath. 'I thought I would move in as her lodger.'

Olive gasped. 'You mean leave home – here – Kettle Street?'

'Only until she can manage again.'

'But when will that be?' Olive's mouth was twitching.

'Mum, Sylvie could move in then. There would be room for all three of them if I went. It would solve a big problem, wouldn't it? And you'd still have all your family round you.'

Olive looked into Connie's eyes. 'I . . . I . . .' she spluttered.

'After all, I'm engaged and I'd be moving out when—'

'When what?' Olive gazed at her incredulously. 'Vic's not coming home, Constance, he's—'

'Olive!' Ebbie interrupted sharply, his face darkening.

Connie shook her head slowly. 'It's all right, Dad.'

Olive looked hurt. 'Well, it's true, isn't it? Everyone is walking around on eggshells, Constance, trying not to upset you by saying the truth. You must face the fact that sooner or later—'

'Olive, that's enough.' Ebbie thrust his hand through his hair and looked at Connie. 'Look, love, we can't stop you from moving in with Pat. But your mother's only got your best interests at heart. You'd be taking on a big responsibility. You've got a kind heart, but you've only just got your . . . well, *freedom* back again after Lucky.'

Connie swallowed hard. 'Dad, I would trade all my so-called freedom for just an hour with Lucky. Without him and Vic, my life is incomplete.'

'But you're only young,' her mother cried. 'You'll find someone else and have a family of your own one day.'

Connie knew they didn't understand. 'I love you both and I don't like upsetting you, but this is a way to help everyone.' She stood up. 'I thought I'd move next Saturday afternoon, if that's all right. Sylvie's baby can have Lucky's bed, though some of the bars that went round its sides need mending.'

Both her parents stared at her. She wanted to throw her arms around them and comfort them, but she knew it was only time that would make sense of what she was doing.

She went upstairs and looked around her room. Did she really want to leave home? Was she ready to take on the responsibility of Pat and the children?

Connie sat down on her bed. She knew that one day she would have to spread her wings. This was a little before time but she had a good reason. Pat, Doris and Lawrence were part of her family now. And they needed her help.

Kevin asked Taffy if he would help to move Connie's things. On Saturday afternoon, Taffy arrived at two o'clock prompt and helped Ebbie to carry Connie's dressing table downstairs and on to the lorry. It was the only article of furniture she was taking with her. All her clothes and personal possessions including Lucky's toys were packed into bags and a large suitcase, loaned to her by Nan.

When all the supplies were loaded, Nan and Lofty stood beside her parents on the pavement.

'I've packed you three good blankets to go with your eiderdown,' Olive told Connie with a heavy sniff. 'A pair of sheets and pillow cases that I'd been saving for a rainy day. And there's a thick pair of brocade curtains that should cover the blackout nicely.' She had been busy all week, occupying herself with a good 'sorting out', pinning little labels on the bags and boxes: 'china', 'bed linen', 'assorted', and a pile of groceries that expanded by the day.

'Don't leave yourself short, Mum,' Connie had assured her. 'Gran left plenty of everything.'

'You're entitled to a good start,' Olive had replied, pushing yet another unidentified parcel into the queue.

Connie had had butterflies all week. Her father had not been his usual self. His jokes were few and far between and Connie found him looking sadly at her before averting his gaze. She knew there would be a big gap in her life when she came home at night, expecting to see him reading his paper in front of the fire.

But she was happy for Kevin and Sylvie. They had set the date for March and Sylvie was going to move into Connie's room next week after Olive had given it a 'good going over'. The young couple were deliriously happy.

Kevin and Sylvie stood hand in hand. 'Dunno what to say, Con, except look after yourself. And anything you want, just name it.' Kevin gave her a kiss on the cheek and Sylvie wrapped her arms around her neck.

'I'll miss you, Connie. I hope your mum gets used to me.'

Connie smiled. 'In a week she'll have forgotten all this.'

'Do you think so?'

'I know so.'

Nan pressed an envelope into Connie's hand. 'Just a little something from Lofty and me, ducks.'

'Nan, you shouldn't.'

'You don't know what it is, yet.'

'I can guess.'

'Just a bit of spare to help you set up home like.'

Connie smiled gratefully. 'Oh, Nan, you've been such a good friend to me.'

'And it's set to continue that way,' Lofty interrupted, his big eyes all watery. 'We expect you to call regular like.'

'I'm coming for tea on Wednesday.'

'We'll pop in, don't you worry.'

Taffy started the engine. The noise rumbled down the street. Connie hugged them all and they stood in line on the pavement to wave her off. Her family and friends.

She waved from the window as Taffy drove them off. What was it going to be like living at Pat's? Could she pay off the arrears of the rent as she had promised? And would she regret leaving home?

Chapter Twenty-Six

After the unexpected snowfall of February, the spell of March sunshine took everyone by surprise. Connie and Pat were debating a walk to the shops. The slush had disappeared and a hint of spring was in the air. It was Lawrence's first birthday and a party was being prepared. Just as they were leaving, there was a knock at the front door.

A young man stood there. 'Telegram for Miss Marsh.'

Pat hurried along the hall. Connie's fingers were shaking as she tore open the envelope. She read it, then slowly handed it to Pat. 'It says that Vic's ship is now classed as being lost and no word had been received of survivors.'

'Oh, Connie!'

'I wrote at Christmas and asked them to let me know if they heard anything. I didn't think it would be this.' Pat reached out and they held each other.

'Mummy, what's the matter?' Doris was standing beside them.

'Nothing, darling.' Pat drew her close.

'What did the letter say?'

'It said that Uncle Vic won't be coming home.'

Lawrence wobbled himself towards them on his bottom, dragging his outstretched leg. Connie lifted him into her arms.

'Are you sad, Auntie Con?'

'Just a bit.'

'Can we still have a party tomorrow?'

'Course we can.' Connie nodded. 'We've made a jelly, haven't we? And we've got presents to wrap up.'

'I wish Daddy could come.'

'I wish he could too,' smiled Pat sadly. She hugged her daughter and Connie saw her discreetly wipe away a tear. She knew that Pat had been living in hope too. They had both refused to believe Vic was dead. Believing that Vic would come home was what had kept Connie going.

The party on Sunday consisted mainly of grown-ups. Kevin, Ebbie and Lofty were enjoying a beer in the kitchen with Albie Cross. Nan, Olive and Sylvie all sat on the couch. Pat was talking to Eve Beale as they watched the children open the presents: a teddy bear with a big blue ribbon round its neck sent from Jenny and Len, a horse carved from wood from Lofty, an embroidered bed cover from Olive and a set of building blocks from Connie. Now Lawrence was banging his fists on a small drum that Ada had sent in the post. He was enjoying himself with all his new things.

The past few months had been surprisingly happy, Connie thought as she passed round the sandwiches and saw smiling faces. The rent was all up to date and Pat and the kids were thriving. Her mother and Sylvie were on the best of terms too. Now they were deep in conversation talking about knitting patterns and baby clothes and the approach of the wedding service to be held in a week's time at the registry office. Connie smiled as she listened to them. Sylvie looked so happy with her nice round bump, despite the fact that a big white wedding wasn't possible.

'Look, that's your friend, isn't it?' Pat said as she glanced out of the window and nudged Connie's arm.

Connie lowered the plate as Clint leaped the steps. 'He asked after you and the kids at work last week. He must have remembered it's Lawrence's birthday,' she added with an embarrassed frown.

When Connie opened the door, Clint dazzled her with a smile. 'Happy birthday to Lawrence.' He held out a big, shiny parcel. 'I have to be honest. I won it from Dalton's Christmas raffle. Heck, it's been sitting in the truck ever since.'

Doris came running up. 'Auntie Con, what's in there?'

'A present for Lawrence.'

She held up her arms and Clint lifted her against his chest. 'Are you coming to our party, Uncle Clint?'

'No. I just called by to give this to your brother.'

'What is it?'

'You'll have to open it to see, honey.'

Doris giggled. 'I'm not honey, I'm Doris.'

Laughing, Clint glanced at Connie. 'Well, guess I'd better be on my way.'

'Ain't you coming in?' Doris demanded as he lowered her to the ground. She tugged Connie's dress. 'Make him stay, Auntie Con.'

'You're welcome to.' Connie nodded. She didn't have the heart to refuse Doris and it was a thoughtful gesture, but Connie guessed he had something else on his mind. What would she say if he asked her to go to the Starlight Club again?

'Please stay!' Doris jumped up and down.

'Come in,' she told him and he grinned even wider.

After saying hello to the women and Lawrence, he joined the men in the kitchen. Doris unwrapped Lawrence's parcel. It was a big, fluffy duck, almost as big as Lawrence himself.

'That was kind of him,' said Pat as she helped Connie fold up the paper and string.

'Yes.'

'Connie, he likes you.'

'I know. He asked me to go to the Starlight with him again.'

'What did you say?'

'I haven't said anything yet.' Connie looked into Pat's gaze. 'There's only one man for me, Pat, and you know who that is.'

Pat nodded slowly. 'I know. But even I have to accept the fact he's not around and isn't likely to be. And you can't live like a widow all your life.'

'Con?' Ebbie's head poked round the door. 'Someone to see you.'

A small, well-dressed woman stood in the hall.

'Peggy!'

'I didn't realize you'd moved,' Peggy Burton said breathlessly. 'I went to Kettle Street first but a neighbour of yours, Mrs Shutler, gave me your new address.'

416

'I'm lodging here with my fiancé's sister, Pat,' Connie explained as her father disappeared back into the kitchen. 'As you can see, it's one of the children's birthdays.'

'I'm sorry to interrupt,' Peggy apologized, 'but I wonder if I could have a quick word. It's important, Connie.'

'Come into the bedroom. It's quieter there.' Connie led the way. 'Is something wrong?' she asked as she gestured Peggy to sit down on the bedside chair.

Peggy lowered herself carefully, removing her leather gloves. 'After I last saw you, I began a new kitchen at Mile End. We were so busy at the Mission Hall, you see. So many travelled long distances. Well, as you know, we always need volunteers and, by the Good Lord's grace, He sent a young girl of fourteen along last October. She brought her small brother, which gave me the idea to begin a nursery. Grace is very reliable and has proved a wonderful help.' He soft eyes looked directly into Connie's. 'I've had my suspicions for some time, but yesterday I decided it was time to call on you. Connie, I think the little boy – her brother – is Lucky.'

Connie sat without expression as she listened to the long story that gradually unfolded. She was trying to keep calm, but emotion was welling up in her.

'I could be wrong of course,' Peggy ended quietly. 'But from what you told me and from what Grace has explained, I think I am correct.'

'But who is this girl called Grace?' Connie asked.

'She claims to be his sister, although that can't be confirmed. I've never yet seen the parents. She says her mother is sick and unable to look after them during the day. The father is rarely mentioned and I've had no proof that he is Gilbert Tucker or that the little boy is Lucky. That is, until yesterday, when we were closing the doors. For the first time he accompanied me to the kitchen, whilst his sister tidied the nursery. He's never spoken and sometimes doesn't seem to hear at all. But yesterday in the kitchen when I gave him a biscuit, he said, quite clearly, "Lucky likes this." I asked him to repeat what he'd said. He did so, twice more. There was no mistaking he was talking about himself.'

'It must be him, then,' Connie breathed. 'Has he got big blue eyes and blond hair?'

'Just as you described.' Peggy nodded. 'Grace has always called him Sydney, which was why I was so astounded when he kept repeating Lucky.'

Connie gasped. 'Sydney was going to be his new name!'

'I questioned Grace as gently as I could,' Peggy continued. 'The man at home is not her father. Her real father died many years ago with her little brother in a boating accident. Though Grace and her mother were left comfortably off, Grace's words to me were, "Mummy never got better after Sydney and Daddy went." Peggy linked her fingers. 'And there is more, I'm afraid. There were bruises on her neck and arms.'

'It was true then, that muddy brown colour,' Connie murmured to herself as she remembered Gran's words. 'It linked Lucky to him . . .'

'What was that, Connie?'

Connie blinked. 'It's just that I know why Rita was so scared of him now. And why I didn't like him from the start. I should have trusted my instincts. Oh, Peggy, what can we do?'

'If Lucky is in danger, then it's up to me to take action as I still have friends in the department. But until tomorrow, Monday, I can do nothing.'

'Can I see Lucky today?' Connie said quickly.

'You have a party going on,' Peggy reminded her. 'And it's a long journey back to Mile End.'

'Pat will understand why I have to leave, and my friend will drive us in his truck.'

Was this little boy really Lucky? she wondered, as she went to find Clint.

Peggy opened the door of the big hall. A smell of boiled cabbage flowed out. Two elderly men passed, their smiles wide as they bid the young volunteers inside goodbye.

She led Connie and Clint through the wooden pews that were still full of people eating hungrily from bowls and chewing on large chunks of bread.

She signalled to a small room. 'This is the nursery,' she warned them as they stood by the door. 'Kitty and Joseph belong to our helpers, but the others are all day visitors. You must try to recognize Lucky amongst them.'

Peggy pushed open the door. It was noisy inside, all the smaller children playing with the toys, unaware of being watched. A young girl sat with them. She stood up, her eyes wide as Peggy beckoned her.

'Grace, this is Miss Marsh.'

'Hello, Grace.' Connie had already noted the bruises on her neck.

'Hello,' Grace answered quietly.

Connie's eyes flew over the room. What if it wasn't Lucky after all?

Then she saw a little boy playing on his own. He was holding a wooden hobby horse made of a single blue stick with a painted horse's head. The child's hair was blond and curly and long. It fell in abundance over his eyes, hiding his face.

Connie moved slowly forward. The children continued to play as she stepped between them. When she was close to the little boy she stopped.

She waited for him to look up at her. Laying the horse gently on the floor, he rubbed his eyes and yawned.

'Lucky?' Connie whispered.

Two very blue eyes slowly met hers.

'Con-Con!' he cried, stretching out his arms and running towards her.

She couldn't bear to let go of him. He sat on her lap, holding her tight.

'I want to take him home,' she told Peggy.

'I'm afraid that would be unwise.' Peggy was insistent. 'You have no legal claim on him and we must proceed through the proper channels or you may never recover him. In the morning,' she continued as they sat in the small office, 'I shall talk to my colleagues at the Welfare Office and insist that an immediate visit is made to the household.'

'But what if he won't let anyone in,' Connie objected.

'Then I shall go to the police and make an official complaint.'

'But all this takes time,' Connie pointed out. 'What if he attacks Grace again, or harms Lucky?'

'I'm afraid it's a risk we'll have to take.' Peggy looked at Grace. 'You must stay home with your mother tomorrow and look after Lucky. And when the man or woman who comes to see you asks how you came by the bruises, you must tell them the truth. In fact, you must be very brave and tell them all you've told me. That your stepfather has been unkind to both you and your mother.'

Grace began to cry. Peggy held her close. 'Grace, dear, you must trust me to help you.'

'But I'm frightened.'

'I know. We would help you if we could now. But surprise – and the law – must be on our side.'

Grace nodded. 'Will you come tomorrow too?'

'I shall try my very best.'

'What will happen to Mummy?'

'She will have to have proper medical help. If what you have told me about her is true, she has needed help for some time.' Peggy stood up and smiled at Clint. 'Young man, may I prevail upon you for one more favour? Would you drive these children home? They've had a tiring day and it's a long way to walk.'

'Sure will, ma'am.'

Lucky began to cry. Connie couldn't bear it. She held him against her, then, taking his little hands, she looked into his face. 'You'll be a good boy for Con-Con now, won't you? Go home with Grace just for tonight.'

'Lucky wants Con-Con.'

'Oh, Lucky, Con-Con wants you too.'

Clint went down on his haunches. 'How do you fancy a ride in the jeep, son? You can sit up front with me if you like.'

Lucky nodded slowly, his eyes wide and tear-filled. Connie released him. She was holding back the tears too. What if their plan went wrong? What if she never saw him again?

She watched Clint carry him out to the truck. Grace stood up slowly. Connie hugged her. 'Don't worry, everything's going to be all right,' she told her, trying to hide the tremble in her voice.

Peggy squeezed the girl's shoulder. 'God bless and keep you safe, Grace.'

As the girl followed Clint, Connie's eyes filled with tears.

It was late when they arrived in East Ferry Road. Connie couldn't stop worrying about Lucky. She wanted to take him away from that dreadful man, Gilbert Tucker.

Clint switched off the engine. 'I guess this isn't the right time to ask you about us.'

Connie gave a little start. 'What do you mean, us? If it's about the Starlight—'

'No,' he said heavily, 'it's not. Connie, I'm leaving London.'

She blinked. 'Leaving?'

'I've been recalled to the States. Guess my time in England is over.'

She was shocked. 'When do you leave?'

'At the end of the week.'

'That's so soon!'

He nodded slowly. 'Connie, I've been wondering how to say this. Guess the only way is to ask outright. You must know the way I feel about you. Since that first day at Paddington, I've not been able to get you out of my head. Darn it, I don't *want* to get you out of my head. I want you to come back with me, you and Lucky. He's a fine kid and he'll love America. No one would take him away from you there. He'll grow up in the best country in the world, and I'll be there to take care of you both. You'll see where I live, meet my sister and her kids, you'll love them, just as you'll love New York. We'll take rides to Fifty-Second Street and Greenwich Village, cosy up in the clubs to Benny Goodman and Dizzy Gillespie and oh, honey, we'll make sweet music together. All you have to do is say yes.' He leaned forward and, taking her in his arms, covered her surprised mouth with his hungry lips.

Chapter Twenty-Seven

The party was over. All the dishes had been washed and put away and Pat was asleep in Gran's chair.

'Oh, it's you, Con.' Pat yawned as she woke up. 'What happened? Did you find Lucky?'

Connie sat on one of the hard-backed chairs. 'Yes, I did.'

Pat blinked the sleep from her eyes. 'Is he all right?'

'I don't know if he is or not. I wanted to bring him home, but Peggy said that nothing can be done till tomorrow. And even then, I don't know what will happen.' She told Pat the story of Grace and Lucky and Peggy's plan of action. 'I'll just have to wait.' She swallowed. 'He didn't want to leave me.'

'Well, at least you've found him.'

'But what good will it do if they can't prove anything against Gilbert Tucker? They could say Grace got the bruises from someone else, even her mother.'

'But won't Grace tell them what's happened?'

'The trouble is she's frightened.'

'What's wrong with her mother?'

'I don't know. She didn't look right when she came to

425

Kettle Street. I think the death of her husband and little boy might have affected her.'

'But what did Gilbert Tucker want to take Lucky for if his wife was ill?'

'I know. None of it makes sense.'

'I'm sure Peggy will sort it all out. Try not to worry.'

Connie nodded, but what would happen tomorrow? What if she didn't hear from Peggy? And would the children be safe in the meantime?

'Where's your friend?' Pat asked curiously.

'Clint? He gave me a lift back and had to get off. He's leaving for America at the end of this week.'

'Oh, that's a shame. He's a really nice young man.'

Connie felt confused as she thought about what had happened between them. Her hand went up to touch her mouth. Had he really kissed her? She had been shocked when he'd asked her and Lucky to go back to America with him. Did he really mean it? Pat was staring at her, a deep frown over her forehead.

'Are you feeling all right, Con?'

'I'm just worried about Lucky.' Clint had promised her that if they took Lucky to America she would never have to fret about losing him again. Was that true? If it was, accepting Clint's offer would be a solution to her problem.

Pat stood up. 'Would you like a cup of tea?'

'That'd be nice.'

Connie let her head rest against the wall. Clint had made America sound appealing. He'd promised her all she could ever dream of – that is, if she didn't have dreams

426

of her own already. What were her dreams now that she didn't have Vic? Was she attracted to Clint?

Pat grasped her hand as she walked by. 'Connie, just think, when Lucky is home, he'll be the brother for Lawrence that I always wanted. Won't that be wonderful? Just think of the big family we'll all be. Our kids will grow up with Sylvie and Kevin's kids – and Billy's kids, too, when he finds a nice girl and gets married – and we'll all be one big happy family, won't we?'

Connie felt a shiver along her spine. It was uncanny, the whisper of fate; it came when you least expected it and perhaps when you needed it most. The island was her home, the place where her heart was and where she was destined to be. She liked Clint but she didn't love him. If ever she'd had a moment's indecision, that moment had passed. It was here on the Isle of Dogs that her future lay.

The hours crawled by. Connie looked at the clock, wishing time away. This morning she had been tempted to board a bus to Mile End instead of Dalton's. But common sense had prevailed. Peggy had said she would find some way of letting Connie know any news and she must be satisfied with that.

But when the warning sounded at two o'clock and everyone ran down into the cellars, she imagined the worst. Lucky was out there somewhere. She wanted to protect him and take care of him.

When the all clear went and they resumed their working stations, Jenny looked at her in concern.

'Is something wrong, Connie?'

Mr Burns was out of the office and Connie told her about yesterday. 'I can't wait to go home,' she ended as Len approached.

'My sentiments entirely,' he agreed as he indicated the accounts they had to catch up on.

'No, it's to do with Lucky,' Jenny said, nudging his arm.

'What's happened?' Len said in surprise.

Connie repeated what she had told Jenny and they both looked startled.

'What that Tucker fellow has done is as good as kidnapping,' Len remarked angrily.

Jenny nodded. 'Except he's the grandfather.'

'And a rotten one at that.'

Connie nodded. 'I was even thinking about running off with Lucky while I had him. I might have if it hadn't been for Peggy telling me it was best for Lucky to do it the proper way.'

'Where would you have gone?'

'Somewhere they couldn't find me. Lots of people disappear in wartime.'

Len frowned. 'You need money for that sort of thing.'

'I would have pawned my engagement ring.'

'What!' Len frowned as he stared at her. 'Vic would have something to say about that.'

Connie felt tears well up in her eyes. 'I had a telegram on Saturday to say his ship is confirmed as lost and no survivors were found.'

Len and Jenny glanced at one another. Connie blinked

hard. She had been in control of her emotions until now, when a sob caught in her throat. 'I know what you're both thinking. That you could have told me it was hopeless six months ago.'

Len sighed softly. 'It's you we worry about, Con.'

'Well you needn't.'

'Connie—'

'I'm going to the cloakroom.' She pushed back her stool. Jenny followed her a few minutes later. 'Connie, are you in there?'

Connie was sitting on the toilet seat in the cubicle listening to the noisy plumbing. She wiped her wet cheeks with her hanky. 'Go back to the office, Jenny, or you'll get into trouble.'

'I don't care about that. Len and me want to help.' When Connie didn't reply she added in a quiet voice, 'I'll just wait quietly out here, then.'

After a while Connie opened the lavatory door. Jenny hugged her tight. 'Have a good cry, Connie. It'll do you good.'

Connie released the anguish inside her. She let the tears fall and used her own hanky and then Jenny's to mop up the flow. When deep sobs came up from her chest she felt empty, as though nothing was left inside her.

'I have to accept Vic's dead, don't I?'

'Take a day at a time. Be patient with yourself.'

They waited until Connie felt calmer then went back to work. Len gave her a wink and when Mr Burns noted Connie's red eyes he refrained from asking them where they had been. Jenny touched her arm as they sat on the stools. Connie realized what a good friend she had turned out to be. The sort of friend that would always be around when times were tough.

The end of the day came and Connie put on her coat. 'We'll walk home with you,' Jenny said as she tied on her headscarf.

'No, it's out of your way.'

'Me and Len were saying we need more exercise.'

Suddenly Connie saw the funny side. 'Oh, Jenny, you can say it with a straight face, too.'

Jenny giggled. Her serious features wrinkled as they both ended up laughing.

'As you can see, I'm fully recovered,' Connie assured them both as they stood at the gates. 'So don't go worrying about me.'

Len raised an eyebrow. 'What are friends for, but to watch out for their mates?'

Just then a tall figure appeared. 'Well if it isn't old twinkle teeth himself,' Len chuckled.

'Hi, Len.' Clint grinned. 'Jenny . . . Connie.'

Connie's cheeks went red. She looked at Len. 'Clint is leaving at the end of the week.'

'You're joking!' exclaimed Len. 'Why's that?'

'We gotta whole heap of trouble brewing in the Pacific. Our bombers raided Guam for the first time since Pearl Harbour. We need personnel at home to shift troops and planes from the States the same way we did to Europe.'

'Now that's spoiled me day,' Len said sadly. 'Will I see you for a pint before you go?'

'Sure will.'

They stood a little awkwardly until Jenny took Len's arm. 'Well, if you're sure you're all right, Connie?'

'Yes, thanks.'

'See you tomorrow then.'

Len punched Clint's arm. 'Don't forget. We'll have one up the Queens, eh?'

When they had gone, Clint frowned. 'Is there any news on the boy?'

Connie shook her head.

'You'd both be safe with me. We could have a good life together, Connie.'

'You don't really know us,' she said gently. 'It's wartime and when you're home with your people you'll forget all about us.'

'I'll never forget you.'

'Thank you for all you've done. And good luck with your music.'

He nodded slowly. Then, looking into her eyes, he chuckled. 'Gee, you Brits are always so polite.'

Connie smiled. She was relieved their friendship had ended this way. She watched him walk back to his truck and jump in. With a little salute he touched his cap and drove out of the gates.

She knew she would never see him again.

'I'm sorry, Con. I thought I'd have something to tell you,' Pat said when Connie walked in that night.

'I thought so too.'

Connie tried not to look too disappointed. But as each hour passed and there was no knock at the door her hopes of recovering Lucky faded. As she lay in bed, regrets filled her. She should have taken action even if it was against the law. What kind of law was it, anyway, that could not prevent a person like Gilbert Tucker from doing the bad things he had done?

When she finally slept it was only to wake up with a start. A new day had dawned. The first thought that came to mind was where was Lucky? And why hadn't she heard from Peggy?

Connie couldn't concentrate on the ledgers spread before her. The rows of figures that she was accustomed to seeing jumbled together. Instead she saw Lucky's face and remembered the way he had held tight to her, not wanting to let her go. Why had she allowed Peggy to convince her to give him up?

She walked home, her steps heavy even though spring seemed to be in the air. Blackbirds fluttered from the plane trees and perched on roofs, making loud clicking noises at the neighbourhood cats. Children played in the streets and on the demolished houses that now grew green grass and weeds over them. No one bothered about unexploded bombs or gas masks any more. There was too much to do without watching your every step and carrying a cumbersome contraption around with you.

Connie took a deep breath as she entered East Ferry Road. She wanted Pat and the children to be sitting on the steps as they did sometimes. Their happy smiles would tell her all she was desperate to hear.

Instead she saw Albie Cross and Eve Beale, each carrying their shopping baskets. They stood in conversation, glancing towards her as she approached.

'Nice evening, ain't it, gel?' Albie lifted his shoulders under his old coat, removing the roll-up from his mouth.

'Could do with a bit of sunshine, though.' Eve smiled as Connie looked up at the house. 'Just seen your Pat. You've got a nice bit of stew for tea.'

Connie walked up the steps. She didn't want to go in. She didn't want to face another long night. The smell of boiling cabbage and a hint of meat trickled out from the kitchen. She could hear Doris's high-pitched voice over the music coming from the radio. Pat would be standing at the stove, the two children positioned at the table waiting eagerly for their meal. Somehow she would have to disguise the sad feelings inside her that yet again she was to be denied Lucky.

She hung up her coat and pushed her hair gently into place. Pat appeared at the kitchen door. Another figure followed and Connie saw it was Peggy. She held a small child in her arms.

'Con-Con!' Lucky screamed. And, wriggling from Peggy's grasp, he ran into her arms.

Chapter Twenty-Eight

June 1944
D-Day

Four hundred and fifty Allied aircraft had dropped 2,500 tons of bombs on French earth, but that hadn't made much difference to Billy's division. In fact, it made things worse. The planes had released their loads well back from the forward line, avoiding their own men. This meant the German defences went almost unscathed. Caen, Monty's prime target, remained occupied territory. And thousands of good men lost already.

Billy threw himself on the ground. He pushed back his helmet as he surveyed the burned, scarred territory in front of him. He wouldn't want to see these last few days again. The landings had been a carve-up. Most of the troops had been buffeted by the tide, many drowned as they struggled ashore. No one knew the result on Omaha beach, only that the 1st Corps were to take Juno and Sword, whilst Billy's infantry division was headed for Caen.

The sky was still raining shells. Men fell and died

where they lay. Only he and Spike had survived the beach, it seemed. Their uniforms were bloody from corpses. They must have eaten half a beach and digested it with seawater as they'd scrambled to safety. Thank God he knew how to swim.

'Lucky we bumped into the Canadians,' Billy muttered as he squinted through the sights of his rifle. 'Gave them panzers something to think about.'

'Yeah, where was our anti-tank support for Christ's sake?'

Billy narrowed his eyes at the concrete hill unsuccessfully camouflaged by nets and greenery. 'What do you reckon on the bunker?'

'Dunno,' Spike whispered beside him. They were on their bellies and only a few burned bushes shielded them.

'It looks quiet.' Billy jerked his head precariously upward. As it wasn't blown off, he decided there might be a chance. 'Who goes first?'

Spike adjusted his helmet strap. Nervously he licked the dirt from his blackened lips. 'Toss for it?'

Billy got out his lucky penny. He had no idea if it was lucky or not, but who cared? 'Heads, I go first. And you give me cover.'

Spike nodded again, the whites of his eyes huge.

Billy flipped the coin. 'Heads.'

'Bad luck, mate.'

Billy grinned. 'Wait till I get over that ridge, then give it all you've got. And don't let up till you see me handsome mug grinning out that hole.'

'Billy?' Spike grabbed his arm.

'What?'

'Shit or bust, eh?'

Billy grinned. 'Shit or bust.' He briefly met Spike's eyes then frowned ahead of him. 'I'm off then, or hallay-feet as the mademoiselles say.'

Spike smiled nervously. 'You ain't gonna find a bit of crumpet in that bunker, you know.'

'I'm not planning to look.'

Billy scrambled on to all fours. He didn't remember counting, or jumping to his feet and running, zig-zagging from one toppled tree to another, listening to the silence broken only by the squelch of mud and the throb of his heart. He didn't remember the first burst of razor fire, but acted on instinct, throwing himself flat and choking as he inhaled the mud.

A warm trickle slithered down his shin. The pain came, hot and piercing. He shifted his leg, surprised he could still move. The fire roared past him, beyond him, ricocheting past his ear. Another volley zipped over his head. Bullets burst through a log in front of him, splintering the bark. He choked on a mouthful and spat out. He was still able to move so whatever had blown a hole in his ankle wasn't killing him. He gritted his teeth on the pain. Singed grass lodged in his teeth. He felt the ground shake and he waited, dazed, expecting the glint of steel in his face.

'Billy?'

'Spike?' He blinked the sweat from his eyes. 'Blimey, I thought you was a Kraut.'

His pal lay beside him, a smile on his face. 'I'm

reinforcements, ain't I?' Then, as gently as a baby, his friend laid his head on the earth. 'I'm done for, Billy.'

'Don't be a silly sod. You're just winded.'

Spike grinned sloppily. 'If you say so, chum.'

Billy listened to the whining and cracking above them. He reached out and laid his fingers on the quiet uniform, felt the warm wetness soaking through his fingers. 'Look, I'm gonna be back for you, mate. But I got to get rid of them sods first so's we can get through to our blokes. Now I want you to stay here and not even fart.'

Spike looked up with glassy eyes.

Once more Billy was on his feet and running. This time he remembered every second, every gulped breath and the sob that rose from his chest. The whistling and zipping of bullets, the nose of the gun in the hole jumping violently as it ate up the snake of ammunition. Turf ripping up in front of him. The puddles of mortar and strangers' blood. A battlefield that refused to die and he with it, hope sailing like a flag beside him.

When his heart seemed to stop beating, he grasped the small round instrument of death tightly in the palm of his hand. Falling flat, he released the pin and spun the metal ball high. As the next – and last – bullet ripped past him, he smiled; the explosion blew the roof off the bunker just like the top coming off a lemonade bottle.

Connie was on her way home from work when she heard the familiar clattering in the distance. The tinny, grating noise grew louder. Her heart stopped still. Everyone's worst dread had come true. There was a new secret weapon after all. The V-1 flying bomb. No one knew which direction the single bomb would come from. Hitler's doodlebugs, as they had been named, had brought a new wave of terror to the country. When the engine cut out there was only fifteen seconds to take shelter before the missile came boring down.

'Go on, you bugger, get out of here!' cried a man on his bicycle. He jumped off and stood staring up at the sky. Connie did the same, selfishly praying the doodlebug would continue its journey.

'Thank the Good Lord it ain't us,' the man muttered to Connie as the missile trundled onward. 'Makes me feel guilty to want it to land elsewhere, but it's every man Jack for hisself, ain't it?' When a distant explosion echoed in the air, his shoulders slumped. 'Someone's copped it,' he sighed. 'God rest their souls.'

When Connie arrived home, the house was quiet. She knew where Pat and the children would be. Quickly she went to the under-stairs cupboard and opened the door. Inside was the old armchair, and Pat and the three kids were huddled in it.

Connie gathered them in her arms. 'You can all come out now.'

'Is it all clear?' Pat asked.

'Until the next one, yes.'

They all scrambled out. 'I heard on the wireless that over seventy have landed on London in the past thirty hours,' Pat said as she lifted Lawrence against her. 'The army is stationing more ack-ack units over Kent and Sussex, trying to shoot them down. But they're too fast.'

'I hate them buzz bombs,' Doris said as she and Lucky ran into the kitchen. 'They make an 'orrible noise.'

'I'm hungry.' Lucky was oblivious to the danger as he climbed on a chair and looked over the empty table.

Connie kissed his cheek hard. 'Your tea will have to be cooked first.'

'I'm hungry too.' Doris sat beside him. They picked up their spoons. 'What have we got today, Aunty Con?'

'Meatloaf and mash, followed by apple pie.'

'You mean that squishy squashy stuff?'

'Squishy squashy,' repeated Lucky. 'I like squishy squashy.'

'Can me and Lucky go out to play while we wait?' Doris asked as Pat lowered Lawrence into his playpen.

'You can sit on the step but if you hear that funny noise in the sky, run in quickly.'

'We will!' both children yelled, and, grabbing hands, they ran out together.

Pat smiled at Connie. 'You can't keep them wrapped in cotton wool you know.'

'I still can't believe he's going to be here when I come home.' Connie shrugged as she took off her coat and tied an apron around her.

Pat nodded. 'It's almost three months since Peggy brought him back but the funny thing is he seems to have been with us for ever.' She glanced at Connie. 'I still find it hard to believe that Gilbert Tucker was only after that poor woman's money and used Lucky to get her to marry him.'

Connie sat down at the table with a bag of vegetables.

Thoughtfully she began to peel them. 'He knew she was mentally ill and convinced her that Lucky would replace Sydney. As soon as they married and Lucky was installed, he took everything he could get his hands on. Now what kind of heartless creature would do that?'

'I only hope the police will catch up with him.'

Connie had her doubts about that. The policeman who had come round afterwards had told her that they believed Gilbert Tucker was a serial bigamist, extorting money from vulnerable women. But so far they hadn't caught up with him.

'What a monster!' Pat exclaimed as she put on the kettle. 'He didn't care about the boy at all. I still get angry when I think about it.'

'Me too,' Connie replied passionately. 'I don't know what he did to Rita and her mother, but it was bad enough for Rita to run away from him and beg me on her dying breath to look after her son. I just wish I'd trusted my instincts and put up a better fight.'

'What beats me,' Pat frowned as she took the milk from the larder, 'is why didn't the authorities discover this when he applied for custody of his grandson? I mean, that was a big mistake on their part.'

Connie sighed. 'Their excuse is that it's wartime and hard to keep track of people. As he went under different names they didn't trace him. And he would have gone on undetected had not Grace taken Lucky to Peggy's soup kitchen.'

'That little girl must have had a dreadful time.'

'I've got her to thank for keeping Lucky safe.'

'At least she's got a good home with Peggy now. The sad thing is her mother will never recover and has to stay in the asylum. Poor Grace.'

Both women sighed as they looked at one another. 'Aren't we lucky to have survived with such a wonderful family?' Pat said, tears in her eyes.

Connie smiled up at her. There had been a change in Pat over the past months. She was her old chatty self again and had regained all her enthusiasm for life. The arrangement of Connie lodging there seemed to be working well. Pat had overcome her worries about Lawrence's leg and even with the threat of the doodle-bugs her spirits didn't flag.

Just then the kids came tumbling in. 'Is tea ready yet?'

Connie laughed. 'You've only just gone out.'

Lucky wriggled himself on to her lap. She gave a slice of carrot to each child. 'Both of you draw us a nice picture,' Connie said, indicating the paper and pencils in the table drawer.

Lucky scribbled happily but Doris frowned as she chewed the end of her pencil. 'What shall I draw?

'A picture of the river and boats on a bright sunny day,' Pat suggested.

Head bent, Doris set to work.

Connie sipped the tea that Pat had made. She smiled into the bottom of the cup. 'I can almost hear Gran telling me to tip up and turn.'

'I seen Gran,' Doris said with a big smile as she continued to draw. 'I seen her a lot.'

Connie and Pat looked at one another.

'Where have you seen her?' Connie asked.

'Dunno. Everywhere really.'

There was silence in the kitchen for a few minutes as this new piece of information was digested. Then Doris held up her picture.

'Look, I didn't do boats. I drawed Gran instead. She showed me her new apron, see? It's all white with frills round the edge.'

Pat and Connie stared at the drawing. Although it was a child's composition, the figure was clearly recognizable as Gran. A lady with a big smile on her face, dressed all in black, the lead pencil having filled in the spaces, leaving the white paper to denote the apron with frills around its edge.

'Th . . . that's beautiful,' Connie stammered.

Pat's eyes were big as saucers. 'You can tell it's Gran all right.'

'Course you can,' Doris said, returning the paper to the table and adding extra flourishes. 'She says I'm gonna be a really good drawer when I go to school. And come top of my class.' She gazed up at the two shocked adult faces. 'Is tea nearly ready now?

At the end of August Paris was liberated. Laurie's letter arrived in September telling Pat he was homeward bound to convalesce from a bout of pneumonia. He'd caught it whilst in the trenches but he was better now after a spell in hospital. He had been granted a weekend's leave, a big surprise for everyone. Pat was so happy that she even went to the market with Connie and bought a new dress.

The Friday evening he arrived there was a rapturous welcome. They all hugged him until he could hardly breathe.

'Are you better now?' everyone demanded, examining him from cap to boot.

'I'll do.' He grinned, showing the kids his muscles and making them laugh. But he looked tired and pale and carefully avoided talking about the things he'd seen and done.

The big surprise for Laurie was his son. It was only the second time he had seen him. Tears came into his eyes as he held the child.

'My beautiful boy,' he called him and, looking at Pat and Doris, his face filled with pride. Pat cleverly disguised the bad leg with a pair of stockings and, other than the way Lawrence crawled around the floor in a clumsy way, there was no evidence of his deformity.

On Saturday morning Laurie and Pat took a walk up to Island Gardens. In the afternoon, Connie looked after the children whilst Laurie and Pat caught a bus to Poplar. Laurie wanted to buy Pat a souvenir from the market. They came home with a second-hand jumper for Doris, a little wooden soldier for Lawrence and a bunch of flowers for Connie. Pat was wearing a small brooch, a posy of flowers that had two stones missing but looked nice all the same. They ate tea all together and played games until the children's bedtime.

'I'm having an early night and leaving you two lovebirds to it,' Connie yawned a little later.

Laurie stood up and took her in his big embrace. 'Sorry if I've been a bit quiet, gel. It's like living in two worlds. The good and normal one here with me family and the one out there somewhere, that I don't want to think about.'

'We understand, Laurie. Just take care of yourself.'

'Thank you for looking after Pat for me,' he told her softly. 'And I'm right pleased you've got your little lad back again. Reckon him and my Larry are going to be best mates.'

As Connie went in to see Lucky, now sleeping next to Lawrence in the big double bed, she wondered when they would all meet up again. Laurie would soon be rejoining his infantry division. After the Normandy landings, stories abounded that German troops were on the run across Europe. But another new Nazi weapon called the V2 rocket had been launched, and one had landed in west London. The blast wave had been felt for miles around. What with the doodlebugs and the rockets could it be true that Germany had a new master plan?

Kissing all three children softly goodnight, she thought of Vic and wondered what he would think of this big brood now. She could almost hear his voice saying how proud he was of them.

Chapter Twenty-Nine

'**Y**our dad and Lofty managed to find us a nice rabbit, though don't ask me where it came from.' Olive raised her eyebrows. 'We'll sit down for dinner as soon as the twins are fed.'

Connie took off her apron and glanced at the clock. 'Dad and Kevin should be home from the pub soon.'

Olive opened the oven door and peered in. 'I told your father I wanted them back for two sharp. No sense in spoiling good food when there's so little of it. Between the rockets and the rationing, we're lucky to get a square meal these days. Nora Hibbert said the vibration of the last V2 cracked her washbasin and sent a cloud of soot from the chimney into the front room. They even felt the floorboards shudder and Nora lives half a mile away from where it was dropped.'

People were terrified of the new weapon. The rockets were much deadlier than doodlebugs, hitting the ground without warning and penetrating deeply into the earth. They caused great destruction, an earthquake effect, and the noise of the sonic boom could be heard all over the capital.

Connie shuddered at the thought of the sight she had witnessed from the top of a bus just the other day. The V2 had demolished a whole row of houses, leaving a steaming crater, the depth of which was later said in the newspapers to extend fifteen feet.

'Shame Pat and the kids couldn't come to dinner today,' Olive sighed as she closed the oven door and mopped her brow. 'Is Doris any better?'

'It's one of those November colds that run all the time,' Connie replied as she shined the knives and forks with a cloth. 'Lawrence had it first and I expect Lucky will get it next. Pat didn't want them to pass it on to Sylvie's twins.'

Olive looked at Connie with a frown. 'Heard anything from Peggy?'

'The police had no luck in tracing Gilbert Tucker.' Connie shrugged. 'It's a lot more difficult in wartime to find someone who doesn't want to be found.'

It was taking time for her parents to accept that Lucky was back for good. She suspected they were still worried he would be removed from her custody again, even though she'd assured them that it wasn't likely to happen, as Gilbert Tucker was a wanted man now and faced the prospect of time in prison when he was caught.

'And no registration of his birth has ever been found?' Olive asked doubtfully.

'Not on the island, anyway. If nothing turns up I'm going to get him registered properly. Peggy said she'd help me go through all the rigmarole when it comes to it.'

Her mother nodded slowly. 'And what of young Grace?'

'She's very happy living with the Burtons.' Connie paused. 'But Peggy doesn't think Sybil will be released from the asylum as the doctors think her condition has got worse. As a last resort they're giving her special treatment like they give to ex-servicemen who have shell shock.'

Olive sighed sadly. 'I suppose they've got to try something. But if you ask me that woman was suffering from a deep-seated grief for her husband and child that nothing earthly can cure.'

Just then Sylvie walked in. Her face looked pink as she rocked five-month-old James in her arms. 'John is fast asleep,' she told them doubtfully, 'but James is still restless. Why does one go off the moment his head hits the pillow and the other scream the house down?'

Connie smiled as she glanced down at the tiny pursed mouth. 'He's just letting you know he's still hungry. Lucky was much better at sleeping when he started on proper food. I can remember piling all sorts into him when we lived down the Anderson. It must have worked as he began to sleep through the raids.'

'Don't mention that awful contraption,' Olive groaned as she strained the potatoes through the colander. 'I still have nightmares about Billy and you being blown to bits inside it. Which, may I remind you, you almost were.'

The Blitz now seemed like a lifetime ago, Connie reflected, as she listened to her mother and Sylvie talking. So much had happened since then that she could hardly believe they were all standing here in the same kitchen of the same house that had had its roof blown in by a bomb, the house next door wrenched from the adjoining wall and both yards and shelters reduced to rubble. In four years she had gained an extended family that she had never dreamed could exist. Before the outbreak of the war she and Ada had nothing more to worry about in their lives than where to go on a Saturday night. Now Ada was living in Kent and had written she'd joined the Land Army. Her letters were full of country life. Surprisingly the fresh, clean air seemed to suit her, as did weekends down the pub with the hale and hearty country lads.

Connie smiled to herself as she took the knives and forks into the front room and placed them on top of the big gateleg table, opened out for Sunday dinner. Even the buzz bombs and rockets hadn't been able to stop this family tradition. Nan and Lofty would be along to tea later that day. A neighbour or two would call in and perhaps Taffy, who always wanted to know how Billy was. Everyone would stop to admire the twins and be force-fed numerous cups of tea and some of Nan's cake. And before Connie left for home, the embers of the fire would warm the room, with all the faces bearing rosy glows. Even the twins would be kept up until she left, handed from lap to lap, the men as much delighted with the two new additions as the women.

The smile flickered slowly from her face. John and James were dear little boys, the apple of everyone's eye. How she had hoped that one day she would be bringing her own family here for Sundays. Vic and her, Lucky and his brothers and sisters. Oh yes, she'd had vivid pictures in her mind once, of the happy family they would all make once the war was ended. Now, of course, that vision had changed.

Her heart gave a frightening tug and she pulled back her mind from the darkness in which her memories of Vic were clouded. She had been given back Lucky. And if the powers above had chosen not to return Vic, then she, like thousands of other women, would have to make new lives, new dreams, new visions, without their men.

'If I get one line every six months I'll be surprised,' Olive was saying to Sylvie when Connie walked back in the kitchen. 'Billy's never been a writer, so I'm not expecting what I've not been used to. As long as he's safe, that's all I want to know.' Her voice shook slightly. Then, lifting her chin, she indicated the mashed potatoes steaming on a small saucer. 'Here, give him to me, Sylvie, and we'll try him with a teaspoon.'

'I don't know what I'd do without your mum,' Sylvie sighed as she handed over the little boy and sat down wearily. 'Delivering two babies at one time was more than a shock, it was a miracle. There's no twins in either of the families. Just goes to show you never know what's round the corner.'

'And where would we be without them!' Olive purred as she wrinkled her nose encouragingly at James and tipped the teaspoon to his lips.

Olive was oblivious to everything around her. The look on her face said it all. The little boy was her blood, as was John upstairs. They meant the world to her and Connie was happy that Sylvie and Kev had brought such fulfilment to her life.

Just as James slapped his lips in appreciation, there was a knock at the door.

'Who can that be, right on dinner time?' Olive demanded, sounding annoyed.

'I'll go.' Connie took off her apron.

'Miss Marsh – Miss Connie Marsh?' A tall, distinguished-looking man wearing an officer's hat and an elegant moustache that grew like a butterfly across his lip smiled down at her.

'Yes.'

'May I introduce myself?' He took off his flat cap. 'I'm Major Adrian Rees-Duncan from GHO . . . er . . . that is, Government Headquarters Overseas. I wonder if I could have a word?'

'Are you sure you've got the right person?'

'Oh yes, indeed. I've just had a chat with Mrs Grant, who directed me here.'

'Pat?' Connie began to be alarmed. 'It's not Laurie, is it?'

'No, no, it's not.' He shook his head ponderously and a shock of light brown hair slipped over his forehead. James let out a great bawl from the kitchen and he glanced over her shoulder. 'I think we should speak privately, if you don't mind.'

If she hadn't felt so worried about what he wanted, Connie would have laughed. Privacy was something you wouldn't find at number thirty-three Kettle Street, or, in fact, in any other house still standing on the Isle of Dogs.

'Perhaps . . . my car?' the Major suggested as the men

came striding up the garden path, politely nodding as Ebbie and Kevin made their way towards them.

'What's going on?' Ebbie demanded as Connie grabbed her coat off the hook.

'I . . . I don't know, Dad. I'll tell you in a minute.'

'You ain't going off in that thing, are you?'

'No. I'm only going to talk in it.'

Connie hurried after the major, who opened the rear door of the big black car. She climbed inside, inhaling the not unpleasant but rather formal smell of cigar smoke and polished upholstery. The watery November sun played through the big back window, giving the atmosphere an unrealistic quality.

'What is it?' Connie stammered as she moved across and he sat beside her. 'What's wrong?'

The major smiled. 'Nothing, nothing at all, but what I have to tell you may come as something of a shock.'

Connie's mouth felt dry. She clenched her hands in her lap.

'Miss Marsh, I am pleased to be able to tell you that your fiancé, Lieutenant Victor Champion . . . is alive.'

Connie stared at him. Was he joking?

'But I must add, after building up your hopes, that he is still in enemy-occupied territory. Italy to be precise.'

'Italy!' Connie exclaimed hoarsely. 'But I was told there were no survivors from his ship.'

'Yes, and that was what we, too, believed, until our sources discovered that your fiancé was recovered from the sea and taken as a prisoner of war to a concentration camp on the Adriatic coast of Italy. Here he recovered from the wounds he had sustained and eventually escaped into the foothills. He joined a number of partisan fighters and continues to this day to oppose the Fascist militia. The longevity of his group, despite unavoidable casualties, is partly due to the fact that the terrain in this area is miserably inhospitable but virtually inaccessible to German troops. Your fiancé, in effect, is now our number one contact inside enemy lines.'

Connie shook her head slowly. After a moment's silence, she whispered, 'Are you *sure* this man is Vic?'

The major smiled again. 'In August of this year our reconnaissance made radio contact with Italian resistance. We formed strategies in order to penetrate behind enemy lines. Our first task was to parachute men and arms into Italy under the cover of darkness and this we did successfully, thanks to the support and information provided by Lieutenant Champion and his group.'

Connie tried to absorb the details the major had given her. The only question she could think of to ask was, 'When will he be coming home?'

'Sadly, I can't say.' The Major frowned. 'You see, your fiancé remains – voluntarily – in Italy. We could get him out now, if he so wished, but he's chosen to stay and help the people who have helped him – and us – in our fight against the enemy.'

Connie felt a stab of dismay as tears sprang to her eyes. Why hadn't he chosen to come to home to her? Hadn't he given enough to his country? They had both endured the torment of being apart and, in her case, even believing he was dead!

'Miss Marsh, I know how painful his decision must be

for you to accept. But may I remind you of something you undoubtedly know? Lieutenant Champion is a very brave man indeed. He is unique in his determination and strength of character and is now invaluable to British Intelligence. Would you really expect any less of him when faced with such a choice?'

Connie looked into his eyes and knew that she would-n't. She was being selfish in wanting Vic's return, but then she was only human and her heart was aching in a very human way. 'Is there anything else you can tell me?' She quickly wiped a tear from her eye.

'Nothing, I'm afraid. And all we have discussed must be kept in the strictest of confidence. Lives depend on the fact that nothing is leaked, not even the slightest word.'

'Did you tell Pat when you saw her?'

'Only that her brother is alive.'

'She must be so happy—' Connie stopped mid-sentence as a thought struck her. 'You needn't have told us, need you?' she breathed haltingly. 'You could have let us go on thinking he was dead.'

The major nodded slowly, quirking an eyebrow. 'Your fiancé had one request, and I vowed to honour it personally. That is why I am here today and have told you all I am able to.'

Connie's face suddenly filled with joy. 'He mentioned me?'

The major smiled but said nothing.

'Can I tell the rest of my family?'

'Yes, but not where – or how. Only that he did not go down with his ship. I'm sorry, but in your fiancé's case, and that of the men working with him, silence is truly golden.'

Connie looked at the man who half an hour ago had not existed in her life. 'So I'll just have to wait until the war is over?

He smiled gently. 'With God's grace, we are winning, Miss Marsh. Hold on to that hope.' He held out his hand. 'I'm very glad – and honoured – to have met you.'

Connie watched the sleek vehicle glide away into the thickening November mist. She wanted to cry, she wanted to laugh. She wanted to jump for joy and run through the houses telling everyone Vic was alive. No one knew if the V2 menace would strengthen the sting in the enemy's tail. No one knew what would happen in Europe or in the Far East. But the major had told her to hang on to hope. And that was what she was going to do.

After the car had driven away, she walked slowly back into the house. She pushed open the front-room door. Her family gazed up at her from the big oval table where all the dirty plates were stacked in a pile, knives and forks balanced on top of them. Olive was dishing the pudding into bowls, an unrecognizable pile on to which Sylvie was pouring condensed cream. Kevin and her father were waiting for seconds, their faces anxious as they stared up at her.

'Well?' they all shouted at once. 'What happened?'

Connie felt tears spring to her eyes once more. Her dad leaped from his chair and hugged her.

'What's wrong, love, what is it?'

'He's alive, Dad. Vic's alive.'

Suddenly she was surrounded, the questions coming from all angles. How dearly she longed to be able to share her news. How much she wanted the war to be over when she could shout from the rooftops that her sweetheart was coming home.

Amidst tears and laughter Connie promised herself she would never lose hope again. She believed that her love had kept him safe and that same love, tenfold in its strength now, would bring him back safely into her loving arms once more.

Epilogue

Vic took a long, slow breath and leaned his arms on the polished oak rails of the cross-channel ferry. The warm sun played on his neck and burned into the cloth of his sports coat. The spray that had moistened his face as he'd gazed over port side was drying on his cheeks, highlighting the slim white scar that began in the centre of his forehead and disappeared under a shock of thick dark hair.

His mind far away, he gazed at the disappearing white cliffs of Dover and his hand went up involuntarily to stroke the pale, twisting thread. Sliding his fingers along to the triangular bump on the pinnacle of his skull he massaged the hard contours. Immediately pictures flew up before his eyes as they did every time he performed this unintentional ritual. After Georgie had died, he'd not noticed the shard of metal sticking up from his own crown, not felt a flicker of pain. He'd been too busy trying not to drown, too occupied in clinging to the wreckage of his little ship and watching it sink before his

459

eyes; listening to the gurgle of water gulp and groan and the metal creak, until nothing was left above the waves. Nothing, that was, of his remaining crew, of the brave lives they had lived and the courage they had shown.

Why had he survived and not them? Why hadn't he sunk to the bottom of the ocean on that sad Sicilian shore? What or who had given him life in the face of death? He'd tried to understand, tried even harder to justify his survival, but even the years he'd spent as a partisan hadn't lessened the guilt he felt. Not even when he'd been repatriated and crossed this same strip of water in a navy cruiser just after VE Day, not even then had he felt justified in walking on English soil once more. Georgie, Tommy Drew, Sammy Kite, they were all gone. Billy too . . .

Vic looked down into the foamy white wake, a healthy sea filled only with fish and the keels of friendly vessels. His eyes skimmed the dancing water and swooping gulls, lifting to the bright blue sky over Dover. He remembered how good it had felt nine years ago to see those liberated cliffs. To inhale the pure air and know that, in the end, the struggle for freedom had been worth it. That Georgie and Billy and the others hadn't died in vain.

But it wasn't until he'd taken Connie in his arms and pressed his lips against hers that he dared to hope it was all real. That he was home again and it was finished. It was over.

'Darling?'

Vic swung round. Connie stood before him, as lovely as the day he'd first met her. Age had delicately added a wise beauty to her features, deepening the colour of her eyes, a thousand shades more intense than the blue of the sea. Her blond waves blew in the breeze over the collar of her shirtwaister dress. She took his hands, placing them on her slim hips hidden elegantly under the fashionable sheath skirt.

'It's beautiful up here,' she whispered. 'But lonely.'

He held her face in his hands. 'Not now you're with me.'

She gave a little tremble and he pulled her against him. 'What's wrong?'

She laid her cheek on his chest. 'It's just that I don't want to get upset when we see his grave.'

'We'll be with you.'

She sighed softly. 'I just can't believe he's gone sometimes. Billy was so full of life.'

Vic looked into her eyes. 'He died a hero, Con. Imagine that. A posthumous medal an' all. Now that's serious business.'

Her soft mouth curved into a wry smile. 'Hark who's talking. You had yours pinned to your chest by the king. I still haven't got over finding myself in Buckingham Palace in that room with all those oil paintings in gold frames and big red velvet chairs. Mum and Dad still go on about it even now.'

'It should've been Georgie and the others there – not me.'

'They were with you, you just couldn't see them.'

He grinned. 'Now I can hear Gran talking.'

'Well, she was there too, although I doubt she'd have

agreed to curtsy, more like she'd have sat on one of those posh chairs and asked for a cup of tea. Served in best china, mind.'

They laughed softly, swaying in the breeze, their arms around one another. 'There'll be so many other graves,' she said suddenly. 'How will we know where he is?'

'Don't worry, they'll show us.'

'Is Normandy far from Calais?'

'Not as the crow flies. We'll stop the car halfway and find somewhere to eat.'

'Don't forget, we've got to drive on the opposite side.'

Vic chuckled. 'Reckon we won't be the first British to make a mistake or two. Now tell me, what's it like being the wife of a successful businessman?'

Connie arched her fine eyebrows. 'Hark at it! Is that what you call yourself these days? Well, don't let it go to your head, Victor Champion. I'm still wondering when I'm going to get those nice new shoes I asked for about a year ago!'

'A year?' He looked mortified. 'Was it that long ago?'

'No, it was only a month, actually. But I'm putting in me order before the queue gets any longer.'

'As if I'd see my lovely wife standing in a queue!' He shook her gently and they laughed again. If anyone had told him when he was a nipper that he would end up a shoemaker, he'd have laughed his head off. But his Italian friends had taught him a thing or two about cobbling and making boots for the partisans, a skill that had set him up for life. He'd opened two workshops now, in Poplar and Stepney, and planned a third near the city centre. The world and his wife wanted good shoes – they never went out of fashion. It was hard to imagine that he'd learned his skills in the foothills of an Italian mountain range, hammering out goatskins!

'I always thought you'd go back to sea, you know,' she murmured as they began to walk arm in arm along the deck. 'I thought you couldn't resist it. The PLA wanted you back and you loved the docks . . .'

'I loved you and the kids more.'

She stopped and the big ship rolled gently. 'It all worked out in the end, didn't it?'

He nodded slowly. 'Yeah, it did.' The silver tail on his forehead disappeared into the furrows of a frown as he spoke hesitantly. 'Con, I know this trip is to see Billy, like we always said we'd do when we could afford it. But coming away like this has made me think. We should have a few good holidays now the business is doing all right. What I mean is, how about somewhere like Switzerland later this year?'

'*Switzerland!*' Connie gasped.

Vic nodded. 'Kev's been with me two years now. He knows the ropes.'

She gave a little cry of delight. 'Oh, Vic, that'd be lovely.'

'We could buy a tent, have a camping holiday if that's what the kids fancy.'

She nodded eagerly. 'Do you really mean it?'

'Course I do. Everyone's going abroad these days. Besides, Lucky'll be fifteen soon. He'll be wanting to get off with his mates. I'd like him to remember one or two good holidays, not just bed and breakfast in Margate with the twins and Pat and the kids. I want to make special memories like this with just the four of us.'

Connie looked into his eyes. 'You're a wonderful dad, the best.'

'Oh, sweetheart, I try to be.'

'Say that again . . . our word . . .'

Slowly he lowered his head and murmured against her lips, 'My darling sweetheart . . .' He kissed her longingly.

'Mum! Dad!'

A tall fair-haired young lad came bounding towards them. He was accompanied by a girl half his size dressed in a blue gingham dress. She had Connie's big blue eyes and long, light brown hair tied in a pony tail. His son and daughter were the apple of his eye. His adopted son, Victor Junior, more often than not still called Lucky, and his seven-year-old daughter, Alice.

'Look in my bag!' cried Alice. 'We've bought funny cards for Grandad and Grandma, a stick of rock each for the twins. And a packet of stamps for Larry's album. Oh, and a bottle of eau de cologne for Grace. Now she's got a boyfriend she wants to smell nice.'

Connie looked impressed. 'I hope you practised your French.'

Alice looked up at her brother. 'Lucky did.'

The handsome young man of fourteen blushed above his white, open-necked shirt. He was as tall as his mother now and dressed in smart grey flannels and a navy blue blazer. 'I only tried out a bit but the lady seemed to understand me.'

'I said merci bucket,' giggled Alice shyly.

'Did you now?' Her father grinned. 'Well, even your old dad might try a word or two of the vernacular when we dock at Calais. I'll start with a quick bonjour mademoiselle to the nearest gendarme.'

Alice slapped her father playfully on the arm. 'Don't be daft, Dad. A gendarme's not a lady. He's a French policeman.'

Vic smirked. 'Clever clogs.'

'So you've both spent all your pocket money?' Connie concluded ruefully.

Alice tutted. 'No, course not, Mum. We've still got to get Auntie Sylvie and Uncle Kev their souvenirs. And Auntie Pat and Uncle Laurie's stinky cheese. And then there's Nan and Lofty, who said they want something nice for their new house in the country.'

Connie grinned. 'It's not the country, love, not really. It's called Osterley Park, in Middlesex. And it's not a house but a flat that's built specially for older folk.'

'Is that where you and Dad are going to live when you're old?'

'Certainly not!' Vic exclaimed, wheeling his daughter forward along the deck. 'Your mum and me are going to live right where we've always lived, in our nice big house on the island, right by the river.' He pulled her pony tail. 'And as far as getting old is concerned, why, we're only spring chickens yet. In fact, I'll have you know we're off to Switzerland very soon, so there!'

Lucky turned to stare at his father. 'You're joking, Dad!'

'Not on your nelly.'

'Where's Switzerland?' Alice asked.

'Turn left after France.' Vic strolled on casually. 'I'm taking your mum up a mountain. Now what do you think of that?'

'What, without us?'

Vic shrugged. 'Well you two wouldn't be interested, not in climbing right up to the top in all that snow and getting all puffed out and moaning that we forced every step out of you.'

Alice jumped in front of him, her freckles glowing. 'Lucky and me never moan. We'd only do that if we was left behind.'

Vic leaned against the rail and winked slyly at Connie, who smothered a grin. Alice flung herself at her father. Squeezing him tight she burst out, 'I knew you was joking!'

Vic hugged his daughter, kissing the top of her silky head. He glanced at Lucky. 'Well, son, what do you say to a stroll in the Alps?'

'Me mates are never gonna believe it.'

'Well, you can thank your Uncle Billy for the inspiration.' Vic glanced at his beautiful wife. 'When we visit him, we'll all say a big thank you.'

'Will he hear us, Dad?' Alice asked.

'He'll hear us. Gran will too. Wouldn't be surprised if a voice didn't boom down in reply either.' Vic ruffled her hair and slid the Brownie box camera from its case strung across his shoulder. 'Now, all of you slap great big smiles across your faces and say cheese to the camera.'

Vic watched his family eagerly arrange themselves for the photograph. Behind them was a vast, clear blue day and, when the ferry dipped, a glimpse of aquamarine ink. And somewhere beyond this was Calais and Caen and Billy's last resting place, soon to be honoured by a long overdue visit from the Champions.

'Right – on the count of three!' Vic lifted the camera. His eye found the viewfinder and he saw his children standing on either side of his wife, arms linked and smiles stretched wide across happy faces. Slowly but surely a layer of pastel colours began to appear around them. Pinks, lemons, greens and blues, a halo that trickled itself around the three people he loved most in the world. The lights grew brighter and more exquisite, until, holding his breath, he blinked, looked again, then snapped the image for posterity.